Apple Queen

Alexandra Lavizzari

Translated by David Hill

Originally published in German as *Somerset*.

Copyright: Zytglogge Verlag, 2015

All rights reserved.

EAN-13: 978-1514341759
ISBN-10: 1514341751

Zytglogge Verlag, Steinentorstrasse 11, CH-4010 Basel

For David

for Steve and Pat
hope you like
the story

Alex H

8.9.2015

Chapter 1

It was already getting dark when Vera reached Taunton and squeezed into the line of commuters who were leaving the motorway as they drove home to their idyllic villages. Nadja had warned her: "Taunton isn't big, Mum, but around Christmas time the rush-hour gets terrible. It takes for ever to reach Southcombe. Make sure you arrive before half-past four. Or else later, about eight."

The clock on the dashboard showed eleven minutes past six. Vera had got it wrong again. Instead of driving directly from Folkestone to Taunton as she had originally planned, she had stopped off in Wells on the spur of the moment and lingered too long in the cathedral and the bishop's palace. And this was the result: after hours of making good progress she was now crawling along at a snail's pace. She inched her way past desolate rows of houses and industrial estates and over a bridge, after which the traffic came to a stop for a good quarter of an hour. But she wasn't expected at her B&B in Southcombe at any particular time, so she didn't mind too much. She even hummed to herself as she stared through the windscreen at the green Ford in front of her and thought about eating crispy fish and chips in the local pub.

What else went through her head during this last stretch of the journey she couldn't easily have said later, but one thing was certain: she had no feeling of premonition. No sudden tightening of her chest, no inner voice warning her to turn round before it was too late. Nothing. On the contrary, she remembered sitting in the traffic jam with a vague smile on her lips, thinking how lucky she was. Yes, for the first time since Robert's death she had felt happiness surging through her body, warm and reassuring, as she realized that she was part of the world again and, though still grieving, more confident and curious about life. Neither the rain nor the wind could have spoiled her mood that evening.

When the traffic came to a halt she rested her chin on the steering wheel and gazed at the autumn leaves and plastic bags swirling around in the chilly breeze, the wheeling and twisting clouds of starlings in the sky, drinking it all in with a sense of thrilled anticipation. And when the last terraced houses were finally behind her and the road was leading through a landscape of undulating fields and meadows, she thought of the warming open fires with which pubs welcomed their customers at this time of year. With a bit of luck Mrs Moore would spoil her by having one ablaze in the B&B.

To judge from her voice on the telephone she was an elderly lady, probably a bit deaf, for she spoke rather loudly and at that ridiculously high pitch that is peculiar to English women, both the very young and the not so young. The directions Vera had been given turned out to be helpful: she had no difficulty finding the turning that led past Southcombe post office into the High Street and from there into Mulberry Lane, where with a sigh of relief she brought the car to a halt at number fifty-seven. It was shortly after seven o'clock.

She had imagined Birch Cottage to be a smart little house, painted white, possibly thatched, with roses scrambling round the windows. So she was taken aback to find a brick-built house in nineteenth-century Gothic style. The house stood gloomily at the end of a gravel path, framed by beech trees. It had clearly seen better days. By the light of the garden lamp, which turned on automatically as Vera entered, she could see a few cracks in the brickwork, and it was clear that the front door and its frame were in urgent need of a new coat of paint. But despite its shabbiness there was something strangely whimsical about its gables and eyecatching corner towers. A light was shining on the ground floor and when Vera rang the bell she heard a cheerful "Come in", followed by the sounds of yapping and panting.

Two terriers jumped up at her, which Mrs Moore immediately chased away with a brusque "Stop it" while she took her visitor's suitcase. "I do apologize. Sam and Maisie are still young and not very well behaved. I hope you don't mind dogs, otherwise I'll shut them up in the garage until tomorrow."

"Oh, please, no. I haven't got a dog of my own, but they don't disturb me in the slightest."

Mrs Moore nodded approvingly and led Vera into the drawing-room. She was younger than Vera had guessed, about fifty perhaps, thin and strikingly tall. Her elegant appearance seemed slightly at odds with such a remote corner of Somerset. From her velvet slippers to the silk scarf knotted around her throat, Mrs Moore was dressed in carefully toning shades of purple, and the only makeup she had on was eye-shadow in the same colour. A large fire opal set in gold drew attention to her left hand. Her wedding ring consisted of two gold circles welded together. So Mrs Moore is a widow, thought Vera, just like me.

By comparison she felt rather scruffy in her jeans, and neither her pullover nor her trainers were exactly new, but Mrs Moore didn't seem to notice. She scrabbled about in a drawer for leaflets about local sights and re-commended a number of restaurants and pubs that could be reached either on foot or by a short car journey. Although there was no fire crackling in the grate, the room with its soft beige and pink decor radiated warmth. Porcelain figures and other ornaments covered the windowsills and the first Christmas cards were lined up on a cupboard between family photographs and vases. The dialogue of a sitcom, punctuated by laughter, came from a neighbouring room. Vera had evidently interrupted Mrs Moore as she was watching television. She was about to apologize when her landlady spoke first, asking her about her trip.

"It was OK, thank you. Three days at the wheel is a pretty long time and for continentals like me driving on the left can be a bit hard to get used to, but all in all I've survived the journey in good shape."

"I'm glad to hear it. I gather this isn't the first time you've been here, is it?"

"No, I've been to Southcombe once before. About a year and a half ago. But I stayed with my daughter that time. Her house is the last one on Church Street, just next to the cemetery."

"Yes, I know it. By the way, your daughter came by in person to reserve your room. A lovely young lady."

"And she's the one who told me about Station House. She said a lot of nice things about it."

"Oh, yes, you'll like it. All my tenants have."

"Can I move in tomorrow?"

"Of course, as we agreed. I checked the central heating, the cooker and the washing machine last week, and my cleaning lady went over it yesterday. Lucy is a jewel. She is in great demand in the village, but if you'd like to make use of her services I'm sure I could put a word in for you."

"That's very kind of you. I'll begin by seeing if I can manage for myself."

"As you please. I thought we might go over about ten tomorrow morning. Would that suit you? And then we can look through the tenancy agreement while we're there."

"Great. There'll be plenty of time after that for me to go into the village and buy what I need for the next few days."

Mrs Moore gave Vera the key to her bedroom and,

after asking her what she wanted for breakfast, left her in front of the door. Vera briefly inspected her room and its smart en suite, which from the tiling down to the towel was mint-green, then threw herself face down on the bed to text Nadja: *Just arrived. B&B excellent. See you tomorrow.* She would have liked to have had a warm bath and gone straight to sleep, but she was hungry, and after the driving she needed to stretch her legs.

A year and a half earlier Vera had spent a long weekend here with Robert, but he had already been very ill and had felt too weak for walks. They had spent most of their time at Nadja's and Tom's house, and occasionally, when it was warm enough, in the garden. The only parts of Southcombe that Vera had seen were a couple of streets around the church and the Co-op, where she had gone shopping with Nadja a few times.

There was a cold wind blowing as she left the B&B. The streets were empty except for a couple of youths in front of the Kings Arms, shivering in their hoodies as they stood silently around a girl who was trying to screw a candle into the lid of an empty beer can.

Vera had planned to walk as far as the end of the village before supper, perhaps with a little detour through Church Street, even though she knew that Nadja and Tom were not at home this evening but were celebrating the marriage of his best friend somewhere on Exmoor. However, just before the church Vera came across a road block. A police car was parked at the side of the road and policemen with walkie-talkies were standing in front of a small terraced house directly opposite the vicarage. From behind her Vera could hear the howl of an ambulance siren. All the windows of the small house were lit up. Beneath the sloping roof one of them stood open, a net curtain blowing restlessly in the wind. Posters of palm-lined beaches decorated the walls inside, and a lamp with a red shade threw an unsteady circle of light on to the ceiling.

Vera looked back at the policemen again and at the blanket laid out by the side of the road. She wanted to look away, but it was too late. She had seen not only the covering but also the crumpled shape underneath, and something peeping out from one side: a pink shoe with a silvery buckle.

"Move along now, please, madam," said a police-man, and pointed to the diversion behind the barricaded row of houses. But Vera did not feel like taking a stroll any more. And she had gone off the idea of fish and chips. She suddenly felt sick, her throat tight and her heart beginning to thump. She watched as the ambulance doors opened and the paramedics approached the shrouded figure on the ground. Then she turned and made her escape.

On the way back to the B&B Vera forced herself to breathe deeply and distract herself by thinking about something else. It was no good. It wasn't even any use counting the house numbers along the High Street. She couldn't rid herself of the image of that blanket and the policemen standing around it. She wasn't superstitious, but this death so soon after her arrival made her fear the worst for her stay in Southcombe. Having arrived in front of the Kings Arms, she gave no further thought to going in but hurried by.

The youths were still standing noiselessly in front of the entrance, their faces under the hoods faintly illuminated by the candle that the girl was trying to shield from the wind with her hands.

The silence all around made Vera feel strangely uneasy. No car, no voice, no radio, nothing. And no sound coming from the pub either. Shaken, she instinctively started walking more quickly. If she had been there a couple of minutes earlier she might have witnessed a woman – or was it a girl? – falling out of the window. But that wasn't the only thing that made her shudder. Standing here now in this complete silence it struck her that there hadn't been a single person at the scene of the accident apart from the police and herself. There were no family members to be seen, nor any of the onlookers who usually linger nearby in such situations. No one had leaned out of the window, and Vera hadn't noticed any witnesses being questioned by the police. But somebody must have seen or heard something, a neighbour or at least a passer-by. There had been lights shining from most of the nearby houses, or at least the bluish glow of television screens.

Why had no neighbouring window been thrown open after the fall? Why had no one reacted to the arrival of policemen and an ambulance? Vera almost began to wonder if she had dreamed the whole thing or was remembering a scene in a film. No, she finally decided, she had not been dreaming. A woman had just died a violent death on the High Street. Vera had seen with her own eyes the body covered with a blanket, and the pink shoe was fixed equally firmly in her memory. Especially the buckle: large and pointed like a butterfly's wing. Not the kind of thing she could have invented.

After this experience Birch Cottage seemed even gloomier than before. She was glad to hear the two terriers barking and to see a strip of light under the drawing-room door. She opened the packet of biscuits that she found beside the kettle in her room and sat down for a moment beside the window. From below she could hear the reassuring sound of women's voices. Mrs Moore was still watching television. And Nadja had left a reply on Vera's mobile: *Great, will be at your place by half nine.*

The thought that in only a few hours she would be holding her daughter in her arms gradually drove the dark images out of Vera's mind. She lay down on the double bed and let herself be carried along by memories and the happy prospect of spending the coming months close to Nadja. Since Robert's death she had found it particularly difficult to live so far away from her only child. Even if she told herself that as a mother she should be pleased to know her daughter was happily married, Vera was sometimes sad that Nadja had moved so far away in order to be with Tom. Vera had nothing against him, no, really not, but as parents she and Robert had both wished that Nadja had stayed in Switzerland – not particularly in Bern, but at least close enough for them to be able to visit her whenever they wanted to.

Nadja had arrived in the world after Vera had given up believing she could ever become pregnant. She and Robert had tried everything, sometimes in a spirit of gritty determination, sometimes good-humouredly, but in truth they were rarely relaxed, and that had perhaps been the reason for their difficulties. They had consulted every imaginable doctor, from specialists to quacks, and each one had blamed something else, had smiled at earlier therapies and promised miracles with their own. But nothing miraculous happened and the years passed by. Vera and Robert became impatient and often used to argue. The word 'separation' hung in the air for a while without either of them daring to speak it out loud. However, luckily they realized in time what was eating away at their relationship.

On Vera's thirtieth birthday, over a bottle of prosecco and some caviar on toast, they finally agreed to consign the disappointments of recent years to the past and solemnly draw a line under their fertility experiments. They would focus instead on the joys of a future without children. By the last glass of prosecco they had reached the point of planning a journey to the Sahara, and enclosing the balcony in glass so as to transform it into a kind of conservatory. They laughed a lot, at themselves most of all, and in the end Vera landed on Robert's lap, put her arms around him and kissed him as she would have kissed a man she had never met before, completely without inhibition.

Nine months later Nadja was born. A true miracle this time. And what a child! She was pretty, with her blonde curls and big eyes, which were not china blue like Robert's, nor boringly brown like Vera's, but a fiery black. They could find no precedent for them amongst their relatives and learned to smile disarmingly and refer to the vagaries of genetics whenever anyone asked. They also learned to deal with comments about an affair on the side or a mix-up in the hospital. They simply refused to take such comments seriously and were only surprised by the way that people always came up with the same tired phrases.

Nadja was a model child, in every respect. When she was five years old Vera was once approached in the middle of the street by a woman who wanted to use Nadja in an advertising campaign. She gave Vera her business card, saying Nadja was a sweetie and bound to appeal to consumers. Vera declined. She and Robert had different ambitions for her. They saw her as a doctor or a solicitor, not as a dumb blonde. Sometimes, too, they dreamed that she would become a chemist like her father, and imagined her in a white coat striding along the corridors of a pharmaceutical company.

As far as Nadja's future was concerned, sensible parents that they were, they were determined to focus on her intellectual development. Not that she had shown any sign of becoming less attractive as she went through the various stages of development from sweet little toddler to a teenager who would turn men's heads in the street. She could never have been described as adolescent. She never had acne or problems with her weight, she never despaired over the injustices of the world, she simply took everything for granted, the good and the less good, with a level-headed acceptance that often left Robert and Vera bewildered. Was this maturity or simply incredible frivolity? Indifference even? They could never quite work it out. Nadja had such an elegant way of sweeping unpleasant things under the carpet and per-suading her parents that everything was just fine. At school, too, she so bewitched her teachers and the other pupils that no parents' evening would go by without comments like, "Your daughter really is extraordinary", or, "Nadja is the sunshine of her class, always in such a good mood, so enthusiastic and so positive. It's a joy to work with her." All that Robert and Vera could do was nod their heads and marvel at the fact that this was their child.

Soon enough Nadja would be confronted with the so-called real world, they thought. In the meantime she should enjoy being young. And in this she had every success, as far as her parents could judge from a distance, including the time she spent in London, where, after much hesitation, they had agreed to let her go and spend an exchange year. Nadja's choice of academic subject was incomprehensible to them. Not medicine, not law and not science, but to Vera's, and especially to Robert's, disappointment, English. How that was to form the basis of a solid career was unclear to them and they repeatedly tried to discourage what they thought was probably a short-lived whim. But it didn't work: English it had to be, English or nothing. Digging her heels in, Nadja finally got her way, and after her first year at university she moved to London – where only a few weeks later she met Tom.

In the morning Vera was awoken by the smell of coffee and fried bacon. The sun was shining, but it must have poured during the night. The gravel path and the lawn were partially under water.

"The first thing you must buy in Somerset is a pair of Wellington boots," Mrs Moore advised Vera as she put a plate of eggs and bacon in front of her. "You can't do anything here without them, we're always inundated. Even in summer."

"I don't mind that. It rains quite often in Switzerland, too."

Mrs Moore, who was wearing a blue-and-green-checked skirt and white twin-set today, produced slices of toast, various kinds of marmalade, jam and honey, as well as yoghurt. While going back and forth between the dining room and the kitchen, she chatted alternately to Vera and the terriers, which impatiently rubbed against her legs. Amongst all this British cosiness, what she had experienced the night before seemed so remote and un-real that Vera felt it would be inappropriate to mention it.

"The little monsters haven't been out yet today. After breakfast I'll have to leave you for a while so I can take them out for a walk."

"My daughter will be coming by in half an hour. Can I let her in?"

"Of course. I'm sure she'll want to be there when

you move into Station House. The three of us can drive over together, with the dogs."

Mrs Moore had three guest rooms that she had no difficulty in letting out during the summer and the school holidays, but the period between November and February was bad for local tourism. Vera was currently the only guest. Apart from the ticking of the clock on the wall there was no sound to be heard. After her last piece of toast and before going back up to her room, she allowed herself a tour of the other rooms on the ground floor which Mrs Moore let her guests use. The walls were hung with landscape watercolours and botanical prints. Of greater interest to Vera were the framed photographs displayed everywhere on occasional tables and chests of drawers.

Mrs Moore was shown on the arm of a man, probably her husband, on a beach, in a field or on a balcony with a view across a stormy sea. Two children appeared frequently, too. The boy was at first rather slight and then, after he had grown into a bean-pole, was shown at his wedding alongside an Asian beauty and finally – very proudly – in military uniform. The girl on the other hand was chubby from early on and as a teenager had piercings in her eyebrows and a green punk hair-do. With the rage in those eyes, those pouting lips, she could not have been an easy child. But what was Mrs Moore's family to Vera? A glance at the clock told her that Nadja would be here at any moment. She dashed upstairs to pack her things and carried her case down to the hall.

Vera would have liked a moment alone with her daughter on first seeing her, but Nadja must have met Mrs Moore on the road. Vera heard the two of them approaching with the terriers. Nadja was playing with the dogs, and from the drawing-room window Vera watched her jumping around the lawn with them. Mrs Moore came in through the door and, standing beside her, said indulgently: "Sam and Maisie seem to be crazy about your daughter – and it's mutual. Just look, isn't that a lovely sight?"

Vera nodded although she didn't find the sight particularly lovely. The dogs were growling excitedly while Nadja, standing in the middle of them, was swinging a twig round, once, twice, three times, and then throwing it high into the bushes. Finally she turned towards the house.

"Mum," she called out when she saw Vera, "there you are!"

Vera kissed her daughter on both cheeks and held her close. Her hair smelled different and the cardigan she wore unbuttoned was one Vera hadn't seen her wear before. But Nadja's face was the same, a shade rounder perhaps but happy and open, and her eyes sparkled with zest for life.

"Come on, let's go straight to Station House. I can't wait to show you your new home," she said.

Mrs Moore drove on ahead in her car. It was further than Vera had thought. Station House was outside the village on the old line of the West Somerset Railway, which since the nineteenth century had connected Taunton with the seaside town of Minehead. Most of the stations on this line were still served by steam or diesel trains as a tourist attraction, but not Southcombe since a detour had been introduced in the seventies.

"And that's where you're going to be living now, Mum," said Nadja excitedly as they turned off down a gravel track and, after about a hundred yards, saw a sandstone cottage, austere in outline but lightened by decorative barge-boarding. Vera liked the old station master's house as soon as she saw it.

Mrs Moore led them through the hall into the kitchen which Vera found inspiring, not so much because of the way in which it was laid out, which was modest, but because of the view across a meadow in which some horses were grazing. In the middle of this stood an oak tree with rooks sitting on its branches, dozens of them, so that it looked as if the tree had produced big black flowers.

"How splendid," said Vera enthusiastically.

"Yes, this house has a special atmosphere. The first station master moved in here in 1862, and when the last one died in 1973 my husband and I bought it and lived in it for thirty years. We loved Station House."

In fact the house was much too big for Vera, a real luxury that she could only afford because of the favourable exchange rate. Two so-called parlours on the ground floor and three rooms on the first floor were much more than she needed. When at the end Mrs Moore was going through the inventory and the tenancy agreement with her, Vera was already wondering which room would work best as a studio and where she would prefer to sleep. She was also thinking about a guest room, for she was sure she would have friends from Switzerland visiting in the course of the next few months.

Mrs Moore had furnished the house in a simple style. The beds and cupboards as well as the crockery were from IKEA, but she must have got the rest from second-hand shops. What Vera liked best were the old sash windows. She only knew them from films. Admittedly her enthusiasm was soon to be tempered when she realized how poorly they insulated the house from cold and rain. For the time being, however, she found it romantic to live in a genuine Victorian house and, after signing the agreement, abandoned herself to the prospect of a happy and creative year spent in it.

"But what about you, Nadja? Tell me, how things are going for you … What you are up to, you and Tom? What was the party like last night?" she asked after Mrs Moore had called her terriers back from the meadow and driven off with them.

Vera was sitting with her daughter on the sofa in the smaller parlour, which, because of the colour of the carpet, she would from now on call the blue room, by contrast with the red room, whose flowery, reddish-orange carpet was a shade too garish for her. She had made a pot of tea – her first English tea – and after she had poured them both a cup, Nadja began to get things off her chest. There was a lot of news to catch up on, not all of it pleasant. There was still no prospect of work for her, it seemed, either as a teacher or in any kind of job where her knowledge of languages would have come in useful.

"No one wants to learn foreign languages here, it's maddening. People even seem to be proud of only being able to speak English. When they find that I can speak three languages and get by in a fourth, they look at me as if I came from Mars."

Vera knew that Tom's parents had offered Nadja a job in their business a couple of months earlier, but mowing machines and other kinds of gardening equipment weren't her thing, and she understood nothing about sales and book-keeping. The parents-in-law meant well and had accepted Nadja's refusal graciously. At the time Vera wrote them a little note thanking them for the gesture.

"Oh, well, I'll get a job sometime. I'm not actually worried about it. And if I don't find anything, then we'll just start a family earlier than we'd planned."

Nadja put her tea-cup back on the tray and got up.

"Come on, Mum, let's go into the garden. Perhaps I can give you a few tips on what to plant so as to brighten it up. Apparently the last tenant completely neglected the garden. Mrs Moore told me how bad it had got, and she's right. It's such a shame."

Nadja and gardening? This was new. But Vera said nothing and followed her out. They stood silently for a while on the grass and looked at the shrubs and trees alongside the wall separating the garden from the land belonging to the railway.

"The forsythias urgently need cutting back. And

over there you need to do some pruning, otherwise there won't be enough light. Do you see? Parts of the lawn are already covered in moss. But you could turn this strip of soil into a wonderful flowerbed. I'll help you, if you like. There are all sorts of bulbs for sale in the village. There's just time to plant them before Christmas so that they flower in spring."

"You really do know a lot. You make me eager to see your garden."

"Don't expect too much. Gardens don't look very special at this time of year. Things only get going in February, and then you'll see. By the way, Southcombe won the local Village in Bloom competition this year. People are really quite proud of that."

"You too?"

Nadja looked down at her toes and said slowly: "A bit, yes … I think so. But you're cold, you're shivering all over. Let's go back into the house."

Together they unpacked Vera's suitcase, and then she went with her daughter as far as the Co-op.

"Shall I help you with the shopping?" Nadja asked.

Vera laughed. "Do I look so helpless?"

"No, not really. So I'll leave you here and we'll see each other tonight at my place. Is half six all right?"

"Of course. I'm looking forward to it. And give Tom my love."

"Will do. Enjoy making yourself at home."

At a quarter past six Vera locked Station House and drove off. On the passenger seat she'd placed the bottle of champagne that she had bought to celebrate meeting up again, together with a pile of Nadja's favourite chocolate from Switzerland. Moonlight fell on the gravel track, just enough to let her avoid the pot-holes. According to the thermometer the temperature outside was minus two, so nine degrees lower than in the morning. Vera shivered. The whole afternoon she hadn't been feeling quite at home in the house, and only now she realized that it must have been because of the cold.

Before she turned into Church Street she slowed down and allowed herself to glance at the house where she had seen the police and the ambulance the evening before. There was no longer any sign of the accident. The barriers had been removed, and where the body had lain, covered in a blanket, there stood a black Shogun. There were even Christmas lights blinking from the ground-floor windows.

Life goes on, she thought, just the same as when Robert lost his battle with cancer. In the weeks after he died, even for months after it, she had been unable to understand that people went to work, that shops opened in the morning and that children laughed on the streets as if nothing bad had happened. It seemed sheer mockery.

As earlier with Mrs Moore, Vera said nothing to Nadja and Tom about what had happened nearby. The pre-Christmas jollity in the house made it impossible. The young couple had already decorated the walls with tinsel, pine twigs and angels made of felt. Not to mention the Christmas cards lined up on a piece of string above the fireplace. All rather kitschy and old-fashioned, Vera thought, not at all the kind of thing Nadja was used to at home. But it's not my house, she told herself, and I haven't come here in order to be the difficult mother-in-law who finds fault with everything. In any case, as Nadja had once explained to her, Tom came from an old Somerset family that was very conscious of tradition. Sooner or later he would probably take over his parents' business even though he had recently found a job in computing and felt, as he put it, more at home in the world of high tech than he did dealing with tipping trailers, irrigation systems and fertilizers.

Vera liked Tom. This evening reminded her how charming and well brought up he was. Head and shoulders above Nadja, with a reddish-blond mop of hair and always rather narrowed eyes as a result of his short-sightedness, he gave the impression of being a big child who never knew exactly what people wanted from him. He was always whistling or humming something to himself, and when he opened his mouth, which was not often, Vera had difficulty understanding him because he spoke so fast and so quietly. But he obviously adored Nadja. He anticipated her every wish and treated her like a princess. As her mother Vera was happy, even if she occasionally wondered if it would do Nadja good in the long term to be so spoiled.

The two of them had prepared a cottage pie, which was under-spiced to Vera's taste but in other respects good. Neither Tom nor Nadja was gifted as a cook, and they were happy to admit that they often ate in the pub or stocked up with frozen pizzas and spring rolls in Taunton, which they then ate in front of the television. All the same, today they were sitting round a table and there was even wine after they had first drunk champagne in a toast to Vera's sabbatical.

"Yes, all the things I would like to do and experience during this year! Painting, getting to know Somerset and Devon – either on my own or together with you – brushing up my English, and as far as possible getting involved in village life."

"We'll help you, Mum. It isn't so easy to mix with people here."

"Unless you go to church on Sundays," Tom added, grinning. "That's the ideal place for getting to know people."

"In that case I'll certainly go, but not for the services. I've read in my guidebook that there are highly prized medieval carvings on the wooden benches in Southcombe church, and plenty of other interesting things to see as well."

"Yes, there's even a window by Burne-Jones, isn't there, Tom?"

He nodded. "There are several in the area. The one in Southcombe isn't the most beautiful, but we do have the most bizarre waterspout, and our porch has some of the best relief carving in the whole of Somerset."

"Well, that sounds promising. Perhaps I really should go to a service next Sunday."

"There's no need for that. Don't worry, Mum, you'll

meet people anyway. The flower shop would be a good place to start. Mr Lee knows everyone in the village, and he's very chatty. And I'm here, too," Nadja told her.

"Have you got a lot of friends in the village?"

"'Friends' is going a bit far. I know plenty of people, but it takes a while before you can really become part of the village. I joined a badminton club a few months ago, and that helps. There are ten or eleven of us women, and we meet every Wednesday afternoon in the village hall to play. It's great fun, and occasionally we go into Taunton in the evening and have a meal together. Of course, I've got to know some people through Tom, too, but they're mainly friends of the family and belong to a different generation."

During the course of the evening Vera learned all kinds of useful things about Southcombe and was able to gain a clearer idea of the life that Nadja had been living there for the past two years. Apart from badminton, walking was one of her favourite occupations when she wasn't busy in the garden, and recently she had bought a bicycle in order to go on outings with Tom at weekends.

"And when the weather's bad I do a bit of craft-work, or else I read."

"Craftwork? You? What do you do, then?"

"Oh, anything. For example, I decorate cards with pressed leaves or cut-outs and then they're sold at bazaars. Or I knit scarves … that's fun, too."

Vera remembered that Nadja had at first regretted leaving London and had even considered going back to the big city. It had been a tense time between her and

Tom. Life in Southcombe was too quiet for her, she had written, and there weren't enough intellectual challenges. However, she had gradually grown accustomed to her new home, and now it seemed to Vera as if she were really blossoming here in the countryside. But whether or not these projects fulfilled her was a different matter. Vera held back from probing too deeply on the first evening.

There was no mention of Robert. Perhaps the memory of those days eighteen months earlier when he had still been sitting at the table with them was so fresh that there was no need to mention it. Vera couldn't help thinking about him the whole time because of the photos Nadja had displayed. Wherever she looked, Vera's eyes met images of him. Here he was holding his little daughter in his arm; there playing with her on the banks of the River Aare in Switzerland. Or climbing a mountain, or waving from a train window. Or else he was standing knee-deep in turquoise water, behind him palm trees and the front of a hotel: the Maldives. Their twentieth wedding anniversary. This photo was the most painful for Vera to see and she shifted in her seat slightly so she would not have to look at it again.

Perhaps that was the reason why she dreamed of Robert in such detail on her first night in Station House. He was still quite young and they were holding hands, walking along a railway line. Then suddenly they found themselves in front of a steep slope and he began to talk her into buying him a toboggan – said he wanted to be a child again and zoom down the slope with her. As he said that, he laughed in such a strange way that Vera became afraid. She heard herself screaming in her sleep. But when she woke up she realized that it hadn't been her screams she'd heard but a bird screeching outside. Probably an owl. Vera sat up and listened. The owl must be near the house, perhaps even sitting on the fir tree at the end of the garden. In any case she could hear more screeching very clearly while she tried to find her bearings in the dark. But the room was still too strange to her, she couldn't make out the door or the cupboard and could only distinguish the curtain, which flapped in the wind.

When had she last heard an owl screech? Had she, as a confirmed townie, ever heard one except in a zoo or in a film? Probably not. However, over breakfast in the morning it occurred to her that on a ski camp in the Grisons when she was perhaps eleven or twelve she had heard a tawny owl and the next day her classmates had laughed at her because she had thought that a wild cat was roaming round the chalet at night.

When Vera got up in the morning, there was snow on the ground. From the room that she had chosen as her studio she could enjoy a view of willows with a stream flowing between them, and in the distance a line of hills. The sky hung low today and was a metallic grey. There was no sign of the sun, just here and there, between the clouds, a strip of pink light. After breakfast Vera took her paint-brushes out of their box, unpacked canvases, paint boxes, oils and thinners, and laid everything out on the desk, which she had first taken care to cover with newspaper. All the same, she wanted to take her time over starting to paint. Despite the cold, she was attracted by the area round about, and even if she didn't yet have any Wellington boots there would surely be no problem with walking around in Swiss hiking boots.

She was mistaken. There was a path over the fields to the next village which Nadja had recommended to her, but it soon became muddy. Vera preferred to turn back before getting stuck.

Instead of returning to the house she decided on a walk into the village, where, amongst other things, she wanted to have a closer look at Southcombe church. She was interested in the Pre-Raphaelite Burne-Jones. She had recently become acquainted with his work at an exhibition in Bern, huge pictures bordering on kitsch, whose renunciation of the everyday world had fascinated her but also left an unpleasant taste in her mouth. Now there was an opportunity to check the ambivalence of her reaction against a stained-glass window of his design.

St Michael's stood on a rectangular plot facing directly on to the High Street between the Co-op and a tiny café that was open at irregular times. With its massive tower, the church seemed to dominate the whole village. Vera opened the iron gate, walked down an avenue bordered by yews up to the main entrance and looked at this for a while before going inside. Tom had aroused her curiosity. The individual figures in the relief did indeed stand out sharply from the stone background. Vera could make out all sorts of legendary grotesques with tails merging into ornamental vegetation. At the top of the doorway these were gathered together and grew upward to become a fruit-bearing tree. An apple tree, thought Vera. After all, Somerset is famous for its cider, and has been since the middle ages.

The interior of the church offered further ornamentation, both chiselled out of the sandstone pillars and carved from the wood of the bench-ends. Looking closer, Vera discovered all sorts of animals: monkeys, lions and various birds, amongst them even a pelican using its beak to cut open its breast so as to feed its young with its own blood, but more often it was vegetation. Here the craftsmen had given free rein to their imagination. They had allowed luxuriant roses, lilies, and other botanically unidentifiable flowers to run wild over the beams and the chancel steps.

Vera could not find the legendary Green Man with vines growing out of his mouth, but what she did find in the chapel was the small recumbent figure of a woman. Sheaves of wheat or flowers grew out of her stomach and her breasts spurted milk in all directions like a fountain. Apart from a wide open mouth the woman had no recognizable facial features, and in general, by contrast with the reliefs on the doorway, her contours seemed to have been smoothed away by the hand of time and could be seen only indistinctly, as if through a fine veil. One foot was broken off, and there was a crack running down the whole of the right arm. Vera had never seen a figure like that before, nor had she come across one in any book. Since the church dated from the thirteenth century she could only assume that this figure, like most of the decorations, stemmed from about the same time.

The Burne-Jones window she had come to see did not seem to belong together with these ancient motifs. Its colours jarred and the composition was too saccharine. It showed the Archangel Michael, to whom the church was dedicated. Winged and graceful, he floated on a cloud, his curly head tilted down towards the earth as he drew his flaming sword from its sheath to brandish it at a dragon cowering meekly at his feet. Vera agreed with Tom that this window was no work of art. Too static and too bloodless, it failed to make any impact in the midst of such an extravagant abundance of plant motifs.

Vera left the church through the side-door. Above her the bell was just beginning to ring out the hour: eleven strokes.

Snowflakes were swirling in the air and a cutting wind chilled her face. With her coat collar turned up, she wandered for a while between the gravestones, reading names and dates as she passed them. Everywhere there was 'In Loving Memory of ...' or 'Sadly Missed by ...', and it soon struck her how tough the people here must be, and had been even two hundred years ago. The majority of them had lived to a considerable age – that is, if they weren't snatched away in childhood. Yes, with a few exceptions, it seemed to her as if in Southcombe you either died before you reached thirty or else you survived until well over eighty. Since the 1950s there was a striking rise in the number of inhabitants who had reached a hundred.

Alongside the wall which separated the cemetery from an adjacent field there was a row of newer graves with clean, simple stones. These were decorated with flowers, even if they couldn't last long in this weather. Brown and limp they hung in the vases, ready to be cleared away. As she headed out of the cemetery it occurred to Vera that the unknown woman who had had the accident a couple of days earlier would soon be lying here. She shuddered at the thought. She didn't know the name of this woman and knew nothing about her life, but the fact that she had only just missed being a witness to her death created an almost tangible link between them. Vera promised herself that she would come back in a couple of days and put flowers on her grave. It was the least she could do, she thought. Now where exactly was Mr Lee's flower-shop?

Immediately beside the café a bright green sign drew her attention. Vera didn't want to buy any flowers today so contented herself with peeping in from the street at the bouquets in the window, which were sprayed with artificial snow. Inside the shop she could see roses glowing, and rows of red and white cyclamen arranged on the shelves. The tulip and daffodil bulbs, which Nadja had particularly recommended to her, were being sold by Mr Lee in big sacks at the entrance, with a little trowel so that people could serve themselves. Another time perhaps, thought Vera, at the same time doubting if she really wanted to become too involved in gardening during her sabbatical year. It didn't seem like the best use of her time. She had planned to do only what she had dreamed of for years, namely paint. With plants you always had to be doing something at a particular time: cutting them back, feeding and spraying them, not to mention the weeding. But cut flowers were something different. Yes, thought Vera, why not get something bright and sweet-smelling for the house from time to time, just like that, just for pleasure?

In the meantime, however, it wasn't flowers that occupied her. The old sash windows of Station House let the draughts in. She had noticed that on the first day, but now the temperature had sunk to minus ten and the air which came through the cracks made it almost unbearably cold in the house. Vera turned on all the radiators, stuffed woollen socks into the cracks and borrowed an electric heater from Nadja. But it wasn't much help, she couldn't get the house cosy, and she caught herself thinking nostalgically of her warm flat in Bern.

She had chanced on the coldest December in England for a hundred years. The television news showed dramatic images of an island crippled by snow, ice and wind. Heathrow and Gatwick airports had to close, and even schools in some parts of the country. There was chaos on the roads where salt and grit ran out. Somerset seemed to be spared the worst of it, but that was little consolation to Vera: she almost froze within her own four walls. It was impossible to sit still for any length of time, whether painting or writing emails. Even with gloves on, her fingers immediately became numb, and she shivered so much that she couldn't hold the paintbrush still, let alone hit the right keys on her computer.

The only thing was to get out and walk herself warm. In moon boots and a quilted coat she would march through the snow, tramping across the fields, in which the sheep no longer looked so white, exploring neighbouring villages and valleys. Sometimes she just felt like going up the hill behind Southcombe to Greenhill Park. The mansion stood in a picturesque setting at the end of an overgrown path rife with brambles and nettles.

Greenhill Park with its stables and annexes was praised in one of Mrs Moore's leaflets as a tourist attraction, less because of its neo-classical architecture than because it had served in the early nineties as the setting for a star-studded thriller. Robert de Niro had been holed up there after a wild chase through the English countryside. From one of the balconies he had shot at Ben Kingsley, who, after staggering a couple of steps, had collapsed, dead, on the staircase. The first signs of decay had been cleverly disguised for the filming, but now the window panes were broken, the doors nailed shut, and entry to the building was forbidden because of the danger of it collapsing. Standing in front of it, though, you could still enjoy a good view of the Quantock Hills and surrounding villages. During her excursions Vera made a series of sketches that she wanted to work into proper pictures later.

Besides the need to keep warm she tried to keep busy because she didn't want to give Nadja the feeling that she had to look after her mother. Her daughter had other things to do, like making cards for the imminent Christmas bazaar, buying presents and preparing a dinner party for Tom's colleagues. Vera offered to help when she bumped into her in front of the vicarage one afternoon on the way back home.

"No, no, I can manage. I'll be all right by myself, thank you. It's just that things are a bit stressful in the run-up to Christmas. There are so many little things to be dealt with that I sometimes lose track."

"Well, I could take a couple of things off your shoulders. For example, we could make these cards together, that would make it go quicker."

"Do you think so? But no, you'll go crazy when you see what I do. By comparison with the pictures you paint, this is kindergarten stuff. I can't ask you to do it."

"Oh, Nadja, don't be like that. In any case, I've got an ulterior motive. Believe me, a couple of hours in your warm house would be a real treat."

This argument seemed to convince her. "OK, then, if it's helping you too. Let's work on these wretched cards together."

"So, when shall I come?"

"Whenever you like."

"How about Monday? Then you'll have a quiet weekend to yourselves first."

Nadja frowned as she did her calculations. "Monday … But that's the twenty-first."

"What about it?"

"The twenty-first isn't any good."

The brusque tone of Nadja's voice took Vera aback.

"Well … You suggest a day, then. It's all the same to me."

"The twenty-second?"

"That's a deal."

Nadja's face brightened at once. "Thanks, Mum, we'll have a cosy day together then, won't we?"

"Of course we will. But in the meantime, back to my refrigerator."

"I forgot to tell you that Tom asked his parents about that. They're friends with Mrs Moore. The day after tomorrow they're flying back from Dubai and then they'll have a word with her so that she does something about it at last. Better insulation or something like that."

"Yes, it really needs something. I wonder how the previous tenants survived the winter."

"That was a man. And he only lived in Station House from spring until the autumn. Otherwise I'm sure Mrs Moore would have done something about the cold long ago. But I must be going, Mum. Tom will be back home very soon, and I haven't got anything ready for tea yet."

As she said this, Nadja dashed off. Not as light-footed as she used to be, Vera noticed. Yes, Nadja had put on a couple of pounds since her mother's last visit. And there was that sudden change of mood, a brief shadow that seemed to pass over her. It probably didn't mean anything, but nevertheless …

Chapter 2

He had time.

The whole night if he wanted it. Nevertheless he acknowledged the body only with a brief, indifferent glance before putting the scissors to the collar of her dress and opening it down to her navel. A thin torso sprinkled with blotches came into view, tiny breasts, a prominent sternum, ribs that one could count at a glance. All in all an easy job, he reckoned. Not like three years ago when he had first had to remove layer after layer of fat.

He avoided the face as he worked. Earlier he used to cover it with a cloth so that he wasn't tempted to let it stick in his memory. But in the meantime he had learned to limit his attention to the few square centimetres he was working on. If his eyes should nevertheless slide higher than the chin he would narrow them and take several deep breaths. He was afraid that the face would haunt him in his sleep. The memory of the first one – she had been called Judith and wasn't even nineteen years old – could still, eight years later, startle him out of his sleep. Her face had been so friendly, filled with a deep sense of trust. And then the freshness of it, the colour of her lips and cheeks, which had scarcely grown pale. He would never have expected such signs of life in a dead person. He had had to force himself not to put down his tools and run off, leaving the job undone. But there was no danger of that tonight. He felt calm and competent. And grateful that for once he didn't know the woman personally.

With his index and middle fingers he felt below the left breast, inserted the knife and slowly began to open the skin. The flesh split apart under the blade and puckered up like a mouth. There was scarcely any blood. He hadn't expected any after four days.

He worked carefully but without precision. There was no need for accurate work here. With a few cuts he separated the left breast from the torso, then he scraped little pieces of flesh off the exposed ribs and used tongs to open the thorax. From the flesh there arose a sharp smell that he knew only too well. He automatically took a step back. He began to sniff and wiped the sweat from his forehead before he collected himself in order to get on with the job.

Outside he could hear the dull sound of footsteps and the voices of passers-by. Then the nine strokes of the church clock opposite. Suddenly he felt tired. He felt a need to sit down. But there was no point in doing things by halves, he had to finish the job, that was the deal. So he bent over the body again and resolutely pushed his hand under the wind-pipe, pressing the left lung against the rib-cage. An involuntary 'Sorry' escaped his lips as he separated the aorta and the caval vein and then, after briefly feeling around, gave the fist-sized heart muscle a tug as he tore it out of the rib-cage.

At twenty to ten he left the house. A few minutes later he pushed open the door of the Kings Arms and ordered a double whisky, which he downed in one. He then looked round, burping, and stared into the distance. There was a sentimental pop song playing on the radio, something sad about unrequited love and loneliness.

Apart from him there were three customers in the pub that evening: John Griffiths, the plumber from Giverton, the old piano builder Rosenbaum and his son Josh. Griffiths was sitting alone by the fire with his back to the room. Every couple of seconds he dipped into his bag of crisps without taking his eyes off his sports newspaper, while the Rosenbaums were using wild gesticulations to express their anger over bankers' bonuses and the imminent rise in VAT.

He didn't exchange a word with any of the customers. After two further double whiskies he slid off his stool and staggered out without anyone paying any attention. It was quarter-past ten.

Chapter 3

In France it was quarter-past eleven. Jason took the watch off his wrist and stepped into the shower. He washed the soil off his hands and the smoke from the open fire out of his hair. He scrubbed sweat and dirt off his legs, belly and upper body, and thought to himself how crap it was that life didn't let you get rid of the past in the same way. Then the nightmares would be washed away, the lies would be shed like layers of skin, and he would be newborn at twenty-nine years old, a blank sheet of paper – and free.

Yes, above all free. Like the seagulls above him driven inland by the bad weather, crying out to each other from the roof of the chateau. They could fly wherever they wanted, those creatures, the whole of the sky belonged to them. But how loud their cries were. Suspiciously loud. Had he left the window open? Or even forgotten to lock the door and push the chest of drawers in front of it?

Covered in soap from head to toe, Jason climbed out of the shower and peered into the adjoining room through the gap in the bathroom door. With the ease of long practice his gaze swept over the carpet – socks, a crumpled paper handkerchief and the thriller he had finished the day before – then on to his bed and finally the edge of the chest of drawers. Everything all right so far, the chest of drawers was in the right position and the door and the window were closed. Of course they were. He suddenly remembered turning the key in the lock and pushing the furniture into place. Over time these actions had become as automatic as breathing. He couldn't imagine that he would ever forget them. And yet he had to check over and over again. It was a compulsion, there was no other word for it.

After his shower Jason let himself collapse on the bed and reached for the zapper. He had put a cheese sandwich and a banana ready on the bedside table together with a two-litre bottle of Cola Light. He took little sips out of it while he zapped through the incomprehensible advertisements and shows.

Three years in Picardy, and the French language was still a closed book to him. He could produce a couple of mangled phrases, '*Merci beaucoup*', '*Au revoir*', '*S'il vous plaît*' and things like that; just enough so that he didn't stand out as rude in the village, just enough to let him buy his croissant at the baker's on a Sunday morning. He didn't need more than that, he scarcely mixed with people. And when he did, he was generally trailing behind Rich and Frances, who needed him to carry what they had bought or to advise them on the choice of new trees in the plant nursery. And for that he really didn't need to dig out his school books again. Rich and Frances hardly spoke any French either. Frances perhaps a little more than Rich,

CUSTOMER RECEIPT

55751 - Barnstaple
89 High Street Barnstaple Devon , EX31 1HR
11/07/2023 11:04:15
RECEIPT NO.: 12656
MID: XXX79154   TID: XXXX6302
AID: A0000000041010
Debit Mastercard
XXXXXXXXXXXX4496
PAN SEQ NO. : 00

SALE :   GBP2.00
TOTAL :   GBP2.00

PLEASE DEBIT MY ACCOUNT
NO CARDHOLDER VERIFICATION
CONTACTLESS
PLEASE KEEP THIS RECEIPT FOR YOUR RECORDS
AUTH CODE:196206

but even in her case Jason had never heard a properly coherent sentence pass her lips.

For more than twenty years the two of them had spent summers in their chateau as if living in an island of Englishness. Somehow it worked. In emergencies the local authorities engaged an interpreter. Like two years ago when parts of the estate were flooded and the insurance company didn't want to pay up for repairs to the swimming pool. And if '*les anglais*', as the pair were referred to locally, had visitors then it was friends from the other side of the Channel, just more '*anglais*'.

When Rich had told him in the pub about his chateau in France and how tricky it was leaving it empty over the winter months, Jason had pricked up his ears. Rich had had a couple of drinks. He was rambling on and Jason didn't take him too seriously at first when he began to describe the estate with its woods, then a swimming pool and tennis court, plus a greenhouse that he wanted to turn into a place to grow succulents. Jason didn't feel he needed to pay much attention. Two years behind the bar had taught him a thing or two: for example, not to take at face value everything he was told after a couple of pints of beer. A chateau! How crazy was that? Lords lived in chateaux, not blokes like Rich who hung around in a pub after work on a Friday evening and poured out their heart to the first friendly barman they came across.

Rich worked in one of those glass skyscrapers behind the famous Gherkin, in some bank or corporation, Jason didn't know which exactly. But one thing was clear.

People who own chateaux don't need to work, so there was definitely something odd about his story. But Rich hadn't finished. The following Friday he took a couple of photos out of his waistcoat pocket and laid them out in front of Jason like a triumphant poker player.

"Well, what do you think of my chateau now?"

"Not bad at all."

Admittedly it wasn't a classic chateau, at least not in Jason's understanding of the word. But with the pillars beside the entrance and its two large, symmetrical wings it certainly gave the impression of being a grand house. It was just that nature round about seemed to have run wild, with brambles over the paths and random gaps in the pine woods.

"And where exactly is this?"

"Not far from the mouth of the Somme, by St Valéry. Does that mean anything to you?"

"No, haven't got a clue."

"Have you ever been to France?"

Jason shook his head. "When I was a kid we used to go on holiday to Spain, but I was little then. I can hardly remember anything except the long drive."

"And later?"

"Later? Nothing. You need money to get away from England. That's what I haven't got."

"So you've never been across the Channel since?"

"No."

"Would you like to go sometime?"

"Don't know. Perhaps. But I've got to work now or else the boss will be shouting at me again. He's been in a terrible mood of late. His wife ran away from him not long ago. Between you and me, I can see why. No normal woman could stand life with a bastard like him."

After this conversation Rich hadn't turned up for a while. But Jason had not forgotten him or his chateau. Why had Rich asked if he would like to go over to France sometime? Could he have fancied him? He wouldn't have been the first man to have hoped for more than just friendship with Jason. But that wasn't his kind of thing at all. And what was Rich thinking of at his age, with that thinning hair, those bags under his eyes and those rotten teeth? Looking back at the scene, Jason almost became angry. But the chateau … that was worth considering. Not that Jason let himself be dazzled by dreams of luxury. Chateau or studio, it was all the same to him really. He was just interested in where it was. In how many hundreds of miles away from his home the chateau was. Perhaps it was fate. When Rich came back into the pub one evening and ordered his usual pint, Jason grabbed his chance.

"Hi, Rich. Haven't seen you for a long time. We've really missed you here. Where have you been hiding? In your French chateau?"

"Dead right. Frances and I only got back the day before yesterday."

Jason looked at him more closely as he filled the beer glass. Rich had caught the sun a little. He seemed less pasty-faced and stressed than usual. And his suit was new, grey rather than the same old dark blue. But basically he hadn't changed. He was and remained a middle-aged man who drank too much and took too little exercise. Jason knew the type. London was full of men like that. Younger ones than Rich too.

"And was it fun?" he asked.

"Yes, great. I've finally made a start on renovating the greenhouse. Hard work, I can tell you. It'll take months yet. But at least it gives me a goal to aim for during the holidays."

Jason listened patiently as Rich boasted of his carpentry skills. He wasn't interested in the greenhouse, and even less in what his customer had to say about the unreliability of French workmen. After a while he managed to get in a few clever questions which turned Rich back to the subject of the chateau.

"So it's going to be empty for the whole winter. Isn't that a pity?"

"There's nothing else for it. Earlier we tried to let it. A real disaster. Broken crockery, torn sheets, scratches everywhere. It was pure vandalism. No, if you're there in person that kind of thing doesn't happen. But we've never found a concierge we could trust."

"*Concierge* … what's that? Having another drink?"

"Yes, thanks. A concierge is something like a house-keeper, butler and odd-job man all rolled into one. I know people in St Valéry who would be keen on the job but I don't trust them. They would just try and impress their friends by playing lord of the manor while we're away."

"You'd need someone who wasn't local then."

"Absolutely. That's the conclusion we've come to as well. But who'd want to spend the winter in an empty mansion two miles from the next village and three from St Valéry … unless they were some kind of crazy hermit? You just find me someone who'd live up there for half the year all on his own."

"Already found, Rich." Jason tapped himself on the chest with his index finger.

Rich smiled awkwardly.

"You joker."

"No, I mean it. Seriously, I do. I'd hand my notice in today if I got the job. I'm sick of it here. The pubs, London, England, the whole lot. A change of scene like that would be just the thing for me."

"You're only saying that."

"No, Rich. Just give me a chance."

"What about your family?"

"You can forget about them. I have."

"Wife or girlfriend?"

"Is this the inquisition? If I was married and had children round my neck I wouldn't be making you this offer."

"OK, OK. Calm down. I was only asking because … because it's so unexpected. I thought a young man like you would want to be around people, partying and so on."

"Nonsense. What do you know about young men?"

"Not a lot, I admit," laughed Rich. "But I can't imagine that someone like you would enjoy living in the middle of nowhere."

"Perhaps I've got my reasons. And in any case I wouldn't be living just anywhere, I'd be in a chateau. That would have its attractions."

It didn't take long to persuade Rich that Jason was the right person for the job. And finally, when he let it slip that he had been used to gardening as a kid at home and now, after three years in the East End of London, longed for nothing more than to spend his time in the fresh air with a spade, a rake and a hoe, Rich was convinced.

"OK, I can see it really could work. But please think if over. And remember especially that you would be entirely cut off there."

"Cut off? I don't know what from."

"From … everything your life has been up to now."

"Up to now it's been crap. My life can only get better."

The move had worked out for Jason. He liked his new life. It proceeded calmly, with nothing special happening, and for the first time since making his hurried getaway from Somerset he felt reasonably free from financial worries and anxiety. What more did he want? Rich and Frances had accepted him like the son they had never had. They arranged a room for him in the right-hand wing of the chateau and allowed him free access everywhere else, from the cellar to the empty rooms in the attics. But Jason didn't make use of them. He wasn't interested in Rich's vintage wines any more than he was in his employer's collection of golf clubs and tennis racquets. He preferred to stay for a while in one of the lounges after supper, leafing through a couple of books, repairing a door handle or wiping spiders' webs from the window recesses. In the summer, when Rich and Frances came, he would occasionally let Rich persuade him to join in a game of chess and would help Frances with her crosswords, but he only really felt comfortable when he could be by himself. He liked his room. The bright modern furniture, the spotless bath and the view across to distant cliffs, lit up in all possible colours in the evening sun, made him forget his shabby studio over a kebab house in Whitechapel.

In particular he liked Rich and Frances. They didn't ask difficult questions, and they didn't use leading comments to provoke him into revealing more about his past than he was comfortable with. In truth the couple knew nothing about him. But soon after Jason had moved in they realized that there was something strangely reciprocal about the arrangement. They had found the ideal man for the job, and Jason had found the ideal place to be left in peace. They didn't want to bother their heads with dreaming up possible reasons why a young man like this should withdraw from the world. As long as he did his job to their satisfaction, that could stay his business. So both sides took care not to disturb this fragile balance. They were as considerate of each other as possible and made numerous gestures to show how much they valued the arrangement.

Jason hadn't been able to provide any references, but did that matter when everything else seemed to fit?

Frances had had reservations at first, but after watching him at work for a couple of days she had been reassured. Jason revealed himself to be an excellent gardener and a landscape designer with an eye for unusual perspectives. In two years he had transformed the approach to the chateau, and thanks to his work dredging the pond at the western end of the estate, which had been nearly suffocating under the onslaught of autumn leaves, frogs slowly began to move back in. Jason, it seemed, didn't merely have the proverbial green fingers, he was a magician: the most troublesome of plants flourished under his supervision.

With Jason on the premises they didn't need to fear trespassers or squatters. Burst pipes, broken windows and patches of mildew on the wallpaper no longer spoiled their return to the house in the summer. They found the lawn mown, the beds made and the refrigerator full. It was almost too good to be true. The only downside was that, year by year, Jason became more indispensable.

He zapped through the television channels and stayed with the images of snowed-up airports and lines of traffic on icy roads. They showed Orly and the A10 around Tours and Blois, perplexed drivers and trees that had snapped under the weight of snow. None of that was very interesting. He went on zapping and for a couple of minutes watched a documentary about catching whales. Finally he turned to an American gangster film full of chases, shooting and blondes in low-cut dresses. When it came to the advertisements he reached over for his cheese sandwich and switched to the BBC. There too there were reports of the disruption of air travel in Europe as a result of the snow. This time Jason recognized the departure lounge at Heathrow. It was full of stranded passengers who all had the same story to tell: they wanted to fly in order to spend Christmas with distant relatives and were now afraid that they would have to celebrate it in the airport instead. An Italian couple seemed relaxed about it, the Spaniard they showed next less so: he struggled with tears at the thought of his mother in Alicante who was dying and whom he would probably never see alive again. Finally a Briton spoke into the microphone.

"I wanted to fly to Paris and, well, it now looks as if I shall have to go back home thanks to a couple of idiots here in airport management. I live in Somerset and that's not just round the corner. I can't afford to spend days in a hotel in London until I can finally get on a plane. That business with the de-icer having run out is just an excuse. It's bad planning. I reckon they don't want to admit that the climate is changing. Last year the airport had problems with snow, too. Is it really so difficult for them to plan ahead? It's not as if this is the first time this has happened."

"And what are you thinking of doing now?"

"I don't know yet. The tunnel isn't the answer. It's hopelessly overbooked. No, I've no idea."

As the man shook his head in despair the camera slowly zoomed in on his face until it filled the whole screen. It was bony and tense-looking, with eyes shadowed by thick brows. A smoker's face, thought Jason, with those typical yellow teeth and the fine lines round the lips. He was glad he didn't smoke. Didn't want to look like that in twenty years' time. But what was he doing listening to the ramblings of a frustrated traveller? What did he care about the man's problems? Jason's finger was already on the zapper to switch off the television, but at the last moment something held him back. A memory was finding its way back into his consciousness. It was unpleasant … no, more than that, it was unsettling. He felt a chill run through him that made his limbs feel weak. Then the fear. Suddenly it was there. Jason swallowed. His mouth went dry, his hands began to sweat. A gust of wind blowing against the window panes made him jump. That voice! Hoarse from smoking and repeatedly cracking. That lazy way of speaking, those long drawn out vowels. Why did it all seem so familiar to him? Where on earth did he know that voice from?

He wanted to look away and close his ears, but forced himself to look more closely at the man. The camera was turning away towards the crowd in the background, but it just caught a helpless shrug and a "What can you do?" before the reporter came into the frame again, this time standing in front of Terminal 5, her breath steaming in the cold air and snowflakes in her hair. Miles! Of course it was. How could Jason have forgotten that face? He really should have recognized it straight away. Miles didn't even look any older, five years on. He was just thinner, as if withered, but it was him, of that Jason had no doubt.

The reporter with her chatter about cancelled flights and the costs for the airlines soon got on his nerves. He turned off the television and sat up in bed. The wind rushing through the trees outside made him feel uneasy. He glanced from the window to the door and pricked up his ears. All was quiet. No, it wasn't entirely quiet. The tap in the bathroom was dripping. But he had turned it off. Obviously not firmly enough, though. Jason heard the drops falling, in a lazy rhythm, one, two, three – like ... He struggled for air as the memory hit him like a thunder-bolt.

Weren't five years enough to let him forget?

He ran his fingers through his hair and began to whimper like an animal. He pressed the pillow to his chest and buried his head in it, deeper and deeper, until he could scarcely breathe and his sight was blocked. But the memory wouldn't go away. Louder and louder the drops fell into the basin and slowly the water began to go red, like the blood that had dripped from Lizzie's fore-head on to the ground. One drop, two, three ... until there was a red pool spreading under his eyes with Liz-zie's hair swimming in it.

If he didn't get up and turn off the tap he would be hearing that sound all night. Until the puddle spread over the whole room, flowed out into the hall and trickled down the stairs, like in his nightmares.

Jason jerked himself up and opened his eyes. The room was spinning, and for a moment he felt like a half-drowned person who has just reached dry land, terrified and astonished still to be alive. But safe? No, never that.

If Miles was searching for Jason after all these years then he would eventually find him. He would hunt him out, even here in the farthest corner of Picardy. Hadn't he sworn that he would? "Sooner or later I'll get you, and when I do I'll kill you. As true as my name is Miles."

That was what he had said, and Jason had taken him at his word. Miles wasn't someone to play games with. There was a good reason why people in the village called him 'the Wolf'.

And now he was on his way to France.

Chapter 4

On the morning of 21 December Southcombe cemetery lay under a thick layer of snow. A flock of starlings flew up from the ground as Vera tramped past some weather-beaten Celtic crosses towards the more recent graves. Thanks to the mass of wreaths and bouquets she immediately found the one that interested her. It consisted of a provisional wooden cross bearing the name and dates of the dead woman: Susan Harper, 5.3.1978 - 20.11.2010.

None of the wreaths had a message attached, and to judge from the untouched layer of snow Vera was the first person to have come here since the burial the day before.

Susan had been thirty-two, Vera worked out, such a young woman. One who wore pink shoes when she died. What had she looked like? Blonde or dark? Slim or podgy? Tall or short? And what had her voice sounded like? Questions to which Vera would probably never have an answer. Perhaps that was the way it should be. The sooner she forgot Susan Harper the better. All the same, today she wanted to pass by the florist's. She could at least buy the unknown woman a poinsettia.

However, to her surprise she found Mr Lee's shop closed, and when she looked further round the village she saw that it wasn't the only one. The butcher's, the newspaper shop, the bistro and a unisex hair salon that Vera found at the end of a side-street were all shut. Only in the Co-op was there any light. There was a sales assistant busy arranging tins on the shelves, but Vera couldn't see a single customer. She bought some fruit, eggs and frozen spinach, and then asked the young man at the till, "Is it a special day today?"

The assistant brushed the hair out of his face and put a finger to his mouth as if he was searching for the right word. Finally he answered in the broadest Somerset accent, "Do you mean a bank holiday? No, not as far as I know."

"But all the other shops are shut."

"They're always shut on the twenty-first. That's how it is here."

"Aha. And why?"

The young man just grinned.

"It's Monday," Vera insisted, "so why?"

"Because it's the twenty-first."

Irritated, she took her change and the receipt and left the shop without replying to the young man as he said good-bye.

It had started to snow again. Except for a blackbird that dived across to the other side of the street, the village seemed deserted. The pub was shut, curtains closed on most of the ground-floor windows, so that Vera had the feeling she was walking through a dream. How could there possibly be such silence on the Monday before Christmas, when the shops were usually striving to boost their sales and everyone was out panic-buying?

Vera did see half a dozen girls playing hopscotch in front of the primary school. She watched them for a while. Despite the cold they were wearing short blue uniform skirts and socks. Under their jackets they wore sweatshirts with the school badge on them. The ones who were not actually doing the hopping stood to one side, shivering, hands clenched into fists, arms crossed over their chests. At least there was school as usual to-day, thought Vera with relief. After seeing no one else on her walk home, though, she decided to check the reason for the village's deserted air.

Searching the internet under 'Southcombe', she found every imaginable bit of information, but no reference to this date. December's 'Events' consisted of three choir evenings, handicraft sessions every Friday, the Christmas bazaar on the twenty-third, and on New Year's Day drinks at a quarter-past six at the vicarage, to which everyone was invited. Vera looked under 'Club Activities'. Clubs were clearly thick on the ground in Southcombe. There was not just the badminton club that Nadja had recently joined, not just pilates, yoga and football clubs, a book group and a Bible group, groups for mothers, groups for women over fifty-five and groups for everything from pottery to knitting, but also a whole list of specialist gardening groups. Vera couldn't help but smile to see these. In Southcombe there really were weekly meetings at which tulip gardeners, friends of the dahlia and rose-lovers could exchange tips. She did however notice that all the usual Tuesday meetings were cancelled on the twenty-first. No one met today, but there was no explanation anywhere for this cancelation of normal activities.

The only thing that occurred to her was that 21 December was the winter solstice, the shortest day of the year. She had found all sorts of information about abstruse rituals across the world, from greeting the light with dance to purifying with incense. Greeting the light? Incense? Here in Southcombe? Vera rejected the idea at once. However, during the afternoon, which dragged on with what seemed to her almost oppressive slowness, she became less certain.

Why not? What did she know about Somerset customs? She had done hardly any research before her journey. After all, she had come here as a mother, not a tourist. And yes, as an artist too, hoping that a sabbatical year would give her some inspiration. If all went well she would go back to Switzerland with enough pictures for an exhibition. That had been her greatest wish even while Robert was still alive.

"When I'm no longer here," he had encouraged her shortly before his death, "you must finally realize this dream of yours. Pack your paints and brushes and go to Nadja. It doesn't have to be for ever."

Vera had now lived for almost a month in the old station master's house in Southcombe and still didn't have a clue about the habits and customs of the place.

She was almost ashamed. Things couldn't go on like this, she had to establish contact, join some club or other. Tom's mother was president of various gardening clubs, Mrs Moore was in charge of the knitting group, and the person responsible for the organisation of the Christmas bazaar, Vera read with a pounding heart, was – Sue Harper. The web page had clearly not been brought up to date.

"How many of you are there in the handicraft group?" Vera asked her daughter the next day as they put the finished cards on the window-sill in order to see them properly.

"Sometimes ten, sometimes only four or five, it just depends. As it gets towards Christmas there are always one or two extra. The Southcombe bazaar is an important occasion. I hope you're coming tomorrow, then I can introduce you to a couple of people from the village. Especially my friends from the badminton group."

"Of course I'm coming. I've already made a note of it."

"Good. And what do you think of our cards?"

"As a matter of fact, I rather like them."

"Come on, tell the truth. You think they're kitsch, don't you?"

"No, not at all. I'm just surprised that everything was laid down so precisely. I thought you'd be able to make the cards in whatever way you wanted."

"That's what I thought in the first year, too. But here everything is done strictly according to tradition.

Decorating the cards with petals goes back centuries, and I'm afraid people aren't keen on anybody deviating from the original patterns."

"But who is it who decides that things have to stay like that?"

"Up to now it was Mrs Harper, she was our group leader, but she died recently and someone else will be taking over the group."

"Did you know her well?"

"No. Why?"

Perhaps Vera was imagining it but it seemed to her that Nadja stiffened almost imperceptibly at the mention of Mrs Harper.

"Because I came across her grave the last time I wandered round the cemetery."

"She was an extraordinary woman. Sometimes terribly over the top, at others listless and gloomy. You never knew quite where you were with her. But otherwise she was nice. I liked her, and I think she liked me. She always called me 'our lovely Swiss girl'."

"And you really are lovely, darling. But to come back to Mrs Harper, was she married … did she have any children?"

"Yes, her husband is the chef at the Kings Arms. I've no idea if she had any children. She never mentioned any or brought them along to the group. But honestly, Mum, why all these questions?"

"I'm just interested in the people you spend time with. Isn't that normal?"

Nadja shrugged her shoulders and disappeared into the kitchen. A few minutes later Vera could here the gentle roaring of the coffee machine.

She had made fifty cards with her daughter but could hardly call the work creative. In Vera's opinion the cards were dull and unimaginative.

"What kind of cards do the other members of the group make?"

"Have a guess," replied Nadja with a mischievous smile as she came into the living-room bringing a tray with steaming coffee cups and biscuits on it.

"Don't tell me they're exactly the same?"

"They're identical. And so it goes on from year to year."

"Is it the same in other villages round here?"

"No, I don't think so. You can see that for yourself from the Christmas cards we've already received. They're printed, meaning people have bought them. Here in Southcombe bought cards are completely frowned upon."

"I'm slowly getting the feeling that this is the weirdest village in England."

"I've thought that for a long time but Tom goes mad when I say it and his parents even more so. Please don't say anything like that at the Christmas dinner, will you?"

"Not a word, I promise."

Vera put down her coffee cup and looked out on to the street. In the garden of the house opposite two boys were trying to build an igloo. They worked hard at forming cubes from the thinly scattered snow and arranged them in rows. Behind the house the tower of St Michael's rose into the sky, and on the right-hand side between two bungalows Vera could see part of the cemetery wall. Sue Harper's grave, she reckoned, was less than fifty metres from Nadja's house.

"Is everything all right, Mum? You look so serious."

"I was thinking about Mrs Harper again. On the evening of the day I arrived here I went for a stroll through the village and saw the police and an ambulance in front of her house."

"You never told me that."

"No, I didn't. But I'm telling you now. She was still lying on the road when I got there. Someone had thrown a blanket over her and there were several policemen shielding her from view. Nevertheless I saw one of her feet. It's not much but it affected me more than I realized. Now I can't get the poor woman out of my head."

"She killed herself," said Nadja in a flat voice.

"I thought she must have. Does anyone know why?"

"I've no idea. Apart from in the handicraft group, I had nothing to do with her. She was older than me and terribly religious. So not really my type."

"People who are terribly religious don't usually commit suicide. But let's not be ghoulish. It's nearly Christmas. Can I do anything to help you get the meal ready? There's going to be quite a crowd of us, I'm sure there's something I could do."

"No, thanks, Tom and I have got everything under control. All you need to do is turn up and enjoy yourself. And how about staying for tea today? It's only leftovers, but at least you won't have to eat all by yourself in your refrigerator."

Station House really was cold. When Vera returned that evening the thermometer showed six degrees in the kitchen and eight in the bedroom. Instead of watching the comedy on television that Nadja had recommended, she crept straight into bed with a hot water bottle and the post that had arrived that day. Salomé had written, good old Salomé who couldn't cope with emails. She told Vera that the headmaster had broken his arm playing squash, that a pupil had been expelled for fighting, and that she with her sixty-two years had finally – perhaps – found the right man. "Cross your fingers for me that it works out. I'm meeting him next Saturday for lunch in town. He's called Ralph and he runs an electrical shop there."

Vera smiled to herself and went over to the art magazine she subscribed to, which had taken a fortnight to get from Switzerland to her front door. Was that because of the Swiss post or the English post? Or was it because of the snow? Her thoughts were interrupted by the phone ringing. A phone call at ten o'clock at night? Vera jumped up and hurried down the stairs into the living room.

"Hello?"

"Good evening. I apologize for ringing so late. Is that Station House?"

"Yes. Who is this?"

"My name is Craig Brett. I used to rent Station House."

"Oh, right. Yes … I …." Vera searched for words, but the caller spoke first.

"Of course you're wondering why I'm ringing you. I'm sorry to call so late. I actually live in London, but at the moment I'm in Somerset and just wondered if I could call by? It would only be for a moment."

"Do you mean in the next few days? Before Christmas? But why?"

"It's a long story. I can understand why you might hesitate, but please believe me, I wouldn't ring you if it were something trivial. When I moved to London in September I left something in Station House that I urgently need."

"If you tell me what you're looking for, I could post it to you. Wouldn't that be simpler? In any case, I've been living here for almost three weeks and haven't found anything that doesn't belong in the house."

"I'd still like to come by and have a look for myself, if you don't mind? Please! I wouldn't disturb you for long."

"I'm rather busy up until Christmas. Really you should contact Mrs Moore. She got the house in order before I arrived and perhaps she found whatever it is you're looking for."

"No, no, Mrs Moore doesn't need to be bothered with this. I'd prefer to come direct to you. How about Boxing Day?"

"Boxing Day?"

"Yes, the twenty-sixth. I'll be staying at the Bell Inn in Watchet then. That's very close to Southcombe."

"All right then, if you really want to. But you'll find the house changed. I've moved some of the furniture round, and my things are everywhere."

"That's all right. I promise not to trouble you for long."

In the end Vera couldn't stop herself from asking why he was travelling the country at Christmas, a time when most people prefer to be at home with their family.

"It's urgent business which I can't put off, unfortunately. So may I come round on the twenty-sixth? At about three?"

Half amused and half anxious, Vera put down the phone and went shivering to bed. The stranger had seemed open and likeable enough, but could she put her trust in a pleasant voice? Hadn't she been rather quick to agree? In order to stifle the doubts rising in her mind, Vera opened her magazine and tried to lose herself in an article about the artists of the Japanese Gutai group, the subject of a major exhibition in Lugano. But it couldn't hold her attention. The telephone conversation went round and round in her head, and the more she thought about it, the more suspicious she became. She was annoyed with herself for having been so compliant. When she turned off the light at eleven and lay in the darkness waiting for sleep that wouldn't come she reached the conclusion that Craig Brett, if that was indeed his name, had not so much requested admission to Station House

61

as insisted on it. But why? And what was he looking for? With these thoughts going round and round her mind there was no question of sleep.

After tossing and turning for a while, Vera turned the light on again and got up. Since Robert's death she slept less well than she used to, but had gradually grown used to it. Even the sight of her weary face when she looked in the mirror the next morning no longer disturbed her. At first the doctor had prescribed tablets, but she had stopped taking them for fear of becoming addicted. It was better to count the strokes of the clock on the bell-tower than sink into that fuzzy unconsciousness she had to struggle out of in the morning. But unlike in Switzerland, here the hours in which she lay awake worrying made her edgy and anxious. Could it be the silence? Station House was too far from the village for her to be able to hear the clock-tower of St Michael's or any traffic. Here she was all by herself, with the wind and the rain and now and then an owl that screeched.

After wandering round the house, Vera sat down in the studio with a cup of tea in front of the picture she had begun the day before. She had chosen a corner of the window as a subject, fascinated by the contrast between the clear lines of the frame and the gently undulating ones of the curtain. Perhaps it was too much for her, though. The various elements of the room did not present her with any particular technical difficulties, but the window-panes and the meadows behind them leading up to the hills were quite a challenge. What colours should she use to paint the frosty background so that the subtle shades of green, grey and brown harmonized with the hard white of the frame and the stylized red and blue pattern of the curtain material? The whole thing should be, as it were, filtered through glass. Vera stared at the sketch and tried to visualize the completed picture. She could see the landscape steeped in dull winter light, framed by white wood and, to the left, the movement introduced by the striped material. She could see everything as clearly as if the picture were already finished. But at the same time she knew that, like every other picture she had previously painted, it would disappoint her.

In a way, disappointment was part of painting. Disappointment spurred her on to learn from her mistakes and do better next time. The difficulty often lay in recognizing and interpreting her mistakes. She noticed at once if something about a picture wasn't right, but what it was, whether the colour composition, the perspectives or simply poor draughtsmanship, only ever became clear much later. Usually she needed the teacher to say, "There, look, that flower in the foreground. It's much too big by comparison with those that are behind it. Where's your sense of proportion?" Werner Raflaub, her teacher for the last two years of her course in Bern, had taught her a lot. He had encouraged her and helped her to develop a style of her own. None of the books she had brought to England would be able to replace his insight and advice. All she had to do was stay long enough in Southcombe and she would end up like Nadja, falling into the trap of producing kitsch.

And as Vera saw the next morning, this was a very real danger. She had hardly crossed the threshold of the village hall in which the Christmas bazaar was being held before she was overwhelmed by the most extraordinary range of kitsch: fashion jewellery, batik scarves, home-made tea-cosies, pictures in acrylic, and plenty more. What clashing colours, what unnecessary cuteness. Luckily she soon made out the card stand next to the coffee and cakes section, and there was Nadja, dressed entirely in black, adding a refreshingly sober note to the scene. Lost in thought, she was gazing over the heads of the crowd while she played with her amber necklace. Vera made her way through the mass of people and gave her daughter a hug.

"Is Tom here too?"

"He's coming later. Bazaars aren't really his thing. But he's promised to take over from me. Look how many of our cards have gone already."

"You're right. But there are heaps more to be sold. Do you think you'll get rid of them all?"

"Of course I will. The bazaar only opened two hours ago. We've got the whole day."

"Now that I'm here, I'll buy a few from you. Will you choose the best patterns for me while I wander round a bit? Perhaps I'll find something I can use. I'll be straight back, probably."

The only things Vera found were in the food section. She bought a jar of home-made marmalade and two packets of ginger biscuits, and finally chose from the wide range of ciders on offer a bottle with a label on it which, instead of the usual manufacturer's name and place, had a picture of the female figure in St Michael's out of which corn grew and milk spurted. Above it was written in Celtic lettering 'Cider', nothing else.

Vera was pleased to see how comfortable Nadja felt in that mass of people, and how many people came up to her individually to have a chat. However when Nadja introduced her to them and proudly explained that her mother was planning to stay for a whole year in South-combe to be near her, Vera was surprised by the looks and comments she received.

"A whole year? Is that possible?" asked Lynn, a friend from the badminton group, with scarcely con-cealed scepticism in her voice. Others went so far as to discourage Vera.

"That's really nice. But are you going to be able to stand it for so long? We're a bit odd in Somerset. People like to come here for their holidays because things are so nice and leisurely. But a year? That's a terribly long time to spend in Southcombe."

"I haven't come here to have a holiday. I want to be with my daughter," Vera tried to explain. But no one in Nadja's circle seemed convinced by this argument.

When Tom turned up at about mid-day so that Nadja could have a break and get something to eat and drink, Vera took the opportunity to express her unease.

"I get the feeling people aren't too keen on having strangers around here. It's different for you and Tom, you live here, but as a visitor I don't seem to be entirely welcome."

"Nonsense, Mum. They just don't express themselves very well. As soon as people see you with Tom's parents they'll open every door to you. Don't worry. You'll see, it'll all be OK."

Vera stirred her coffee without saying anything. While they were talking Nadja had quietly ordered a second slice of marble cake, which she now accepted gratefully from the girl who was serving.

"Will you stay behind afterwards for a bit? At two o'clock the raffle takes place outside, and you mustn't miss that. The whole village gathers on the grass and takes part. There are fantastic prizes to be won."

"I've always wanted to win a flight. To New York or Tokyo, for example. But I don't suppose you can win something like that here."

"No, I'm afraid there are no trips to be won. But you can win overnight stays in local hotels, vouchers for a pub meal, and all sorts of local products."

"But first you need tickets. Where can you buy them?"

"Oh, they were sold out long ago. But I went and got ten in advance, five for you and five for me."

Nadja had in the meantime eaten the second slice of cake and was now scrabbling around in her bag for the tickets.

"I'll keep them all for the moment. But in case we win something, which numbers do you want?"

Vera decided on the lower numbers and wanted to press a £5 note into Nadja's hand.

"No, that's much too much. You owe me just a pound."

"One pound for five numbers? In that case you could have bought more and given us a better chance."

"Not allowed to. Five numbers per person is the maximum. I expect they want to avoid any one person grabbing all the prizes."

That seemed logical to Vera. But when she looked round before the draw began she saw a man standing in front of the entrance holding bundles of tickets in his hand. Green tickets, though, not pink ones like theirs.

Chapter 5

Previously he had always avoided the raffle. Tombola didn't interest him, and he had never won anything – he simply wasn't one of those lucky beggars who went home after such events with armfuls of booty. Once, as a child, he had won a bag of tulip bulbs, but how is a six year old supposed to get excited over a bag of bulbs? Disappointed, he had handed the prize over to his mother, who planted the bulbs in two big pots in front of the annexes and by the time they flowered had long forgotten who had given them to her.

It was only since he had started his additional line of work – it was Judith in 1997 – that he had begun to take any interest in the raffle, and then purely for professional reasons. There was nothing about it in his contract, but here and there he had picked up comments to the effect that it was in his interest to attend the raffle. So that he could understand the deeper meaning of his task.

Understand! That was the wrong word. Everyone in the village knew that he didn't understand a thing. He could weld, he could hammer nails in and he could lay bricks, not much else. And he could drink. But understand? That was asking too much. Nevertheless he obeyed without asking questions. From now on he bought tickets like everyone else in the village, up to twenty at a time when he was in the right mood, and watched as the numbers were called out and people clapped and cheered as if it were a play being performed in front of him that did not involve him. He hardly bothered to check whether the numbers matched his tickets. They never did.

At some stage, however, it had begun to dawn on him that there were patterns. There was no sudden flash of realization but rather the feeling crept up on him that what happened during the raffle, despite all the laughter and despite the beaming faces, in reality hid something darker. Every year it was the same apparently harmless ritual. It was always Mrs Moore who took the box with the slips of paper over to the children and selected one child to draw the winning ticket. This year her choice fell on Kevin, a pale, fair-haired boy with glasses.

First the tickets for the smaller prizes were drawn. One after another the winners came on to the stage and collected their boxes of chocolates, baskets of fruit, and the inevitable bottles of cider.

Then it was time for the more interesting prizes, which were sponsored by various firms and hotels in the county. Mrs Moore played her part well. She knew the right moment to leave a pause in order to increase the tension and spoke into the microphone in a professional tone of voice, reading out the numbers extra clearly so that there could be no misunderstanding. The next hour saw the distribution of various rose bushes as well as tickets for local races and theatre productions. Helen Dean, the waitress at the bistro, went home with a voucher for a dinner for two at the best restaurant in Bristol, and Bill Lee with a voucher for a luxury weekend for two by the sea in Lyme Regis. Typical Bill, he thought enviously. A murmur ran through the crowd as Mr Lee collected his prize: a question hung in the air. Who would the unmarried and possibly gay florist be spending his weekend away with? It did not seem to worry Mr Lee. On the contrary, he enjoyed the applause and stood for a moment on the stage, basking in self-congratulation. Then with a broad grin he waved the voucher in the air before leaving the stage and mingling with the crowd again.

Mrs Moore was visibly agitated as, in a solemn tone of voice, she requested silence. The great moment had arrived, she announced, the moment that everyone in the village was awaiting with keen anticipation.

"Yes, ladies and gentlemen, the time has come. In a few moments I shall have the honour of announcing the name of the lady who has won this year's first prize. But before I do so I should like to ask you, as custom dictates, to dedicate a minute's silence to our dear Sue Harper. Sue returned her soul to the Lord a month ago. Let us remember her today in love and gratitude."

At Sue Harper's name everyone suddenly fell silent. Even the children jumping around between the rows of spectators stood as still as statues. All eyes were on Mrs Moore. She stared at her watch. How long a minute could last, he reflected wearily. Finally Mrs Moore raised her head, gave a brief sigh and asked Kevin to draw the last and most important ticket. Was the boy aware of the solemnity of the occasion? He seemed to hesitate as if he feared that a dangerous animal might leap out of the box at him.

"Come along then, Kevin. There's nothing to be afraid of," said Mrs Moore encouragingly.

People held their breath, ready to clap as the number was announced. But when Kevin fished out a green ticket a sigh of disappointment went round. Mrs Moore put the ticket on one side and said, "Once more, Kevin. It's sure to work this time."

Once again the boy selected a green ticket, and once again Mrs Moore put it to one side without reading it. At the third green ticket she started to betray impatience.

"Now, now. Why do you keep on drawing the wrong one? Come on, lad, make a bit of an effort, please."

Kevin gave several vigorous nods before he once again reached into the box and in slow motion drew out a ticket. A pink one this time. A murmur of relief swept round.

"Well done, Kevin, you've done a good job. Give it to me, and then you can go back to your place."

The tension rose. Women nestled up closer to their partners. Some of them bit their lips, other shut their eyes or held their breath. Mrs Moore was excited, too. Several times she looked around the mass of people before taking off her glasses and, with a tense smile, raising the ticket to her eyes so that she could read it.

"The number is ... four hundred and thirty-one. Four, three, one."

He had seen enough, but with the tumult caused by the announcement of the number there was no way out for him. Everyone began to talk at the same time and move towards a woman dressed in black who was frantically waving a ticket in the air.

"No, no, not me, the number's not mine," shouted the woman, but no one paid her any attention. Even Mrs Moore, as she forced a way to her through the crowd, did not seem to take the woman's protestations seriously. She checked the ticket number and summoned the reluctant winner on to the stage.

"But I'm telling you, it's not my number. I bought this ticket for my mother. It's she who won, not me," the young woman insisted. Mrs Moore shook her head.

"The ticket is in your possession, so you are the winner. Please don't cause any unnecessary fuss. Just come with me."

He found the scene amusing. He had never seen a reluctant winner before. On the contrary, everyone was usually desperate to win the first prize. But here was a winner who said she was willing to give it up. That was unheard of. Didn't she know what an honour it was? Or was she somehow afraid of this prize? In any case she was behaving in complete ignorance of local customs. A pity, because she was young and strikingly pretty. Not local, though – she had a strong accent – and possibly not even English. But, he went on wondering, was an outsider entitled to accept the prize at all?

This didn't seem to be Mrs Moore's main concern. Having for years been responsible for the smooth management of the raffle, she was facing other problems. Standing on the stage between the winner who refused to be one and the woman's mother, she went on trying to convince the younger of the two to accept the prize. The mother even added her support, but the daughter remained stubborn, insisting that she would never in her life accept a prize that was not hers by rights.

The public reacted with shouts and catcalls. Someone called out, "We want the young one," and another, "That's enough of this nonsense! Just draw another ticket!"

But the ticket had been drawn. "There is absolutely no question of drawing a second one. The statutes forbid it," said Mrs Moore, ending all speculation. But when, after a lot of dithering, she apologetically shrugged her shoulders and whispered into the microphone that she had no choice but to declare Vera Wyler the winner, her announcement was drowned out by boos.

"Quiet, please! I hereby declare that Nadja Skinner's statement is accepted and her mother, Mrs Vera Wyler, is declared the rightful winner of the first prize. There can be no objection to that, even if Mrs Wyler doesn't live in Southcombe. After all, she is intending to spend the whole of the coming year with us. So that's settled. May I present to you, Mrs Wyler from Switzerland."

He clapped half-heartedly, but after all the controversy didn't want to miss the moment where the stranger received the bouquet of roses and the sealed envelope.

She seemed to be genuinely pleased, he thought as he made his way out. All the better. The time of uncertainty would come soon enough.

Chapter 6

On the afternoon of Christmas Eve, a Friday, Jason cycled into St Valéry. He bought himself a slice of lobster terrine and a steak, together with a bottle of champagne, and then, in the finest patisserie of the town, a chocolate éclair. Twice a year, once at Christmas and once on his birthday in February, he allowed himself a banquet, which he ate not in his room but at the huge mahogany table in the dining-room.

Enthralled by the town's Christmas lights, he parked his bicycle at the Quai Lejoille and after doing his shopping strolled on through the streets. He stopped in front of particularly well-decorated shop-windows and thought about earlier Christmases in Somerset. Finally he ordered a coffee in La Civette and drank it standing at the window. The tide was coming in and he could see how the level of the sea gradually rose, grey like the sand it swallowed up, and the sky above.

Jason was no sailor. He found boats and yachts boring, and the continual screeching of the seagulls got on his nerves. Nevertheless he stayed standing there for a long time, the empty cup in his hand, enjoying the sensation of not being alone. For once in a while there were voices around him that didn't come from either a radio or a television. He could hear men laughing behind him while a child grizzled and the barman threw in sentences that he didn't understand. It didn't worry him that the words in his ears were just sounds. On the contrary, it helped him relax because it saved him from talking and the trouble of lying. In this way he could be sure that no one was observing him.

No one? He pricked up his ears. He wondered if he had just heard an English sentence in the midst of the confusion of French voices. A question which couldn't be directed at him because he didn't know a soul in St Valéry, but nevertheless a clearly understandable English sentence.

"Hey, you. Back again?"

Jason stared fixedly at the sea and forced himself to stay calm. The question didn't have anything to do with him, no, it couldn't have been aimed at him. In any case the voice was a woman's.

He didn't know any women here. But English? Who on earth spoke English in St Valéry?

"Aren't you the guy from the chateau? The mysterious hermit?" the woman went on, undeterred.

At these words a cold shudder ran down his back. His first thought was to rush out of that door, pedal back to the chateau as quickly as possible and barricade himself in his room. He tried to move but his legs felt like lead. He stood there rooted to the spot, quivering with anxiety but also raging against himself for having been so stupid as to go into the bar. Now it was too late. He had to confront the person asking the question if he wasn't going to draw further attention to himself. Slowly he turned his head until he met the laughing eyes of a girl standing beside him at the counter. She looked seventeen, eighteen at most. Almost a child, thank God. He smiled back at her, relieved. The girl was wearing jeans, a baggy roll-neck sweater and a knitted beanie cap from which strands of dark hair were peeping out.

"Can you talk?" she asked him, with a grin on her face.

"Yes, I can talk, I'm just surprised."

"Why? Because I'm talking English?"

"Well, yes. After all, we're in France."

"You don't honestly think you're the only English person here, do you?"

"Yes, until just now that's exactly what I thought."

"Well, you're quite wrong. I'm half-English and my father is English. That's one and a half more for a start. And outside St Valéry there are plenty of English people."

"I'd never have thought that."

"That's because you so rarely leave your castle. Like I said, you're a hermit. No wonder you don't know what's going on out here."

The girl swept off her cap, passed her hand through her hair a couple of times and ordered a hot chocolate. Her French was faultless.

"Why are you standing there rooted to the spot? Have I said the wrong thing?"

"How do you know I live like a hermit?"

"Everyone here knows that. Isn't that right, Jean? People all know that, don't they?"

The barman nodded, with a sideways glance at Jason, and placed the steaming cup in front of the girl.

"Come on, don't be so shy," she said. "Sit down. I'm not going to bite you."

He couldn't decline the invitation without being rude. So he sat down next to her and ordered a second coffee.

"I live on the other side of the bay," she told him. "Towards Le Crotoy. You won't believe it, but I've seen you several times in St Valéry. And do you know what I thought each time?"

"No."

"How strange you look. Sort of hunted-looking, like there's a pack of hounds after you. That's how you look now too."

Jason shrugged his shoulders and tried to smile.

"That's just the way I am."

"Why don't you just chill, like I do? It makes more sense. The less you stress, the longer you'll live. Things are going great for me at the moment. No more prissy French school for me, thank God, and since I've got no idea what to do next I'm just going with the flow. Perhaps I'll go abroad in the New Year. South America … somewhere like that."

As long as the girl was talking about herself Jason had no objection to sitting beside her and occasionally nodding or smiling. But when she suddenly asked him what he was doing in the chateau and loudly announced that he must be bored to death up there alone, he felt trapped. He stared into his coffee cup, absent-mindedly stirring the spoon and muttering things like, *don't know ... maybe ... not really*. Inside, though, he was trembling. How could he have been so stupid as to let himself be sucked into a conversation with this loudmouth? Sure, she looked innocent enough. But no one was really innocent, were they? Least of all someone who asked so many questions.

"Aha! *Not really* ... That has to mean *bored out of my brain*, doesn't it? Come on, you can tell me."

The girl was laughing at him. Jason briefly caught sight of her tongue, like glistening pink fruit between her pointed little teeth, and felt a sudden deep longing to place his lips on hers. Would their kiss be as beautiful and easy as it had been with Lizzie? Or would the girl draw back from him, appalled, perhaps even give him a slap? Lizzie ... Terrified suddenly, he raised his hand to his mouth and struggled for air. He hadn't kissed a girl since Lizzie. Simply couldn't. Because of Lizzie's blood, which went on dripping in his head, and because of the enormous indifferent silence in which his cry still echoed without response: "Lizzie, Lizzie, no!"

"Why are you looking at me so strangely?" the annoying stranger was asking him.

"Nothing. I ..."

"You want to make a dash for it, don't you? Am I so bloody boring?"

She rested her elbows on the counter and leaned her chin on top of her folded hands, looking up at him with unconcealed curiosity.

"You are really weird. What's your name?"

"Jason."

"And I'm Zoë. Rich and Frances spent a long time looking for a decent live-in handyman, in case you didn't know. As soon as they found a new one he either did a runner or else they had to get rid of him because he drank all the best wine or had some other bad habit. But they seem to like you, and you seem to manage all right here, too. How's it working out for you?"

"The chateau's really great. There are plenty of jobs to be done, and I like that."

"So do you want spend the rest of your life working for Rich and Frances?"

Jason shrugged his shoulders again and said nothing. He must be on his guard. The girl was talking about his employers as if they were old friends. And she was half-English. That unsettled him.

Later, on his bicycle, he was annoyed that he hadn't realized that the ripples on the water were the warning of a storm to come and had stayed too long in La Civette. He hadn't even reached Noyelles sur Mer when the wind threatened to blow him off his saddle. With an effort he managed to pedal across the flat stretch alongside the bay. He persuaded himself that he would be able to get back to the chateau in time, but when he reached the crossroads before the road branched and had to go uphill the storm exploded over his head with an ear-shattering crash. The rain was so heavy that he could scarcely see more than a yard ahead of him. He had to get off. As he pushed the bicycle along he thought of the girl in the café. Zoë. He had liked her even if she was a pest. If things had been different he would have allowed himself to fancy her. But she probably had no interest in him – other than to spy on him.

Ever since Lizzie he had been suspicious of any girl who showed an interest in him. So he had turned down Zoë's request to come and see the chateau from inside.

"OK. But we could meet after the Christmas rush is over … here in La Civette, for example. I come here every now and then," she insisted. But then Jason had simply shaken his head and muttered, "No, better not." He had tried to explain that he had very little time, but it sounded so far-fetched that she simply laughed in his face.

"Hey, it's OK. I'm not your type. No big deal."

He hadn't contradicted her. But as they parted he told a lie and said that he too often came to the café and it would be good if they could bump into each other again.

He thought about this lie now. How threadbare it had been, how idiotic. Chance meetings never happen when you want them to. So in all likelihood he would never see the girl again. If only he had at least asked for her full name and address. He knew nothing about her except for her first name, and that wouldn't help him find out her phone number. Idiot! He cursed himself.

When he pushed open the gate at the end of the drive and heard the wet gravel crunch under his feet, this evidence of his isolation gave him a shock. It was so silent out here, so dark. Like a huge grave. For the first time since he had fled Somerset he felt a longing for a proper home. And for love.

Chapter 7

Nadja and Tom had not spared with the Christmas decorations. Above the entrance there flickered a team of illuminated reindeer pulling a large sleigh, and inside the house there were golden garlands gleaming on every wall, candles were burning, and carols were playing on the iPod.

Vera could not help expressing surprise when she saw all the coloured stars and snow-flakes. How much must all this have cost? However, before she could give it any further thought, Nadja came out of the kitchen, hugged her and steered her immediately into the living room, where Tom's parents were standing round the table admiring the decorations. Marion was a large, middle-aged lady with a friendly face and strikingly beautiful hair – fairer than her son's, it glowed a fiery orange under the hall light.

"Vera, so good to see you again."

By contrast with her husband, who hovered behind the table with a stiff smile on his face, Marion Skinner came up to Vera to shake her hand. A cloud of heavy perfume enveloped her. Like her low-cut chiffon dress, it was a shade too formal for a family occasion.

Vera couldn't remember Tom's parents being so jovial on previous occasions. After his first glass of sherry even Geoffrey began an amusing account about the time when, as a clumsy teenager who always had his head in the clouds, he had begun to work in his father's firm.

"I'm afraid Tom takes after you, my dear," sighed Marion, and told a couple of funny stories about their son in order to make her point.

"Better than taking after you, my dear. Otherwise we'd have …"

"Here he goes again! Come on, Geoffrey, out with it."

"No, calm down. I'm only joking."

"A romantic dreamer. Isn't that what you wanted to say? Go on, admit it, you always say I'm a hopeless romantic. My husband is jealous, you see, Vera. Just imagine that, he's still jealous, just as he was when I worked as a nurse in the clinic at Greenhill Park. That's decades ago, but Geoffrey insists I only ever worked there because of the director. Well, I ask you. Even if it were true, that man was a genius. Which, I'm afraid, you are not, Geoffrey," said his giggling wife. "But let's not talk about that. After all, it's Christmas. Let's be happy and grateful to be sitting round this table together."

As Nadja began to carve the goose there was a relaxed and warm atmosphere that Vera hadn't known since her husband's death.

"Oh, how Robert would have liked to be spending Christmas with us," she said sadly. "How glad he would have been to see Nadja and Tom so happy."

To Vera's surprise Nadja threw her a disapproving glance across the table and quickly changed the subject: "Isn't it wonderful that it's Mum who won the first prize in the raffle?" she said.

"You should have followed Mrs Moore's advice and taken it yourself," responded Marion Skinner.

"But heavens, no, I'd never do such a thing. It was Mum's ticket. We'd agreed on the numbers beforehand."

"Nevertheless."

"But—"

"It would be better. You can still change your mind."

"Yes, darling. It really doesn't matter to me. I'm happy not to have the prize. I don't even know what I'm supposed to have won. The envelope only contains a kind of document. You're welcome to that," Vera told her daughter.

"The real prize comes later, Vera," Marion old her. "You will be astonished at everything you're given."

"Whatever it is, I am very willing to hand it over to Nadja. At my age I've got more than enough."

"I don't understand the lot of you. Tom, say something! This is absolute nonsense," Nadja burst out. "Mum won and so she should receive the prize. Whatever it is."

But he just gave his parents an embarrassed look and muttered something along the lines of, "Not now, darling, it's Christmas."

"You English, I'll never understand you," said Nadja, rolling her eyes and determinedly sticking her fork into a piece of meat. She was smiling, but Vera knew her daughter too well not to recognize an element of irritation there too. And indeed from this moment on Nadja took hardly any part in the conversation – but was all the more assiduous in playing the role of perfect hostess and daughter-in-law.

It wasn't until they reached the Christmas pudding, when the usual subjects of conversation had been exhausted and even the bad weather had played its proper part in the discussion, that she started to thaw out and told Vera that she and Tom were planning to drive to the sea at Hartland on the following day.

"It's at its most impressive at this time of year. Last year the sea was so rough that the spray came up to the window of our hotel room."

"So, do you go every year?" Vera wanted to know.

"Yes, every Boxing Day. Over the years it's turned into a kind of tradition. And what are you doing tomorrow? Anything special?"

"No, I expect I'll stay at home and paint. In the afternoon I'm expecting a visit from the previous tenant. He wants to collect something from the house that he forgot when he moved out. It sounds as if it's of vital importance to him."

"Craig Brett?" interjected Geoffrey.

"That's right. Do you know him?"

"It's a bit much to say we know him, isn't it, Marion? We saw him two or three times at village events. A journalist if I'm not mistaken. One of those fellows who asks people lots of questions and then writes articles about them without getting their permission. But I suppose good journalists stick their noses in other people's affairs because they wouldn't have anything to write about otherwise.

"So Craig Brett is coming to Southcombe tomorrow, is he? Well, I'm surprised. Doesn't he live in London? That's quite a distance away."

"Oh, Geoff, it's no great distance nowadays. With a car you're there in a few hours."

"He said he was in the area anyway. He's spending the night in Watchet. Where is that exactly?"

"Haven't you ever been there? That's a place you really mustn't miss. Charming. One of the most beautiful poems in English literature has its origins there."

"Geoff, don't start on that now. Otherwise we'll be sitting here at the table until after midnight."

"No, no," Vera interjected, "that's very interesting. Do tell me, Geoffrey, what poem is that?"

"It's 'The Rhyme of the Ancient Mariner' by Samuel Taylor Coleridge. He is supposed to have written part of it in the Bell Inn in Watchet."

"What a coincidence! That's the very hotel Craig Brett mentioned. Perhaps he wants to write something about Coleridge."

"'The Ancient Mariner' is a wonderful Romantic ballad. Every child used to learn it at school. At the harbour in Watchet there is a bronze statue to commemorate it, showing an old sailor, the one from the poem, and, clinging to him, a huge albatross."

Vera had to admit that she hadn't heard of Coleridge.

"Right, we must see to that. There are reminders of Coleridge everywhere in Somerset. Not far from here, in a village on the other side of the Quantock Hills, you can still visit his cottage."

"We could all drive to Nether Stowey together," suggested Marion Skinner. "It's worth visiting. The village itself is a real jewel."

Vera nodded agreement with all the plans that were proposed. And if it was to be Nether Stowey, Tom said, then they had to make a stop in Holford.

"Virginia Woolf spent some of her honeymoon in the pub there. And don't let's forget Alfoxton House nearby, where William Wordsworth lived with his sister for a while."

"Yes, Vera," added Marion in support of her son, "Somerset is an extremely interesting county from a literary point of view. If you like, we'd be very pleased to show you all these places. Not now in the depths of winter, but as soon as spring comes along we can set off."

Vera promised to do some reading first, beginning with Coleridge whose ballad she liked the sound of.

"I'll lend you a book of his poems, Mum. Don't forget to remind me." Saying this, Nadja got up and began to distribute the Christmas presents. Vera had brought everyone chocolate from Switzerland. She gave Tom's parents embroidered towels and to the young couple a picture of Lake Thun that she had painted in the summer. She herself went home rather later than she had intended with a book of Somerset recipes, various jars of preserves and a magnificently illustrated book about English garden design. She leafed through it before going to sleep and at every picture was astonished anew by how luxuriant, how wildly rampant, these gardens looked at first sight, and how on closer inspection all the flowers, from the simple daffodil to the most sophisticated iris, obeyed a precisely calculated pattern.

The flowers pursued Vera into her dreams. She saw Nadja walking in the cemetery at Southcombe with a basket full of roses – or was it carnations? – which she laid on the graves, laughing as she explained, "They were all my friends, you understand, I miss them. But they don't believe me because I haven't brought any lilies today." She laughed again and placed the last flowers, which suddenly changed into spoons and forks, in a circle around herself on the grass. That was how Vera knew that Nadja too belonged among the dead.

The nightmare made Vera wake up with an oppressive feeling of anxiety. Her first thought was to phone her daughter to make sure that nothing had happened to her. But what could have happened during the night? Vera forced herself to be calm and lay in bed for a few minutes more, her eyes wide open, until she got up and tackled the new day with its strange name, Boxing Day. She would be receiving her visitor at three. Until then there was more than enough time to do some painting.

A week earlier she had begun a new still life that was causing her quite a headache: oranges, lemons and a mango in a glass bowl. Perhaps she was asking too much of herself again. The diamond pattern of the table-cloth, distorted in the glass, seemed unrealistic by comparison with the fruit, and the shadow of the lemons on the oranges had too much blue in it. She had been inclined to discard this attempt as an exercise that had failed, but during the day she kept on hearing Werner Raflaub's voice in her ear: "Never give up, do your best. And when you think you have done your best, do more work, do something even better. Go on until your last doubt has been dispelled."

For a long time she had thought Raflaub was stubborn, but in time she came to see that he was right and that his way allowed her to get a lot more out of herself and her pictures. So she attacked the work with renewed energy and corrected the mistakes as best she could. It was simpler than she had thought, and the clear improvement gave her so much satisfaction that she would have liked best of all to carry on working until the evening.

However, at two o'clock, for good or ill, she turned away from the picture, cleaned her brushes and put the tea things on the table. What could it be that the journalist was so desperate to have back? And where could this important object be? Clutching a cheese sandwich in her hand, Vera went from room to room and checked all the corners. But there were no hidden niches, cracks or holes that she hadn't noticed when she moved in. And the fitted carpets were firmly fixed.

Vera's curiosity grew. If a journalist made the effort to visit, specially at Christmas, he must smell a scandal.

But what kind of scandal? Financial? Something crooked with local estate agents? Or was it something more private? Did it have something to do with a particular person in the village? With someone who had lived here earlier, or – yes, that was possible – someone the house had once belonged to? Mrs Moore?

Vera shook her head and smiled to herself at the thought that the good lady could be caught up in a scandal. It was high time that her visitor arrived and drove such absurd ideas out of her head. In the end it would be something quite banal, heirloom cufflinks, a signet ring or something like that.

Shortly before three Vera put the kettle on, arranged a few biscuits on a plate and killed time with a sudoku that she had cut out of the latest number of the *Guardian*. It was a rather tricky one, and before she noticed it half an hour had passed. Craig Brett was late.

For the rest of the afternoon she was on tenterhooks. She did a few household jobs, which she could have interrupted at any time. At the slightest sound she peeped out of the kitchen window to see if there was a car coming up the gravel drive. But no sign of Craig Brett. And he evidently didn't think it necessary to ring up and apologize for his absence. At seven o'clock Vera put away the tea things and the biscuits and drowned her irritation in a glass of wine while she watched the BBC news. There was further talk of snow, of traffic problems across the country, of villages being cut off and schools being shut. She started to find all this excitement over a few snowflakes exaggerated. Could snow be the reason why Craig Brett hadn't managed to reach Southcombe?

Or had he perhaps managed to get there? When Vera cast a final glance out of the window before going to bed she could see in the moonlight the marks of tyres on the snow covering the gravel drive, broad lines which made a loop in front of the entrance. So the journalist really had come and she hadn't heard the doorbell. Now it was Vera who would have liked to apologize to him.

However, when the next day she found a big cardboard box with a card from Mrs Moore on the front doorstep she decided not to ring Craig Brett in Watchet. If the thing he had lost really was important to him he would contact her.

The cardboard box contained fresh fruit and vegetables, and the note read: *"First instalment of the raffle prize, with warmest greetings from Eileen Moore."*

I'll never be able to eat all that myself, thought Vera, when she looked through the contents of the box. There were apples, pears, bananas, grapes and oranges, carrots, potatoes, cabbage, swedes and parsnips, in quantities that would easily have fed a family of four for a week.

Was she pleased with the gift? Wasn't there also in her pleasure a certain disappointment that the prize didn't contain something more original, for example an excursion or a pub meal in a village she didn't know, something that would have given her the opportunity to explore new areas? She didn't convey anything of her muted happiness to Mrs Moore when she telephoned her, but thanked her extravagantly.

"Don't mention it, Mrs Wyler. It's all yours."

"But it's much too much. Especially the apples. There are so many different varieties, I'll never get through them all on my own."

"Apples are good for you."

"Yes, of course, but ..."

"Go on, eat them. Please."

"Yes, I certainly will. I like apples. But there are really more than enough. I've already put some of them on one side for my daughter."

"But it was agreed that you won the prize, not your daughter. Sharing the prize is against the regulations."

"Surely I can give my daughter some apples and potatoes without breaking the rules?"

"You could give up your entitlement to the prize, that would solve all the problems with the regulations. And it would be the best thing anyway."

"I obviously don't understand this whole business with the raffle, Mrs Moore. As far as I am concerned, my daughter is welcome to the prize. I offered it to her myself at Christmas but she refused and so now Tom and Nadja are going to join me in sharing this first instalment – since there are apparently to be further surprises. In the light of the extreme quantity that seems to me only sensible."

"As you wish, Mrs Wyler. But the prize has never been shared before, and I must warn you that it won't meet with approval in the village."

Mrs Moore's displeasure was unmistakable. During the conversation her tone had become increasingly sharp, and individual sentences echoed in Vera's head. Nevertheless she drove over to Nadja's house in the early evening and dropped off half of the gifts at her front door. The pair hadn't yet returned from Hartland, and in the garden there was only a cat stalking the birds that Nadja had put out food for.

Vera stroked the cat as she walked past. The fur felt silky, and because it purred so trustingly she took it into her arms and tickled its neck. The cat had a leather collar with name, telephone number and address.

"So, you're called Tony and you live – let's see – in the High Street, at number nineteen. With Rupert and Sue Harper."

Vera pressed her nose into the soft fur and breathed in the warm smell of the animal. Sue Harper's cat. How strange to read the name on a cat's collar. It was as if Sue Harper were still alive. Perhaps Tony roamed around in the cemetery, not suspecting that his owner was buried there.

Meeting the cat darkened Vera's mood. With the memories of that first evening in Southcombe in her head, she didn't feel like going back to her cold, lonely house, and so she briefly went into the Kings Arms. This was the first time she had been in the pub. A couple of men stood by the bar and watched with curiosity as she ordered a glass of merlot and then sat down with it by herself at a table next to the fire. She stared into the flames and felt not only a pleasing warmth spread through her body but also the images of the dead Sue Harper gradually becoming paler and less real in her mind, as if she had dreamed the whole thing.

"Don't we know you?"

Vera looked up. The two men had come up to her table and were smiling at her inquisitively.

"I don't think so."

The older one, bald and with a wild and curly beard, lifted up his glass of cider as if to drink her health and said, "But of course we do. You're the lady who won first prize in our raffle. Here's to your health and fortune."

"Thank you."

"By the way, I'm Paddy, and this is Greg."

"And I'm Vera. Pleased to meet you."

Her pleasure was limited, however, and she tried to convey the fact to the pair through her monosyllabic replies. But neither Paddy nor Greg seemed to notice how uncommunicative she was trying to be.

"You're Mrs Moore's tenant, aren't you?"

"My goodness, people seem to know all about me in the village."

"No. Only that Nadja is your daughter and that for the time being you are living in Station House. That isn't much."

Vera took a sip from her glass without replying. The two men were quite nice, and the younger one, Greg, in particular had a winning smile and something cheeky about his eyes that vaguely reminded her of Robert.

"Station House is a good place," he said. "Mrs Moore never has any difficulty letting it. In the summer there's a real scrum to get it. I know because I look after her website. She gets no end of enquiries."

Vera pricked up her ears. "But the actual arrangements go directly through Mrs Moore, don't they? At least, I never had any dealings with anyone else."

"You're an exception. Nadja fixed things up and vouched for you. Otherwise it's me that deals with the administrative bits and pieces."

"Oh, right. So that's what you did in the case of Craig Brett?"

"Yes, but it was simple. He's pretty well known and Mrs Moore didn't need to be afraid of the house being vandalized or anything."

"Famous?"

"Well, he's not exactly Piers Morgan or anyone like that, but he's pretty well known. He writes for *The Times* and other broadsheets, and regularly appears on television. Mrs Moore did without references, as I'm sure she did with you. As a police constable I could reassure her on that one. 'Brett's clean,' I told her, and that was quite enough for her as a guarantee."

"Do you mind?" Paddy had taken a chair from the next table and sat down next to Vera, who nodded in a non-committal kind of way. If he had been alone she would have turned him down, but Greg had interesting things to say.

"Craig came here almost every evening and listened out for stories. At one stage he wrote an article about

Greenhill Park. He spent days on end up there in those dilapidated sheds, photographing every little detail, and then he had the old people in the village tell him how things were before the war."

"And how were they?"

"Have you ever been up there? Seen the place from close up?"

"No, only from a distance. It must have been a very grand mansion in the old days."

"Yes, way back I'm sure it was. But before and after the Second World War Greenhill Park was used as a funny farm for children who weren't quite ..., well, who were a bit soft in the head, Down's Syndrome and stuff like that. The clinic didn't close until the early 1990s. Bloody hell, so many children living there, poor little mites. And half of Southcombe had a job there. Anyone not in the cider business worked as security guard, nurse, plumber, whatever. Dr Lee was a ..."

"Dr Lee the florist?"

"No, his father. One way or another he involved everyone in the village and gave them a helping hand. An impressive man, Dr Lee. Anyone here would have gone through hell and high water for him. In any case the clinic had a very good reputation, thanks to him."

"And that's what Craig Brett was researching?"

"Researching is going a bit far," Paddy objected. "He just sniffed around. Greenhill Park is full of stories. People even say there are ghosts there. It's supposed to be haunted by the souls of children who disappeared without trace in the middle of the night. And ..."

"Nonsense, Paddy. You don't even believe that yourself."

"I certainly do. There are people in the village who have seen ghosts like that. Rose who lives in Mill Street, for example. She was a nurse there and told me how she once saw a child on the steps of the mansion. All pale and wearing a blue nightdress, and when she got nearer it disappeared, just like that, as if it had dissolved. It was always girls who …"

"Hold your trap now, Paddy. You've drunk too much cider. You mustn't believe these stories, Vera. It's just stupid nonsense. I'm afraid people are very super-stitious round here."

"I can't take stories like that too seriously, but it's not too surprising to hear that there are ghosts in Green-hill Park. At least, I can understand how rumours like that start up. It's not exactly a cheerful place."

"It certainly isn't. The children were well looked after, though. Mr Lee made sure that they didn't lack for anything. But some of them were just odd in the head and after they were grown up they'd come back to take revenge. There was lots of arson, windows were broken and walls knocked down. Poor beggars. Part of me can understand it. It's no life being in a home like that."

Slowly the pub filled up, becoming hot and loud, and Vera began to wonder how she would get rid of the two men without being rude. She looked at her watch several times while Paddy tried to explain the rules of cricket to her, and during a pause she even made a move to get up but Greg got in first by ordering a second round of drinks. He also gave her a glance across the full glasses that she rather enjoyed. It was a long time since a man had looked at her so intensely and shown so openly that he liked what he saw. And she had never before received that kind of attention from a policeman.

Chapter 8

Jason spent the morning of 27 December clearing out the greenhouse. He got rid of dried out plants, filled empty flower-pots with new soil and cleaned the tiled floor and the windows. Rich had phoned the day before and announced his plans for the greenhouse during the summer: "Vegetables, Jason, lots of vegetables. And Frances wants to have another go at orchids. In the past they've never worked out, but now she's counting on your green fingers."

Orchids! Everyone knew how difficult it was to grow exotic plants in a temperate climate, and you had to expect disappointments. Jason had shaken his head but kept his doubts to himself. He didn't know anything about orchids and had had hardly anything to do with them at home in Southcombe. But if Frances wanted orchids, that was it. At the end of the day she was mistress of the house and her whims were more or less his orders. In any case he had until July to read up on the subject.

At midday Jason stopped work and ate a sandwich in his room, sitting by the window as he let his eyes range with satisfaction over the land that he almost considered his own. After three years he could say that knew every tree and every shrub in this garden, and with most of the animals – birds, rabbits, frogs or hedgehogs – he knew where they spent the winter and where they brought up their young. He had become part of this world and had grown so deeply rooted in it that it was only here he felt secure and happy, far from other people, alone in the society of animals that wanted nothing from him and let him live as if he were one of them. He missed them in the winter and consoled himself with their tracks in the snow, which told him that they were still there. Deer came at night, and sometimes foxes too. Every day he discovered new tracks on top of older ones, crossing and erasing them.

From the bird's eye view offered by his room, Jason could look down today on the crazy pattern of tracks glistening in the midday sun. He had gazed at them earlier in the morning and realized how soon after the heavy snowfalls he had lost any sense of which track was which. And yet he had the feeling that something had changed since the morning. Jason looked more closely. There were the icy prints of the rabbits from the day before, over there by the oak trees there were the tracks from a herd of deer, and everywhere the usual ones from the birds. But alongside the roses and diagonally across the field up to the entrance to the chateau he saw prints he could have sworn weren't there in the morning.

Prints made by shoes with grooved soles!

Someone had forced their way in while he was working in the glasshouse. The realization hit Jason with the force of a blow. He thought of Miles on the television before Christmas, stuck in Heathrow on his way to France. Miles, who five years earlier had screamed at him, "Run, go on! You'll never get away from me. Sooner or later I'll get you, and then ..."

Had the Wolf finally found him out? But how? How could he know where Jason lived? How did he get here?

Jason stared at the new tracks in the snow with eyes wide open, unable to move from the spot. His heart began to race. He could see Lizzie again, on that decrepit sofa with her head hanging down, the pool of blood on the ground and the splinters of glass scattered over it, Lizzie's matted hair, her eyes still shining, her mouth open, twisted into a grimace. So much blood everywhere, on her neck, her beautiful white neck ... no, no, not again! He had to forget them, these agonizing memories. He had tried to bury them so deep that they would never come to the surface again, so that he could finally let go of the past and live in freedom again. Free and without fear.

In vain Jason tried to think of something different, Frances' orchids or Rich's vegetables, for example, but Lizzie and Miles refused to go away. They were there, in his head and everywhere. Wherever he turned he encountered them, and each time he was shocked by the clarity with which their faces gazed back at him: the smooth, young face of the girl and the leathery smoker's face of his pursuer. Miles hadn't even made the effort to run after him, so confident was he of catching him in the end.

And he, Jason, what had he done? He had let Lizzie down. She was dead. Could he ever forgive himself for having left her alone because he was afraid for his own life? Miles had simply watched with contempt as Jason had run out of the shed, straight down Greenhill Way to the Kings Arms, insane with grief and horror. Never in his life had he run so far or so fast. Then in front of the pub he had …

But stop, why was he wasting time with these memories? Perhaps Miles had already gained entry to the chateau and was at this very moment lying in wait for him behind the door. Jason listened hard for suspicious sounds in the house. He heard only a thin, gurgling noise from the gutter over the window and had the distinct sensation of a slight draft creeping under the door and round his legs.

The silence only partly calmed him. Silence itself could be suspicious. He slowly turned round, looked into every corner of the room and was about to accept that he would be spending the rest of the day locked in, in front of the television, when he heard a voice calling from outside: "Hello, are you there?"

A girl's voice, light, joyful, young.

"Zoë!"

"Hello, loner. So you remember my name! That's more than I expected."

The young woman stood in front of the main entrance with her head on one side and blinked up at him. She was wearing a red gilet and matching boots up to her knees over her jeans. As she spoke she swept off her black cap and shook out her hair.

"May I come in?"

"No, wait. I'm just coming down."

The hairs were still standing up on the back of Jason's neck, but at the same time he felt light with relief and joy as he rushed down the two floors, taking several steps at a time, and unlocked the door.

"Hey, are you so afraid of burglars you have to lock yourself in in broad daylight? So many keys. Show me. Fourteen? Wow, that's almost like a prison warder."

Jason looked down, embarrassed. To be standing opposite her so unexpectedly made him speechless.

"Whoah, what's up? Don't panic. I'm not going to attack you. I just came by to invite you to my New Year's party. A few of us are getting together at my place. I thought it would be a change for you."

Jason's gaze wandered slowly up Zoë's long legs and trim waist. Under the gilet she wore a long cashmere scarf wound elaborately around her neck. He couldn't bring himself to give her the answer he longed to. Instead he stammered something along the lines of, "Thanks, it's good of you to have thought of me, but I … I just can't manage that day."

Zoë laughed. "Lying really isn't your thing, is it? But never mind. You can think about it. Here are the details … time and place, my phone number and so on."

"But why?"

"Well, duh! Why do you think? Because I happen to like you. Haven't you noticed?"

Of course he had, of course he had noticed. And it flattered him and filled him with a sensation that, however familiar it was, he couldn't quite trust.

"There's not much to like about me," he heard himself say, and immediately regretted it as Zoë replied with a sigh of impatience: "You let me be the judge of that. But I'd better be off. I left my bike outside the gate and, judging from your key ring, I guess I should worry about it being stolen. See you soon, I hope. Don't think about it for too long, though, or you're bound to find a hundred reasons why you can't come."

"OK, I'll … I'll think about it."

"And next time perhaps you'd be gracious enough to let me have a look inside this place. Firstly it's not very polite to leave a lady standing outside in the cold, and secondly I'm really keen to see what life's like in a palace like this. But for now, you can see me out as far as the gate."

Together they tramped through the snow, he tongue-tied and pleasantly light-headed to find himself walking alongside this lively girl while she told him about all the people she had invited to her party.

"There's my cousin Michel and Christine, his new girl-friend. You'll like her, they're both very … how shall I put it? … intellectual and artistic. A bit odd, but good mates. Then Laure and Alice, two school-friends, Jacqueline, my father's secretary, Sabine, Vanessa and Régine ,who I went trekking with in the Atlas Mountains last autumn, and Patrice, my ex-boyfriend. As you can see, we're short of a few men. Which, of course, is the main reason why I'd be pleased if you came."

The light in Zoë's eyes told him she was joking.

When they reached the gate she didn't wait for Jason to find the right key in order to open it but climbed nimbly over the stone wall, got on her bicycle and blew him a kiss before pedalling off. He could hear her singing as she cycled down the hill.

Chapter 9

The cry of a buzzard roused Vera from her sleep later than usual. Where am I? she thought, opening one eye and seeing nothing but blurred outlines around her. She felt unwell, and her head hurt whenever she moved it. She tried to keep her eyes open and could make out a curtain in the general haze, and then the chair with her clothes hanging on one of its arms, but everything turned and swayed, making her feel even worse.

At least she was in her bed in Station House, that was clear. But how had she got home after spending the evening before in the pub? She had a vague memory of Paddy and Greg but could no longer reconstruct how she had got into conversation with them or what they had talked about. They had spoken about cricket – or was it rugby? And one of the two men had enthused about a cottage in Yorkshire. Paddy? Greg? She had no idea. Equally she had no idea how many glasses of wine she had drunk. And it was only a few hours ago.

She shut her eyes and tried to go to sleep again. The buzzard had stopped crying or flown away. Apart from the distant sound of cars on the main road, everything was silent. But Vera tossed and turned in her bed, and she couldn't get to sleep. Her head ached too much, and she had a dull feeling of nausea when she thought of the evening before.

Something important had happened. Something unexpected, something sudden. A young man, yes, he had been young, scarcely twenty, with long, dishevelled hair and a T-shirt … that's right, the idea that someone could run around in the cold of December wearing a T-shirt! So this young man had stormed into the pub and ordered a cider at the bar. And then … what had happened then? He had made an announcement in a loud and excited voice. And these words had produced silence in the room. Even Paddy and Greg had stopped talking and sat for a while as if frozen to their seats. But what was it that the young man had said? Had she even understood him? Or had Greg had to explain it to her? But there was no sense in thinking about it any more. The more she tried, the more she worried about it, the faster her memories evaporated.

A glance at her alarm clock finally raised her out of her drowsiness. Twenty-past ten! She had slept for half the morning, all that time had gone. But did she need to feel guilty about it? She only had herself to answer to, after all.

Vera groped her way into the bathroom, showered and brushed her teeth, doing her best to avoid the two mirrors in which she would normally give herself a thorough examination in the morning. With a hangover her face was bound to look even more lined than usual. She didn't want to have to confront that on top of everything else. A headache and memory lapses were quite enough as consequences of an evening that she was in any case beginning to regret. She swilled down two headache tablets with a glass of orange juice, had a black coffee, and spent the rest of the morning ironing and vacuum cleaning. The telephone rang twice downstairs, and on both occasions she just left it to ring. She was afraid it could be Greg. Who knows what she could have said to him in the pub. Unfortunately she was one of those people that wine made tearful and it was possible that after a couple of glasses she could have wept all over his coat and confessed to him how miserable she was, how alone, how lost without a man. The thought made her blush.

Once before, years ago, during a winter holiday in the Bernese Oberland, she had made a fool of herself like that. She and Robert had quarrelled over something trivial and so she had gone out by herself in the evening, full of defiance and rage, and attached herself to the first available man she came across in a bar. It wasn't until he had made unambiguous advances to her that she got a grip of herself and ran out. She had been so ashamed of the incident that she never confessed it to Robert. And now that he was no longer here she was even more ashamed.

Ah, Robert. There were days on which she didn't think of him at all, but usually she felt his presence so distinctly that she carried on conversations with him aloud, asking his advice or his opinion.

By contrast with Nadja, who put up photos of her father all over the house, Vera had no pictures of him around her. If she wanted to see his face she just used Google to search for his name. One click and the screen filled with the list of his publications, books which she had on her shelves at home in multiple copies, books dealing with molecules, heterogeneous catalysis or cata-lytic processes on surfaces: books with seven seals, as far as she was concerned. But when she clicked on Images he appeared in person as if he had jumped out of a magic box, so alive that it made her heart leap every time. She felt herself caught out as she looked at him more closely, as if she had done something forbidden or summoned up dark spirits. And he smiled so harmlessly on the passport photo that he had had taken for the home-page of the university. Or else, engrossed in the material, he was squinting at his notes during a lecture that he had given in Heidelberg shortly before he became ill. There were already signs of the illness, but it was unmistakably Robert, the academic in glasses and tweed jacket, his tie always a little crooked. She would often speak to this pic-ture while she gazed at it. In the meantime she was so fa-miliar with every detail of it that she had gradually come to feel that she herself had sat among that audience.

Yes, thought Vera, as she rolled up the cable after having finished the ironing, I miss you, Robert, even if I did flirt with a stranger last night, I miss you so desper-ately. What am I supposed to do with this emptiness in my heart? How am I supposed to resist these attacks of utter helplessness and fear of the future without the strength your friendship gave me?

Vera stood in the corridor with the iron in her hand and abandoned herself to her tears.

Still weeping, she put away the ironing and wondered whether an outing to somewhere new would drive away her blues, somewhere by the sea, perhaps – after all, it wasn't so far away. But first she must see Robert. She needed to pour out her heart to him and tell him about the evening before and about Greg.

To her surprise she found her lap-top open on the desk and beside the keyboard there was a torn out scrap of paper with an internet address scribbled on it: *www.somersetcountygazette.co.uk.*

The writing was clearly her own, but when had she written the note? And above all, why?

She had obviously forgotten to switch the lap-top off over night because she had hardly touched the keyboard before the newspaper's home-page appeared on the screen. Vera's eyes passed over announcements of Christmas bazaars and church concerts, over weather forecasts for the next few days and a speech by the mayor of Taunton, as well as various advertisements for local pubs before she came to the miscellaneous news items. The word 'Watchet' jumped out at her. Watchet, that was where … And now it suddenly struck her like a thunderbolt as she remembered the words of the young man in the pub on the evening before which had shaken everyone so much. "That journalist Craig Brett … You remember him, guys?" he had asked. And without waiting for a response added, "He's dead."

The report in the *Gazette* was brief: "On Thursday Sam Blake, a retired greengrocer from Watchet, discovered the body of a man while on an early-morning walk in Helwell Bay. The deceased was later identified as a forty-four-year-old news reporter, Craig Brett, from London, who in recent years had made a name for himself by producing documentaries on social abuses both in Britain and abroad. He was best known to television audiences through his appearance on the satirical programme *Have I Got News For You?* The police have not yet revealed the cause of death. A press conference has been announced for Friday, 30 December, in Taunton."

Vera had probably read the report before going to bed but forgotten it because of the wine. Now, however, the various fragments began to fit together like the pieces of a jigsaw puzzle. The young man had explained that he had spent the day working on a building site in Watchet and had heard the news at the harbour.

"Everyone was talking about it," he had said. Paddy and Greg had proposed various possible reasons for the accident. She herself just sat there silently, taking sips from her glass. Paddy thought it most likely that the reporter had fallen off a cliff, while Greg doubted that he would have been such a fool and thought that a heart attack was more likely.

Vera had kept her mouth shut, but now she shook her head pensively and muttered, "If that was an accident, I'm the Queen." In order to discover more, she typed in 'Craig Brett' instead of Robert's name. There were more than three hundred thousands hits, beginning with Wikipedia, which gave her the basic information about his place of birth, education and career. Vera could also read several articles of his on-line, including the one about Greenhill Park, which she saved for later. Despite the tiresome fuzziness of her head, she decided there were better ways of using the afternoon than sitting in front of the screen.

The road to Watchet ran parallel to the Quantock Hills between meadows and arable land covered by snow, past cottages with smoke coming out of their chimneys. The idyll was almost perfect. Almost. Vera had scarcely passed the first few bends in the road when she began to feel horrified by the scale of the roadkill lying by the side of the carriageway: badgers, pheasants, a rabbit – every mile or two there was another body, the fur shiny brown or the feathers squashed flat in the frozen blood. After Williton the view extended over the Bristol Channel, a greyish-brown strip of water, and beyond it Wales.

The journey lasted more than half an hour. Vera parked the car behind the railway station and found a signpost pointing to the harbour. It wasn't far but nor was it particularly attractive, with the dark Methodist chapel on her left rising above the bus station and bar-rack-like commercial premises. It was only when she turned into the Esplanade and noticed the salty smell of the sea in her nostrils that she began to understand why Tom's parents had recommended this place at Christmas. The harbour consisted of a moderately sized marina with souvenir shops, pubs and some old fishermen's cottages that had been spruced up. But the wind struck her so forcefully that she had to lean into it in order to make progress amongst the swirling scraps of paper and polystyrene.

It was high tide. The boats were rocking in the dark water, their masts swaying wildly against the background of the harbour wall. As Vera had discovered from her guidebook, Watchet had the second largest variation of height between high and low tide of anywhere in the world. As she gazed out across the sea from the harbour wall, she found that hard to believe. The Bristol Channel looked more like a lake than a sea, brownish, tamely wedged in between the British and the Welsh coasts, its surface scarcely ruffled.

A metal ladder at the end of the marina led down to the beach. Beach! The word made Vera think of sand, palms and sun. Helwell Bay, by contrast, consisted of huge blocks of stone covered with algae. A notice warned against bathing – not because of the risk of drowning in the water but because of the mud. As if anyone would think of swimming here. Vera could scarcely imagine a less hospitable bay. And yet she saw people tottering across the stones. Couples, a woman with a dog, a family whose members were all poking around in the stones, occasionally picking one up, examining them and then either throwing them away or slipping them into their canvas bags. Fossils for certain.

According to the guidebook the bay was a treasure-trove for amateur palaeontologists.

So it was here, in this grey wasteland of stone, that Craig Brett had met his death. One section had been cordoned off by the police, and curious onlookers crowded round the barriers. Vera didn't want to joint them, and so she returned to the marina.

The Bell Inn was at the end of the Esplanade in Market Street, a yellow-rendered house from the sixteenth century with a roaring fire in the dining section. Vera enquired about the prices of rooms, but the landlord simply shook his head without looking away from the beer glasses he was filling.

"A single room. How much would that cost?" she repeated her question.

"This isn't a hotel, madam. If you're looking for a room in Watchet you'd best go over there to the West Somerset Hotel."

"But a friend of mine spent the night here and recommended this place to me."

"Impossible. He must have meant the West Somerset, or else one of the many B&Bs. There's a tourist office on the Esplanade. I'm sure they'll help you find a room for the night."

Vera persisted. "Craig Brett …," she said casually and waited eagerly for the landlord's reaction. He just shook his head again and said, "Craig Brett. You're the second person to ask after him. Poor devil. Of course I knew him, everybody in Watchet did. But he didn't stay here, I've already told the police that. Over the Christmas period he would eat here and he had his post sent here, but he spent the night somewhere else. No idea where. A friend of yours?"

"Not really a friend. But he was supposed to visit me and … well, he just didn't turn up."

The landlord had filled his glasses by now and was taking fresh orders. Vera noticed that his interest was waning.

"He was on the track of a sensational story, wasn't he?" she asked speculatively.

"Don't know. He didn't talk to me about things like that. If you really want to find out more you'll have to ask his partner. He arrived from London today and is staying in the West Somerset."

"His partner?"

The landlord smirked. "Yes, Ahmed something. A Paki. You often saw the two of them together on television. One of them made the films and the other wrote the scripts. You know, a team. But come on, why are you asking all these questions about the poor bugger? For somebody who claims to know him, you don't seem to know a great deal about him. Are you from the police, too?"

"No, no. I really am just an acquaintance. But his death has affected me."

"It's affected us all. A nice chap, Craig. Real shame it is."

There was nothing more to be got out of the landlord other than expressions of regret. Perhaps she would have more luck in the West Somerset.

There were three policemen standing at the bar there, one of them shouting various instructions into his walkie-talkie while the other two compared notes. The place was full and correspondingly loud, so that Vera had difficulty understanding the barmaid.

"One or two pounds?" she asked.

"One pound ten for a cup, two pounds for a pot," repeated the girl.

Vera ordered a pot of tea and sat down on the only empty seat in the pub, next to a young family with twin babies. She could feel that the painkillers were beginning to lose their effectiveness and tiredness was spreading through her limbs. She longed for her bed in Station House and would have liked best of all to set off there at once. But going back to Southcombe with unfinished business was out of the question.

The tea tasted bitter and the twins next to her began to rub the sleep from their eyes and to grizzle. Vera left her tea half finished and made her way over to the girl at the bar.

"Excuse me," she said quite shamelessly, "could you put me in touch with a guest by the name of Ahmed? Please, it's important. I think he's in his room at the moment."

The girl looked sceptical but obeyed without asking questions. Like so many others that Vera had seen in the area, she had that porcelain skin the English are famous for, but the piercings in her lips and eyebrows were in marked contrast. While she keyed in the number and looked up at the ceiling as she waited for the phone to ring, Vera thought how glad she was that Nadja had never thought of piercings when she had been a teenager. How would she and Robert have reacted? Robert would probably have shrugged his shoulders and said, "If that's what you want, so be it, but if I were you I'd think about it again." She herself wouldn't have been so …

"Here you are, madam. Mr Haider is on the phone."

"Hello, who's speaking?"

The man sounded cautious but not unfriendly. Vera summoned up all her courage and explained in carefully chosen English, "You don't know me. I am Swiss and at the moment I'm living in the house in Southcombe that Mr Brett rented last summer. He contacted me before Christmas and wanted to come and see me."

"I know all about that. Thank you for coming. I'll be down in a moment."

That's how easy it is, thought Vera triumphantly. Just a bit of chutzpah and you make progress. Sure enough, she didn't need to wait long before a man appeared in the doorway and, after casting his eyes around, walked straight up to her.

"My name is Ahmed Haider, Madame …?"

"I'm Vera Wyler. Pleased to meet you."

Vera's seat had been taken in the meantime, but they found a table by the window where an elderly couple had just been sitting. Ahmed Haider pushed the empty cups and dirty plates to one side and let Vera take her seat before he himself sat down, folding his arms expectantly.

"Well, where shall I start? I have to admit that I asked for you quite spontaneously and now I don't quite know what I should say," she faltered.

Ahmed Haider didn't make it easy for her. While she struggled to find the right words he looked into her eyes, making no effort to conceal his curiosity. The term 'urban chic' occurred to her as she surreptitiously examined his well-cut suit. He was strikingly good-looking with his grey-green eyes and fine but by no means feminine features. And then his teeth, dazzlingly white and entirely regular. Had this slim, handsome man been Craig's life partner? She had assumed so from the landlord's words, but now she wasn't so certain. He could simply be a work colleague.

"I think it's best if I start at the beginning."

"Right, but let me get some drinks first. What would you like?"

"Oh, thank you. I don't know … I've just had a cup of tea."

"A glass of wine? Or cider perhaps? That's meant to be particularly good in Somerset."

"All right, if you insist, yes, a glass of cider would be nice. I haven't tried one since being here."

Ahmed Haider came back carrying two pints.

"What we're going to be drinking doesn't exactly sound appetising, but I've had it recommended to me as one of the best brews."

"You're making me curious. What's it called then?"

"Do you really want to know? It's called Black Rat. A strange name for a drink, don't you think?"

"It certainly is."

"So, to the Black Rat!"

A Pakistani drinking alcohol! Vera didn't dare to ask the question that was on the tip of her tongue. Instead she took a gulp of cider. It tasted mild and fruity, but a touch too sour for her taste.

They sat silent for a moment, looking into their glasses.

"Good, isn't it?"

Vera nodded. But her thoughts were elsewhere. It had just occurred to her that within the past twenty-four hours she had been drinking in pubs with a variety of strangers. In Switzerland she hadn't been out for a drink with anyone since Robert's death except her friend Salomé and members of her art circle. What was happening to her? What was different here? It couldn't just be the holiday atmosphere.

She cleared her throat and finally began to tell her story. It wasn't much, and at the end Vera apologized for having been so bold as to seek a meeting simply because of a phone call from a journalist she didn't know.

"Perhaps you won't understand my unease, but I've got the feeling that Mr Brett's request is somehow connected with his … with his death. Since I heard what happened to him I've been wondering if I should go to the police."

"The police?"

"Well, when all's said and done, Mr Brett is now dead. Perhaps it would help the police to know everything he was doing in the last few days and who he contacted."

"The police will come to you. If Craig rang you, your phone number will be stored on his mobile."

"Of course you're right. So should I just wait?"

Ahmed Haider took a deep breath before suddenly bending forward and asking, "Do you have any idea what Craig wanted to pick up from your house?"

Vera shrugged her shoulders. "Not the faintest. Do you know?"

"Me? No, I'm afraid not. He only used to let me in on his research when he had the complete story. He rang me from Watchet before Christmas to say that he would be getting back to London later than planned because he had to stop off in Southcombe. There was just one crucial thing he needed before he could finish off his next scoop. He wouldn't say anything more. Not to me anyway."

Was it Vera's imagination or was there bitterness in his tone?

"So you can't say what Mr Brett was researching?"

"No. Or only vaguely. In the summer he mentioned that he was on the trail of something crazy in a Somerset village, but for him that could mean anything from murder to gossip."

"Do they know how Mr Brett … died? I mean, do the police have any evidence?"

"As far as I'm concerned, Mrs Wyler, you don't have to be so reverential about Craig. He and I were just work colleagues, not friends. As you can see, I am neither shaken nor especially sad that he has died. I am just astonished that something could have happened to him. He wasn't a man to fall for anybody's tricks, he was much too mistrustful and cunning. And he was … let's talk about something else, shall we? What are you going to do now? Turn the house upside down and search until the mysterious object appears?"

"Hardly. I wouldn't know what I was looking for."

"Perhaps I could help."

Vera smiled doubtfully. "You mean drive to Southcombe with me so as to join in the search? No, thank you, Mr Haider. If I'm going to do it, I'd prefer to do it by myself."

"I'm sorry, I didn't mean it like that. But I'd be very interested to know what turns up."

"Really? If you're as much in the dark as I am, Mr Haider, and your colleague evidently doesn't mean a great deal to you, I don't quite understand your interest."

Ahmed Haider seemed to realize he had gone too far. He shook his head, in Vera's opinion rather too energetically to be convincing.

"I'm afraid I didn't express myself very well. My suggestion is, if you find whatever it is that Craig was looking for then we should meet again. It doesn't have to be in London. I could come to Southcombe."

"Thank you, that won't be necessary. I had hoped you could tell me what Mr Brett was working on, but that doesn't matter. In the end it's not important."

Haider put on his most charming smile.

"Yes, I understand. You're quite right. You see, at the moment I'm making a documentary about forced marriages in this country, and the misery I can see in some families is so indescribable, so unspeakably inhumane, that the death of a journalist – the natural death, mind you – is by comparison pretty trivial."

"But a moment ago you shared my view that Mr Brett must have been the victim of a crime."

"No, no, I never said that, Mrs Wyler. Please don't misquote me. I only expressed my surprise at the idea that Craig might have let himself be lured into a trap. He knew his business much too well, and something like that would never have happened to him."

Whether it was the cider or Ahmed Haider's distant politeness, Vera sensed that she was gradually losing the thread of this conversation and even had the feeling that Haider was wringing information out of her rather than vice versa. By asking a question about his career in film she finally managed to focus on a different subject.

"I've been working for Channel 4 for three years. Short films, half an hour or less, broadcast as part of the seven o'clock news."

"I usually watch the BBC but from now on I'll look out for you on Channel 4. Is anything of yours going to be shown in the near future?"

"Yes, in about two weeks' time. A short film about the National Health Service. Nothing particularly interesting for a non-Briton, I should think, but the new coalition government is planning a thorough reform of the NHS that is pretty contentious. Channel 4 wants to use a number of short films to show how different people are going to be affected by these reforms."

"And the film about forced marriages?"

"That's in the editing suite. Craig had finished the script, I just need two more sequences, and the editor will do the rest. Then I can turn to something new."

Ahmed Haider seemed perfectly happy to discuss his work. He described to her his next film project about the families of three soldiers who had recently been killed in Afghanistan and wanted to know what the Swiss thought about the war.

"I don't represent Switzerland," said Vera evasively.

"But you've got an opinion, haven't you?"

"Any war is nonsense, and this one more than most. No one has been able to conquer Afghanistan. Things are so complicated there that we in the West don't know half of what's going on."

Ahmed Haider's face darkened. "I'm half Afghan. My mother came from Jellalabad. The fate of this country is particularly close to my heart."

Aha, thought Vera, that explains the grey-green eyes. She knew an Afghan refugee in Bern who had the same attractive eye colour. He helped out in the local carpet shop, and for a while she had given him German lessons. Robert had teased her for this weakness: "How's your Afghan with the beautiful emerald eyes? Is he making good progress?"

"Mr Haider, it's getting late and I've got a half-hour drive ahead of me. I'd like to get home before it's dark.

How much longer are you thinking of staying in Watchet?"

"That depends on the police. I have made myself available for the duration of the investigation. That could be several days. Would you be so kind as to give me your mobile number? You never know, perhaps …"

"I haven't yet got round to getting an English mobile, and so I'm not keen on receiving calls. It's just too expensive."

"Your landline?" he persisted, and Vera gave in.

Even from a distance Vera could see something white stuck to her front door. A letter, too big for the letter-box, she thought. Once before the postman had used sticky tape to fix an envelope from Switzerland to the door.

Vera always looked forward to receiving post. Here in England she even liked to read advertising leaflets before recycling them. They were brighter and tackier than at home and helped her to form a more precise impression of English taste.

She opened the door, switched on the light in the corridor and looked at the sheet of paper, which had been attached to the door at eye level with a nail. It consisted of tissue paper on which cut out letters formed three unsteady lines. *"Dear Miss,"* Vera read. *"You did not win. Please give the raffle prize to your daughter immediately. Or else."*

The words 'not' and 'immediately' were underlined in red, and of course there was no indication of who the message was from.

So, an anonymous message. Classic, just like an Agatha Christie mystery. But frightening? No, certainly not. Ridiculous, rather. Chuckling to herself, Vera tore the paper off the nail, sniffed it and took it up to her room. She would deal with that later, the next day or the day after, but not now with the headache, which had hit her again during the journey back from Watchet.

There was also the unpleasant feeling of failure that had dogged her during the course of her conversation with Ahmed Haider. Instead of finding out more about Craig Brett, she had blurted out things which she would have done better to keep to herself. Once again she had been too trusting. And stupid, so unspeakably stupid, to drink cider on top of a hangover.

Chapter 10

The programme *Come Dine With Me* had got to him. Four people who don't know each other cook a meal in turn. They are given points by their fellow diners and at the end choose a winner who takes home £1,000. That was just the kind of entertainment he liked: moderately exciting, not annoying like *Top Gear* and not boring like the soaps, in which he in any case could scarcely distinguish one character from another because they all looked equally young and insipid. What he liked best about the cooking programme was that it allowed him to see inside the fantastic kitchens and sitting rooms of the participants. He sometimes toyed with the idea of applying to take part. When he compared the well-intentioned but often unsuccessful menus that were cooked in front of the cameras, he imagined that he stood a good chance. He would serve breast of pheasant flambé accompanied by steamed apples and mashed turnips, and to drink he would offer cider – obvious: what else could it be in Somerset? The only problem was his house. He couldn't invite anyone else here. No one but he could stand it.

Miles had almost been sick when he came round for the first time. "Hey, are you crazy, living in a pigsty like

127

this? It's bloody dangerous. Come on, let's go to the Kings Arms, I'm not going to stay here a second longer than I have to." Since then they'd always met in the pub.

If even Miles complained, what would the television people say when they came to check out his house? The pile of newspapers and the empty bottles in the hall would probably be enough to make them turn round and go out without even looking at the kitchen. Could he blame them when he himself avoided it because of the mouldy remains of food and dirty plates – not because he was revolted by them, no, he was well used to the stink – but the flies! The maggots! The continual smell of rot that even came through closed doors. It was the same rot that did its work over there in the cemetery, the same rot that ate its way remorselessly through the bodies, the undamaged ones no less than the ones whose hearts he had cut out: by now there were four of those.

He could forget all that for an hour while he watch-ed *Come Dine With Me*. He lived in the brightly lit, spot-less rooms of the participants, he used their new pans and mixers, free from scratches or gravy smears; he poured champagne into their sparkling glasses and drank to the health of the assembled company before eating at their beautifully laid table with their best cutlery.

Over the months the idea of taking part in the pro-gramme had come to be his big dream. Bigger than a trip to Australia or the purchase of a luxury car. Every even-ing he had the dream, eating his pizza or his Chinese takeaway while watching the participants cooking and tasting their most tried and tested dishes. And every time, at the end, he slipped into the skin of the winner and felt the pride and happiness rise up in him when he triumphantly took a handful of twenty-pound notes and threw them around as if they were confetti. One day he would succeed in winning. He would succeed in achieving something that he didn't need to keep secret from everyone. He would fry, purée and flambé in front of the whole world, instead of doing things in Miles' darkened workshop that no one could bear to hear about.

Chapter 11

"No, absolutely not."

"But just think. Everyone in the village would be happy and they wouldn't write such silly anonymous letters. I'd really prefer it. I don't want to get on the wrong side of Southcombe and do you harm by my living here."

"But of course you're not doing me harm! That's not the village, it's just an individual nutter. Tom agrees with me entirely. You keep your prize, and if you're given too much you can pass some of it on to us. By the way, the apples were excellent. After being in Somerset, I don't know if I'll ever be able to eat a Swiss apple again."

"Now you're exaggerating. There's nothing wrong with our apples."

"Somerset apples are better."

"They are very sweet and juicy, I agree. But better? I think you've forgotten how our apples taste, our Chläuslers, Gravensteiners and Reinettes."

"Maybe," said Nadja, with a show of truculence. "Somerset apples are still better."

She locked the front door and hooked arms with Vera, laughing at her expression.

"Admit it, Mum. It gets on your nerves when I talk like this."

"No, that's putting it too strongly. Perhaps I find it a bit strange. You didn't used to be so …"

"Obstinate?"

"So one-sided in your opinions. So partisan."

"But you should be happy that I fit in here."

"And I am, Nadja. As long as you're happy, that's the main thing."

"I am happy, Mum, in every respect. And not least because I've got the best mum in the world."

Nadja planted a kiss on Vera's cheek and suggested a walk to Greenhill Park, stopping off at the bistro in the village on the way back.

"Helen makes the best scones in the neighbourhood. You must try them. Scones with strawberry jam and clotted cream. You'll see, there's nothing more blissful on a winter's day. Come on, it's my treat."

The biting cold had relaxed a little overnight. Patches of earth began to appear in the fields. Snow slid down from the roofs and dripped from the trees. Vera and Nadja left Southcombe behind them and after the Kings Arms turned into the avenue that led up the hill to Greenhill.

"Tom and I often do this walk in the summer. Greenhill itself is a bit creepy, but the park is wonderful, especially when there are horses grazing in it."

To Vera's astonishment, Nadja paid absolutely no attention to a sign which forbade access to unauthorized persons. After reaching the main building she went straight through under the security tape and waited for Vera to do the same.

"I can see cameras above the entrance pillars. We could run into difficulties."

"Nonsense. They're just there to scare people off and don't even work. Anyway Tom and I have never had any problems. Come over here, nothing's going to happen."

Together they walked round the main building. Nadja went ahead, jumping over splintered glass, rubble and boards. Vera, with a queasy feeling in her stomach, crept alongside the walls, which were covered in weather-worn graffiti. Above them ruined balconies jutted out, a few stone slabs still clinging to them.

"The police are right to close this place off. You could be killed here at any moment. Come on, let's get out," she insisted.

But Nadja had already slipped ahead through the brambles to the outbuildings. Vera could count eight barracks arranged in a straight line, all as ready for demolition as the main building itself. The sight of such dilapidation was oppressive, but she could also understand the fascination that Greenhill held for the inhabitants of Southcombe. She didn't believe in ghosts, good heavens no, but the fragments of wall rising up out of rampant undergrowth, with broken window-panes, rotten doors and sooty beams, made it seem like a bewitched landscape in a fairy-tale. A kingdom on which a curse seemed to have been laid in payback for the generations of wretches – the mentally disabled children, the wounded soldiers – who had suffered and left their lives there.

Vera stood surveying it for a moment longer.

"I don't really understand why you brought me here. It's terribly depressing."

"Yes, it is. But behind the last wall there's a way past the wire netting. From there you can walk through the woods back to Southcombe. That way we can return by a different route."

As she left the house, Vera felt she had to peer through the empty window-frames. What she saw was unsettling, but it was nevertheless a relief to discover some signs of life in the desolate rooms. There weren't many, but she saw a couple of broken office chairs, some shelves, rusty radiators and broken toilets, files, the body of a plastic doll. There was even an ancient sofa standing in a corner, its arms still intact, though there were marks on the damask cover and the springs were sticking through it. Who could this impressive piece of furniture once have belonged to?

"Come on, Mum. First you complain that I drag you here, and then I can't get you away from the place."

Beyond the wire netting sloping fields led down towards the valley. A pheasant flew up into the air as Nadja stumbled over a stone, fell over laughing and lay for a moment on her back with her arms outstretched. Vera helped her back on to her feet and wiped the soil and leaves from her back.

"Tell me, have you made any plans for the New Year? Finding a job or something like that?" Vera said.

"No, not really. Why do you ask?"

"Just asking. I think a job would do you good."

"I'm fine as I am."

"I can see that, Nadja. But where's your ambition? A job would give you more of a purpose in life. More satisfaction."

"Mum, I know you mean well, but I don't like it when you worry about me and get involved in my life. I've got plenty to do at the moment."

"Plenty?"

"Yes. For example, the gardening course starts at the beginning of January, and this year we're going to go through the different varieties of roses. For a long time now I've wanted a bed of roses in front of the house. Tea roses. It's not as simple as you think."

"You can't be serious, Nadja? You can't fill your life with such … hobbies. Roses are all fine and well, but you've been to university and you ought to be using your skills."

"Tom's parents are convinced that I'm a born gardener."

"I'm slowly coming to the conclusion that the only thing that counts in Southcombe is gardening. There's something not quite right about that."

"Huh, you're talking just like that journalist who lived in Station House before you. Brett, that man they found three days ago on the beach at Watchet. Watch out. Go on talking like that and you'll end up the same way."

"Well, well, what strange thoughts are these?"

Nadja poked her mother in the ribs and tried to change the subject. "That's not what I meant. Can't you take a joke any longer?"

"It all depends. So what exactly did this Brett say?"

"Oh, him. Tom's father got him right: a snooper of the worst kind. There was no stopping his questions. Really pushy. He interviewed me twice. Wanted to know what I as a foreigner thought of life in Southcombe. How are you supposed to answer a question like that? All I could say was that I feel entirely at ease and welcome here. If I'd said anything else, let alone gone so far as to complain about individual people, it would have been in the papers next morning. Just imagine the fuss that would have caused."

In the meantime they had reached the last farm before the village: Upcott Farm, offering B&B, riding lessons, fresh eggs and seasonal vegetables delivered to one's front door. Nadja greeted the farmer who was just leading his horse out of the stable. He squinted at her and, briefly raising his hand to his cap, turned back to the animal without a word.

"Not exactly friendly, that man," observed Vera.

"You mustn't take it personally. They're all a bit withdrawn here. On a Friday evening in the pub they thaw out. But let's go to the café and see Helen. I'm starving, aren't you?"

The café was tiny and had an old-fashioned kind of cosiness about it. Four cast-iron tables stood along the pink-striped carpet and above them reproductions of Victorian engravings in decorated gold frames. There were plastic flowers in mock-Tiffany vases and the whole place smelled of a mixture of coffee, cakes and fried bacon.

"Pure nostalgia," Vera exclaimed as she laid her coat over the arm of the nearest chair.

"Do you like it?"

Vera would have liked to have given an honest answer, but she didn't want to hurt Nadja. Also she had the impression that her daughter was friendly with the owner of the café. The atmosphere of this place gave Vera an unpleasant feeling. It was trying so hard to be dainty that it had lost all authenticity.

But Helen's café wasn't important. Why should Vera be bothered by a bistro with retro frills? No, what bothered her more was Nadja, her own daughter, who was just now standing at the counter and, with childish excitement in her eyes, pointing at scones and pots of jam. How perfectly she fitted the décor! All too perfectly.

Should Vera broach the subject with her? Should she once more, after so many years, introduce one of those liberating mother-daughter discussions and clear away her lingering unease once and for all? There was nothing specific that Vera could point to. There were just vague anxieties which had weighed more and more on her since her arrival in Southcombe without her being able to say exactly why.

Here in the café, waiting for Nadja, who was now having various kinds of cake explained to her and was nodding eagerly at each of them, Vera suddenly realized what was disturbing her about her daughter. Since being in Southcombe, Nadja had acclimatized herself to the extent that she was losing all her natural effervescence and becoming dulled by the comfortable cocoon around her. As her mother, Vera could not and would not just sit there and watch that happen.

When Nadja sat down and had poured out the tea, Vera made a tentative advance: "I've noticed, Nadja, that you …"

"Mum, please focus on these wonderful scones. Helen has just taken them out of the oven. You need to eat them warm, that's when they taste best."

Vera sighed, sliced her scone in two and began spreading it with jam. Nadja was once again using cheerfulness as a way of warding off serious questions. Vera knew this tactic of old and recalled only too well how nimbly her daughter would evade her when she sensed something unpleasant about to be said.

"Nadja, listen to me now. The scones will taste just as good cold. There are more important things in the world."

Nadja winced. She wanted to make an objection, but thought better of it. Her head down, she let Vera talk without interruption. Just occasionally she nibbled at her scone and dared a glance through the window at the street outside. Vera didn't stop talking until finally she drew the raffle ticket out of her bag, smoothed it with her fist and passed it across.

"There. And no arguing, now! If you absolutely insist on turning into a country bumpkin, then be my guest.

From now on you can be at the receiving end of mountains of local produce. I have decided to stay clear of the whole nonsense. Anonymous letters! I mean, how childish can you get?

"Tomorrow I'll go and see Mrs Moore and tell her to deliver the fruit and vegetables to your address in future. And as far as you're concerned, Nadja, my advice is that you should give some serious thought to your situation. You have changed since you've lived here and there is nothing unusual about that – you are getting older and maturing. Believe me, the last thing I want to do is intrude in your life. But I must admit that I wonder what you're doing with it. You seem to have reached a bit of a dead end. Don't you see it, or don't you want to see it?"

"Mum! What are you saying? I don't know what you're talking about."

"Please don't pretend. Of course you know what I mean. Here you are, living in this hole in the depths of Somerset, no career prospects, no intellectual stimulation, no …"

"That's not for you to pronounce on! You don't live here permanently and have no idea of all the things there are to do in Southcombe. In any case, as you said, I'm grown up and can do what I want. That's exactly what I'm doing here. I play badminton, I go to various gardening and craftwork courses, and I've got my life with Tom. What else do you want? Go on, tell me, what do you want from me? Do you want me to write a doctorate about Shakespeare or start studying quantum physics just so you can be satisfied that I'm getting enough intellectual stimulation?"

Vera shook her head gently. "Oh, Nadja, is it really so difficult for you to see what I mean?"

"If Father were alive he'd have made you shut up long ago. He would never have talked such rubbish. He'd just be happy that things are going well for me. But not you, with your endless nagging and pushing …"

"Nadja, I beg you, calm down."

"No, it's my turn to talk now."

"But don't shout, I can't bear it."

Nadja stood up to leave. "What a lot of things you can't bear, Mum. I'd better not say anything, then. You wouldn't understand anyway."

Chapter 12

Vera didn't wait until the next day to inform Mrs Moore of her decision. The awkwardness over the raffle ticket had already lasted far too long, and when on her way back to Station House she saw light in the windows of Birch Cottage, she marched up the garden path. Even before she had rung the bell she heard the two dogs run to the door barking. They were followed by Mrs Moore, who muttered a cautious and, it seemed to Vera, not entirely welcoming 'Who is it?' before opening the door a crack.

"Oh, it's you. Come in, come in. Maisie, heel! These dogs, they really are too much sometimes."

Vera followed her into the living room. The table was already laid for four people for the following morning.

"I don't want to interrupt you, Mrs Moore. I can see you've got visitors and I'm sure you're busy. I've just come to give you back the raffle ticket. I've thought about it again and I want to pass the ticket on to my daughter."

"The ticket … oh, yes, I'd almost forgotten it. Let's just go into the next room, it's more comfortable there.

Please sit down, Mrs Wyler. A cup of tea?" Vera shook her head. Did one always have to drink tea in this country? She followed Mrs Moore into the room that she had inspected on that first morning in Southcombe while her landlady was out. Six by no means untroubled weeks ago, bearing in mind the two deaths and now the argument with Nadja.

Subdued lighting gave the room a warmth that Vera had missed previously. If it weren't for the watercolours, prints and photos, which Vera remembered quite clearly, she would scarcely have recognized it. But there was the picture with the beautiful ripe quinces, and the one of the coast, and she recalled the people in the photos, too, the elderly gentleman and the two young people, particularly the boy – Mrs Moore had put out so many more photos of him than of the girl. A case of overt preference?

Yes, thought Vera, how is it when you have more than one child? How do you distribute your love? Her own mother had always said that true mother-love is multiplied every time a new child arrives: two children, twice as much, three children, three times as much, and so on for ever. Quite different from the way it is with men or siblings. How could her mother know that so precisely when she too had had only one daughter? Perhaps this maternal multiplication of love wasn't as self-evident as people assumed. Vera counted four photos of the girl on the chest of drawers, while the boy was there to be admired at every stage of his life from nappy-changing to the wedding banquet to army career.

"Mrs Wyler?"

Mrs Moore held a file of papers in her hands and had just taken a sheet out.

"Would you sign here? It's just a formality and I'm sure it seems trivial, but it will stop the club members from disputing the transfer to your daughter. I assume you have cleared it with her, haven't you?"

"Yes, we were just talking about it in the village café. That is to say, I gave her the ticket but because there was rather a serious difference of opinion between us as we parted she either forgot the ticket or else left it there on purpose. I'm sure you know how children can be: one wrong word and they go through the roof."

Mrs Moore nodded and followed the direction of Vera's gaze.

"Are those your children?"

"Yes."

Vera went up to the chest of drawers and allowed herself to pick up a photo. The boy, with a tooth missing, standing in front of a fish and chip stall by the sea.

"That was during a summer holiday in Aldeburgh. Stanley was ten then."

"Does he still live here in Southcombe or at least nearby?"

"No. Stanley has been living in London for many years. He and his wife run a Thai restaurant in Bethnal Green these days. That's her, by the way, on the other photo. Lek comes from Thailand, a charming girl."

"And your daughter?"

"Lizzie? She … is no longer with us, I'm sad to say. It's five years since we … lost her."

Vera was annoyed with herself for not even considering that possibility when wondering why there were comparatively few photographs of the girl.

"Excuse my curiosity, Mrs Moore. How tactless of me. I'm so sorry."

For a moment Mrs Moore stared silently into the void with eyes wide open. Vera could only guess what images were going through her head.

She didn't dare to move or to apologize again for fear of invoking further painful memories.

"A ball-point," Mrs Moore said at last. As if waking out of a trance, she turned away abruptly and began to root around in various drawers.

"Drat, if you need something to write with you can never find it."

"Don't worry, I've got something here. I only hope I don't make Nadja even more angry by signing the prize away. But what's to be done? You obviously can't please everyone at the same time in Southcombe. At least, I don't seem able to."

Vera told Mrs Moore the story of the anonymous letter and was pleased when she took the whole business as lightly as Vera herself did.

"It's something and nothing, Mrs Wyler. I know a few people in the village who might be capable of acting as stupidly as that. I only hope we haven't frightened you off."

" Frightened me? Oh, no, it would take more than an anonymous letter to do that."

Mrs Moore had pulled herself together again, the worry line on her forehead smoothed away. As Vera signed the sheet of paper and passed it to her, the flicker of a smile crossed Mrs Moore's discreetly painted pink lips.

"Thank you, Mrs Wyler, on behalf of myself and of the other club members. You have done the right thing, believe me."

"That's good. Now I just need to talk to Nadja. But not today. I'd prefer to wait until she has calmed down."

"Children can sometimes be a bit impetuous and stubborn."

Had Lizzie been an impetuous and stubborn child? A difficult child? Vera wondered as Mrs Moore led her to the door.

"'Bye for now, Mrs Wyler. See you on the evening of the twelfth, if not before. All right?"

"Twelfth Night? That's by Shakespeare if I'm not much mistaken."

"That's correct, but not what I mean. I'm talking about our festival in Greenhill Park which takes place on the eve of Epiphany, the twelfth night. Next Wednesday, at about eight. Your daughter knows all about it and I'm sure she'll explain it to you."

As things stood at the moment, Nadja wouldn't want to explain anything to Vera. Might Greg perhaps? Hadn't he said he wanted to visit her in Station House sometime? Why not this evening, now?

But Greg didn't come, and the phone call that Vera had hoped for from Nadja didn't materialize. Vera sat down in front of the television with a small bag of crisps and a glass of wine, spent some time zapping through the various channels and ended up with the Al Jazeera coverage of Guantánamo, NATO troops in Afghanistan and the continuing snowfall in Scotland, but none of these could hold her attention. Vera was on tenterhooks, waiting for the call that didn't come. Should she make the first move, even apologize to Nadja? She spent the night arguing the point with herself.

When the telephone finally rang the next morning she jumped up from the breakfast table with relief and was about to congratulate her daughter on her reasonableness.

"Hello, sorry to disturb you so early. It's me, Tom."

"Tom? But why … has something happened to Nadja?"

"No. She's just left the house to go shopping so I took the opportunity to give you a quick call."

"You've heard about our silly argument, I suppose. It's very nice of you to break the ice like this, but in all honesty I think Nadja should do it herself."

"Argument? I don't know anything about that. Nadja didn't say anything about an argument. Is it because of the raffle ticket?"

Vera laughed out loud.

"Oh, that stupid ticket! We've dealt with that now, thank goodness. No, our argument was about something quite different, but I'm not sure I want to talk about it behind Nadja's back. You understand, don't you?"

"Yes, of course. But it's because of the raffle ticket that I'm phoning you."

"Don't tell me she's decided to give it back to me? That really would be too absurd."

"No, no. She doesn't mind keeping it, but I … well, I'd much prefer it if you'd take it back."

"Why?"

"Because it's not the right way to do things. You won the ticket and that's it."

"But you'll be getting tons of fruit and vegetables, all of it organic, free and delivered to your front door. You'd be silly not to accept it. And in any case, it's too late."

"Too late?"

"Yes, I was at Mrs Moore's yesterday and formally signed away the ticket, making it over to Nadja."

"No! That's impossible …"

"Tom, why are you so shocked? It's just some fruit and vegetables. I don't understand why there's so much fuss."

There was silence for a moment. His voice sounded cold and remote when he replied.

"It sounds like there's nothing to be done. Unless you return to Mrs Moore and ask if you can take it back?"

"I'm certainly *not* going to do that. I find this whole business a waste of time."

"What if I try and talk to her?"

"Please don't do that. I consider the whole thing done and dusted. I'd prefer not to talk about it any more."

"If you insist."

If Vera hadn't sensed that Tom was close to tears she would have liked to ask him for details of the festival that Mrs Moore had referred to. However, it wasn't long before he found an excuse to end the conversation and hung up abruptly. His behaviour worried Vera more than she liked to admit to herself. She didn't understand it, but she felt convinced that Tom had withheld something important from her. But what? And above all, why? And did this have anything to do with Craig Brett's discovery in Southcombe?

The unanswered questions wouldn't allow her any peace. After breakfast she set off for the village, her head full of dark forebodings, determined once and for all to confront Nadja and Tom.

However, the two of them were out. But at least on her way Vera saw on the village hall noticeboard the announcement of Twelfth Night in Greenhill Park. People were told to assemble in front of the barrier at 7 p.m. on 5 January. After the wassailing ceremony there would be a torch-lit procession to the Kings Arms, where a local band would provide music until late.

Chapter 13

Jason had hesitated until the last minute before deciding to go to Zoë's New Year party. On the day before he had washed and ironed the only presentable shirt he possessed. He realized he would need to give his hostess something and potted up one of the orchids he had been experimenting with in readiness for Frances' arrival. Although his preparations were made, he couldn't quite believe he would actually break his usual caution and go. Nevertheless, at seven o'clock on New Year's Eve he managed to lock the door behind him and cycle through the dark and cold down to St Valéry. Despite the snow swirling into his face, making it difficult to see, there was the suggestion of a smile on his lips.

The party was already in full swing when Jason reached one of the last houses in St Valéry in the direction of Crotoy, a grand Art Nouveau villa overlooking the sea. In the illuminated windows of the first floor he could see garlands glittering and candles flickering, and the shadows of people dancing to muffled rhythms.

Zoë opened the door, looking almost unrecognizable in a figure-hugging black sequined dress and a pair of towering heels.

"Hello, Jason. What a surprise!" she greeted him. "I've told everyone about you, but the way I described you no one really believed you'd turn up. I didn't either, to be honest. But don't stand out there in the cold. Come in and let me introduce you to my friends."

Jason followed her up the stairs. Couples were dancing, others sitting around the room chattering excitedly, holding glasses and cigarettes. Zoë went round introducing him, repeating each time, "English, please. Jason doesn't speak French."

To his surprise, her friends kept at it and made a big effort not to exclude him. When they were near him they talked whatever English they could manage, even among themselves. Only Zoë's ex-boyfriend Patrice, who had in any case sensed that Jason was to be his replacement and seemed far from pleased about the fact, spoke such a garbled English that they could hardly keep up a conversation. After a couple of attempts they shrugged their shoulders and gave up, spending the rest of the evening trying to avoid each other's eye.

Jason wasn't comfortable among so many people. If it hadn't been for Zoë, who kept on coming back to sit and chat with him, he would have sidled into a corner and taken the first sign of the party breaking up as his excuse to leave.

But she was there, among the sea of unfamiliar faces, lit up like a lighthouse in her sparkling dress. He could scarcely take his eyes off her, she was so lively and – thank God – so reassuringly different from Lizzie. In fact, Zoë was the opposite of her. Dark hair, but otherwise a creature of light, easygoing, uncomplicated. Lizzie had been blonde and fair-skinned – his 'Fairy Queen' he liked to call her – but inwardly plagued by doubts and worries and a deeply embedded anger against everything that restricted her freedom: her parents, her school, the Church, and finally, of course, the 'circle'.

"Well, Jason, how do you like my party?" Zoë asked, steering him into a quiet corner where her friends would hopefully leave them undisturbed.

"Yeah, it's good. Thanks for inviting me."

"Have you chatted to Patrice a bit? I think you'd be interested in what he's up to. He organizes hiking holidays in Holland and Scandinavia and is thinking about branching out into Britain. Perhaps you could give him a couple of tips."

"Hiking? That's not my thing, really. Cycling, yes, but hiking … that's too slow for me."

"No, I mean help him with British destinations. You could suggest parts of the country that are off the tourist radar. Where exactly do you come from anyway?"

Was this a trap? Could she have invited him here tonight just so she could question him? For a moment he tried to think of a plausible lie. 'I used to live in the Lake District,' he could have said, but didn't like the idea of lying to Zoë. So he pretended not to have heard the question and disappeared to offer more wine to her girlfriends.

"*Il est mignon, l'Anglais, tu trouves pas?*" one of them had just whispered to the other, giggling. Jason under-

150

stood only that they were talking about him and smiled back politely. He knew from Zoë that Sabine and Vanessa were former schoolfriends of hers, but because of their heavily made-up faces and something ladylike about their manner the two of them seemed much older, especially Vanessa who began to boast that she was planning to study 'Sciences Po' in Paris next year.

"What's that?' he asked.

"Political Science," Sabine explained. "That's something for brain-boxes like Van. Ordinary mortals like me and Zoë, we're happy with languages, art, things like that."

"Does Zoë want to go to university?"

"Well," laughed Vanessa, "she'll have to do something sometime. She's so casual, Zoë. Or maybe she'll manage to float along as usual, doing nothing, very elegantly."

"Aha, talking about me behind my back? So which of my secrets are you betraying to Jason? Make sure you don't put him off me."

"It's a pity we don't know any secrets about you that we could betray," said Vanessa thoughtfully. "Otherwise of course we'd have shared them."

"If it's secrets you want then you should ask Jason. I'm sure he's got heaps of them, he just smells of secrets."

As if to underline her words, Zoë moved closer to him and buried her face in his shirt, inhaling deeply.

"And?" enquired Sabine.

" Perfume too. Something very sexy. I reckon it's Armani, 1001 Nights. Am I right?"

Jason nodded, amused. Perhaps because of the wine, which was gradually going to his head, or simply because Zoë was so close to him, instead of his usual instinctive mistrust he suddenly felt calm and in control. He put one arm round his hostess who didn't resist, and even heard himself say, "Here's to our secrets."

"Yes, may we reveal them to each other. All our secrets, in fact."

"Aha, so you've got that far already," blurted out Vanessa. "Come on, Sabine, let's leave them to it. They need a bit of together time."

"No need," replied Jason, embarrassed. "That's not what we meant. We were just talking generally."

"Oh, people always say that. But …"

"No, really."

The more he insisted that Sabine and Vanessa should stay where they were, the further into sulky silence Zoë retreated. "So you're still afraid of me?" she said, raising an eyebrow. "Actually I wanted to dance with you, but never mind. I should talk to my other guests."

She walked off without a backward glance, leaving him feeling bereft.

Vanessa giggled. "You're afraid of Zoë? What a strange idea."

Jason shrugged his shoulders, embarrassed. He still couldn't entirely relax in Zoë's presence; needed other people around to keep him steady, so that he didn't …

"May I?"

Michel, Zoë's cousin, stood by the sofa and waited for Sabine and Vanessa to move closer together and give him room to sit down. He was the only one there who was wearing a suit, and under it he had on a white, open-necked shirt, which revealed a smooth, sun-tanned chest. He could have been Zoë's brother, Jason thought. He had the same narrow face, the same finely marked eyebrows. And like Zoë, he too seemed to be thoroughly at ease with himself.

From him Jason discovered more about Zoë's family. Since her parents' divorce ten years earlier she had lived with her father, while her younger brother lived with their mother near Nice.

"The divorce was tough. I can remember it well because my father, Zoë's uncle, got dragged into it. Contact with her mother and brother has been minimal since then, which bothers Zoë a lot. She doesn't complain, but I know she misses Edmond a lot. As children the two of them were inseparable." Jason listened carefully, grateful for the information.

"You wouldn't think so to hear her being so casual and laid back but Zoë is actually a very gifted dancer and acrobat. That's from her mother's side, of course. She used to teach dance therapy in Abbeville, not far from here. It's a pity Zoë hasn't taken it any further. And you? She tells me that you look after the chateau of the two English people above Noyelle sur Mer. Are you a professional butler?"

"No, I kind of slipped into the role. I used to be a medical assistant."

"Ah, so you handed out medicines and gave injections?"

"Among other things."

Michel took a gulp of wine and said, laughing, "I couldn't do that. If I see blood, that's the end for me. I prefer to deal with beautiful things. I run a small but select gallery in the town, specializing in sculpture by local artists."

"Can you live from that?"

"It's all right in the summer, we've got the tourists then. They want souvenirs to take back from their holidays. But in the winter it's more difficult, and I have to do all sorts of things to stay above water. Christine … that's the woman in the green dress … has just opened a restaurant by the harbour. In due course she wants to offer cultural events there, concerts, readings, small exhibitions. If it does well I may sell the gallery and get involved with that."

It was getting on for midnight. "Three minutes to go," announced Zoë as she came out of the kitchen with two bottles of champagne and triumphantly held them up in the air. The music was turned down, the dancing stopped and everyone gathered round the table.

"Take care now," she warned, "these are Dad's favourite glasses. Genuine Bohemian crystal."

"So where is he tonight?" asked Patrice.

"In Paris with a friend of his. I've got the house to myself for at least two weeks because after that he's going to visit relations in England. But it's nearly time now. Come on, Jason, give me a hand opening the bottles."

A few seconds before midnight everyone began counting out loud, and then people clinked glasses and kissed each other on the cheek before going to the window to admire the fireworks over the sea. Zoë stood next to Jason and slid her arm round his waist. She repeatedly looked up at him, laughing, and whenever he didn't immediately turn away from the spectacle outside and answer her look she would give him a friendly poke in the stomach.

"Jason," she whispered. "You're welcome to stay here for the night rather than riding home in the dark. Régine is staying too because she lives so far away."

Jason hesitated. In three years he hadn't once spent a night away from the chateau. What if there were a break-in? Could he risk it?

"So?" Zoë pressed him.

"I don't know."

"Oh, you and your don't knows! If you imagine I'm going to come creeping into your room, you don't need to flatter yourself. You're quite safe here, promise."

Jacqueline was the last to leave, and when she had gone Zoë, Régine and Jason sat in the living room for a while, yawning as they stared at the bottles and glasses, the remains of the festive cake and the wilting decorations around them.

"Just think," said Zoë. "Last year I was still with Patrice. God, that was exhausting!"

"Yes, I can remember the two of you having an argument at midnight precisely and you running out of the room, crying," said Régine.

"Isn't it strange how he used to get on my nerves then, and what good friends we have become since we're no longer together? Have you ever known anything like that?" Zoë asked her friend.

"No, if I finish a relationship that's it. And if he finishes it, that's really it."

Régine lifted up a paper decoration from the floor and wrapped it absent-mindedly round her finger.

"And how was it with you?" she asked Jason.

"I can't really say. I've only had one girlfriend up to now."

"What? Only one?" Zoë looked slightly dismayed to hear this. "Régine, do you believe him?"

"If he says so, I expect he knows."

"But you're over thirty, Jason. That's … that's not normal."

"Don't make me older than I am. I'm only twenty-nine."

"All the same … Perhaps you prefer men?"

He shook his head, grinning.

Zoë glanced sideways at Régine then up at Jason under lowered lashes.

"So can I hope that you like me, just a bit?"

Régine hooted with laughter at her friend's bare-faced cheekiness.

"Behave yourself, Zoë! If you go on like this you'll scare him off for sure. Now I need some sleep. Can you show me where I'm staying? I'm really tired, aren't you?"

"Right, let's get off to bed. Come on, Jason, I'll show you your room. It's my brother's but he hasn't lived here for a long time."

As soon as Zoë closed the door behind her, Jason began to regret not having gone home. What was he doing in a child's bedroom? In the half-light he could make out a bookshelf full of comics, a chest of drawers boasting a yellow and red Lego mountain surrounded by all sorts of robots, posters of pop stars on the walls.

Outside there were explosions and bright lights. St Valéry was lighting fireworks while he tried in vain to sleep in a narrow, unfamiliar bed.

Zoë's presence in the house put him on edge. Without knowing where her room was he sensed her near to him, almost thought he could hear her breathing. Was she already asleep, or was she too thinking about the evening and everything that had happened? And where was Régine sleeping? Could it be in the same room as Zoë, even in the same bed, and were they whispering to each other, perhaps talking about him?

Finally he slept, deeply and with no dreams, until a gentle knock on the door and Zoë's voice woke him: "Jason, are you awake?"

So she is coming to me after all, was his first thought, and he didn't know whether to be pleased or disappointed that she had broken her promise.

"Mmm."

"I don't know if you've got any plans for today, but it's already two in the afternoon. I thought I'd just let you know. Régine and I had breakfast ages ago."

Two in the afternoon!

"Give me a couple of minutes. I'll be straight down," he called to her.

"Tea or coffee?"

"Tea, please. Thanks."

"No problem." He heard Zoë race downstairs. She had kept her word. She hadn't visited him in the night; hadn't opened the door even a crack in order to speak to him now. Was this a sign that he could trust her?

Chapter 14

Fresh snow had fallen over Somerset. Behind the Kings Arms, at Greenhill Park, there was a bluish tinge to the glistening of the lawns leading up to the main building. The forecourt had been turned into a temporary car park, and people stood around with hands in pockets, their heads shielded from the cold under woollen hats and balaclavas. Two torches were burning in front of the last of the outbuildings. Behind them a twisted apple tree reached up into the sky, its lichen-covered branches like outstretched arms.

Vera had gone on foot, armed with an electric torch, and reached Greenhill Park just as Tom's mother, Mrs Moore and two other people were getting out of their car. Tom and Nadja were presumably not with them. As Vera went up to Marion she began to have the feeling that Nadja wouldn't be coming to the ceremony and that she was the reason why. Since that argument in the café they hadn't spoken together, and even Tom had seemed unusually chilly during their most recent telephone conversation.

"Welcome to our wassailing ceremony, Vera," said his mother. "I'm sure you're going to think we're completely crazy, but we're willing to put up with that. In any case you won't be the first person to shake their head over Somerset customs, and I don't suppose you'll be the last."

Marion laughed with delight as she spoke, excitement written all over her face. She linked arms with Vera and led her away from the others.

"Vera, you must be prepared not to recognize your daughter tonight. But I can guarantee that Nadja will be an absolute delight to see. The most beautiful for years."

"But …"

"Oh, please, I'm sorry. I didn't want to suggest she isn't always a delight to the eyes. She is, truly. I just wanted to prepare you for your daughter looking special tonight … different."

"At least she's coming. A couple of days ago we had a bit of a … falling out, if you know what I mean."

"Oh, yes, I know about that. It's nothing serious, believe me. A little difference of opinion, nothing more. Nadja has already got over it."

Vera tried to free herself but Marion held firm and went on talking about Nadja's many good qualities as if she were her own daughter. Finally Vera had heard enough.

"You don't need to tell me about Nadja. If there's anyone in the world who knows her it's me. After all, I am her mother."

Vera wanted to sound firm and decisive, but this didn't have the desired effect. Mrs Skinner just made a dismissive gesture and said, "Oh, but these ideas about family ties are all relative, don't you think? And the possessiveness! People should be much more open-minded about such things. After all, our children don't actually belong to us so much as to the community. But keep your eyes open – at any moment the Lord of Misrule will appear."

"Who?"

"Our master of ceremonies. We call him the Lord of Misrule. A kind of carnival figure."

In the meantime they had reached the apple tree, around which most of the residents of Southcombe had already assembled in a circle. Vera recognized many of the faces from her walks through the village, but apart from the Skinners and Mrs Moore she didn't know anyone personally. She knew that the tall man opposite her was the postman and that the woman in the ill-fitting dress with two children hanging on to her skirt, sucking their thumbs, was the butcher's daughter, but she had never spoken to either of them. However, her eyes soon passed from these two and wandered across the other spectators. What wouldn't she have given to see Nadja in the crowd! She saw Tom, though, sitting by himself away from the crowd, a blank expression on his normally cheerful face.

She wanted to shout across to him, but suddenly a murmur ran round the crowd and from the barracks there came the distant sound of a violin. A male figure had emerged from the darkness and now began to lurch towards the tree. His green velvet cloak, under which light-coloured clothing could be seen, moved in waves, following the rhythm of his movements, and as he requested admission to the centre of the circle Vera saw that the rod he was brandishing in the air was in reality a gun. But it was less the weapon than the man himself that astonished Vera. Although his face was painted dark green, the bushy eyebrows and the thin, ash-blond hair revealed who this in fact was – Tom's father. In his primitive dress Geoff Skinner seemed to belong to another time, and Vera found it difficult to believe the change in him. And yet it was he, the otherwise dignified and proper Mr Geoffrey Skinner, who as the Lord of Misrule danced and sang merrily as he spun round and round.

Vera turned to Marion to convey her surprise. However she was already straining her neck to look in another direction. A band of musicians with fiddles, accordions and drums had started to move forward, followed by a group of dancers dressed in white with strings of bells around their knees, which rang out into the night with every step they took.

Vera watched the strange procession with mixed feelings as it made its way into the circle of onlookers. As they played, the musicians began to dance round the apple tree and the crowd to clap and sing. Wasn't this a trifle ridiculous? Nostalgia of the weirder kind?

"What's it all supposed to mean?" she finally decided to ask.

"Those are our Morris dancers. An ancient English popular tradition that you probably don't know about. There are dancers like these everywhere in England. They perform at every important village event."

"Yes, but why are they doing it tonight? What is it that's being celebrated?"

"Just be patient. You'll understand soon enough. It's all to do with the apple tree. This is the oldest one in the village."

All very well, thought Vera. But what do I care about an apple tree when Nadja isn't here?

The Morris men danced in groups of four, following the gun, which Geoff Skinner used like a conductor's baton. One of them was Greg, and his boyishness, which had struck Vera when she'd met him in the pub, was even more apparent during this dance. He laughed with the whole of his face, his movements were exuberant and seemed to express a childlike joy. The crowd joined in, clapping and cheering, but not for long. Suddenly there was a deafening drum roll which made both dancers and spectators freeze. For a moment time seemed to be suspended. In the silence two men stepped out of the circle and carried a chest over to the foot of the apple tree. They took trowels out of their trouser pockets and began to dig a hole between the roots of the tree. Not a sound was to be heard while they were working. When the hole seemed deep enough, they opened the chest and took from it a jug, a leather purse and a silver goblet, and placed them on a cloth. One of the men was Paddy. He was wearing the same glowing orange jacket as he had done that time in the pub, but even without it Vera would have recognized him by his tousled beard.

Slowly the music began again, at first just a couple of tentative bars but soon a lilting melody underlined by dull drum-beats, which Vera felt vibrating in her whole body. It's like a circus, she thought. As the music gradually gets louder and more insistent it arouses the expectations of the audience, until the star of the show leaps out from behind the curtain and begins his number in the glare of the spotlights.

"Now, watch," whispered Marion. And indeed, into the middle of the circle there stepped a young woman, as if conjured up out of nowhere, who smiled shyly round at them as she skipped up to the tree. On her feet glistened green ankle boots, matching her coat and the ivy wreath which decorated her head. Vera held her breath in joy and astonishment. She would have liked to cry out, 'Nadja, what on earth are you doing?' but the mood of the crowd, which a moment ago had been exuberant, had turned unaccountably solemn. People watched her closely with serious, withdrawn expressions on their faces, as if she were being subjected to a test. Marion had been right. Nadja looked special this evening. Special and, yes, somehow different. Perhaps it was because of her hair which she wasn't wearing down, as she usually did, but twisted into long ropes so that she looked like a medieval princess. That Nadja should agree to appear in such an absurd spectacle surprised Vera. But there stood her daughter, revelling in her role, while the crowd inspected her silently from all sides – for an age, it seemed to Vera, until finally, on a sign from the Lord of Misrule, a frenzy of joy broke out.

"Long live our Apple Queen! Hip, hip, hurrah! Hip, hip, hurrah! Long live our Apple Queen!"

"Our Apple Queen. What a beauty!" said Marion, more to herself than to Vera.

"Oh, is that what this is all about? My daughter is your Apple Queen?"

"Yes, exactly, our Apple Queen. And what a splendid one!"

"I'm sorry but more than anything else I find this whole spectacle … odd."

"You're not jealous, are you? Nadja can be both things, you know, your daughter and our Apple Queen. But in any case, the spectacle, as you call it, isn't yet over. The most important part is still to come."

What followed did little to appease Vera. Nadja's slow and stately movements resembled those of a priestess and she had to carry out a series of actions that would have been incomprehensible to Vera if Marion hadn't now and then given explanatory comments.

"The Apple Queen is now pouring cider on to slices of toast and hanging them on the branches of the apple tree. And what the Lord of Misrule is reciting is an invocation of the robin."

Vera tried to remain straight-faced throughout all this, but couldn't suppress an ironic tone of voice when she asked, "Did I hear you right? An invocation of the robin? That sounds deeply heathen."

"For centuries the robin has been regarded as the good spirit of the apple tree. The toast is for him."

When Nadja had hung up the last slice amidst clapping and singing, she lifted the leather bag and laid it carefully in the hole that had been dug at the foot of the tree, strewing the turned soil back over it. For the fraction of a second she was illuminated by a series of flashlights, which produced a general muttering from the crowd.

"No cameras, please," shouted Geoff, but the photographer paid no attention to the Lord of Misrule and carried on taking pictures until a couple of nearby spectators snatched his camera from him and trampled it to pieces in front of his eyes. The photographer merely raised his hands in a gesture of apology.

"Well, I never. Did you see that? What a cheek! He can't be one of us. What's he doing here?" Marion was breathless with indignation.

"I must say, the crowd's reaction seems a bit extreme to me," replied Vera. "They've just destroyed the poor man's camera."

"Quite right, too. There is no photography allowed at our wassailing. I know that other villages like Carhampton or Kenilston even publicize their ceremonies on YouTube, but we don't approve of that kind of exhibitionism. Our ceremony must not travel beyond Southcombe."

The photographer meanwhile had rejoined the spectators as if nothing had happened and awaited, apparently quite relaxed, the next stage of the ceremony.

"But that is …" began Vera.

"What? Do you know this miserable wretch?"

"I don't exactly know him though I think I spoke to him once. But now I look more closely, I'm not sure."

Surely Vera had been mistaken and that was not Ahmed Haider as she had at first thought? What would he be doing in Southcombe?

During this episode Nadja had been standing passively by the tree. As soon as the crowd had calmed down she continued with her duties.

"The jug the Apple Queen is holding contains cider. She's going to pour it over the roots of the tree," explained Marion. "The cider will remind the tree of the taste of cider so that it gives a good crop in the coming year."

"Do you really believe that?"

Marion gave Vera a severe look and shrugged her shoulders. In the meantime Nadja had indeed lifted the jug and was carefully anointing the base of the tree. Meanwhile the Lord of Misrule intoned the invocation in a loud voice:

"All health to thee, thou ancient apple tree,

We wish thee buds and blossoms

And apples, apples, apples.

Hats full! Caps full!

Sacks and sacks and sacks full!

And my pockets full, full, full! Hurrah!"

At the word 'Hurrah' Geoff fired his gun four times into the air and broke into peals of laughter. Vera shuddered.

"He is rejoicing," explained Marion, "because he has driven the evil spirits out of the tree."

"And not only the evil spirits, I see," replied Vera. "Listen to the flapping over there by the oak tree. The poor rooks must have been scared to death. And so was I, to tell the truth. It was so unexpected. And that laughter, it sounded so … creepy."

"You don't like this ceremony, just admit it. But how could you? After all, you're not one of us."

"But neither is Nadja. And yet she seems to feel right at home playing the part of your Apple Queen."

"Nadja is a clever girl. It didn't take her long to understand what an honour it is."

But was it really such a great honour to stand up in front of everyone and pour cider on to the roots of an apple tree, and then, after the celebratory shots had been fired, fill a goblet, drink from it and pass it round the circle of participants in an anti-clockwise direction? By the time the goblet reached Vera it was almost empty. She merely wetted her lips with it, but the bitter smell of the cider at once reminded her of meeting Ahmed Haider in Watchet. Strange, she thought, as she passed the goblet on to Mrs Skinner, that cider should also play a part at her second meeting with Ahmed Haider.

As the torch-lit procession led back into the village, Vera tried to approach Nadja, but couldn't reach her. The Morris men danced close around her and the yelling crowd formed a second impenetrable barrier. Even later on in the pub, when people were sitting comfortably drinking cider and singing songs, it seemed to Vera that she was being prevented from reaching her daughter. Nadja, still surrounded by Morris men as if by bodyguards, sat beside Mr Skinner on a dais raised above the level of the villagers, who at every new pint lifted their glasses and cried, "Hail to thee, our most lovely Apple Queen."

The serenity with which she received this homage awoke in Vera memories of earlier years when Nadja had taken part in small-scale theatrical performances at school and always shone in the principal role. Anything less than that had been out of the question. Wasn't she the prettiest child? The most accomplished? The villagers of Southcombe must have reached the same conclusion as the school: who could possibly compete with her for the role of Apple Queen this year?

As Nadja's mother, Vera should have been proud of her daughter, Marion was continually suggesting it to her, but in reality she found the sight of Nadja's serenely smiling face disturbing. And even more so the behaviour of the revellers, who after a couple of pints of cider began to slur their speech and even fall off their stools. They took no notice of Vera's disapproval, and she couldn't escape the feeling that she was tolerated in this gathering merely because she was the mother of their Queen. Apart from Marion no one spoke to her. Greg gave her a little smile but was busy with the other Morris dancers paying homage to Nadja, Tom sat with them on the dais, and the only other person who might possibly have given Vera an honest account of the background to this strange evening seemed to have disappeared, possibly sent packing by the organizers.

"It's getting late, Marion. I think I should go home," Vera told her. "Many thanks for a most interesting evening. And once again I wish you and Geoff a Happy New Year."

"Happy New Year to you too, Vera. When shall we meet again?"

Vera smiled politely, hoping to slip away without making any definite arrangement.

"Come and have tea with us one day," Tom's mother was saying. "You know where we live: Quantock View, number fourteen. We've got a conservatory with wonderful views, a one-hundred-and-eighty-degree panorama. And perhaps I'll have the opportunity to give you a bit of an introduction to the mentality of our village and help you to reconcile yourself to it."

"Yes, perhaps. Who knows?"

But Vera didn't want to be reconciled, she wanted to understand what was going on here.

She wanted to understand why Nadja was on the point of slipping away from her. Nothing else bothered her. The villagers of Southcombe could pray to their apple trees and indulge in any kind of New Age nonsense they wanted to. So long as they didn't drag Nadja into it, Vera could live with it and even get some amusement from it. If Nadja wanted to spend an evening being feted as the Apple Queen of Southcombe all very well, but in the real world she was still Vera's daughter. She couldn't simply shake off that tie because her mother didn't fit into this new environment.

While Vera was stomping back home through the snow, the darkest thoughts ran through her head. Half aloud she talked with Robert, told him of her fears and at the same time tried to rid from her mind the mask-like smile that Nadja had worn throughout the whole evening. She couldn't stop thinking about it, though, and increasingly it filled her with fear.

Although she could scarcely keep her eyes open, Vera had no thought of going to bed. She was too agitated to sleep and decided that she must finally collect some factual information about Southcombe and its strange practices. Haider's presence at the wassailing ceremony was significant, she was sure of that. When she recalled what had recently happened to his partner Craig Brett she couldn't believe that the film-maker had come purely out of curiosity. Was it possible that wassailing was at the centre of Craig Brett's research and that Haider now wanted to continue this work on his own?

Vera could find nothing by Brett on the internet about wassailing, but in the last months before his death the journalist had nevertheless published several articles about Somerset that were publicly available. Together with Haider he had even made a film about the wild ponies on the Quantock Hills, and Vera was able to see a substantial excerpt from it in the internet archive of Channel 4 News. However, it was clear to her after a few minutes that it had little relevance to the many questions that were worrying her.

She chose to pass over an article on the restoration of Coleridge's cottage in Nether Stowey and engrossed herself instead in an essay that Brett had written for a local studies paper. The name 'Southcombe' leaped out at her on several occasions. The essay, which was entitled 'The Green Man', was concerned among other things with St Michael's in Southcombe, and in addition contained a series of interesting reproductions of an ancient figure that was widely to be found even outside England: a male face carved from wood or chiselled out of stone, from whose mouth, nose and ears the tendrils of plants grew.

In his essay Brett had been less concerned with questions of belief than with establishing a historical timeline for this Green Man. During 2010 he had visited the most important churches in Somerset, had photographed the representations of the figure there and made a stylistic comparison. Southcombe church, as Tom had told Vera, possessed no such figure, and she found this confirmed by Brett:

"Interestingly, St Michael's Southcombe lacks any reference to a Green Man. In the chapel, however, there is a niche at eye-level in which it is possible to identify a figure that may represent a female equivalent of the traditional male fertility symbol, a recumbent woman from whose body wheat is sprouting and from whose breasts milk is flowing (see fig. 11). Incidentally, the same figure is also to be found on gravestones there of a more recent date (see fig. 12). According to a survey undertaken in Southcombe, the figure is a representation of St Aldusa, patron saint of farmers. There is however no source material to confirm this: there is no reference to a St Aldusa either in local chronicles or in Somerset folk-songs, and in the neighbouring villages this figure is completely un-known."

In figure eleven Vera recognized the worn features that had caught her attention on her visit to St Michael's.

Brett had photographed the female figure from the side and, Vera guessed, enhanced the contrasts digitally in order to bring out the contours more clearly. Nevertheless parts of the woman, especially her face and the feet, were indistinct because of the porosity of the stone. The gravestone shown in figure twelve was quite different. A miniature version of the original, the black lines engraved in the marble stood out sharply from the milky white background. Vera leaned back in her chair and rubbed her eyes. What was she doing, worrying about abstruse scrawls at this time of night instead of sleeping like any normal human being? The clock on the computer showed 2:13 in the morning. She hadn't stayed up as late as this for years.

Her eyes slid from the numbers back to the computer screen, which was completely filled by a close-up of the white marble slab. Above there was the stylized Aldusa, and lower down in golden letters the name and dates of the deceased: Elizabeth Karen Moore, 20 April 1988 - 26 July 2005.

Lizzie! The blonde girl with the pout and the piercing in her eyebrow, Mrs Moore's daughter.

Unfortunately there was no word about the person herself. What Brett had concentrated on here was merely the design on her gravestone, although his text clearly spoke of gravestones in the plural. That meant that Lizzie's grave wasn't the only one to have this symbol. There were others, but which ones? And how many?

Vera was suddenly wide awake. If it had been daytime she would have set off at once for the cemetery in order to look for the other graves, but it was snowing again and by torchlight it would have been of little use. For good or evil she would have to be patient until the following morning, 6 January: Robert's birthday.

That was of itself enough of a reason to visit a cemetery. If she couldn't place any flowers on his grave she would at least finally make good her omission and put some on Sue Harper's. Mr Lee's shop was open this time, the owner behind the counter doing some photocopying. Beside him a door stood half open, and through the gap Vera could see a long conference table with a glass and a blue brochure laid out in every place. Nadja had described Mr Lee as extremely jovial and chatty, but, after checking who it was, he only briefly lifted his head from the machine as Vera came in and looked around the shop.

She decided on yellow roses.

"Five, please. And you don't need to wrap them, I'm taking them straight to the cemetery."

"Thirteen pounds fifty, please. Or let's say thirteen pounds since you're my first customer today. Are you driving through?"

"No, I'm living temporarily in Southcombe. In Station House at the end of the village."

"Station House? Aha, Mrs Moore's new tenant."

"Not so new. I've been here since November."

"Not exactly the best time for enjoying Somerset. I mean, from the point of the view of the weather. We've not had such a filthy winter as this for years and years."

"Yes, that's what I keep reading in the papers."

"Actually I wanted to drive to Lyme Regis this weekend, but with this bitter cold I think it's better to stay at home."

"Right. You won the weekend in Lyme Regis in the raffle, didn't you?"

"Exactly, but how did you know? Were you there when the numbers were drawn?"

"Yes, I was, and I had a winning ticket like you. That is to say, my daughter had the winning ticket. I'm afraid we caused a bit of a commotion in the end."

Mr Lee began to laugh a shade too loudly to be entirely convincing. Vera could have sworn that he'd recognized her as soon as she came into the shop.

"Of course, the argument about the main prize! I certainly couldn't forget that. Believe me, it's already gone into the annals of Southcombe. You see, ever since we've had the raffle we've never had anything like it. So, you're the mother of this year's Apple Queen …"

Mr Lee left the end of his sentence hanging in the air and, instead of speaking, spontaneously put together a large bouquet of brightly coloured flowers, which he put down beside the roses.

"There, would you take this bouquet to your daughter, please? A small gift from us."

"Us?"

"Yes, from us villagers. I take the liberty of acting as representative of Southcombe. Our Apple Queen deserves the very best flowers!"

"Thank you. I'm sure Nadja will be delighted to receive them."

Vera was in fact expressing her own delight that Mr Lee had given her a plausible reason for looking in on Nadja. But first on her agenda was Sue Harper's grave.

Several people were visiting the cemetery this morning, some cleaning graves, others standing reverently in front of them, their hands joined in silent prayer. On this occasion Sue Harper's grave stood out even from a distance because it was so richly adorned. Flowers, both genuine and plastic, wreaths, candle ends and a lantern covered the grave. The gravestone itself stood free and on it – hadn't she half expected it? – a simple, black design stood out: St Aldusa, the same figure that Vera had seen on her computer a few hours earlier. Yes, without quite being able to say why, she had been almost certain she would find it here. Nevertheless she was unnerved to find her hunch confirmed. Absent-mindedly she placed the roses on top of the other flowers and, despite the persistent snow, set off in search of Lizzie's grave and possible others with the same figure represented on them. She found Lizzie's near the entrance to the church, in the shadow of a yew tree. The gravestone was smaller than she remembered it being from the internet. Almost as white as the snow around, it made the engraved pattern stand out particularly sharply.

Vera found three more graves with the same pattern on them. Behind the church, near the village hall, lay Judith Selwyn, who had died aged nineteen on 27 October, 2002, and, a little further along there was an Alice Jane Wilcox, who had died, at the age of sixty-four on 8 November, 1997. Finally Vera found, a few yards from the exit, Janet Rees Mogg, who had died on 30 November, 2000, aged forty-one. Was there a connection between these women? Could they have belonged to a secret religious group, a St Aldusa sect?

On her way to Nadja's house, Vera thought about who she could ask without arousing suspicion. Apart from Ahmed Haider, no one occurred to her. But when she recalled how insistently he had questioned her about whatever it was that had been lost in her house when she met him in Watchet, she shrank back from the idea of another meeting with him. And when she stood in front of Nadja's and Tom's house and the latter greeted her at the door with a rather joyless smile, it suddenly struck her that she didn't really trust anybody any longer, not even Tom.

"Is Nadja in?"

"Yes, come in. She's awake, but she's still in bed. Last night rather took it out of her. We didn't get home until four in the morning."

There was an unusual disorder in the living-room. She must have interrupted Tom while he was ironing. Washing was piled up on the sofa, and the ironing-board had taken the place of the dining-table, which was push-

ed up diagonally against the wall. In the corner Vera recognized the same kind of large cardboard box as the
one that Mrs Moore had put in front of her door before
Christmas.

"Ah, I can see that Nadja has received another instalment of her raffle prize."

"Yes, it arrived yesterday. Again there's an enormous amount of fruit and vegetables, too much for two
people, really. But wait a moment, I think Nadja's getting
up. I'll tell her you're here."

Her heart beating faster, Vera listened to the noises
from the next room, whispers, then a chair being moved.
Finally Nadja opened the door and stood in front of her,
barefoot, still wearing pyjamas, her hair tousled and her
eyes red from lack of sleep. Or had she been crying?

"Mum … it's so good that you've come." She threw
her arms round Vera and buried her face in her neck, but
then at once drew back with a cry: "You're soaking wet
from the snow. Take your coat off and sit down next to
the radiator. Oh, I'm so sorry for being such an impossible daughter. I don't know what got into me that
time we were in the café."

"Don't worry, it's fine. I didn't exactly behave like
the ideal mother either. Let's forget that silly argument.
Look, here are some flowers for you. Not from me, I'm
afraid, but from Mr Lee."

Nadja's face brightened up at the sight of them.
"Gladioli … lilies ... at this time of year! That's incredible.
Look, Tom, how wonderful." She took the bouquet from

Vera, carried it into the kitchen and came back with a vase.

"There's nothing more beautiful than flowers. But tell me, Mum, what did you think of me last night as the Apple Queen?"

"Enchanting, although I can't take the whole thing entirely seriously. It reminded me a bit of a carnival procession."

"Tom, did you hear what my mother said?" called Nadja to her husband who was in the kitchen making coffee. "Carnival! Your sacred wassailing compared with a carnival!"

"You mustn't talk like that in the village, they take wassailing extremely seriously," he commented.

"And you?" Vera asked her daughter.

"Me? I haven't really thought about it. I just enjoy it. And to tell the truth, it's exciting to be a queen once in a while, even if it's only an Apple Queen. I've really been lucky of late. First the main prize in the raffle, and now I'm the Apple Queen."

Vera frowned. There was a question burning on her lips, but she held back and instead took the cup of coffee from Tom, thanking him, while Nadja pushed a couple of ironed shirts to the side of the table so that he could put down the tray with the coffee pot and a plate of biscuits.

"Dad would have been sixty-seven today," said Vera after a brief silence. "Did you remember?"

Nadja shook her head. She looked down at her feet and gazed absent-mindedly at her toenails, each of which was painted a different shade of green. With a sigh she admitted that today was the first year she had woken up on this date without immediately thinking of his birthday.

"Perhaps because I'm not properly awake yet. But we'll light a candle for him. I always do that on his birthday. Darling, would you get us a candle? I think there are some left in the spare-room chest of drawers. And have you by chance seen my vitamin pills? I've got no idea where I put them down yesterday."

Tom laughed. "You've been so distracted recently. It's not like you."

"You're right, I've become dreadful. Recently I left my shopping in the Co-op, and I would have just missed the first lesson of my gardening course if Mrs Moore hadn't been so kind as to ring me up beforehand and remind me."

Tom had in the meantime fetched the candle and found the vitamin tablets in the kitchen cupboard behind the bag of coffee, it was a white bottle out of which he counted three little round objects into Nadja's hand.

"What kind of vitamins are those?" asked Vera, bending forward to look more closely.

"Just don't worry about it, Mum. It's a special compound that you can't buy commercially."

"And you just swallow that stuff without knowing what's in it?"

Nadja suppressed a sigh of impatience and turned to Tom: "You explain it to her. And while you do that I'll nip up and have a shower."

When Nadja had gone out of the room Vera asked, "Do you take them as well?"

Instead of a direct answer, Tom began to explain that the compound consisted of natural herbs. "Valerian, nettle extract and who knows what else. Mr Lee puts the stuff together and sells it in the village at a pretty high price. But Nadja didn't have to pay. The bottle was in the box together with the fruit and vegetables."

"Is he to be trusted?"

"Absolutely. He's the best authority there is on local plants. A real expert! He was even interviewed by the BBC once."

"Right. I'm sure the BBC will vouch for him not being a charlatan."

Tom also looked tired this morning, Vera thought, and, yes, a little lost, too. He didn't whistle to himself and he didn't walk restlessly from room to room as he usually did, but sat at the table with hunched shoulders and stared at the candle he had just lit. He was so unforth-coming that he couldn't have made it clearer what a bad time his mother-in-law had chosen for her visit.

"Actually I just dropped by to bring the flowers and to wish you both a Happy New Year," she said. "I won't interrupt you any longer. But it would be nice if you would come and have a meal with me at Station House sometime."

"Great idea, Mum," said Nadja, who at that moment came into the room wearing jeans and a thick Shetland pullover. She had wound a bath towel round her wet hair and held a newspaper that she gave to Vera.

"I've been keeping this for you for a long time. You'll find information about all the cultural events in the region for the next few months. Exhibitions, for example. In the Brewhouse there are always interesting things going on. We could go to something together."

So Nadja was not yet so wrapped up in village affairs that she couldn't be persuaded to go to an exhibition, thought Vera, relieved.

"I'll set off straight away, otherwise I'll get stuck in the snow on the way back. It's real stay-at-home weather, isn't it?"

"I don't have much choice," said Tom, laughing. "As you can see, I've got piles of stuff to iron."

"Yes, the poor man is on duty this afternoon, while I'm invited to Mrs Moore's for a cream tea. Without Tom. She'll do things properly, Eileen Moore is a stickler for making an effort when she entertains. She likes telling me about the times when she worked as ward sister in the Greenhill Park clinic. I think she must have been pretty crazy about the director. 'Mr Lee said this … Mr Lee thought that.' When she starts on that tack you can hardly stop her. A bit like Tom's mother. Marion was a cook in the clinic and, if you ask me, besotted by the great man – yes, she was, Tom, you've said as much yourself. Mrs Moore is much more restrained, but I like it when she talks about her time there. And she always serves such delicious teas."

Nadja and Mrs Moore in a cosy tête-à-tête … Vera could picture the living-room of Birch Cottage in her mind's eye, and Nadja sitting there, so eager to please, almost playing the role of daughter to her gracious hostess.

Vera found the image painful. Perhaps Marion had been right to suggest that she was jealous. That without wanting to be, she was one of those women who keep their daughters entirely to themselves and resent their having friendships with other women. But no, that was not fair. What unsettled Vera lay deeper than mere possessiveness. She was becoming more and more uneasy in Southcombe without understanding why, feeling trouble approaching her like a storm but unsure as yet in which direction it lay.

Chapter 15

He took the fifty-pound notes out of the envelope and put them down beside each other on the table. Three hundred pounds. One hundred for the work, two hundred for his silence. Or vice versa, he couldn't remember any more what Miles had told him the first time round. He had been happy enough to put the money in his pocket then. Ten years ago three hundred pounds had been a lot of money. Who else, he had thought at the time, gets so much money for twenty minutes' work?

Today, however, the six notes seemed shabby recompense. One was brand new, the others – God knows how many hands they had already been through. Grubby, folded and refolded, they disgusted him. It was a miracle that they were still worth the fifty that was written on them.

Three hundred pounds – ridiculous! It wasn't even half of his monthly mortgage payment. The members of the committee he worked for spent this kind of money every month on their horses, or blew it on a weekend in London or Cornwall. Who did they think he was? For ten years he had been doing things that everyone in the village shied away from. But they had to be done. Didn't it occur to them that he might think differently one day? Did these people in their neat little cottages and their manor houses never ask themselves what would happen if he decided he didn't like the work and simply opted out? He had said as much to Miles, who had shouted and made threats, said it would be an absolute catastrophe and would affect the whole village: "It's too late to pull out now, just get that idea out of your head. Understand?" he'd warned.

Miles had suddenly become very edgy when questioned about the terms of the job. So, for fear of provoking a further outburst he had just nodded like a good boy and promised that he would stick with it until the end of his life if that was what people wanted. "Swear it!" Miles had ordered him, and he had obeyed.

Today, after fourteen years of loyal service, he was no longer certain whether he wanted to carry on for another fourteen. Anyway what did a promise like that amount to? There hadn't been any witnesses.

The whole of Southcombe slept the sleep of the just, while for weeks after a job he spent nights tormented by mental images which kept him awake until morning. They should give him a thousand pounds in consideration of that, let alone the fact that the well-being of Southcombe depended on it. In fact, why should he be thinking of a specific sum? They couldn't put a price on his silence, and that meant that whatever he requested was justified, a hundred, a thousand or a million. Why on earth hadn't he thought of that argument before?

In the light of all this his measly six notes were a mockery! He should not – he could not tolerate it any longer. Something had to change, and change radically. He needed a new television. And he would have logs delivered to his house for the winter instead of going up the Quantocks in the autumn and secretly filling his cart with rotten wood that in any case didn't burn well. And – above all – he needed a cleaning lady. She would clear all the rubbish out of the house, then scrub and polish it until this run-down hole was properly habitable again. Then he would be able to apply for the next series of *Come Dine With Me*.

He took the six notes and held them up to the light. They were genuine enough, no question of that, but – he had made his mind up – there were definitely too few of them. If he was ever going to cook pheasant breast with apple in front of a television camera there would have to be at least ten times as many in future.

Feverishly he grabbed his mobile and keyed in Miles' number.

At the other end there was an unusual dialling tone.

"Miles?"

"Yes, what is it? Make it quick, I'm in France now and phone calls cost a bomb."

"Aha, Paris, night clubs, girls, champagne! You're a lucky devil."

"Chance would be a fine thing. No, I'm stuck in some dump in the middle of Picardy. But go on, what do you want?"

"I've got my pay. – You know what I'm talking about."

"Yes, well?"

"I've been thinking about it, Miles, and three hundred just isn't enough. Not for what I'm called on to do."

"Don't talk nonsense. Three hundred's more than enough for a little bit of cutting."

"That's what you say but I don't agree. The cost of living is going up for everybody, remember. I'm no exception."

There was a thoughtful silence then Miles said, mildly for him, "Let me sort it out with the committee. But I'm not going to do it from here."

"When are you coming back?"

"Don't know yet. It all depends. How much do you want then?"

"A lot more."

"Four hundred? Five?"

"Add a nought on and you'll be getting nearer the mark."

"Are you crazy?"

"No. I've thought it all through. Five thousand seems the right amount to me. But I could easily ask for more."

"You really are crazy! The committee won't stand for this, I'm warning you."

"It's not nonsense. And don't shout like that, Miles. Not at me."

"You just wait. I'm telling you, you'd better bloody well watch your …"

But he didn't wait any longer. With the press of a button he silenced the Wolf, the most feared man in the village, and it felt good.

Chapter 16

Zoë stuck to her guns, but she took her time.

A good month had passed since the New Year's Eve party before Jason saw her again. He was working in the greenhouse when she climbed over the garden wall one morning, dressed all in black, like a Ninja temptress. He put the flower-pot he had just filled with soil back on the staging, rubbed his hands clean on his apron and waved her over.

She took her time, giving him the chance to admire her endless legs in skinny jeans and the way her hair glinted like the blue-black of a raven's wing in the low winter sun. "So," she said, when she joined him in the steam heat of the greenhouse, "did you miss me?"

But he wasn't going to let her wrong-foot him into admitting the shameful truth: that for the whole of January he'd been on tenterhooks, wondering whether to make the next move or force himself to wait. Relief filled him as he glanced away from her mischievous gaze and forced himself to concentrate on misting a fine spray over the leaves of the cymbidiums.

"Frances wants to grow orchids in the summer. She's lost interest in cacti. I'm just getting the pots ready for her," he explained, knowing this evasion would annoy Zoë.

"Oh, orchids are just too complicated for me," she said with a wave of her hand, peeling off her leather gloves as she spoke. "They look wonderful in the shop, but you only have to have them at home for a couple of weeks and then the petals drop off and that's it. Never flower again."

Jason laughed: "You need patience if you're going to work with plants. A bit of knowledge and a lot of patience."

"And you're the patient type, aren't you? I've worked that out for myself."

"That's why Rich and Frances gave me the job," he replied blandly, inwardly exulting at the way she had showed her hand.

Zoë looked around in the greenhouse, which was empty except for a few cacti, some moth-eaten palms in pots and the two neat trial rows of orchids, like jewel-coloured butterflies poised for flight at any moment.

She shivered with cold as she looked up at their rich green fronds. She hugged herself and buried her chin in her roll-neck jumper. "Brrr. Can't you see how cold I am? I wouldn't mind drinking something hot … – that is, if you are going to offer me something. It was a real effort to get here. And what a wind today – terrible."

Without waiting for his answer, she stepped out and headed for the chateau. Jason hesitated. Perhaps the hot drink was a pretext, and behind her haste to escape the cold was really the hope of searching the chateau and seeing where he lived, which of the seventeen rooms was his.

On the other hand she looked so harmless, jiggling from one foot to the other as she waved to him from the door while he followed her tracks across the lawn. So harmless and so damned loveable. What should he do? There was nothing for it but to take the key-ring out of his pocket. She had won. This time he couldn't think of any excuse to keep her out of the house.

"Aha, the jailer with his fourteen keys," giggled Zoë as he put the key into the lock. "But do hurry up, I'm really on the point of freezing solid."

It wasn't a great deal warmer inside the chateau. Jason only heated the rooms he was actually living in, his own, the large drawing room and the kitchen. He kept the other rooms bolted shut. Nevertheless an icy draft blew through the high arched corridor that led to the staircase.

"Come into the kitchen. It's warm there."

Zoë went after him, eyes widening as she gazed around at the splendour of the furnishings. "Wow, Jason, I had no idea Rich and Frances were as rich as this. These vases … the tapestries on the walls. And look at the candelabra! It's like a historical film. Louis XIV could have lived here, or Marie Antoinette."

"Now you're exaggerating."

But her astonishment and delight seemed to be genuine. Cautiously she let her fingers pass over a porcelain figure on a commode, touched a silk lamp-shade surmounting an ormolu and marble urn-shaped lamp.

"Amazing," she said, shaking her head. "This place is like a palace."

How often he had dreamed of this moment since Zoë had entered his life. The two of them alone in the chateau. In his imagination he had painted her in the wildest colours, beautiful but a danger to the defences he had built up around himself, his hard-won equilibrium. Now it felt like the most natural thing in the world to be here with her. He couldn't quite leave his old fears behind, felt them flare up as a dull pain in his stomach, but he trusted himself to keep them in check for the duration of Zoë's visit.

He still believed it when Zoë spontaneously put her arms around him from behind and rested her head against his back. She stayed in that position without saying a word while he froze, a tumult of thoughts and images in his head. But no images of Lizzie, no, not of her. Not yet.

"Jason …"

Zoë's hand gently felt under his pullover. She had scarcely stroked his back when she withdrew her hand and continued, "Jason, we don't know anything about each other, do we?"

"No, we don't."

"So how is it that I like you so much?"

He could not open his mouth.

"I mean, who have I fallen in love with if I don't even know who you are?"

He wanted to tell her then, tell her everything, but couldn't bring himself to run the risk.

"Why don't you say anything? It's the same for you, admit it? I'm sure you fancy me, too. In fact, I *know* you do. But you don't show it. That's the difference between us."

He made a sound then, muffled and inarticulate, full of the longing he couldn't express. "What do you think? Say something. And please turn round. I want to see your face."

Her eyes were not in fact blue, as he thought he remembered from the New Year party, but grey like a cloudy sky and surrounded by precisely mascaraed lashes which reminded him of the branches of a tree in winter.

"Jason, I'm doing all the talking and acting like I'm the most confident woman in the world. But I'm not," she protested. "To tell the truth, you're making me nervous. Why is that? I don't understand. There's nothing wrong with you, but whenever I ask you anything personal you seem to slide away out of reach. I want to put my trust in you but I don't even know if that's what you want."

She was asking to be allowed to trust him. Of all things. It was almost too good to be true. He could have laughed or sung for joy. What a release! He felt it in his whole body, this release, it was overwhelming, cleansing, a blessing, a miracle! He could scarcely comprehend it, but that was how it was. Without knowing it, Zoë had found amongst all words the single one that at a stroke freed him from the pressure he had been suffering under for the past five years. The word 'trust' was like a magician's spell. It transformed him and made him human again, it made him the man he had once been before that fateful summer. "Tell me, can I put my trust in you?" repeated Zoë uncertainly.

"Yes," he stammered. "Yes, of course. Together …"

But Zoë did not let him finish his sentence. She stood on tiptoe and cupped his face in her hands. Her skin smelled of soap, and her breath of cherries. He felt her relax in his arms, but the kiss that she gave him then took him by surprise. It wasn't abandoned, or passionate, but rather a shy testing of the trust he had refused to put in her until now. He had not previously known her so serious, so restrained. What she said next was such a shock it almost robbed him of the breath to reply.

"Jason … there's someone standing in front of the main door as if he wants to come in. Are you expecting anyone?"

Jason was instantly back in the clutches of his old fear, washed by Lizzie's blood, Miles' wolf's eyes looking straight through him. Miles, who had hunted him then and had now unearthed him in the remotest corner of France. Had Jason seriously thought he could escape? Had he during all those years been so naïve as to think that the walls of a chateau could protect him? Walls that were no barrier against even a delicate creature like Zoë.

Jason cautiously stretched his neck to see out of the window, but it was too late. There was no one standing in front of the door, just a magpie strutting across the snow. Another one had just landed on the branch of a tree, setting off a small shower of snow. Otherwise, as far as he could see, everything round about was as quiet as usual.

"Strange," whispered Zoë. "Earlier, when I parked my bike, a man walked past and slowed down in front of the gate to look into the park. I think it was the same one."

"A-Are you sure?" stammered Jason.

Zoë nodded. Although he had known at once who the man must be, he only now took it in properly. He gasped for breath, wanting to say something, but how could he explain to Zoë in a few words the hurt he had suffered for five years? Perhaps there weren't even words to express it and the events of that distant day would have to stay locked inside him for ever, never told to anyone, a wound that got neither better nor worse but was simply there and ached and ached.

He could not afford to waste time thinking. Every second that he let pass was a second that Miles could be making use of. He quickly grabbed Zoë by the arm and rushed her out of the kitchen, dragging her because she resisted him with a force he had not expected of her.

"It's OK, Zoë," he said, trying to reassure her as he rushed up the stairs and unlocked his room. "Please, I know what I'm doing. Trust me." As gently as he could, he pulled her inside, turned the key and leaned panting against the door.

"Jason, what's all this nonsense? You're frightening me. Open the door at once!"

"No, I can't just now. Help me move this chest of drawers in front of it."

Jason worked feverishly. He pushed and dragged furniture across the room without paying attention to Zoë, who watched him in fear and surprise.

"Come on, help me!"

"No, I'm not going to move until you open that door."

"Shhh … Don't talk so loud."

"What? You think you can lock me in here and tell me to be quiet? Have you lost your mind? I'll show you …"

Zoë leaped for the window and opened the catch. But before she could make a sound Jason was after her, holding his hand over her mouth, dragging her away. Once again he was astonished by her strength. She struggled and fought like a fury, bit, scratched and waved her arms about wildly. Jason was stronger and at last succeeded in throwing her on to the bed, face down, and holding her there. For a while there was a hostile silence in the air. Zoë stared at the wall without expression, panting. Tears of rage and disappointment ran down her cheeks, which were blackened by mascara. At last she opened her mouth and said, "Let me go or else you'll break my arm."

Jason loosened his grip but did not dare release her.

"What a creep you are. I'd have gone to bed with you without any of this. Without being forced, do you understand? But now …"

Tears filled her eyes and she choked on her words. She tried to turn round, but Jason pressed her deeper into the pillows.

"What you're thinking is quite wrong, Zoë. You must believe that. I'll explain everything later, I promise. But first you must be quiet and co-operate."

"Later? After this mysterious man has dealt with us first?" she said, mocking him.

Jason lowered his head, ashamed of his behaviour towards her but wanting to make her see. "Miles isn't someone to mess with. He's after me. Has been for years."

"What kind of a spy thriller are we in, then? No, really, Jason. You won't convince me with stories like this. Violence is the one thing I hate above all else. God, I've been bloody stupid chasing after you, haven't I? But you didn't look the kind of man who'd need to force a woman."

He didn't release her. Instead he sighed and said, "I suppose I've ruined everything between us, haven't I?"

"Do you really need to ask?"

Zoë was working herself up into another rage. Every time he attempted to calm her down she responded with a wave of curses, not all of which he understood because she produced them in a mixture of English and French. When she could think of nothing further to say she began to flail around in fury and hit herself against the headboard. Jason had had enough. He released her. She slowly got up, rubbing her bruised arms, and went over to the window.

"In case you're interested, there's not a soul to be seen out there. I honestly think you've got a screw loose. Someone called Miles has been after you for years? Surely you could have come up with something better than that."

"Five years ago he slit my girlfriend's throat."

Zoë flinched and Jason saw her inner struggle. She stood motionless, staring out into the distance, and he waited to see how she would react. Once again it was a question of trust. Scarcely had it been built up between them than he had destroyed it. Anything else he said now would only make the breach deeper. Still sitting on the edge of the bed, he waited for her to make up her mind. Their relationship, if that's what it was, lay entirely in her hands. She, too, seemed to know that, for she took her time. An agonizing amount of it. His uncertainty mounted with every second that passed.

When she finally sighed and pressed her forehead against the glass he thought he could breathe again. She wanted to believe him. She trusted him. Why else would she have hesitated so long and stayed in his room?

"Zoë …"

"No, Jason, don't say anything else. Let me go now. I want to go home. Now, please."

Zoë had gone around midday. All he was left with was the faint scent of soap in his pillow and the imprint of her body on his bed. He had lain down on it and hoped she would change her mind, but the door downstairs had banged shut and the crunching of Zoë's shoes in the snow had become gradually fainter until he could hear nothing more. Nothing? Not steps anyway.

Later he could not forgive himself for mistaking the sound he heard next for the cry of a bird. It had been short and piercing, perhaps it had even been two cries, he couldn't remember exactly.

He probably wouldn't have gone out of the house again that day if he hadn't remembered the temperature dial in the greenhouse, which he usually checked before leaving. The silence of the afternoon had calmed him and he had come to the conclusion that Zoë must have imagined the man's interest in the chateau. If someone really had stared through the iron gates it must only have been a curious passer-by. There were people like that all the time, especially now that the borders along the driveway had been planted up.

The sight of his and Zoë's footsteps in the snow gave Jason a deep sense of loss. A few hours earlier they had walked together in the opposite direction, in the unspoken knowledge that they would soon fall into each other's arms. But here he stood in front of the greenhouse, alone again, as he had been for years, abandoned even before the relationship had had a chance to flourish. He checked the heating swiftly and methodically but his mind was elsewhere, circling around the moment in which he had lost Zoë for ever.

She hadn't trusted him. And he had done nothing to deserve her trust. It was as simple as that, and it was unspeakably depressing. With a gesture of irritation Jason flung the last pot into the corner and buried his face in his hands, about to give way to despair. Then he heard it.

Not the pot as it broke, not the soil as it trickled on to the ground, but a soft whimpering that he couldn't place.

He peered through his fingers in all directions but saw only sacks of soil, pots and palms and, through the glass, the deep red sun, just touching the horizon. It seemed to him that the whimpering came from the willows by the pond that Frances was so proud of.

He did not consider the possibility that it was a trap, convinced by now that he knew who was making those stifled cries for help.

"Zoë, where are you? Wait … I'm coming. Zoë!"

Jason was out of the door and running across the grass. At his back the sun had already half disappeared behind the hills. How fast it was sinking! The shadows of the trees were reaching out to swallow him up. When he arrived at the pond one last ice-covered patch of reeds glowed in the dying rays. Then, from one moment to the next, darkness engulfed him and he was experiencing for a second time what had all but cost him his sanity five years earlier. And yet it was different this time. The whimpering told him Zoë was still alive.

On the last occasion no sound had come from Lizzie's mouth, no breath, and there was already a veil across her eyes when he reached her. It had been a muggy evening, the air had smelled of warm grass and of the horses grazing nearby.

But Zoë was lying on snow. Her legs were bent at a strange angle and her arms pressed protectively to her chest. Her blood, too, had flowed. When Jason crouched down and bent over her he could only smell it at first, but then in the half-light he saw the red stains against the white. His stomach turned. He had to look away, look up to the sky – there was no blood there, only the lights of an aeroplane flashing, and the first evening star. But this girl could be helped, he swiftly realized. It gave him the strength to stay at Zoë's side and relive his nightmares. Carefully he reached one arm under her head and with the other gripped her under her legs. The black cap she had been lying on was stuck to her cheek by congealed blood. Zoë let out a muffled cry of pain as he rose to his feet and began to walk.

"Shhh. Be calm. It's me, Jason. I'm looking after you," he told her.

He walked slowly in order to spare her. In the meantime it had become so dark that he could no longer see the surface of the path and repeatedly sank knee-deep into the snow. Every time he did so she moaned, but when he asked her where it hurt there was no answer. As he walked on all he could feel were the clumps of ice in her hair melting under the warmth of his hand, and he imagined her gradually thawing out in his arms until they both, as in a fairy tale, awoke from a bad dream.

He carried her into his room and laid her on the bed. She still didn't speak, not even when her eyes were open and she could move her fingers. After he had bolted the door and pushed the chest of drawers back in front of it he sat on the edge of the mattress beside her, uncertain what he should do next. Tentatively he began to take off her shoes and socks. When he held her wet feet in his hands he realized that she urgently needed dry clothes.

"Zoë, I must … get your clothes off. Otherwise you'll catch pneumonia. You can have my pyjamas for the moment so that you're warm."

She gave a weak nod. She did not resist, but nor was she in any state to help him. Like a broken doll, she allowed him to remove her clothes one by one and finally to rub her bruised and trembling body with a bath towel before he put her in flannel pyjamas that were much too big for her. She had not weighed much on the way into the chateau, but when he saw her lying naked in front of him he was surprised to see how muscular her thighs and shoulders were. She must have been sun-bathing topless in the summer. Only her pubic hair, which she had shaved into a vertical stripe, was paler than the rest of her body, and also her breasts, which in his day-dreams he had always imagined to be smaller.

"The police," breathed Zoë when she came to herself again under the warming blanket. "Call them."

"Mmm."

Zoë groaned. She used gestures to show where it hurt. He had seen the scratches and bruises on her body and wondered if she had broken any ribs and whether he should call a doctor. But what could he tell him? And even more difficult, what could he tell the police?

Zoë reached out one arm from under the blanket and sought his hand.

"Jason, I'm sorry. You were right and I didn't believe you."

"Lie still, it's all right."

"That man – he could have killed me."

"But he didn't. That's the main thing. And I'm here now."

He bent over her and kissed her forehead. She still smelled of blood although he had used a damp cloth to wipe the graze at her hairline.

"You should have seen how I fought! The bastard didn't get away unscathed." She smiled crookedly so as not to pull the tear in one of her lips.

Jason forced a smile too though it was anything but funny. Miles wasn't someone you fought. If he wanted to kill you he'd whip out his flick knife, and then there'd be no way out. It was lucky for Zoë that he hadn't used it this time.

"He was waiting for me behind a tree. I was grabbed from behind and …"

"Take it easy, Zoë. We can talk about it later. You're still suffering from shock, you need to recover first."

"No, let me finish! And then you must phone for the police. Someone like that can't be left free."

"He won't do anyone else any harm. Only me."

"Yes, he asked about you. Oh, Jason, it was … terrible. At first I thought it wasn't real. Only when he started to hit me did I realize how serious it was. He wanted to know who lived in the chateau, but then he mentioned your name and asked what your daily routine was, when you go out and so on."

"And?"

"I don't know why, but suddenly I knew that I had to lie to him. I acted dumb and told him that I wanted to visit the cook in the chateau. But that just worked him up even more. He snarled at me like an animal, saying I shouldn't talk such nonsense. He said he couldn't give a damn about the cook, he wanted information about Jason Collings and no one else. That's you, isn't it?"

"Yes, but …"

"I said, 'Jason Collings? Never heard of him. In the winter there's just a cook in the chateau.' And because he was staring at me doubtfully I told him that I thought someone had got the job of butler but last spring he had made off with a valuable painting, no one knew where."

Despite her pain, Zoë was pleased enough with herself to manage a smile.

"He completely swallowed it. I actually saw his jaw drop. But then … then he suddenly began hitting me again like a lunatic. He beat the living daylights out of me. At some stage I must have lost consciousness. I've got a vague memory that he dragged me by the legs through the snow and then everything went black. I don't know what happened then until you arrived."

Zoë hesitated for a moment and looked questioningly into Jason's face.

"What I'm telling you doesn't even seem to upset you. Why?"

"Of course it does! Of course it upsets me to see you like this. But I'm not surprised. I know Miles. He's an animal. In my village people used to call him 'the Wolf'. The slightest provocation and he'd go for you."

204

"So that was Miles, was it? And what does he do when he's not coming after people like a wild beast?"

"He helps in his brother's flower shop. Cuts roses and tulips, arranges the shop window, that kind of thing, but he's rarely seen in the village. Most of the time he's out and about, drives to flower markets and spends the day doing odd jobs here and there."

"Not exactly the usual job for a thug. And that's the bloke who killed your girlfriend? God, I can't believe I'm actually saying this."

"Yes, it was him."

"But if he's a murderer, why isn't he behind bars?"

"It's complicated."

"And because it's complicated you don't want to call the police. Is that right?"

Jason looked past her out of the darkened window and then down at the floor where Zoë's clothes lay in a heap, everything black except for a scrap of turquoise lace that was peeping out from under the pullover.

"Go on. That's right, isn't it? You've no intention of calling them, have you? Not even for my sake."

She became agitated as she spoke and tried to sit up in the bed, but didn't have the strength for it. Sighing, she fell back on the pillows and shut her eyes.

"Zoë, I would have to tell you a long, long story for you to understand why I can't do anything to stop Miles. But it's such a monstrous story I'm afraid that you would never believe me."

"All right, then, don't tell me. Well done. Your girl-friend is dead, I very nearly kicked the bucket too, but your plan is to do nothing. To tell the truth, Jason, that's more difficult to understand than the most mind-bending story you could possibly tell me."

He tried to defend himself. "It's not mind-bending! It's just that … I've sworn an oath of silence. I mean they made me …"

"Who are 'they'? And anyway, what is this? Some sick sort of love-triangle?"

"No, nothing like that. I don't think Miles even knew Lizzie personally."

Zoë frowned, thought for a moment and then dug deeper.

"So you were enemies and he wanted to get at you through her?"

"It's not that either. You could spend the whole night guessing and you would never hit on it. Let's leave it for the moment, OK?"

"But do you promise to explain everything to me soon?"

"I promise, Zoë. And then I hope you'll understand why I acted as I did this afternoon."

"All right then, but I've got your promise to explain as soon as you can, haven't I?"

Jason lifted her hand to his lips and kissed it solemnly.

"Yes, you have my promise. Thank you for being so understanding. Stay lying down for a bit while I pack a bag."

"Are you going away?"

"We've both got to get away. As soon as Miles finds out that you've been lying to him he'll be back. That could be tonight."

"Where are you going?"

"No idea. It doesn't matter as long as it's away from here."

"We could go to my place. Dad's in England and he's in no hurry to get back. I think he's met someone there. I hope for his sake that it's the right one this time. I've got the place to myself for the time being."

"I'll have to let Rich and Frances know. They wouldn't like me to leave without telling them."

"God, you're conscientious! That should be the least of your worries at the moment."

The warmth of the room had brought colour to her cheeks. But when she threw the blanket aside and tried to swing her feet on to the floor a sharp stabbing pain in her side took away her breath.

" I can't stand up. Everything is going round and round in my ..."

He had stuffed a pair of jeans, a shirt and pullover into his bag and was on his way to the bathroom. He was just in time to turn back and catch Zoë before she fell forward. He gently put her back on the bed and waited until she came round. If he had been alone, his old fears would long ago have driven him out of the chateau. Defenceless as she was, lying there, Zoë gave him the confidence and courage to put his bag down and wait patiently beside her, the whole night if need be, irrespective of the danger of Miles returning.

That night Jason didn't close his eyes. He spent it sitting in the wicker chair next to the chest of drawers, a blanket over his knees, listening to Zoë's gentle, piping breath and the scrabbling of the tree branches in the wind. There was one occasion when he jumped; sometime after midnight a deer stalked through the snow beneath his window, but apart from that the hours until daylight passed in silent monotony.

It was the second time that he had spent a night near Zoë without being able to touch her. This time at least he could see her as she slept, but the disarming trust in him that she had shown as she snuggled down into the pillows made her as unreachable as she had been after the New Year's party. There was no doubt in Jason's mind that Zoë had saved his life. She had shown courage and had done something that he wouldn't have trusted anyone, least of all himself, to do: she had defied Miles. In the last resort it was unimportant whether Zoë had done so out of love or out of ignorance of the dangers involved. What counted was her fearlessness, which had diverted the danger away from him and restored the relationship between the two of them. He felt that he was in debt to her, and there was nothing unpleasant about this feeling.

As he watched Zoë slowly wake up – frowning because of the pain and at the same time smiling because she vaguely remembered that he was in the room, too – he wondered how long he could keep the story of Lizzie from her. Zoë was waiting for an explanation, even if she had promised not to ask him any more questions. But that meant the ball was now in his court. Sooner or later he would have to come clean. But where should he start? And, in particular, how?

He didn't want to paint Lizzie in darker colours than was necessary. She had been difficult, he wanted to admit that, difficult and with a tendency to wild outbursts of rage. One wrong word, one strange look, would be enough to make her rant and rave. She couldn't tolerate anything that ran contrary to her plans. But he had soon discovered the other side of Lizzie: her gentleness, her enthusiasm for anything beautiful, and especially her hunger for life. This hunger had been so intense and so infectious that when she was beside him she seemed to lend him some special energy that allowed him to live more fully, more wholeheartedly. She had had an incredible zest that awoke an equal hunger for life in him, and for months on end he had felt himself glowing, actually glowing, with joy and astonishment that he had met someone like her in Southcombe.

But that wasn't what Zoë wanted to hear. And in the last resort it didn't belong to the story that he had to tell her. But that evening in March did, that cold, damp evening when Lizzie had staggered out of the Kings Arms and, after taking a few steps, collapsed beside him on the pavement. That had been the first crack, the first sign of the weakness she had had implanted in her. She had been drinking cider, three pints, four maybe. Too much for a teenager, as she admitted the next day, but she showed no regret or embarrassment and was almost proud when she said, "It's true, I drank too much and that's why I feel like puking now. All the same, I've decided to go on drinking … shhh, let me go on, right? I've decided to go on getting drunk, and I'll go on until I'm ready to face up to things without needing alcohol to help me. And there's one more thing you need to know: I've stopped taking Mr Lee's magic pills. There's something wrong with them. They take all my fight away. And I want to fight, do you understand? I don't want to be a daughter of your St Aldusa. If you think you can argue me round you've got another think coming. So forget about it. I'd rather die straight away."

He could tell Zoë that these words of Lizzie's had shattered his happiness. It wouldn't even be an untruth, but it wouldn't be the whole truth, either. The whole truth was that from the middle of February onwards Lizzie had begged him for help and he had insisted on waiting in order to keep his conscience clear.

"Conscience?" Lizzie had screamed at him. "Conscience! But we're not talking about an abortion or something like that. It's me. We're talking about me, don't you get it? And I can tell you, I'm not going through with this under any circumstances and I'm not going to let my will be broken. Not by anyone, is that clear? Not even by my mother. I refuse! I shall go on strike. When it gets to that point, I'll … I'll … I'll rebel and I'll talk. Yes, I swear I'll talk, and no one will be able to stop me. – Oh, Jason, if only you weren't so stubborn, so blind, it wouldn't have to get to that point. I need your help. I can't do this on my own. What do I need to do to get you on my side?"

By April he had finally reached the point where he was ready to agree, but by then it was too late and Lizzie's zest for life was already weakened, muted.

On the day when he noticed it for the first time they had driven up on to the Quantocks and walked from the car park near Crowcombe Park Gate to Will's Neck. There was no one else to be seen from the viewpoint, only hilly heathland around them, and in the distance the line of the Welsh coast with the two islands in front of it, Steep Holm and Flat Holm, which stood out from the reflecting surface of the sea like the back of an underwater monster. The sun shone through the drizzle, and he had shown her a pale rainbow.

Earlier in their relationship this view would have roused Lizzie to ecstasy. Often she had stood on tiptoe beside the trig point, spread out her arms and, with her eyes closed, abandoned herself to the wind, imagining she was a bird flying across to Swansea where her grandmother lived. And with her coat flapping in the wind she had even looked a bit like a bird. A sea-gull or, because of her blonde hair, a golden pheasant. But on this occasion she hadn't even changed her expression. She just stared silently across to Wales, and on the journey back to Southcombe had sat brooding wordlessly in the car.

That was the day he had promised to help her.

"Jason?"

Zoë was trying to sit up in bed.

"Yes?"

"Did you spend the whole night on that chair for my sake? You didn't need to do that. I'm sure there would have been room for both of us in the bed."

By the light of the morning it became clear how much violence Zoë had had to suffer for his sake. Her whole face was bruised and puffy, her left eye almost entirely hidden by the violet-green swelling of the lid, and quantities of blood had come out of her nose during the night and drawn a dark line across her cheek. And there was blood on the pillow.

Chapter 17

The last half-hour documentary that Craig Brett and Ahmed Haider had made together was broadcast in the middle of February during Channel 4 News. Vera made sure she watched it, especially since the *Radio Times* noted that the film would be followed by a brief tribute to the recently deceased journalist.

The film was an enquiry into the effects of cost-cutting in the NHS instituted by the Conservative-Liberal coalition government. Craig Brett's perspective was that the consequences would be devastating across the country. Vera immediately recognized his sharp, clear voice, but as the camera turned to him during his interview with the Health Minister she didn't find it easy to match the person she saw with that voice. There was something gnome-like about Craig Brett, and not just because of his beard, which, grey and wiry, covered a good part of his cheeks. It was also the stocky little body stuck in a suit of indefinable cut that made her think of gnomes. But how clever and quick he was. At the slightest hesitation by his interviewee he would probe further, dig deeper and find ways to drive him into a corner. In Vera's opinion this journalistic skill was reason enough to make the film worth seeing.

But the tribute to his life and work was the most enlightening part of the coverage. Jon Snow, star announcer of Channel 4 News, had put it together, a brilliant kaleidoscope of biographical and professional sketches which in the end portrayed a journalist for whom a private life had never been a priority – if he had had one at all. Writing documentaries attacking social abuses and uncovering dodgy deals: that had been Craig Brett's life.

"He was a quiet, retiring man who preferred to spend his time in the archives," said the voiceover. And in order to support his statement, Snow then spoke to a woman from the Somerset Archive and Record Office, which Brett had visited shortly before his death.

"Yes, Mr Brett spent whole afternoons in our archive over several months last autumn. Usually he made notes from documentary sources, but sometimes he played recordings of conversations with local people that we keep in our oral history department. I gather he wanted to make a film about the wassailing customs of Somerset. One area in particular seemed to fascinate him, the countryside around Taunton."

Vera made a note of the name of the woman and of the archive she worked in and put the slip of paper on the computer keyboard before going to bed.

Since witnessing the wassailing ritual nearly two weeks earlier, she had been struggling against the temptation to contact Ahmed Haider in London. She was preoccupied by the fact that he'd been undercover at the ceremony, trying to photograph it. He must have seen something in it that had escaped her notice, something Craig Brett also had seen and which was important enough to justify his coming all the way from London. Something, she suspected, that Ahmed Haider wanted to keep to himself.

Thanks to Snow's tribute film, which to Vera's surprise only mentioned Haider in passing as an occasional collaborator of Brett's, Vera now saw an opportunity to bypass him.

On the phone the archivist Brett had visited turned out to be friendly and co-operative. But she was unwilling to give out information about which material in particular he had been concentrating on. Instead she invited Vera to come and see her. The documents, books and tapes Mr Brett had borrowed weren't a state secret, she said, but there were legal reasons why she was unable to give exact details unless Vera was from the police or could show a press pass.

"No, neither of those applies to me. It's just a private interest."

"Oh, right, I understand."

Whatever it was that Mrs Fox thought she understood, Vera preferred to leave her uncorrected and try her luck in person.

On the morning of 18 February therefore she got into her car and drove to Taunton. She went straight to the Somerset Archive and Records Office located in two modern buildings a short distance outside the main town centre.

Vera had not been in an archive since her student days. Earlier there had been alphabetically organised card catalogues, and she had known her way around those, but nowadays searches were done digitally and this made her unsure of herself, especially being in England.

Mrs Fox was waiting for her in her office and welcomed Vera with a well-intentioned comment about Swiss punctuality.

"As far as I know, you are the first Swiss person to have visited our new archive. You are very welcome."

She was a slim red-head with freckles on her face and a narrow mouth bracketed by smile lines.

"The police have already been here and made a copy of the list of documents Mr Brett was studying. As I told you on the phone, I'm afraid I can't give you that list. On the other hand, I can show you several documents concerning Somerset customs if you would like to read them. I just need some identification from you first."

Vera didn't usually take her passport when she left the house, but since she had withdrawn money from the cash machine in Southcombe the day before, she was still carrying her purse with her, which had various cards in it.

"Here's proof of my identity."

Mrs Fox looked at the credit card and made an exaggerated gesture of regret.

"I'm sorry but this card isn't enough by itself. The archive needs an official document with your address on it. An NHS card or gas bill, for example."

"But I haven't got anything like that. I'm only renting here temporarily, my landlady pays my bills and I go to the doctor in Switzerland."

"I'm sorry, we're not going to be able to help you without proper documentation."

"What about my Swiss bank statements? They're sent to me at my address in Southcombe. Would you accept these?"

"No, foreign documents don't count. Just imagine if a Chinese person came along and presented his bank statements from China. No one here understands Chinese."

"But maybe someone understands German?"

"No, Mrs Wyler, I'm very sorry, it's a question of regulations."

Vera's disappointment must have been plain to see on her face. As she left, Mrs Fox spontaneously came out from behind her desk and whispered in a conspiratorial tone of voice: "Just between you and me, in the last days before his death Mr Brett was particularly preoccupied with a clinic for mentally disabled children and also with the wassailing ceremony in Southcombe. I don't know if there's any connection. By the way, Southcombe is quite near here."

"Yes, I know. That's where I've been living for the past few weeks."

"Oh, right. Then of course I understand your interest. Mind you, Mr Brett thought that Southcombe's wassailing ceremony deviated significantly from the pattern of local traditions. Southcombe is known round here for being a bit odd, you know. The back of beyond – and then some."

"Did Mr Brett say what made wassailing there different?"

Mrs Fox shook her head.

"No, and I didn't ask him. If I questioned everyone who visits our archive, where would that get me?"

Mrs Fox was similarly evasive about answering further questions, and her glances at the clock were clear hints that she should be getting back to her work.

Dissatisfied, Vera opened up her umbrella and for a while wandered aimlessly through the streets of Taunton, accompanied by the drumming of the rain. In the end she went into one of the numerous charity shops and bought a well-worn copy of Coleridge's poems for fifty pence – seeing that since their conversation at New Year Nadja still hadn't remembered to lend her the volume – and sat down with it in the first café she came across. For the most trivial of reasons she had been refused access to the archival material, but Vera wasn't someone to give up so easily. There must be other ways to follow Brett's trail.

The rain was falling in slanting rods, heavily and without pause. Puddles were forming in the pot-holes, people were finding shelter under overhanging roofs and ran with their heads down through the motionless traffic into the nearest shop. The café soon filled. Vera had to press herself against the window in order to make room for a group of men who, after placing their orders, unfolded the plans of a new estate and began to discuss them heatedly.

Sitting in front of her vegetable quiche, which she left untouched for a while, Vera did her best to forget the noise around her and organise her thoughts. Once again she recalled all the strange little things of the past months which had given her this foreboding of a danger that she could not quite identify. She certainly couldn't go to the police with two deaths which were evidently not even considered suspicious, or a threatening letter that she was the first to dismiss as ridiculous. They would just laugh at her and send her home. Or ask her what she was afraid of and whether she didn't have anything more concrete to show than a confused theory about a St Aldusa that nobody had ever heard of. Would Greg be an exception? How could she know? – He had never contacted her, which didn't seem exactly an argument in his favour.

No, she had absolutely nothing that could arouse the interest of the police in Southcombe, not the slightest hint of proof that anything fishy was going on in the village. And yet she knew she was right. She was certainly not going to just sit there until something happened that confirmed her suspicions. If the archive shut its door in her face, then she would find other doors. There were archives on-line, too.

Thanks to her new-found determination she felt buoyed up on her way back to Southcombe, but this came to an abrupt end as she entered the drive leading to Station House. At first she saw the starlings rise screeching from the chimney as if the car had frightened them on its approach. But it wasn't the car that had made the birds fly away, it was Mrs Moore's two terriers which ran up to Vera, barking, and jumped up so boisterously as she tried to get out of the car that she would have preferred to get back in and drive away again. Mrs Moore here? Why? She was the last person Vera wanted to meet just now. But her landlady wasn't alone. Nadja's yellow anorak was hanging on the garden gate and Nadja herself was standing in her Wellingtons and thick pullover next to the flowerbeds.

"Mum! Where have you been? We wanted to pay you a visit."

As she spoke, Mrs Moore came out of the shed and walked across the lawn to greet Vera. "Good afternoon, Mrs Wyler. Yes, it's true, we wanted to give you a surprise. I hope you don't mind that we've made ourselves at home even though you weren't here? I suggested to Nadja that we might come and see how the garden's getting on. Not that I want to intrude on your plans for it. Good heavens, no. But when tenants come and go the garden tends to get a bit wild. This one's really suffered. The last tenant paid absolutely no attention to it, and I'm afraid the results are all too easy to see the following year."

"Yes, Mum. Look over there at the bed I've raked for you. Now you can have whatever vegetables you like there. And I've brought you a rose. 'Princess Diana', a wonderful variety. If you look after it you'll have a mass of snow-white flowers in the summer. It was the nicest rose in Mr Lee's shop."

The bush stood next to the garden gate in a pot. Nadja had already dug a hole near the back door and was now getting ready to put the rose in it.

"Can you give me a hand, please? Hold the rose upright while I cover the roots with soil."

"It's not much fun gardening in the rain, and it's not good for the garden either. You could have waited a day or two, couldn't you?"

"Rain? No, it hasn't rained here at all."

Mrs Moore stood to one side of the lawn, the two terriers panting at her feet, while Vera and Nadja planted the rose. It struck Vera how rough Nadja's hands had become since living in the country. There had been a time when she had thought it important to file her nails and varnish them, but there was no sign of that now. Her hands had calluses and scratches, and there was a black rim of soil under the nails. But the movements of her fingers as Nadja finally smoothed the soil over the roots were gentle and careful. It struck Vera exactly as it had done a few weeks earlier during the wassailing ceremony. There too she had noticed how Nadja handled the soil. Respectfully, she thought now, as if her daughter felt there was something sacred about the earth.

"Mrs Wyler," said Mrs Moore, interrupting her thoughts, "I suggest cutting the wisteria back a bit. The last time I was here I noticed that it's growing dangerously near the gutter. You shouldn't underestimate the strength of a wisteria. In spring it could pull down the gutter, and the drainpipe with it."

"As you wish. It's your garden after all. I'm sure you know what's best."

Even though she was dressed for the country, Mrs Moore conveyed a certain elegance. Her Wellingtons, which were decorated with a flower motif, were Laura Ashley perhaps, and her coat a classic Burberry with matching scarf. Maybe her own garden provided the perfect setting for this style, but here, in the somewhat rundown surroundings of Station House, there was a suggestion of arrogance about her well-groomed appearance. Vera particularly felt the contrast with Nadja, who had arrived in her well-worn old clothes.

"Good. So if you're agreeable, I'll ask Mr Lee to drop in. He's got the proper lopping shears, and he'll bring his ladder. Can I tell him to get in touch with you to agree a time? And he can help you with planting too, if you want."

"Let's see. I haven't given any thought to the garden yet. In any case there are plenty of crocuses and hyacinths popping up. I'm quite happy with them, actually."

Mrs Moore nodded indulgently and began to take her dogs out of the garden.

"Can you stay for a moment?" Vera asked her daughter.

She didn't seem to hear but stood bent over the edge of a flowerbed scraping patches of moss from the earth with a hoe.

"Your iris roots need to be uncovered. There's so much moss here it'll smother them. They have to be able to breathe, otherwise you'll have only leaves and no flowers in the summer."

"Oh, don't worry about the irises, I'll see to them later. Look, can you stay? Mrs Moore seems ready to go."

"Sorry, not today. I've got a class very soon."

"Class? Another of your rose courses?"

"More or less. I know you find it ridiculous, but I enjoy it. I get a lot of useful tips there. Don't be angry. If you like, I'll drop in afterwards. OK?"

Mrs Moore waited by the gate until Nadja had said goodbye to Vera. She watched her dogs with apparent indifference as they chased a rabbit, which desperately zigzagged across the rails and finally found refuge behind the signal box.

"See you then, Mum. I'll be back about three."

When Vera opened the door of Station House she realized immediately that someone had entered in her absence. They hadn't made any effort to hide their traces, in fact they had intentionally left some. Vera found her post, not as usual stuffed in the letter-box or scattered on the floor but neatly piled up on the chest of drawers in the hall. And in the kitchen she found the window shut after leaving it open a crack on purpose because of the smell of fried bacon.

In Switzerland Vera would at once have picked up the telephone and indignantly accused her landlord of failing to respect her privacy. But in the case of Mrs Moore she was uncertain. Perhaps the owner of a UK holiday home had the right to do this, or perhaps Nadja

223

had given her permission. In any case, as Vera established after going round the house, Mrs Moore had been in every room. Vera didn't find concrete evidence, but everywhere there was the elusive hint of someone else's perfume.

Vera found the clearest signs in her study. Her pictures had been examined and her sketchbook leafed through. The letters and notes on her desk were lying not quite where she had left them.

What had made Mrs Moore go through the house? Could she have been searching for the same thing as Craig Brett?

Nadja was only partly able to calm her mother when, as promised, she dropped in for a chat after her course.

"Yes, Mrs Moore asked me if it was all right for her to go into the house. She wanted to read the gas meter. Why should I say no to her? It's her house. As far as I know you haven't got any secrets you want to hide, have you?"

"Did you come in together, or did you let her come in alone?"

"I came in with her, but just briefly. I wanted to rake the flowerbed for you."

"And she stayed in the house for how long?"

"I don't know exactly. Why are you asking all these questions? Has she broken or stolen something?" asked Nadja in a tone of irritation.

"No, that's not it. It just seems strange to me that she should go through all the rooms and look at my things."

"But I showed her your pictures. I'm really proud of your painting. The still life with oranges is fantastic. And Eileen – Mrs Moore – was crazy about the small landscape with hills in the background. She told me that she used to paint when she was younger – watercolours, though. The memory made her go all nostalgic. You could paint a nice Somerset picture for Tom and me. I'd hang it in the sitting-room above the sofa."

"Did you know that Mrs Moore had a daughter?"

"Lizzie, yes. But she's dead. Almost exactly a year before I came to Southcombe, I believe."

Nadja pulled a sad expression and went on, "It must be terrible to lose your own child, mustn't it?"

"Yes, so terrible that as a mother you can't bear to imagine it. How did Lizzie die?"

"No idea. Somehow it's never the right moment to ask Eileen. You can understand that she doesn't like talking about it. And that may be connected to her former job too. As a nurse she probably had to develop a pretty thick skin. After all, she was working with disabled children in Greenhill Park and must have seen a lot of misery there."

"And Lizzie's father? I thought Mrs Moore was a widow."

"Yes, she is. Her husband died soon after Lizzie – of grief, or so she told me."

"Have you ever been to the graveyard? It's strange that father and daughter aren't buried together. I've seen Lizzie's grave, but it's all alone."

"I've no idea. I never go to the graveyard. But how come you are so interested in the Moores?"

"Well, they did live in this house as a family. I sometimes wonder how it was furnished and who had which room. Perhaps the one I work in was Lizzie's and I sleep in her brother's."

"Stanley? He hasn't lived in Southcombe for ages. I'm not so keen on him, actually. When he comes to visit he hangs around with strange types. It's not easy to believe that he's Eileen's son."

"You obviously feel close to her."

"She's very nice to me. Do you mind?"

"No. Of course I'm pleased that you're made so welcome in the village."

"Oh, Mum, just listen to your tone of voice. You're not jealous, are you? Please don't be. We have our differences of opinion, but they don't mean a thing. You are and always will be …"

"Yes, I know. I am and always will be the best mum in the world."

How many times Nadja had used that phrase before, not always with the degree of conviction that Vera would have liked to hear. Now too it sounded clichéed, like a hurried reassurance intended to distract her. This time, however, it had the opposite effect.

As soon as Nadja had gone, Vera sat down at her computer and began her search. Whichever way she turned, it always came back to Lizzie. She had spent her short life in Station House. Her grave, like those of Sue Harper and a small number of other women, had on it the mysterious Aldusa motif that Craig Brett had explored in his article. And last but not least, it was from Lizzie's house that the journalist had wanted to reclaim something important.

There were thousands of Lizzie Moores on the internet, however, ranging from Australian teenagers to an English professor of archaeology at SOAS in London, and Facebook too provided a discouragingly long list of Lizzie or Elizabeth Moores. Since the Lizzie Moore in question had died five years ago, Facebook wasn't likely to be helpful. In fact the search had to be the other way round: it had to begin with the dead, not the living, Lizzie.

Not many local newspapers offered an on-line archive. The *Somerset County Gazette* had set one up in 1995, the *West Somerset Free Press* three years later. Vera entered the year 2005 in the *Free Press*, and, one click later, the month. Lizzie had died on 26 July, so Vera left earlier news to one side and began with the first on-line date after that, 29 July. There was column after column containing news of the events of the previous week, listed in no particular order: a burglary in Bagborough, a crash in Cotford St Luke, cricket in Taunton and Wellington, and the news that Princess Zara Phillips, who had taken part

227

in the horse-racing at Stockland Lovell, had failed to win a prize.

Vera smiled: these English and their royals! That was a subject in its own right, and one that she, coming from Switzerland, would never fully understand. She clicked on the article and scanned the lines describing the race. The reporter had had the delicate task of writing something complimentary about Princess Zara despite the fact of her losing.

She then let her eyes run across the page, restricting her attention to possible key-words – of which there were scarcely any. Instead there was news about things like the renovation of the Watchet library or road-works, which she could pass over. Only the report of a farewell party for Sue Nash made Vera's heart beat faster for a moment. But Sue Nash had nothing to do with Sue Harper. This Sue had been headmistress of a local school for forty years and was being congratulated on her retirement by colleagues and pupils.

My God, the things that people here think worth reporting, thought Vera, bored. Although the endless columns of miscellaneous news items gradually began to undermine her concentration, she forced herself to keep going until the end. Up to now she had not been quite clear what it was she was looking for, whether it was the story of Lizzie's fateful battle against a malicious disease or the report of a car accident. But then a headline on the last page but one of the web-site jumped out at her. It contained the phrase 'Greenhill Park' and jerked Vera out of her lethargy. There it stood, in between the announcement of a garden show and the opening of a health food shop in Minehead: 'Gruesome Murder in Greenhill Park'. So it was murder! Not illness, not an accident, but murder.

There were two pictures alongside the article. The first showed the main building of Greenhill Park with a police barrier in front of it, and the second a young blonde girl with a piercing in her left eyebrow. So it was her. This was the same photo as the one on Mrs Moore's chest of drawers and bore the caption 'The victim, Eliza-beth Moore (17) from Southcombe'.

Lizzie, Vera found out, had been a pupil at King's College, Taunton, and on 26 July had travelled back to Southcombe as usual after the last class of the day. When questioned, her school-mates Carol Lamb and Wynn Davies said that Lizzie hadn't taken her usual route from the bus stop by the railway bridge, which involved cross-ing the lines to get to Station House where she lived, but had set off in the opposite direction towards the village. Neither of the girls knew the reason why. An assistant at the Co-op, Sarah Griffith, and the hairdresser whose business was opposite Helen Dean's café, had seen Lizzie wandering up and down the High Street at twenty to five. She'd looked indecisive, the hairdresser thought. Mrs Griffith, on the other hand, described the girl as 'ex-tremely edgy and agitated' and added that there was no-thing unusual about this for her. It was the last time she had been seen alive. She was later found in the second from last of the barracks at Greenhill Park by a pair of lovers who didn't want to be named in the newspaper.

Her throat had been cut and she was lying on a scruffy sofa in a corner of the room, wearing school uniform, the upper part of her body hanging down. The local CID, it was said, were working flat out.

At the same time readers were reminded that Greenhill Park estate above Southcombe, which had been owned by the aristocratic Amory family since 1714, had been purchased by West Somerset District Council in 1929 and turned into a clinic for children with Downs Syndrome and other relatively mild forms of mental disability. With the exception of the years 1941-45, the building and various annexes had served this purpose until the clinic was closed in 1991. Since then the Neoclassical property had been up for sale again, but repeated acts of vandalism by unknown perpetrators had pushed up the costs of renovation year by year and frightened off potential purchasers. For this reason there had recently been discussions about demolishing it in order to use the land for social housing.

The scanty facts of the case were followed by statements from friends and acquaintances of the victim. Lizzie did not seem to have been especially popular. Her teachers characterized her as clever, but most of her fellow pupils had to make an effort to find something positive to say. Her parents and elder brother had declined to be interviewed. They were apparently still suffering from shock.

Vera had to pause for a moment in order to digest the significance of this information.

In the following week's edition, it was reported that the post mortem had revealed no signs of sexual violence.

Lizzie seemed to have been murdered not because she was a pretty young thing who had caught the eye of a sexual predator but – according to the officer in charge of the investigation, Detective Chief Inspector Moffatt – for personal reasons. That is, because she knew something compromising or had somehow stood in the way of the perpetrator. In conclusion Moffat appealed to the inhabitants of Southcombe to think carefully about the afternoon and evening of 26 July and to inform the police of anything unusual they might have witnessed, however insignificant it seemed.

In the following days hundreds of sightings were reported. Lizzie was supposed to have been seen in the evening not only on the High Street but also in Ashmead and outside Southcombe on the unlit road to the next village. One person swore to having seen her get into a light-coloured BMW, another to having seen her in Bristol on the arm of an Asian. Every sighting was checked, but the perpetrator, who had done his work with the utmost precision and had shown an almost professional attention to detail in hiding all traces of himself, was for the time being on the loose. No, not just for the time being, Vera discovered, but up to the present day.

She consulted every edition of the *West Somerset Free Press* from July to December 2005 and after that every July on the anniversary of the event. After a few weeks there were only occasional references to 'the Elizabeth

Moore case'. The articles became shorter and by Christmas consisted of a mere three or four lines, which repeated the few known facts.

Five years ago Southcombe had been shaken by the murder of a young girl. That was not so long ago, reflected Vera. And yet village life had gone on just the same, as calm and orderly as if the atrocity had taken place on another planet. The parish web-site provided Vera with a complete list of local activities. The Christmas Bazaar with the big tombola had taken place in 2005, and on 5 January of the following year the wassailing ritual. In February Tom's parents had announced the coming garden season with offers of discounts on equipment, as they did every year, and in the village hall not a single course was cancelled. What Vera found particularly shocking was that the 'Family Fun Day' had gone ahead as usual: children's games, stalls with snacks and a big flower display organized by Mr Lee had managed to attract the whole village a mere two weeks after Lizzie's death. Did these people not know what mourning was? Did they have no respect for the dead?

And no one seemed to be troubled by the thought that Lizzie's murderer could be one of them, living unrecognized in Southcombe. Not Mrs Moore, who stood out as the driving force of the village's cultural life, and not Tom's parents, who took every opportunity to profile their mowing machines at any festival or special occasion. Even Mr Lee with his love of flowers and Greg, who as police constable should have viewed the case as a personal challenge, behaved no differently.

Chapter 18

"This gate, the one we're heading for," explained Zoë, "is the one that Joan of Arc was taken through as a prisoner of the English. I wanted to show it you today. If it doesn't put you on edge too much we can go down to the bay through the lower part of town and walk along the harbour a bit. What do you think? I know a walk would do me good."

Without waiting for Jason's answer, she put her arm through his and at the end of the Rue de l'Abbaye steered him between two squat towers towards the arch giving access to the old part of town.

"I'd prefer not to stay outside too long. We can always look at the bay tomorrow," he told her.

"I understand," said Zoë quietly and pressed herself closer to him, but Jason had heard the disappointment in her voice. She thought she understood, she tried to, but in the end she had no idea how exposed and vulnerable he felt. And how could she? It wasn't something that he spoke about, at least not directly.

It was the first time he had gone for a walk since he had fled the chateau with her and holed up in her villa; it was the first walk he had ever had in St Valéry. Before knowing Zoë it would never have occurred to him to stay in the little town any longer than necessary. And now that Miles was on his heels it seemed more dangerous than ever to let himself be seen in the place. For Miles was still prowling around in the area, of that Jason was certain. And he was equally certain that Miles would not return to Southcombe without completing his mission. He was still there, somewhere in the neighbourhood, perhaps even just around the next corner, waiting for the right moment to strike again.

But after four days Zoë had had enough of this perpetual hide-and-seek and insisted on getting some fresh air with Jason.

"Only a short one, Jason. Otherwise you're going to go crazy. If I were in your shoes I'd have gone off my rocker long ago. And, you know, the more the days go by the more I'm convinced that Miles isn't here any longer. Otherwise he'd have found us long ago. So, agreed? We'll do the short walk round the old part of town and then come straight back home. There's a gate there that ought to interest you as an Englishman. I bet you don't know it."

They had caught the bus in Crotoy, had been dropped off a quarter of an hour later at the square in front of St Valéry railway station and had walked up to the Porte Guillaume. At the gate, Zoë pointed to an information board dedicated to Joan of Arc.

"I said it was in December 1430," Zoë announced after checking the date on the information board.

"I didn't know you were such an expert in history."

"Oh, it's no big deal in a town like this. You get your ears stuffed full of Joan of Arc at school – even at kindergarten. St Valéry is incredibly proud of its role in history, even if it isn't exactly a glorious one. Poor old Joan was kept for weeks in the castle of Le Crotoy while the French haggled over her with you guys."

Jason laughed. "'You guys'? That's good coming from you! You're English too. Half- English, at least."

"But I've never lived in England, that's the difference. Although I talk English with my father I feel a hundred per cent French. Always have done."

He thought he knew what she meant. He had never before given any thought to what it was that distinguished the French from the English apart from their respective languages. But since being with Zoë, her way of living fascinated him. It was so different from his, and he could find no explanation for it other than to say that she was through and through un-English. It was clearest in everyday little unconscious gestures, such as the care she took with her make-up in the mornings, the way she colour-coordinated her clothes, or the delight she took in laying out the food she had bought and surveying it before putting it away in the fridge. She would brim with enthusiasm over the bright red of a tomato or the shimmering scales of a trout. Every kind of food that had colour or smell or even just a particular pattern, like the tree-like shape of a halved cauliflower, commanded her respect.

And there was the sheer pleasure she took in it. She only tolerated sandwiches as an exception, and simple meals like fried eggs or bread and cheese were acceptable only at lunchtime. For the evening meal it was important to her to have a nicely laid table and meat or fish dishes, preferably ones she had cooked herself. This was such a cliché that Jason was at first surprised and even a little unsettled by it. Cooking had up to now been a pure waste of time for him and certainly not something he expected a beautiful girl to concern herself with. In England he didn't know anyone, least of all anyone young, who would make such a fuss about food. But Zoë was just different; she came to life in the kitchen, he could hear her whistling and singing while she busied herself with pots and pans. Occasionally she would shout across that she loved him, and in the next breath ask him how he liked the meat cooked and whether he wanted red or white wine with it. She got irritated if he replied that he didn't mind, and so he had learned to express clear opinions. But really he was embarrassed. He didn't have any particular wishes with regard to food, and hanging around in the sitting-room waiting to be served like a pasha wasn't his thing either.

"Please, just let me do it. It's my pleasure," Zoë had said, dismissing his reservations. "After all, we've agreed that I'll do the shopping, cooking and washing up. If you want to, you can do the cleaning and clearing up. But you don't have to. We've got a cleaning lady who comes every ten days and gets the house into shape."

Now Zoë let go of Jason's arm and walked ahead for a couple of steps to look at the bay, in which at this time of day land and water formed patterns of grey lines snaking into each other. She was wearing a padded coat, beanie and scarf, all in various shades of grey, and against that background seemed to merge with the colours of the sand and the clouds.

"The tide will soon be coming in," she said, and was about to turn away and start walking back home when Jason suddenly pulled her towards him and covered her face, including the grazes and the green and purple bruises, with kisses. Like the tide of which Zoë had just spoken, he felt his desire for her grow in him, warm and dangerous, a surge that would uproot him and wash him away far from himself. But perhaps it had already happened and this welling up of love was just a physical response to the shocking realization that he was another person these days and finally ready for a new relationship.

"Zoë, my wonderful Zoë. I love you, … love you like crazy. Have I already told you today?"

"No, not yet today. But you told me yesterday, and the day before, and every night you've told me."

"So the thrill has gone already, has it?"

"Silly boy," she replied, kissing him on the tip of his nose. "Tell me a thousand times a day and it will always be new and wonderful to me."

She was laughing up at him when she saw his face begin to cloud over.

"What is it? Have I said the wrong thing? Sometimes you become so serious, so … sad. That scares me because I don't know what's going on inside your head."

"I just can't get over how incredibly lucky I am, Zoë. I still can't really believe it. Sometimes I wonder if you aren't a mirage."

"A mirage? Nonsense! I'm here all right. Touch me, look, I really am flesh and blood. And now I'll hug you and kiss you – you see?"

"Yes, but you said yourself once that you know nothing about me."

Ever since he had moved in with Zoë he had looked for opportunities to turn the conversation in this direction. Nothing had come of them. When he saw her lying naked beside him, her eyes glowing with the intoxication of love, her beautiful body relaxed, shining with tiny pearls of sweat, he could not bring himself to disturb the moment by talking. Sex was so much simpler than explanations.

When they made love, even in the spirit of wild desire that Zoë favoured, they observed a balance between giving and taking. In the revelation of their pasts there was, however, no such balance. His past was so much weightier than hers. Apart from the separation of her parents, Zoë had had no traumatic experiences and said herself that the only shadow over her life concerned Mathieu, her brother in Nice whom she had not been able to grow up with.

"It's true, I only know as much as you want to tell me. That's not much, admittedly, but you've given me to understand that it's got to be enough for the moment," she said, smiling to show that she was prepared to wait in order to learn the truth. "That's right, isn't it?"

"I'm sorry, Zoë, I've left you in the dark for too long. Let's go home, I owe you ..."

"You don't owe me anything, Jason. I'm with you of my own free will."

"Yes, I know. But that's why you deserve something better than a friend who is burdened by guilt and secrets."

"Not a friend, Jason: a lover. I've got plenty of friends already."

Chapter 19

"OK, OK, calm down, I'm on my way already. I've just gone past Stogumber. But honestly, expecting me to drive to the coast at Blue Anchor in this weather … it's a damn cheek. Couldn't you just post me the money as usual?"

"That's the hundredth time you've asked. What do you want me to say? That's the way they want it, perhaps because it's so much this time. But you follow my directions precisely, understand? If you don't, even I can't help you."

"You least of all. When are you coming back?"

"Earlier than planned. They've called me back."

"Called you back? You?"

"Yes, there are more urgent things to be dealt with. That idiot in France can wait. He's not going to get away from me."

"Where are you, Miles?"

"That's for me to ask you. You're late and you know they don't like waiting."

"Damn it, give me a bit of time. You can't just zoom down these lanes. Since passing Crowcombe I've been crawling along behind a tractor and trailer. If he doesn't stop somewhere soon I'll be at least half an hour late."

"Can't you overtake?"

"Nope, not safely. And not when I'm talking to you on the phone at the same time."

"Then I'll hang up. But hurry, there's not much time! And don't forget what I told you about the mobile, will you? We can't allow ourselves any mistakes now."

"OK. But if you ask me, you're all a bit crazy. To be as over-cautious as this …"

"No one asked for your opinion, so shut your trap! And put your foot down, for heaven's sake."

That was easier said than done. The tractor gave no sign of leaving the A358. Only when both vehicles had left Williton behind them and were on the B3191 heading for Watchet did it occur to the farmer to pull in to the left and let him pass. The patches of fog were thicker now, so that even with the fog-lights he couldn't see more than ten yards in front of him. Blue Anchor, what nonsense! Who did they think he was, these idiots? He cursed aloud to himself as he drove, but at the same time the images of earlier summers ran through his head, images of three boys who just there, on the Blue Anchor beach, had set off, armed with buckets and spades, to collect crabs under the supervision of Bill's and Miles' father.

The brothers had always been more skilful than he was. They used a stick to poke around in the pebbles until the crabs crawled out of their hiding places, and then they went for them so quickly that they didn't have time to bury themselves in the sand again. They caught dozens like this, but none of them wondered what the purpose of it all was. After a few days the crabs perished in the buckets, Bill poured the stinking brew on to the compost heap, and he – yes, it was always he – had to clean out the bucket for next time. Catching crabs, collecting seaweed, it was just what you did on those days on a beach where you couldn't swim because of the mud. But what he preferred was collecting fossils, not snails and certainly not the stones with the imprint of grasses or worms in them, no, his ambition as a child had always been to discover the bones of dinosaurs, big thigh bones, perhaps a skull, even a whole animal with rib-cage, spine and tail, teeth and everything. Other people sometimes found skeletons like that on the beach, so why shouldn't he one day be lucky enough to become famous? Somewhere in his sitting-room there must still be the fragment of bone lying around that he and Miles really did find one day. He wondered whether Miles remembered how proud they had been of their discovery. He at least had scarcely been able to sleep that night for sheer joy and excitement.

He couldn't remember there ever before being a fog like there was this year. In his memory Blue Anchor had always been sunny and light, a place to be carefree. But as children they had never been taken there in the winter, only in the summer when, as Bill's and Miles' father explained to them, the days were long and warm enough to make the drive worthwhile.

One or two miles after Watchet the fog became impenetrable. The feeling of being enclosed in his car as if it were a cage began to darken his mood. When he finally stopped in the car park at Blue Anchor and opened the car door, the stagnant air flowed into his lungs like syrup and enveloped him in the sharp tang of seaweed and moor. He had to cough as he looked around and was startled by how little he saw and how silent the bay lay in the darkness. He briefly glimpsed the green anorak of a woman taking a dog for a walk, and then that too was swallowed up by the fog and he was alone again between the invisible sea and a road which, emerging out of nothingness, returned to nothingness after only a few yards.

He hadn't thought of taking a torch. How could he have guessed that the light would be so bad at twenty to seven? He still had his mobile with him that lit up the path, but not for long. Miles' instructions on that had been clear, almost threatening: "No mobile, understand? Under no circumstances!" And exactly as it had been described to him, he found at the entrance to the car park the litter bin he had to leave his mobile in. He did so reluctantly. However, Miles had assured him that it would be safe there and he would be able to take it out later.

"Apart from the fact that you'll be able to buy a new one with all the money you're earning. How about an iPhone?"

It was easy for Miles to talk, he didn't have to stumble around in the fog like a blind man, looking for the ramp that led down to the beach. At that very moment, he was sure, Miles would be sitting in a comfortable restaurant drinking top-class wine together with French delicacies of one kind or another, oysters, snails, something like that.

The concrete ramp that he finally came to was steep and slippery with seaweed. He had to hold on to the rail in order not to fall over, and strain his eyes to see where to put his feet. The gentle sound of swishing and sucking to his left made him guess that the tide was coming in, but he had time. In any case Miles had reassured him that he wouldn't have to wait long. "Someone will be looking out for you by the alabaster cliff. The whole business will take less than five minutes and then, my friend, … you'll be a rich friend."

It wasn't far to that cliff, he knew from earlier where it was, but with every step the jagged outline of the great piece of rock seemed to move further away. He tried to go straight towards it but outcrops of rock and inlets of water in the sand forced him to make detours. He stumbled, went in deeper, and every time he cursed and called himself an idiot for agreeing to this ridiculous meeting.

"Why does it have to be Blue Anchor?" he had asked repeatedly. "I don't understand." But it wasn't a good idea to argue with Miles. That had always been the case. Even his brother Bill, who was two years older, had been afraid of him earlier. Probably still was while they sorted flowers in the shop.

Anyway he counted himself lucky that Miles was in France at that moment. Wouldn't he otherwise have had to fear that it was the Wolf waiting for him at the alabaster cliff? Dealing with Miles in this thick fog – the very thought of it made him shudder. By now he was panting with the effort. Hip-high outcrops of rock had been obstructing his path for a while now. He had alternately to climb up and slide down them in the dark. He'd scraped his hands and was bleeding, but there was no going back. The alabaster cliff loomed above him, big and black, and by now significantly nearer than the ramp up to the car park that he had left a good quarter of an hour ago. Only a couple of minutes more and he would be at his goal.

He risked a half-hearted shout, which was lost in the fog and was not answered. A seagull shrieked in the distance, a second one responded with the same drawn-out sound, and then once more he could only hear his own panting and the sound of his feet as he stumbled over the stones and finally came on to sand again.

When he reached the cliff he began to think he had been the victim of a practical joke. Contrary to Miles' assurance, no one seemed to be waiting for him.

"Anyone there?" he asked as he began to pick his way round the cliff. There was no reply but he asked the question twice more, so as to hear a voice in the midst of this silent desolation. It did not reassure him. Instead he felt a dull sense of helplessness growing inside him, which could at any moment tip over into panic. He continued waiting for a response. In vain. Around him all he could hear was the soft rustling sound of shrimps burrowing in the mud and, by the cliff, the drops of condensation falling on sand and stone.

But if Miles said that someone would be waiting for him, then that would be the case. Someone must be there, someone must be very nearby, perhaps just behind him or over there, less than two yards away, in that dark recess in the cliff. But why didn't he make himself known, why didn't he speak? Miles had said that the thing would only take five minutes. Five minutes had already passed. He was freezing now, sweating too, and didn't want to spend any longer in this savage place, with the swishing of the sea in his ears gradually coming closer, frothing nearer and nearer. Yes, he could hear it coming in, the sea, and he knew that … – but no, there was enough time to reach the next alabaster cliff. Perhaps he had been mistaken and was expected there. That's how things must be, yes, bound to be.

He laughed in relief and began to run, more quickly this time because of the rising tide. The sand felt soft under his feet, softer than it had a few minutes earlier, so that in places he sank in up to his ankles. He had to search out rocky islands in order to make any progress and kept increasing to the right by the steeply towering cliffs, although the danger of erosion made it unsafe. But at least it was dry there.

Once again he took courage and laughed. This time an echo replied. He heard it come from behind and, out of sheer joy at hearing a sound that did not come from his own mouth, wanted to laugh again, more loudly, so as to produce a second echo. But the sudden realization that there could not possibly be any echo in this place and in this weather made him freeze on the spot. He had been mistaken. He was not alone. Someone had been watching him from the beginning and was standing not far from him. But where?

"Who's there?" he asked anxiously, and turned towards the sea, where he thought the sound had come from. As if through a veil he could see a row of tiny, pale lights flickering across from Wales, filling him with a desperate longing. If only he could swim across the Bristol Channel to those lights and mingle with those people. Because he'd be safe there. Suddenly the lights didn't seem so far away, with a bit of luck … But no, he was standing on the dark, dangerous side of an estuary, drawn there by the prospect of thousands of pounds, and now it was too late to turn round.

Slowly he began to creep along the edge of the cliff-face away from where he thought he had heard the echo. He didn't get far. Whoever was after him caught up with him in a single leap and was suddenly standing so close behind that he could smell them – a mixture of stale tobacco smoke and aftershave. He wanted to turn round, but at his first movement he felt something hard boring into his ribs and heard a voice just behind his neck whisper:

"Not a word. Just walk on, straight on."

Did he know the voice? He wasn't sure. Apart from Miles he could think of no one who spoke with that air of cold indifference. But Miles wasn't here. Bill, perhaps? Why would Bill treat him so roughly?

"You must be confusing me with someone else. I'm not …"

"Quiet! Straight on, I said. And not a word."

He had to resist. Whoever it was was taking the two of them straight towards the sea, towards the incoming tide, towards the middle of the mud. Didn't he know the danger for both of them?

"Sorry, but I'm not going any further."

"Aren't you? Then my knife will have to help you along. Don't make me do that, please, just get on. Move!"

What could he do? You couldn't mess around with a knife in your back. So he cautiously put one foot in front of the other. But between each of the stones there was sodden sand, a cold sludge that clung in clumps to his shoes and dragged him down. With each step he sank a fraction of an inch deeper and it cost him more strength to pull his foot out for the next step. It was still only up to his calves, there were still occasional islands of stone that he could put his trust in, but he knew that a single step into deeper mud would be enough to engulf him. Sweat ran down his face, fear threatened to paralyse him, the slightest wrong move could be the end of him. In front of him the relentless sea was approaching. Was this the last thing in the world he would see? A couple of distant lights in the fog, an indistinct awareness of the water. Was that all?

"Please let me turn round," he heard himself whine. "Please, please, I take it all back, I'll do without …' And as he desperately struggled for breath it struck him like a blow to the face: he did not need to turn round to see who was standing behind him, he knew who it was, that chilly silence spoke clearer than words.

But the horror of it had made him miss the moment when the pressure in his back disappeared and the salty sea-breeze replaced the smell of tobacco and perfume. His tormentor had left him and retreated to safety. He was alone. He was stuck in the mud over his knees, and the sea was advancing threateningly towards him.

Chapter 20

Up on the Quantock Hills the last of the snow had melted. Primroses and wild crocuses added the first splash of colour to clearings in the woods. Daffodils had sprung up in the gardens and by the sides of the road. And so in fog-bound Southcombe the word 'spring' was on everyone's lips even though there was a good month to wait before the season officially began. The people queuing to pay at the Co-op were talking about it, and at the post office and at Helen Dean's café, which Vera sometimes visited alone despite the unpleasant memory of her argument there with Nadja, the word seemed to be part of people's standard greeting to each other.

In these first mild days Tom's mother recalled her suggestion that she should show Vera the sights of Somerset. The cottage in Nether Stowey where the young Coleridge had lived and written the *Lyrical Ballads* together with William Wordsworth was unfortunately still being restored, so Marion proposed a trip to the Somerset Levels instead.

"There are several nature reserves there, Vera, and you will see that the Levels breathe an atmosphere of calm that's good for the soul. And apart from that I know a pub there that serves excellent food. Come on, let me treat you. What about next Monday or Tuesday, say about ten? Tom will have to work but I'm sure we can at least persuade Nadja to come along with us. To tell you the truth, I've already asked her."

Did Vera have any choice?

The journey began under an oppressively low mass of cloud. At any moment the rain could come pelting down on land that was in many places already under-water. To both sides of the road stretched canals over-grown with reeds and willows. Herons flew up at the ap-proach of the car, and in the distance, towards the Pol-den Hills, flocks of starlings blackened the sky.

Marion Skinner, wearing jeans and a quilted jacket that was the same flaming red as her hair, sat at the wheel and made occasional comments on the sights they pass-ed, albeit much too fast, so that Vera could only catch a glimpse of them. She would have liked to get out at Bur-rowbridge, where the few houses and the pub which made up the village were clustered round the foot of an artificially created hill with sheep grazing on it, crowned by a romantic ruin. When she asked if it was possible to climb up to the ruin and get a good view of the sur-rounding countryside, Marion nodded, without however thinking of stopping.

Vera felt as if the two of them were alone in the car. Nadja sat in the back seat, her eyes closed and her hands in her lap, presenting an image of complete indifference.

From time to time Vera looked at her questioningly in the mirror but said nothing.

However, it upset her to see her daughter slouched in her seat, looking so disinterested. Earlier, in Switzerland, Nadja had loved driving through the countryside. On Sundays Robert would suggest somewhere to go to, perhaps the Napf or perhaps the Greyerzer region, it didn't matter where, Nadja was always excited about discovering new places and ending up in a café eating an ice cream.

"Nadja?" In the end Vera could not bear it any longer and leaned back to touch her daughter's knee.

"Mmm, what is it?"

"Are you all right?"

"Yes, why? I just feel a bit queasy from the travelling, but it's not bad, really. It's better when I shut my eyes."

That was new, too. Vera couldn't remember Nadja ever having suffered from car sickness.

"Oh, don't worry, Vera" interjected Marion. "She'll be all right. Wait until we're sitting in the Crown Inn. Then she'll be herself again. Isn't that right, Nadja? Do you remember last time – when was that, in October? – how good our game pie was?"

Nadja murmured agreement and fell back into half-sleep again. The journey led from Burrowbridge across a low-lying plain on roads full of puddles and pot-holes. The Levels might well be of interest to bird-watchers, but as long as Vera could not get out and take in the countryside for herself, smell the air and hear the rustling of the leaves and the twittering of the birds, it all seemed monotonous, almost eerie.

It was as if Marion had read her thoughts as she began to talk again. "There are lots of legends about ghosts on the Levels. Not only in Glastonbury, the one-time Avalon and spiritual centre of England, but also in these swamps and fields. Three hundred years ago, the king crushed an army of rebels here and lots of people say they've seen the ghosts of dead soldiers from those days. Are you sceptical? Of course I am, too, but if you come here on a foggy winter's day you can easily see how such legends arise."

They had been in the car for almost an hour when Marion decided to stop at the end of a track and invited Vera and Nadja to get out and stretch their legs.

"If we're lucky we'll be able to see lapwings here in Catcott. Come on, they're really worth seeing."

Nadja and Vera stood in front of a board which listed the various species of bird – egret, lapwing, kingfisher and ducks of all sorts – while Marion turned the car round in the tiny parking area, ready to drive out again. The nature reserve stretched out in front of them with ponds covered in reeds and copses of pussy willow, and gave the impression that not a soul had been there since time immemorial. It was peaceful but also desolate, and by comparison with the lush fields and woods of the Somerset that Vera had got to know there was something forlorn about it. Marion had brought two pairs of binoculars with her and hung them round Vera's and Nadja's necks, saying encouragingly:

"There. Now you look like genuine twitchers."

Her enthusiasm for the bleak, windswept stretch of land seemed genuine. She pointed to the wet patches where they might catch sight of a lapwing and allowed herself to push Vera and Nadja in various directions so that they would have a better view over the wire netting fence, and after a while the two did in fact get a glimpse of the black tip of a bird's tail before it disappeared into the reeds.

Had Marion really thought that the view across a desolate landscape of reeds would justify an hour's journey? Dubiously, Vera cast her eyes over the Levels, which at this time of year still showed signs of the recent weeks of hard winter weather. Many plants had been frozen and rose, brown and split, from the ponds. A small number of ducks slid alongside the banks, something narrow and hairy emerged briefly from the water, probably an otter. Then there was no movement anywhere.

Nadja was the first to lose her patience and return to the car. Vera waited a while longer, but when she heard the sound of the engine starting behind her she also turned away and sat herself in the passenger seat next to Marion.

"Impressive, isn't it?" said the latter as she engaged first gear. When neither Vera nor Nadja replied she also fell silent.

The village of Catcott that the reserve was named after was less than five minutes' drive away. From outside the Crown Inn didn't make much of an impression, and the way it was furnished scarcely differed from the other local pubs that Vera already knew. Dark, exposed beams, white walls, and for decoration everywhere there were highly polished metal objects – spurs, horseshoes and containers of every shape and size.

"It doesn't look like anything special, but wait till you've tasted the food. And then read at home what Tripadvisor has to say about it. Really first class, the Crown Inn."

At first Nadja didn't want to eat anything at all, but Vera coaxed her to at least choose soup from the menu.

"It'll warm you up. But why don't you feel like eating? Is it because of travel sickness?"

"Yes, a bit. I feel faint, too. Most of all I'd like to stretch out on this bench and go to sleep."

Nadja didn't say a word more during the whole meal. She looked out of the window or sent text messages while Vera and Marion enjoyed their poached salmon and had a lively discussion about the progress that English cooking had made.

However, Vera became increasingly uncomfortable. She kept expecting Marion to come out with a more important topic of conversation, the actual reason for this strange excursion. But she seemed content to make small talk and for a long time didn't notice that Vera was looking increasingly anxiously towards Nadja. Only when the clock struck half-past one in the farthest corner of the room did she suddenly say, "As late as that? Would you mind if we miss out on coffee and dessert today, Vera? I think we should take Nadja home. She needs to lie down."

Nadja protested weakly, but Marion had scarcely paid the bill when Nadja got up from the table and made rather unsteadily for the exit. Her face was chalky and her eyes shone as if she had a temperature.

But she didn't have a temperature, Vera confirmed as she touched her forehead on the way out. She was probably just tired after a sleepless night. Unless – but no, if there was joyful news about an addition to the family her daughter would have told her long ago.

Nadja could scarcely stand when she got out of the car in Southcombe and made her way alone from the garden gate to the front door. On the way back Vera had offered to stop off with her to make a pot of tea and help her get into bed: to do the kind of thing that mothers do for their children in situations like this. It would have given her the opportunity, too, to find out a bit more a-bout the strange state of apathy that her daughter seemed to be slipping into. Nadja hesitated for a moment and gave Marion a questioning look before declining. As she left the car, her mother-in-law patted Nadja's cheek in a gesture of maternal affection, which did not escape Vera. Marion dropped her in front of Station House and, be-fore driving away, wound down the window and called out, "'Bye, Vera. Don't worry, I'm sure Nadja will feel better soon."

She left Vera with the unpleasant feeling that she hadn't done the right thing as a mother and should have gone into the house with Nadja when they got back. But it was too late for that now, she reflected, as she put the key in the door.

Before going into the house she looked up at it and watched for a while as two doves cooing immediately above her head scuttled up and down the porch roof. Yes, spring was on the way, tulips were bursting out of the ground, the rose that Nadja had given her was forming its first tiny leaves and the wisteria was beginning to go green – but Vera was astonished to see that the branches were freshly pruned. The weeds that had been growing round the down-pipe had disappeared and the gutter was clear. What remained of the wisteria was a six-foot-high twisted stem with stumps of branches sticking out, the recently sawed surfaces bright and still damp. Mr Lee must just have finished his work. Without the agreed advance notice. And, above all, in her absence.

Eileen Moore tried to reassure her on the telephone.

"What are you thinking of, Mrs Wyler? There's absolutely nothing malicious behind it. Mr Lee just happened to have a free minute this morning. I tried to ring you at about ten and when you didn't answer I presumed I was doing the right thing in giving him the go-ahead. I even thought you would prefer it like this so as to be spared the noise of the saw and all the coming and going."

"What coming and going?" asked Vera abruptly.

"Well, collecting the prunings and sweeping the yard. Mr Lee is very thorough and takes his time with jobs like this. It could have disturbed you."

"I don't think so."

"If I've annoyed you then I'm very sorry and apologize. On Mr Lee's behalf, too. We only wanted to do what was best for you."

That might be the case. Or not. It was time for Vera to swallow her pride and go and find Greg. The man who had said he would get in touch and never had.

The Kings Arms was scarcely ever full during the week, but on Friday and Saturday evenings almost the whole of Southcombe would gather in the pub for a round of cider. At least pubs were no longer the forbidden territory for women that they had once been. On one occasion when Vera had been on a language course in London at the age of seventeen, she had wanted to go into a pub on her own, but the men at the bar looked her over so disapprovingly that she went straight out of the door again, deeply ashamed, as if she had done something disreputable.

It was still early, and Vera found herself alone in the pub with the exception of an elderly couple silently eating fish and chips in a corner. She sat down at the bar, ordered a glass of merlot and asked the barman if he knew someone called Greg.

"I think he's a policeman."

"Greg Jones?"

"I don't know his surname, but I saw him here with Paddy once."

"Yes, Paddy Bale and Greg Jones. The two of them are often here. Greg lives diagonally opposite – the big white thatched cottage next to the post office, over there, that's where he lives."

"Alone?"

The barman grinned.

"In theory, yes."

Vera sipped at her merlot and prayed that Greg would come through the door this evening. Every time someone came into the pub she turned hopefully towards the door, but the only people who came in this evening sat themselves in groups around tables in the next room and, having placed orders, pulled out their pencils. Of course, how could Vera have forgotten? It was Thursday, quiz night. Questions about sport, geography, film and the royal family, as the quiz master announced, and he was already starting with the first question: "Which horse won the Hennessy Gold Cup in the three successive years: 1999, 2000 and 2001? And next, …"

Vera didn't need to hear any more. After the last sip she put her coat on and thanked the barman once again for the information. He could be my son, he's so young, she thought as she admired the skill with which he washed glasses and poured out beer at the same time. He might be young, almost a teenager, but he managed to embarrass her with an almost imperceptible lift of one eyebrow.

Greg was at home. There was a light on upstairs, but not on the ground floor where Vera guessed the kitchen and sitting-room were. Looking in from the street, she could make out a vase and various photograph frames on the window-ledge and behind the net curtain a sofa with brightly coloured cushions. It was nine o'clock at night, too late just to drop in. Vera dug an old receipt out of her bag and wrote on the back of it: "Can I have a word with you, please? My number is 01823 431 472. Best wishes, Vera (Station House)." She opened the garden gate as quietly as she could, went on tip-toe up to the front door and pushed the note into the letter-box.

To her relief no excuses were necessary. Greg rang her the next morning from the police station in Taunton and didn't conceal his pleasure at hearing from her. His voice, even in the first words he spoke, made her shiver. She had forgotten how deep and warm it was.

"Sorry, Vera. It should have been me getting in touch with you."

"No, that doesn't matter. I've done it now. It just occurred to me yesterday that you may be able to help me with a couple of things that I don't understand."

"Things?"

"I mean incidents in the village."

"Huh, it'd be good if there *were* incidents in South-combe. It's such a sleepy little hole that nothing much happens here apart from tea parties and the occasional charity bazaar."

"That's not true. I'm serious, Greg. I'd really be very grateful if you could reassure me about certain … how shall I put it? … suspicions that have arisen in my mind. Would you do that for me?"

"Today?"

"Yes, if that's possible."

"OK. No problem. Drop by this evening. You obviously know where I live."

"I don't want to disturb you at home. We could meet in the pub."

"Oh, why not at my place? That way we can stop the tongues from wagging. I get home about half-past six. Come along whenever you like after that. But don't expect too much, I'm terrible at housework."

As she put the phone down Vera felt as if a weight had been lifted off her. If only she had thought of consulting him earlier. Greg knew the villagers, he was one of them, and yet as a policeman he was on the side of the law. If she couldn't trust him, who could she trust?

The prospect of a discussion that would clarify things for her filled Vera with renewed energy.

She made a note of the gravestones on which she had seen an image of St Aldusa. She wanted to show Greg her list in the evening so as to prove that there was some factual basis to her worries and she wasn't just imagining things.

Five dead women whose only connection was St Aldusa — what was that all about? If it hadn't been for Lizzie, who'd died in the summer, Vera would have been tempted to see a link in the time of year when they died. For, listed one under the other, it occurred to her for the first time that not only Sue Harper but also three other women had died in the autumn, one in October, the other three in November. However, Lizzie did not fit this pattern, nor did the fact that she had been so brutally murdered. Was it possible that Craig Brett had seen another connection and paid for it with his life?

Vera still had the whole afternoon to kill until she could visit Greg. She wasn't sure whether she was being invited for a meal or simply a drink, so she bought a box of Belgian chocolates at the Co-op in order to cover herself and, giving way to temptation, also bought herself a bar of Swiss chocolate, which she opened as soon as she reached the road. How good it tasted, that chocolate, how lightly it dissolved on the tongue.

The taste brought back memories of the time before she left Bern. They had been weeks of hectic organization that now seemed further back in the past than last autumn, especially when she recalled everything she had experienced in recent months. But if she thought about the neat little stone-built houses of Southcombe's High Street, 'Poppy Cottage' and 'Hill View' on one side, 'Swan House' and 'Ashculme' on the other, she didn't feel she belonged here now any more than she had when she had just arrived. She still had no idea who lived in those houses, she still only knew Nadja's family and Eileen Moore, and when people greeted her on the street it was out of automatic politeness, not because they really took any interest in her.

But perhaps things weren't really so bad. Mr Lee, who was in the process of arranging crates of violets and primroses on a stand, turned round to greet her with a polite smile as she walked past. He at least, it seemed, recognized her.

"Does that taste good?" he asked, to which Vera nodded with her mouth full and, on impulse, came to a halt.

"By the way, thank you for pruning the wisteria. Actually I was waiting for you to ring."

"To ring?"

"Yes. Mrs Moore said you would warn me beforehand."

"I don't need to warn people if I'm carrying out Mrs Moore's orders. It had to be done at once, and so I just trotted along and didn't worry whether you were at home or not. It wasn't relevant, you see.

"You do see, don't you?" he repeated in a different tone of voice after a short pause.

He was virtually demanding her agreement. It made her feel uncomfortable.

"Yes, of course I understand," Vera found herself saying, when really she did not.

"Good," he said, a note of dismissal in his voice.

He clearly considered that to be the end of the matter. But instead of leaving, Vera stared directly into his deep-set hazel eyes and added: "You've done the job perfectly, I congratulate you. And now if I could go into your shop, please, I'd like to look around for some flowers."

"No problem. Please come in."

Inside there was the sound of whispering from an adjoining room. For a while Vera acted as if she couldn't decide between yellow and white tulips. Or should it be a mixed bunch? In the end perhaps not tulips at all, but lilies? Not that it mattered to her: what she was really looking for was not flowers but white jars containing the vitamin pills which, according to Tom, Mr Lee sold to half the village. Wherever she looked, though, Vera saw nothing that resembled the little jar she had seen in Tom's hands. There were glass vases in various shapes, plant food, slug bait without metaldehyde or other dubious ingredients, as well as shelves full of gardening books, but no white jars.

"Mr Lee," she finally decided to ask after placing a bunch of yellow tulips on the counter to be wrapped, "I've heard that there's a wonder medicine that you sell in the village. I believe it's made of natural extracts that you put together yourself and it once featured on the BBC. I'd really like to try it. Can I buy it here?"

"Of course you can."

Mr Lee seemed visibly flattered to be asked. Reaching under the counter, he produced one of his white jars and gave it to Vera. By contrast with the one she had seen at Nadja and Tom's, this jar had a label giving the name and the proportions of the ingredients. Also a printed price: £14.99.

"That makes £17.49 together."

As Vera was counting out the money from her purse, a burst of laughter broke through the steady level of background noise from the next room, which she had up to then taken for a radio broadcast. There were people in there. And now she clearly heard the shifting of a chair. Vera could distinguish at least three women's voices, but it could have been more. And one of them dominated, intoning the sentences in a monotonous voice and then giving individual words a particular emphasis. These were the only ones that Vera could make out, the rest were submerged in a general murmur. There was talk of 'nutrition', of 'mildew', 'mites' and 'greenfly', of 'harmful substances' and of various chemical compounds.

"Is that one of your funny gardening courses?" asked Vera as she took the wrapped bunch of tulips. Perhaps she had unintentionally put a shade too much mockery into her question, for Mr Lee snapped back in a rather ill-tempered way, "And who told you that our gardening courses are funny?"

It was only as she left the shop that Vera realized he hadn't given a direct reply to her question. What a strange bunch of people they are here, she thought, mystery-mongers every one of them.

With her hand already on the door-handle and on her face the obligatory smile of farewell, she still hesitated to leave. Hadn't she heard a familiar voice in the muted conversation next door?

"Goodbye, Mrs Wyler. Don't forget: cut the stems and not too much water."

Vera nodded but stood by the door, listening.

"I think I just heard Nadja."

"Nadja?"

"My daughter. Is she next door?"

"It's possible. I don't know who goes to which course. I make the room available, that's all."

"Ah, so you don't give any courses yourself? And yet you would be the best qualified teacher in the village."

Mr Lee gave an exaggerated bow.

"Too kind, madam, but there are plenty of people in the village who understand as much about nature as I do."

"Do you mind if I have a quick look?"

Vera was already moving towards the adjacent room when Mr Lee stepped across and blocked her way: "Sorry, I can't allow that. It would be against the regulations."

Against the regulations! Wasn't that the phrase that Eileen Moore had used when she tried to prevent Vera from sharing the first instalment of the raffle prize? What kind of regulations were they? Another question Vera hoped Greg would be able to help her with, she reflected on her way home.

Mr Lee's jar contained not pills but greenish lozenges about the size of a five-pence piece. The recommended dose was one each morning and evening for a complete cycle of the moon, from one new moon to the next, preferably in the enervating period between All Souls and Christmas. The lozenges contained extracts of sage, sea buckthorn, nettle, dandelion, mallow, St John's wort, algae, mistletoe, wormwood and other herbs. The various components were poorly fused and the lozenges crumbled immediately on the tongue, leaving a bitter taste behind. Vera had no compunctions about taking them. She was sure the lozenges could do her no harm even if the ideal time had passed. She had seen the moon through the shifting veil of cloud the evening before and it was unmistakably waning.

Fifteen pounds for a handful of herbal tablets, thought Vera, while she settled down in the blue sitting-room with the art magazine she had received the day before, that's a ridiculous price. Even more than the price, though, what really made her think was the fact that Nadja had received a different medication, one without the names and amounts of the ingredients listed. Before opening the article about a Segantini exhibition Vera turned the jar in every direction and read the small print, which said that because of the high proportion of extract of algae the lozenges should be used with caution in cases of thyroid dysfunction. That had the ring of medical professionalism, but Mr Lee was no doctor. He ran a flower shop and did some gardening. As a non-professional, was he even permitted to sell home-made medications?

Vera stretched out on the sofa, put her legs up on the arm, consigned all the awkward questions to the back of her mind and became engrossed in the richly illustrated article. However, an occasional rustling noise in the room, which had struck her as she came in, prevented her from concentrating entirely on what she was reading. From time to time she looked up and listened. She could clearly distinguish that the sound came from inside the room. But was it really rustling or more perhaps a scratching or pecking noise? Sometimes it sounded like wings beating.

She tried to concentrate on Segantini again, read about his love for the mountains and studied the large-scale reproduction of 'Brown Cow at Trough' until the rustling became so loud that there could no longer be any doubt: there was a living creature with her in the room. Involuntarily she thought of a rat that might have squeezed through the gap between the stone floor and the front door and drew her legs up, shuddering. She held her breath and pricked her ears in order to locate the rustling more precisely, but now it sounded more like the sound of wings beating against a wall. Then there was a gentle squawk, then a moment of silence before the rustling began again. It came from the fireplace.

Despite the cold, Vera had not used it this winter. She was put off by the work – ordering wood, lighting the fire and then cleaning the fireplace – since it was easier to press the button on an electric heater. And so she had always regarded the fireplace as nothing more than a bit of decorative nostalgia and had never wondered why wind, rain and snow did not fall down the chimney into the room. But when she kneeled down in front of it and felt up the flue with her hand she knew at once why. Balls of newspaper had been used to block the opening, and now she could hear distinctly that a bird had fallen down inside the chimney and was scratching and fluttering for its life.

Tentatively she began to tug at the newspaper and pulled out scrap after scrap. The higher she reached, the damper and sootier it all became until, with the last piece, a bird came tumbling down and landed on the mountain of paper with a loud squawk. It was probably one of the many starlings that gathered on the chimney pot in the mornings and evenings. It didn't stay still for long. Vera just had time to admire its feathers sparkling through the soot and its bright button eyes when the bird spread its wings and flew past her, banging into the window-pane. Vera scrambled after it, praying it had not broken its neck or a wing. The bird had landed on the window ledge and seemed to be scrabbling at it as she carefully reached past and opened the window. Scarcely had cold air begun to seep in through the gap than it ducked out and flapped unsteadily to a perch on the nearest tree, where it immediately began to clean its feathers.

She was glad to have rescued it, but what chaos it had left behind: droppings on the carpet, down floating in the air and masses of newspaper on the floor. Vera filled two large plastic bags and was just wondering whether to fetch a third for the rest of the mess when, under the last crumpled scraps of paper, she saw something blue with pink dots shining through. It was a book or notebook with a shiny laminated cover. Vera knew at once what chance had placed in her hands. With beating heart she extracted the book from the mass of paper and looked at it for a moment without opening it. She had seen similar books in local paper-shops with covers designed for every possible taste. The pink dots indicated a female owner, probably young. Lizzie.

This was the thing Craig Brett had wanted to come back for, and this was the reason Mrs Moore had recently

270

been through the house, not to mention Mr Lee who had in all probability been searching for it when he ostensibly came to prune the wisteria.

Brett had hidden it well. If the starling hadn't fallen down the chimney it could have been years before anyone found it. But what was so special about the book that he had to die for it?

The thought of the dead journalist made Vera want to put the book back into its hiding place and ignore it. But no. Nevertheless she faced an uncomfortable dilemma. She had at last come into possession of a document that might possibly provide answers to some or all of the questions about Southcombe that were nagging at her. It might even give an indication of the identity of Lizzie's murderer. If she kept the diary and said nothing about it, might Vera make herself guilty of withholding evidence? What should she do? If she mentioned it to Greg he would probably ask her to hand it over to him, and she could see that that was the most sensible thing to do.

While she put the plastic bags full of paper into the rubbish bin and cleared away the bird droppings she thought about taking her find with her and looking at it together with Greg. But when she reached the point of leaving the house Vera changed her mind again. She would read the diary alone and in peace and only then, depending on what it contained, decide what to do with it. But what should she do with it until she got back? After long reflection she stuffed the book back into the chimney together with fresh newspaper and then got changed. She briefly checked her hair in the mirror and left the house at about seven, aware of a current of excitement within her which she could not check. Ridiculous! she told herself, but part of her felt glad she could still feel like this.

A narrow strip of moon lit the way to Greg's cottage. Vera had smartened herself up to meet him. For the first time in weeks she had put on proper make-up and was wearing a dress instead of jeans and a sweater, the dark green one with a slit up the side which fortunately went with the only shoes she could walk in at all naturally after spending weeks in Wellingtons or trainers.

Even before she had entered his house, however, she realized that she had made a big mistake. Her whole outfit screamed that she had made a special effort whereas Greg greeted her in worn-out jeans and a lumberjack shirt, a glass of cider in his hand that he had already drunk from. Was he expecting her at all? She could see no sign of his having prepared for her visit. How out of place she felt, how ridiculous in her urban elegance! But Greg had warned her, she remembered. He had said he was terrible at housework, and that did indeed seem to be the case. A quick glance into the sitting-room confirmed it. The room was filled with all sorts of ill-matched second-hand furniture that had seen better days. There were piles of newspapers on the sofa, post on the dining table, and in the corner shirts, underpants and socks were hanging on a drying rack. The only source of light was the neon-lit aquarium in which fish of all colours floated amongst luminous green plants.

"An aquarium, how nice," said Vera as she walked in. She went up to the glass and peered into a spotlessly clean tropical scene full of grottoes and tree trunks, a kind of miniature paradise for fish and snails. This was a world for which Greg seemed to have plenty of time and energy.

"Yes, it's my pride and joy. When I get home from work in the evening I find it relaxing to look after my fish. They're my television, so to speak. But do sit down … wherever there's room. That chair's fairly comfortable still."

Vera pushed a rumpled blanket to one side and seated herself cautiously on the edge of the chair. She could feel the springs beneath the threadbare material and see greasy marks on the arms.

"Sorry," said Greg. "I keep meaning to give the place a proper sort out."

"Not at all, I'm fine," insisted Vera. "I won't keep you long anyway."

"But you'll have a cider with me, won't you?"

"To tell the truth, I'm not so keen on cider. I'd prefer water."

"You can't be serious! Apart from the fact that there's no fancy water in the house. I can offer you wine or whisky."

"In that case a glass of wine, please. Red, if you've got it."

While Greg opened the bottle Vera checked her stockings and pulled her bra straight, and even had time to check her reflection briefly in her handbag mirror.

Eyeliner still intact, mascara too, and by briefly pressing her lips together she made sure her lipstick was even. Though why she was bothering she didn't know. This had clearly been a mistake.

"Here you are. I don't know if it's any good," said Greg, returning with a bottle of red. French, Vera noted. "A friend of mine brought it along recently, but I don't often drink wine so I don't know a lot about it."

The wine was too young and acidic but Vera didn't react, just said, "It's good, thank you," before clearing her throat to show that she was now ready to get down to the matter in hand.

"I'd like to ask you a couple of questions about the village if you don't mind," she began. "Because I get the feeling there's something unpleasant going on here … something I don't understand."

Greg pushed the next best chair close to hers and sat down opposite her. He looked younger than she remembered and the colour of his hair lighter, maybe because of the glimmer from the harsh aquarium light. The difference in age unsettled her even if Greg himself seemed oblivious to it. He looked her over with the same open curiosity he had shown in the pub, not bothering to hide the fact that he found her attractive.

"Oh, that sounds exciting. What's been bothering you then? Why don't you tell me everything and I'll do my best to set your mind at rest."

Vera tried to tell her story in chronological sequence. She began with Sue Harper's death on the day of her arrival, explained to Greg that she found Nadja disturbingly changed, talked about the anonymous letter and her suspicion that Craig Brett's death in Watchet had been no accident. Finally she drew Mr Lee's lozenges from her bag and said, "And these are vitamins Mr Lee sells in his shop. My daughter has been given some by him but they look very different, and in any case I don't believe Mr Lee has any business manufacturing and selling medicines like these."

Greg listened without interrupting, occasionally raising an eyebrow or pursing his lips. As she spoke, however, Vera became uneasily aware that her worries could easily be dismissed as the work of an over-active imagination. Her voice faltered and she fell silent, waiting for Greg to speak.

"My dear lady," he said gently, "allow me to set your mind at rest immediately by making two things clear. Sue Harper was deeply depressed in the last months of her life, and there is absolutely no doubt at all that she killed herself. Her husband was out of the house, working in the kitchen of the Kings Arms, and she had given her baby to her mother to look after, which was not something she usually did. Believe me, Vera, it was suicide. The post-mortem report and the police enquiry both reached the same conclusion. The same applies to Craig Brett. He had an accident and fell, that's all there is to it. Perhaps it will reassure you to learn that I was personally involved in both cases."

Vera bit her lip in embarrassment and tried to gather her arguments together.

"But Mr Lee's lozenges – they're not right. I'm sure you're not allowed to sell medicines if you're not at least a chemist, which as far as I know he isn't. And he certainly isn't a doctor."

"No, he isn't. But his father, Reginald Lee, was. Haven't people told you about him? He was a real character."

Vera shook her head in embarrassment, though at the back of her mind she realized someone had spoken to her about Mr Lee. Was it Tom's mother?

"He was in charge of Greenhill Park when it was still a clinic for mentally disabled children, and at the same time acted as a kind of local guru, healing people with his herbal mixtures, laying hands on them and performing all sorts of … well, they were seen hereabouts as miracles. I don't know all the details, it was before my time, but he was much loved and respected, I know that much.

"Good old Bill here in the village is cut from the same cloth. He may only run a flower shop but he understands a thing or two about herbs. Old Mr Lee taught him all about them in the cradle, so to speak. And if he wants to earn a bit of money from his knowledge, what's wrong with that? In these difficult financial times you can't blame him, especially since not a single person besides you has complained so far. Satisfied?"

"And what about Lizzie … Mrs Moore's daughter? You're not telling me *she* died a natural death!"

"OK, that really is a tragic story." Greg took a sip of cider and stared past Vera, eyes fixed at a point on the wall behind her. He seemed to be searching for the right words and repeated, as if to himself, "Yes, extremely tragic." Then he sat up straight in his chair and turned his attention back to Vera. It was less admiring now and his voice seemed less sleepy. "How come you're asking about Lizzie, though? That's a long time ago, well before you and your daughter came to live here. What's the connection?"

"You probably think I'm putting together some kind of conspiracy theory, don't you?"

"No, I wouldn't dismiss anyone's worries out of hand. But I don't understand why you're getting so het up about a quiet little place like Southcombe."

"Greg, Mrs Moore recently searched my house. Why? And this morning my daughter's mother-in-law insisted I accompany her on a trip to the Levels. I kept on asking myself why, but when I got back I realized the answer. It was so that I would be out when Mr Lee came round to the house. He easily had enough time to search it, but neither of them found what they were looking for. I know that much at least."

She stopped herself from saying any more. Greg shook his head at her in amusement.

"Vera, I have to admit none of this makes any sense to me. I'm sure you're just imagining things. Mrs Moore's your landlady. Of course she has to look in on her property once in a while. And Bill Lee's a good friend to her, lending a hand with some tricky pruning, that's all. Please stop seeing anything more sinister in it than that. Though I must admit, I'm glad you came to me with your worries. I think I could enjoy setting your mind at rest even further, if you catch my drift? You're a good-looking woman, Vera … I find you very attractive, sitting in front of me with this expression of despair in your pretty face, extremely attractive. I have to control myself to stop myself taking you in my arms. – But what you're trying to tell me makes no sense at all."

She felt her face flood with heat. Avoiding his insistent gaze, she drank a gulp of wine to give her strength and, with a smile that was half apologetic and half triumphant, took the anonymous letter out of her bag, together with the list of names and dates from the St Aldusa gravestones in the cemetery.

Greg reluctantly turned his gaze to the letter. "Hmm," he said. "Well, yes, this is a malicious communication, no doubt about it. But you say yourself this arrived weeks ago and there's been nothing similar since. And it's hardly at the most threatening end of the spectrum. You're not taking it seriously, surely?"

"Yes, but the list. Five women's graves with the Aldusa motif on them … that must mean something."

"Where did you get the name Aldusa from?"

"From the internet, where else? Craig Brett did some research on it."

"And you've been doing some research on Craig Brett. Is that it?"

Greg's tone was less flirtatious than before and his face wore the beginnings of a frown. This encounter was not going at all the way Vera had hoped it would.

" In the end it's my daughter I'm most concerned about," she pleaded with him to understand. "People here seem to feel oddly possessive about her. She was this year's Apple Queen, for instance."

"Still is," said Greg, smiling again.

"But why Nadja – a comparative newcomer to the village? Heaven knows how the choice was made."

"There's no choosing involved. Whoever wins the main prize in the grand November raffle becomes our Apple Queen. If you hadn't passed your ticket on to your daughter, you would now be Queen."

"So it was pure chance?"

"Yes, if you want to put it like that. Now does this put an end to your worries? Is everything clear now?"

"No," said Vera stubbornly. "Because Lizzie's murder still hasn't been solved. Were you involved in that case too?"

"Of course. I'm the local officer. Poor kid," he sighed.

"Isn't there even a suspect?"

"Vera, I'm afraid I must draw a line here. Much as I like you, I can't and won't overstep the bounds of professional confidentiality. I'm sure you understand. Now, how about you and me have something to eat? It's nothing much, I'm afraid. Wish I'd made more of an effort, with you getting yourself all dressed up for me."

As Vera blushed for the second time that evening Greg stood up and let his hand rest briefly on her shoulder as he walked past.

"Let me give you some good advice, Vera," he said, leaning closer. "Leave Lizzie in peace. You didn't even know her."

That was clearly the end of it as far as Greg was concerned. Disappointed, Vera followed him into the kitchen and watched him empty a bag of salad on to two plates, arrange cherry tomatoes and cubes of cheese on top and then pour a ready-made dressing over the whole thing while bread was browning in the toaster behind him.

"I've got smoked salmon too, if you'd like some?"

He carried the two plates into the sitting-room and looked around in vain for a place to put them down. Both the dining table and the one in front of the sofa were covered with papers, on top of which a variety of everyday objects had ended up, from torches to electric cables and squash rackets.

"Do you mind if we eat with the plates on our laps?" he said, with a grin on his face that was meant to convey his carefree refusal to observe the social niceties. "I usually do."

Vera didn't know how to reply. She had imagined this evening so differently; had been prepared for some romantic overtures. Candles on a well-laid table, a simple but carefully prepared meal. Instead they sat beside each other on the uncomfortable sofa and poked around in oversize lettuce leaves, with the bubbling of the aquarium pump for background and only random flashes of illumination from the headlights of cars passing by outside.

Greg seemed to be in a good mood. He chatted volubly about his two failed marriages and how at peace he felt since he'd started living alone. He'd always lived in Somerset, it seemed. Couldn't imagine ever living anywhere else. He didn't show any particular interest in her life before Southcombe.

After she had swallowed the last piece of toast and gulped down another mouthful of sour wine, Vera took advantage of a moment of silence to return to her enquiries.

"Craig Brett made a thorough study of the wassailing ritual in Southcombe before he died. He even wanted to make a film about it. Did he ask you any questions relating to it? After all, as a Morris dancer you played an active role in it."

"Brett asked all us Morris dancers."

"What kind of questions did he ask you?"

"The usual ones about wassailing, as far as I remember. We told him it's all about the apples. They're Somerset's gold, and without wassailing there wouldn't be a good apple crop. Or that's what we reckon."

"But you don't really believe that apple trees need to have cider poured on them in order to bear fruit?"

"To bear especially juicy fruit, you should say. Yes, I believe that. We all do. The word 'wassail' comes from an Anglo-Saxon term which means more or less 'Be well' or 'Be healthy'. So all we're doing is wishing our trees good health."

"And what do you need an Apple Queen for?"

"What a question! Doesn't every ritual need a priest? The Apple Queen is our priestess. She makes the miracle of rebirth possible. If it really interests you I can lend you a little book on the subject. Everything's in there."

"That would help a lot, thank you. But I presume it doesn't contain any photos. The photographer who wanted to take pictures of this year's wassailing wasn't very well treated by the spectators."

"Oh, Vera, you worry too much. Can't you simply enjoy staying in Southcombe? Can't you enjoy just being here with me now?"

While he was speaking, Greg had put his empty plate on the floor and slipped his arm round her shoulders. She could feel his breath in her ear as he whispered, "Come on, Vera. Loosen up a bit. You're too serious. I can make you forget your worries. You're very elegant tonight. Can I flatter myself that it's for my sake?"

"I couldn't say that it's exactly for your sake. I normally get changed when I'm invited out, or when I go anywhere in the evening."

"But you weren't so chic that time in the pub when we got to know each other."

He gave the foreign word an exaggerated French accent and, visibly satisfied with the effect, added, "I've not held a woman as beautiful as you for a long time. You really are very special, Vera."

"Nonsense, Greg, I …"

She wanted to believe him although she knew that he was exaggerating and that the word 'beautiful' was simply a lie. She attempted to relax and give herself over to the tingling feeling of sitting next to a man who desired her. But when Greg without further ado buried his nose in her hair and began longingly to breathe in her scent and nibble at her ear lobe she suddenly felt a wave of disenchantment sweep over her. She looked at the two plates on the floor with the dampened crumbs of toast lying in the salad dressing, the desolation and disorder round about, the clichéed hunting prints on the walls, heard the bubbling pump of the aquarium and it was immediately clear to her: no, not with this man. Never.

"Greg, please, no. It's all too fast for me. I … I'm not yet ready for this."

Greg stopped at once. Was he annoyed? Or just disappointed? Vera didn't know. In any case he made no attempt to get her to change her mind but just said, "Pity," as with a loud sigh he withdrew his arm. Then he collected the plates from the floor and carried them into the kitchen.

"Please don't be angry,' she called after him.

"Why angry?"

"I mean, perhaps you thought that I …"

"Yes, I did think that, but it doesn't matter. Things don't always go the way you want them to. Shall I drive you home?"

"No, thank you. The short walk home will do me good."

"But it's raining."

"Doesn't matter. As you just said, things don't always go the way you want them to."

Chapter 21

"So you've lived with this business for five years – five years, Jason – and haven't done a thing about it? Just cleared off to France and hidden away in a chateau? In-credible."

"So what would you have done in my place?"

"Me?"

Zoë raised her glass and swirled the wine around it for a moment, thinking. She hesitated before answering, taking a long time to savour the aroma of the wine and smoothing the table-cloth before looking into his eyes and admitting sheepishly:

"To tell the truth, I don't know."

For the first time since he had moved in with her they were sitting opposite each other in a restaurant. It had been Zoë's idea. She had listened to his story for half the night until finally he lay exhausted in her arms, his face stained with tears. The following day they both felt drained.

"Come on, let's go out," Zoë said that evening. "I know a good restaurant in St Valéry that has the best mussels in the bay. It'll do us good. And there's been no sign of Miles, has there? I'm sure he's gone."

Sea mussels – another of Zoë's favourite dishes that he couldn't get used to. Like scallops and ox tongue, not to mention the horse steak she had once served up to him almost raw. Fortunately Nicol's also offered food acceptable to the English palate, and so he finally agreed to drive into town in Zoë's father's car that evening. Not that he was in a mood to eat or celebrate, God knows, but how could he turn down her request after she had listened to him so patiently and sympathetically for hours on end? And perhaps a proper meal and a change of scenery really would clear his mind.

Zoë looked especially eye-catching this evening. In her classic little black dress and a tightly cut velvet jacket, also black, which emphasized her figure, she looked like Audrey Hepburn in *Breakfast at Tiffany's*. As they walked into the restaurant Jason tried to make a compliment out of it, but she just turned round and shrugged her shoulders in surprise, asking, "Audrey Hepburn? No idea what she looked like. Did she have a black eye like mine?"

Was she really too young to know the film?

"But it's fine. If you want to call me Audrey, go ahead," she told him. "I've got nothing against it, it's a nice name."

"No, for me you'll always be Zoë. It's a lovely name."

"Perhaps. But not to me. It's my mother's name, too."

"And does that disturb you?"

"Oh, yes, very much so. I don't get on with her. She wanted to turn me into a dancer like she was, but that's not for me. I've never wanted to be what my mother is."

"Your cousin told me that you're a very talented dacer."

"Oh, Michel. What does he know about it? He's got no idea what it feels like to spend years being trained in something you're quite unsuited to."

"Couldn't you have refused?"

"You don't know my mother! She's as hard as nails. I'm glad she lives so far away. Things have been going much better for me since I've been living with my father. I just dance when I feel like it now, and that's less and less."

"I thought you wanted a career in dancing."

Zoë laughed aloud: "Not one bit."

"What do you want do in life then?"

"No idea at the moment. Before I got to know you I wanted to go travelling for a year. I'd so much like to see the Brazilian rain forest. The parrots, the Indians, the carnival, that must all be great fun and so colourful. But now I think I'd prefer to stay here."

As long as they talked about Zoë's life and plans, Jason could feel free of worries. He was genuinely interested in finding out what her hopes for the future were, and he was pleased that there was a place in it for him. Above all, though, he was loved. Every one of her glances, every gesture confirmed it, and that filled him with a confidence that was new. He at once understood what people meant when they said that they could move mountains.

"South America? There's an idea. I could go with you."

"No, Jason, we can't think of South America now. Not yet. There's something to be dealt with in Somerset first. That must come first."

She made it sound so simple.

"Luckily there's still some time before the autumn," he said, thinking aloud.

Zoë looked thoughtful.

"But that's not the crucial thing, is it? If it's true that your village needs an Apple Queen every year then one inhabitant is already in danger. Now, not just in the autumn."

"But we only choose an Apple Queen after years when there has been a bad crop. So it depends on last year's harvest. I can remember several years in succession in the past when there was no Apple Queen."

"All the same, you can't take the risk. How can you be certain there isn't one this year?"

He wasn't. And in any case he had already promised Zoë that for Lizzie's sake he would do everything he possibly could to put an end to the custom. Oh, Lizzie! His brave Lizzie! He had spent the whole afternoon telling Zoë about her and since then she felt more alive and real in his memory than she had for years.

Zoë reached out for his hand under the table and gently stroked his fingers. "Jason, I know you're still very hung up over what to do. After all, you grew up in that creepy village and lived exactly the same way as everyone else there. I get it. I'd probably have done the same in your position. But let an outsider appeal to your conscience: this wassailing of yours, this passion for apples and cider … it's absolutely crazy, it's warped and it's murderous. It can't go on, Jason. Think of your poor girlfriend."

He nodded, his head bent.

"I think of Lizzie the whole time. I've done nothing else for the past five years."

"That's the problem, isn't it? For as long as you don't actually do something about getting justice for Lizzie, you'll be trapped with your feelings of guilt and regret. And," Zoë added tentatively, "the two of us won't have a chance together. Your feelings of guilt will always lie between us and sooner or later they'll drive us apart."

She looked very sad as she said this, and suddenly older. He was responsible for that, he realized. He had to break this vicious cycle.

"I promise you, I'm going back to Southcombe to expose the whole business. But I've got to be careful how I go about it. You've seen for yourself what I'm up against."

She shuddered at the reminder and gently touched the bruise around her eye.

"The wassailing ritual is the key. As soon as we've got concrete evidence, you can go to the police with it. God, Jason, it makes me feel so sick to think about it! It's so … so brutal, so inhuman. When did it all start? Something criminal like this can't stretch back to the Middle

Ages. Someone would have spoken out against it, surely? It must have gone off the rails or been corrupted in the course of time. In the past your wassailing must have been just another harmless festival."

"I can't say how it was before the nineties, but for as long as I can remember there's been a raffle in the autumn after a bad harvest and then the Apple Queen is selected. I'm pretty sure everyone in the village knew about it. My family certainly did."

"Jason, I've got an idea. My father will be coming back from London at some point. You won't be able to stay here then anyway. Dad is pretty liberal but he has his limits. A boy-friend, OK, but then moving in with his daughter, he wouldn't like that."

"Right. But I can't go back to the chateau again. Miles is sure to have found out in the meantime that you were lying and he'll be waiting for me there."

"I wasn't thinking of the chateau. I was thinking of Somerset."

"You mean I should leave?"

"Not you. We. And the sooner we go the better."

"And what will your father say?"

"My father? Not a lot. A daughter who jumps into an aeroplane disturbs him much less than one who puts her boyfriend up in his house while he's away. Last year I once let Patrice stay the night and after that he really read me the riot act. Whoo, that was something! But travelling is different. I've often gone away without warning, and he doesn't even notice. His job in Abbeville completely monopolises him. You see, he's high up in an insurance company. Dark suit, white shirt, Yves Saint Laurent tie – that's how he goes around, my dad. Like the wicked bosses in films, with the difference that he's the softest hearted man in the world. And that he loves me above all else."

"I can understand that."

"But how are things on your side? To be specific: if we go to Somerset together, who is there who'll put you up? Have you still got family in the village – what's it called again?"

"Southcombe. Yes, my sister lives there. Our parents both died a couple of years ago. A ferry accident in the Baltic."

"Oh, how terrible. I'm so sorry, Jason."

"It's OK, it's some time ago now."

"But could we stay with your sister for a couple of days at least?"

"I'd rather not. Don't forget that I disappeared without trace from one day to the next. I expect she's still angry with me about that. She isn't exactly a straightforward person herself and her husband never particularly liked me. As far as he's concerned I'm an upstart simply because I decided to study medicine while he never got further than being assistant cook. So I don't really think it'd be a good idea to knock on her door as if nothing had happened. And there are other people in the village too, remember. Going there is dangerous for me."

"In that case we'll do things differently. We'll base ourselves in a B&B nearby and I'll go there on a recce. I can easily spend a couple of nights in the B&B belonging to your girlfriend's mother, which puts me right at the centre of things, though to tell the truth I'm dreading the apple tree … But there's no avoiding it, is there?"

"It's our best card, Zoë. But if you'd rather not …"

"Well, you can't stay with her, obviously. No, leave it to me, I'll do it. And perhaps I'll find something else that will help us at Mrs Moore's."

Zoë was visibly pleased with her idea and was getting impatient to sit down at the computer and plan the journey. However, she had ordered each of them a floating island as dessert, and when it arrived at the table with a glass of armagnac on the house she clapped her hands in delight and right up to the last spoonful forgot everything that had to do with Somerset and its dark secrets.

Chapter 22

Having arrived back home, Vera was almost able to laugh about her non-adventure with Greg. She was slipping into bed not with him, but at least with a document that promised to be more informative than he was. It helped her to get over the worst of the embarrassment.

Lizzie had a typical teenager's handwriting. It bore the signs of someone who had been trained at school to make their writing legible but at the same time rebellious touches signalled her need to assert her own personality: circles instead of dots over the i's, lapses into text spelling and frequent underlinings. It took a while for Vera to accustom herself to the style and rhythm of Lizzie's innermost thoughts.

The diary covered almost two years from April 2003 to July 2005. But Lizzie had not been able to fill more than half of the sixty pages, dying, Vera calculated, some two months after the last entry.

She had to make an effort to read it. As a mother she had always laid value on respecting her daughter's private realm. Nadja's letters and diaries had been a taboo, and if, when she was clearing up her room, he eyes lighted by chance on lines that were not intended for her she would blush as if she had been caught red-handed.

But Lizzie isn't my daughter, Vera thought to herself, as she tried to dismiss her scruples, and in any case she's been dead for nearly six years. But it was this last fact that caused Vera unease. Opening the book again on the first page, she felt like a voyeur secretly looking in on the world of a young girl. But that's not the case, she reassured herself. In the end it wasn't about Lizzie, who could no longer be helped, it was about Nadja.

The entries of the first months surprised Vera by their triviality. There was nothing sensational that anyone could have found gripping, not the slightest hint of a scandal and no unspeakable shame. Lizzie's life had followed the normal middle-class pattern of school and home. Now and then there were holidays in Cornwall or a birthday party, which were the cause of moderate degrees of happiness, and conversely there were minor tragedies like the death of Oscar, the old cat, or the departure of her best friend to northern England, things that seemed to have moved Lizzie but not to have shaken her.

Vera was surprised and shocked to discover that the predominant emotion that had driven Lizzie Moore was hatred: hatred of her mother, her brother, her teachers and her fellow pupils. With the exception of her father there was no one she did not secretly despise. It was everywhere, this hatred, spreading its feelers in every imaginable direction. Life was shit, she wrote, South-combe made her want to puke, the whole world was crap. And she herself was rubbish, scum, a freak, and other things that Vera would have had to look up in the dictionary in order to understand them.

However, after the first summer that was described there seemed to be a change in Lizzie's everyday life. She became more moderate in her expression, the swearing became rarer, and she occasionally included descriptions of minor highlights in her life. The mood was still dark, but not entirely without hope. The reason for this was a man whom Lizzie never actually named for fear that her mother – aka the Old Witch – would pry into her diary.

"I think he fancies me," a clearly blissful Lizzie confided to her diary on 16 October. Two weeks later she drank espresso with him at Starbucks in Taunton. And so it went on until December with sentences like, "I find him totally irresistible, especially his eyes." "He's much, much older than I am." "He's written me a love-letter." "I can't wait for him to kiss me. I mean properly kiss." And, "I'm so fucking in love I can't bear it."

Vera couldn't help smiling as she read on. Nadja had probably written similar things about her first boy-friends, lanky Lorenzo with that hangdog expression, and Jürg, a tennis fanatic from Langenthal, for whose sake she had had tennis lessons for a while. And she herself, Vera, hadn't she too had a girlish passion for a school-leaver that she had got to know at the leaving ball and straight after their first kiss had declared to be the man of her life? And thirty-eight years later she no longer knew what he was called or what he looked like.

Vera had already read a good third of the diary and was gradually losing interest in Lizzie's teenage woes when the entry for 21 December, 2003, made her sit up and pay attention.

"The 21st is absolute SHIT. Every year the same. Sitting around at home, hands folded in laps, best behaviour and God knows what other weird stuff. The worst thing: no music!! No television!! Nothing, absolutely NOTHING that's fun. That's what I call really over the top. And then the olds – what idiots! They drift around the house like ghosts and make a fuss if I talk too loud or go up the stairs too fast. The whole thing is stupid, STUPID! Believing nature needs this rest in order to recover. Recover from what? Well, they know where they can stick it. Thank God I'm seeing him tomorrow! First visit to the cinema together!"

So this was the explanation of a puzzle that Vera had never quite stopped thinking about. Now at last she knew why Southcombe seemed so deserted on 21 December, why all the shops were shut except for the Co-op and the state primary school, and why she hadn't met a soul on the streets. The reason why Nadja hadn't wanted to make Christmas cards that day. Vera leafed forward a year and for 21 December 2004 came across the following sentences: "Won the big lottery on Sunday! (Which is why the Old Witch is totally doing her nut.) So I thought that as Apple Queen I'd be let off this day-of-rest nonsense, but no: silence and boredom at home even for me. It's enough to make you scream!!!!"

Lizzie as Apple Queen. Vera found it difficult to imagine the sullen, rebellious girl playing this part. With so much rage in her belly, so much contempt for her parents and for the village, how could she have taken the role seriously?

Vera leafed back and read on expectantly. The love story with the unnamed man took its course and seemed wholly to absorb Lizzie. He lived in the village, worked as a medical assistant at Musgrove Hospital in Taunton, and liked taking her on walks into the Quantock and Blackdown Hills, on "real treks", as she wrote, "with rucksack and binoculars and a camera with a mega lens to take pictures of wild horses and birds".

Up until the raffle in December 2004 Lizzie had been a defiant brat, hopelessly in love, struggling with the usual problems of her age group. But her selection as Apple Queen, which at first made her happy, was just the start of more serious problems. The following February she complained for the first time of attacks of weakness. She felt funny, she wrote on 24 February, and didn't really want to eat all the fruit and vegetables that the Old Witch wanted to stuff her with. A few days later she had headaches: "Me and headaches! That's something totally new!"

After that there was a two-week gap, after which she confided to her diary: "Mr Lee has prescribed me pills. They're supposed to help. But I still feel sick, and I'm tired the whole time. And I look a total wreck. If this goes on he won't fancy me any longer. I told him but he said no, not at all, he was very proud that I was this year's Apple Queen."

That had been March 3. Nothing more until the 19th. On that day, a Friday, Lizzie described a visit to Mr Lee: "From now on I have to go to Mr Lee's a couple of times a week for lessons. I like him, actually, he can be funny, but what he is trying to teach me is crazy. Nature, always stupid nature. He says I must learn to identify with it. I don't want to do that at all. I'm not nature or an apple tree, I'm Elizabeth Moore. I don't want to drink weird tea and sit still with my eyes shut, feeling how my skin becomes bark and my feet become roots reaching into the earth. It's absolute nonsense. Even my olds believe it, at least the Old Witch and Stan do. Pops a bit less, perhaps, but what he says doesn't count, poor old Pops."

Having reached this point, Vera was strongly tempted to pick up the phone and rouse Nadja from her sleep. She had to take several deep breaths before she was calm enough to read any further. Lizzie's symptoms persisted. Tired, jaded, listless, she dragged herself through April and May until suddenly a spark of the old rebellious girl flared up again.

"I am now 100% certain that Mr Lee's pills are having an effect on me. The Old Witch says that's nonsense but I haven't taken any for the past three days and the world seems almost normal again. More or less. That's proof. In any case, I'm not going to just let things happen to me like before. I haven't got that wanting to die feeling either. That's gone, too. It was the damned pills that made me like that. He doesn't believe me. Pity. We often argue about it now. He thinks I shouldn't have run away from my training weekend in Washford. But he didn't have to be locked in that old cider farm and spend day and night listening to Mr Lee's family rubbish: his mother and his unborn sister and the father who had re-introduced wassailing after it having been forgotten for so many hundreds of years, and so on. Mr Lee has got a screw missing, no doubt about that, and his brothers, too. It's a good thing I ran away, otherwise I'd be a zombie by now. Three days of having that nonsense rammed down my throat and then the weird drinks … that would have been the end of me. One day was too much. It really did my head in. I did actually faint and when I came round I went on pretending to be unconscious, so he went back into the kitchen and I heard the damned mixer running and that was my chance. I ran like never before and hitched a lift back to Southcombe. The Old Witch's face was a picture when she saw me on the doorstep, I nearly fell over laughing."

Lizzie didn't seem to have told her parents anything about her doubts. On 28 May she definitely stopped taking the pills but continued attending Mr Lee's course, each time having to swear blind that she was following his schedule: three pills in the morning, at least two apples during the day, preferably uncooked, and in the evening before bed the mental identification exercises. Sometimes Mr Lee also invited other women from the village to his classes. A certain Miss Crabb was supposed to help Lizzie get to know the tradition of wassailing better, and Sue Harper the varieties of apples that were grown around Southcombe for the production of local cider. The same ones that Lizzie had to ingest.

"The Harper woman actually used the word 'ingest'! She must be from another planet. Unfortunately I can't avoid eating the stupid apples, the Old Witch keeps watch over me like the devil and I have to eat them in front of her, but I can cheat with the other stuff. He is still refusing to help me find out what the pills contain. And there's a laboratory in Musgrove he could use. What a wimp. I'd do anything for him, even if the whole of Southcombe condemned me for it. But he's still shilly-shallying. He thinks that as Apple Queen I've just got to go through with it, that it's an honour. Honour!!! Don't make me laugh. If he won't help me, I'll have to manage by myself. I don't need anyone. I'm strong. Pops always said I was."

Vera came to the last entry, dated 2 July. Lizzie was triumphant: "Yesterday on our way back, after we'd been for our walk on the Quantocks, he finally agreed to help me. I gave him the pills today and in a couple of days he'll be able to tell me everything that's in them. I know I'm right, those pills are pure poison. They did something to my head and I know that if I'd carried on taking them, I'd be believing all this nonsense Mr Lee is trying to drum into me. He must be crazy. Recently he hasn't been as jolly as he used to be and tells lots of gloomy stories about Greenhill. He wants me to go to the old apple tree sometimes in order to 'feel' it. That made me laugh in his face, and he scowled at me and said I was a little idiot. He never used to talk to me like that. I guess I offended him by laughing. In the end I had to promise to go and visit Greenhill Park one day. That calmed him down. But I'm not really going. It's different for him, he grew up there. The place is totally derelict, what is there for me there?"

Three weeks later Lizzie had been murdered in Greenhill Park. The diary didn't contain a direct reference to the identity of her murderer, but neither was it exactly what Greg would have called mundane stuff. At the very least, Mr Lee would have several questions to answer if Vera gave it to the police. By which, of course, she meant the area force, not Greg.

She would have given a great deal for someone to confide in, but after her last experience she was unsure who to turn to. What about Ahmed Haider? He had already tried twice to contact her, leaving messages on her answer-phone asking her to ring him back, saying it was urgent. She hadn't yet decided whether she would or not. He wouldn't want to help, she was sure, just to try and drag more information out of her.

A spontaneous visit to Nadja the next morning did nothing to calm Vera's fears. She found her daughter in pyjamas in the kitchen, busy crushing egg-shells that she mixed with a brownish liquid.

"I'm making fertilizer for the flowerbed at the back. The dahlias didn't do so well last year, this should help.

But don't just stand there, I'm sure you'd like a coffee. I'll make you one in a moment."

"No, you stay where you are. I can make the coffee. After all, you're the Apple Queen and I'm sure you're not supposed to be waiting on other people. If anything it's the other way round."

Vera leaned over her daughter from behind, put her arms round her and kissed her on the back of the head.

"I really, really love you, Nadja. I hope you know that."

"And I love you, Mum. Just think how nice it would be if you lived here. I mean, for ever. Then you could drop in at any time, or I could drop in on you. And in the summer you could come on bicycle rides with us."

After Nadja had squashed the last eggshell, she pushed the pestle and mortar to one side and rested her cheek on the table-cloth, sighing. The sun fell on her face and lit up the first sign of a crow's foot near her temple.

"Don't you want to think about getting dressed? It's almost ten. You never used to sleep this late," fretted Vera.

"I've been up since eight. In case you're interested, I've already cleared the sitting-room, put out bird food and filled the washing machine. And now I'm busy making fertilizer. Oh, Mum, I've just remembered something. Actually I've been wanting to ring you up these past few days to discuss it. I mentioned that Tom and I might want to start a family sooner than we originally planned. Do you remember?"

"Nadja, you're pregnant, how wonderful! That's why you've felt so tired recently. I'm so pleased for both of you."

"Wait a moment, don't get too excited. I'm not pregnant. That's what the problem is. Tom was the one who was pushing for it. I was more in favour of waiting a bit, but now it suddenly seems to be the other way round, and I don't understand it."

Vera hugged Nadja closer and rocked her back and forth a little.

"Come on, come on, I'm sure you're just imagining it."

"No. Tom told me quite clearly, he doesn't want a child. Just when I'm ready to try, he isn't. Isn't that silly?"

"I'm sure he's got his reasons for wanting to wait."

"But he didn't say anything about waiting, just that he doesn't want a child, full stop. We discussed it until late last night, but I can't change his mind. He's suddenly terribly stubborn about it. It's such a pity … But weren't you going to make us a coffee?"

"Yes, of course."

"It's on the lower shelf on the left. I'll just nip out into the garden with the fertilizer. Back in a moment."

Vera watched her go, surprised that Nadja could apparently dismiss the subject of children so easily. Presumably she was confident of getting round Tom, one way or another. Vera found the coffee behind a row of nutritional supplements: zinc, phosphorus, vitamin B complex and Mr Lee's jar of pills. It was almost empty already, Vera found, and there was the next one waiting.

"You really ought to be bursting with vitality after all the supplements you're taking," she said as Nadja came back into the kitchen. "Don't you think that all the fruit and vegetables from your raffle prize should be enough?"

But Nadja had clearly been weeping. So Vera had been wrong about her not taking Tom's refusal seriously. Vera felt angry on her daughter's behalf. What was wrong with Tom, chopping and changing like this?

Would there ever be a more suitable moment for a proper discussion? For the first time since their argument in the café Nadja was evidently ready to pour out her heart and ask for Vera's advice.

"Come on, Nadja, sit down next to me and let's have a chat. Like we used to in Bern. Do you remember how well we got on together then?"

Nadja's eyes filled with tears again. She nodded silently and wiped her face dry with her sleeve.

"Do you really think I haven't noticed the change in you? I'm worried, Nadja. Please forget what I said in the café that time. I'm not concerned about your career, really I'm not, only about your health. Your well-being. That's so much more important, believe me."

"But there's nothing wrong with me, Mum. I can promise you that. I'm as fit as a fiddle. Just … sad. Yes, that's it really. Sometimes I think I'd like to die, then I'd have peace. Did you ever feel like that?"

Vera didn't like the sound of that, Nadja talking about death. But she wasn't going to risk their new-found closeness by saying so and chose her words carefully.

"I've known sadness, Nadja. Of course I have. I miss your father very much. Still haven't got used to the idea that he will never be with us again. That often makes me very sad."

"Of course, I often think about Dad too. But I don't think that's the reason why I'm so down. After all, things are going well for me. I've got Tom, you're here now, and I fit into the village so well that I can't imagine living anywhere else."

"How long have you been feeling depressed, then?"

"I don't know exactly. It's not the kind of thing that happens from one day to the next. For a couple of weeks or so, I reckon."

"Since you've been taking Mr Lee's pills, perhaps?"

Nadja recoiled in surprise. "What makes you say that?"

"Just an idea. Intuition if you like."

"No, Mr Lee's pills are excellent. I think I'd feel much worse without them."

"Nadja, I'm not so sure, and I want you to listen carefully to what I'm going to say. I didn't want to talk about it to you yet because I don't understand everything myself, but there's one thing I do know for certain: there's something very wrong about the wassailing ritual in which you played the part of the Apple Queen. In fact, it's quite possible that you're in danger."

"In danger? What kind of nonsense is this?"

"You're taking lessons from Mr Lee, aren't you?"

"Yes, isn't that allowed?"

"You're supposed to learn from him how to identify with nature?"

"Well, yes, but …"

"Contradict me if I'm wrong, but during these lessons, if that's the right word, you have to sit there with your eyes shut and imagine that you're an apple tree or something like that. Am I right?"

"How do you know? Who told you?"

"I've read it, Nadja."

"No one writes about it. Mr Lee says that everything that happens during our lessons remains the Apple Queen's secret."

"But you aren't the only Apple Queen. Remember, there have been others before you. One of them has written about it."

"Who? Sue Harper?"

"Sue Harper! No, but why her in particular?"

"Well, because she was last year's Apple Queen."

"And now she's dead. Like Lizzie. You see, she too was an Apple Queen. Did you know that?"

Nadja stared out of the window and for a long time said nothing.

"Lizzie?" she finally asked. "Eileen's daughter? No, I didn't know that. But now I understand better why she takes such special care of me. She must miss her daughter very much."

"Nadja, please think about this. Two Apple Queens dead – don't you find that worrying?"

"It's pure chance. And what's it got to do with me? One of them I didn't know and the other threw herself out of a window."

"Sue Harper was depressed. Or, if you prefer, sad. Just like you."

"But I've got no intention of jumping out of a window, if that's what you're afraid of."

"Perhaps that wasn't her intention either. Nadja, I don't know what to make of all this, but perhaps you can help me at least to understand the wassailing ritual better. Do you remember the journalist who died, Craig Brett? He wanted to make a film or publish an article about the Southcombe ceremony. He was firmly convinced that there was something special about wassailing here."

"Yes, I remember him. He really pumped us dry on that one."

"Try to remember his questions if you can. It's important, Nadja."

She stared into her cup while she tried to remember more precisely the conversations with Brett.

"What interested him most, I think, was the role of the Apple Queen during the ritual. Helen Dean, the woman from the café, described it in detail to him. Now I understand the ritual myself much better, but at that time I let Helen do the talking because she knew more about it than I did. I had watched Sue Harper the year before, but without paying attention to details. To tell the truth, the whole business left me pretty cold. I found it a bit weird, like you do now."

"Can you tell me what instructions you were given for your role?"

Nadja stared out of the window. Even while she was speaking she didn't look away from the garden gate, at which passers-by would occasional stop to admire the flaming yellow daffodils running the whole length of the Apple Queen's garden path.

"You were at the wassailing yourself," she said, defensive at first, but eventually she gave in and began to list the individual tasks: "So, first I had to dip five slices of toast in cider and hang these on the tree. Then the roots of the tree had to have cider poured over them – no, first there was the leather purse. I had to bury that between the roots."

"What was in the purse?"

"No idea. It wasn't very heavy anyway. But I remember that I was told to be particularly careful with it because it was valuable or something like that. And then the tree roots. That's all, really. If wassailing interests you so much, I'll give you a little book about it. Wait, I'll just fetch it before I forget."

"Like Coleridge's ballads, I suppose?" said Vera, joking.

"Oh, right. How silly of me. I'll give you them at the same time."

"You don't need to. I bought myself a copy in Taunton. But they're not so easy to read, those ballads. Maybe you ought to give me some English lessons. I'm sure they taught you all about Coleridge's Romantic vocabulary at university."

Nadja stood up and shuffled over to the drawing-room bookcase. Vera felt sad to see her lovely young daughter moving like an old woman. Whatever was wrong with Nadja, Vera was sure it was nothing as simple as mild depression.

"It must be here somewhere. But … here we are, Tom was looking at it recently and didn't put it back in the right place."

The booklet about the wassailing ritual was the same as the one Greg had given Vera, which she had intentionally left behind. The last thing she needed after the disappointment of her evening with him was the thought that she would have to take it back to him.

"Thank you, Nadja. I'm sure this will be useful."

"Mum, were you serious when you said I could be in danger? That sounds so melodramatic. Everyone's so nice to me here in Southcombe, people like me, and since I've become Apple Queen even more so."

"All the same, I'd prefer it if for a start you'd stop taking Mr Lee's funny pills. I don't trust them."

"But I do. Mr Lee is THE herb man in Somerset. He is thinking seriously about opening a clinic for alternative medicine in the village. People here admire him, and they all go to him rather than the doctor in Taunton."

"In that case I'm sure he'll give me all the details when I ask him directly what the pills he gives you contain. There's no information at all on the jar, and the ones he sells over the counter have their ingredients listed."

"But you won't find Mr Lee in the shop today. It's shut until further notice. His brother or half-brother or some other near relative died the day before yesterday. Didn't you hear about it?"

"No, how could I?"

"There's a big item in the *Somerset Gazette* about it, and yesterday there was even something about it on the local television news. The man was drowned in Blue Anchor the night before last. Got stuck in the mud, the tide came in over him and he couldn't get away."

"That's horrific."

"Yes, just imagine … terrible. That's why there are those warning signs all down the coast. People often don't take them seriously and then helicopters have to be sent to rescue people caught on the sand. That's always happening."

Vera remembered having seen signs like that on the beach at Watchet. She had thought the warnings exaggerated. The sand seemed so harmless, so reliably firm. Though Craig Brett had died there.

"Shall I come some of the way home with you? I can be ready in three minutes."

"But I'm not going home, Nadja. I want to get out of the village today. The sun is shining for practically the first time since I arrived. The sky is even blue, look, not a cloud to be seen. I want to take advantage of that before it rains again. Why don't you come with me?"

Her daughter looked anxious.

"But isn't it too windy? How long do you want to stay away?"

"Just a couple of hours. We could drive up on to the Quantocks together. I've never been up there. And we'll stay as long as you want to, you can decide."

"OK, Mum. You have a look at the booklet while I have a shower and get dressed. It won't take you long."

Vera parked the car where Nadja recommended, at the top of a steep hill near Crowcombe Park Gate. Wild ponies were standing in the shade of a beech grove and sheep were nibbling the grass. A path led over the range of hills down to Holford. Nadja explained that more than two hundred years ago the two writers Coleridge and Wordsworth had met on this path almost every day to discuss the ballads they were writing together.

"Coleridge came from over there – without his wife because she had to stay at home and look after their baby – and Wordsworth and his sister Dorothy came from Holford. For a while the three of them were inseparable, as you can read in Dorothy's diary. She describes the Quantocks in all kinds of weather, including at night by moonlight. It's a wonderful read. Although she stood in the shadow of the two men, as was inevitable in those days, she writes very lyrical English."

Nadja became animated and let herself be sufficiently carried away to recite a couple of stanzas of Coleridge's 'Ancient Mariner'. Vera listened without interrupting, grateful that her daughter's enthusiasm for English literature hadn't been entirely extinguished. Nadja seemed more relaxed here than she had been in a long time. She was enjoying the view over to the sea, just visible between the tree-covered hills, and said she was looking forward to Easter when she was going to drive to Oxford with Tom for a couple of days.

"But the first thing is to make some Easter cards," she said, laughing. "I got the materials a few days ago. With precise instructions, of course."

"So even as Apple Queen you are not free from all tasks in the village."

"Clearly not. Will you help me again? It's more fun together than alone."

Nadja had begun the walk full of zest, but before the path descended through sparse beech woods to Holford she begged to turn round.

"I'm tired, always am at this time of day. I usually have a little midday nap, and then I'm on my feet again. But the wet grass here isn't any good for lying on."

They had been walking for three-quarters of an hour on level ground but needed longer on the way back because Nadja kept on stopping to get her breath back and rub her legs.

"I don't know if you really are as fit as you claim to be," Vera told her. "A walk like this ought to be as easy as pie at your age."

"Mr Lee takes my pulse regularly and listens to my heart. He says that everything's fine, and I believe him. He knows what he's talking about."

"But I don't see why a man who runs a flower-shop should be concerned with your health. I'd prefer it if you went to a proper doctor. I'm happy to take you to Taunton."

"There's no need for that, Mum. Really."

"Do it for my sake, then. Please."

By now they had reached the car. The horses were still standing at the same place, three mares and a foal that hid anxiously behind its mother when Nadja went up to it with outstretched hand.

The horses were a useful pretext for not replying to Vera. On the way back she spent the whole time talking about them, saying that one day she would love to go to the auction at London Farm in September when Quantock ponies like those were sold.

"If I had the money I'd buy one. They're not only very beautiful but also ideally suited to bad weather conditions because they spend the whole winter up here in the open …"

"Nadja, that's enough about horses! I asked you if you'd let a doctor examine you, for my sake, and I'm still waiting for an answer. I'm asking you again: please."

However, Vera received no reply until they drove into Church Street. Only as she was about to get out did Nadja lean over briefly, kiss Vera on the cheek and say in a non-committal kind of way:

"If I do it, then it's really only for you, Mum. And in return you must promise to stop fussing over me. I'll think about it. Bye, and thanks for the trip."

Chapter 23

The plane was late landing at Bristol because of strong winds over the Channel. When they reached the baggage reclaim area Zoë suggested spending the night in a hotel nearby before catching the train across to the north-west of Somerset.

Jason worried about the cost, but she interrupted him after the first sentence: "Come on, a few pounds more won't make much difference. It's not as if you did so badly out of Rich and Frances, and I've got my own money."

"I *didn't* do so badly out of them. I can't bank on them wanting me back now when I tell them I've spent so long away from the chateau."

"Huh, that's one thing you don't have to worry about. They'll never find anyone else who's willing to stick it out alone there. They'll welcome you back with open arms – if that's what you want, of course."

When Zoë's rucksack appeared on the carousel – a splash of brilliant red in the middle of indistinguishable dark bags and suitcases – she put her arms round Jason's neck, kissed him on the mouth and whispered, "Now our adventure can begin. Don't worry, we'll manage it together."

She had noticed his increasing restlessness but stopped herself from commenting on it. He had scarcely spoken a word on the plane, just leafed through the EasyJet magazine or sat with his eyes closed. The prospect of soon being back on English soil awoke the old sense of claustrophobia and panic. His hand, which Zoë had held in hers during the whole of the flight, felt cold and damp. But now that they were at the airport exit, battling through wind and rain to find the bus into town, he was in control of himself again. The country that he had avoided for five long years received him with its familiar smells and the language of his childhood. Suddenly he was no longer a foreigner, he knew where he was truly at home. Zoë, on the other hand, had seen nothing of this country apart from London and Brighton, where she had once spent a holiday as a child, and was curious about everything.

"It's a pity it's so dark that we can't see a thing apart from traffic lights and trees," she said as the bus drove out of the airport. "We might just as well be in France."

From the window of the hotel room, too, she looked out in the vain hope of seeing something 'typically English'.

"I don't know what I imagined, but all I can see is a motorway loop, a forest of road signs, and over there a McDonald's. I'm sure that's not what you see in picture books about England."

"But you can't expect to find the perfect rural idyll ten minutes from an airport."

"No, I suppose not."

Disappointed, she turned away from the window and inspected the bathroom while Jason took his shoes off and collapsed on the bed.

"Unbelievably clean, the bathroom. And there's even a good selection of bathy things. Have a smell. Which do you like best, pomegranate, lavender or rose?"

"Mmm, do I have to? They all smell pretty much the same to me."

"No, come on, tell me, which do you like best? I'm going to treat myself to half an hour in the bath and when I get out I'll smell of something you like. Or even better, you get into the bath with me, and then we'll both smell good."

"What? Now? At a quarter to eleven?"

But Zoë was already back in the bathroom filling the bath with water and called, "Which one, then?"

"I don't mind. Pomegranate."

"It's all the same to you, isn't it? Like with food. Pomegranate or lavender, trout *au bleu* or *à la meunière*, chocolate black or milk. How boring, Jason. Is it all the same to you which item of clothing I begin with? With the jacket or the tights?"

While she was talking, Zoë had already begun to get undressed in front of him. Her eyes shining seductively, she slowly undid the zip on her knitted jacket, hesitated for a moment as if changing her mind, and then pulled it down a little further, finally letting the jacket slip to the floor. Jason wanted to express his approval, but Zoë told him to be patient and was now swinging her hips in circles as she undid the buttons of her jeans, peeling them off, inch by inch. She had told him that she didn't enjoy dancing any more, but there was no sign of that now. Every one of her movements was graceful and followed an inner rhythm of controlled excitement. There was no need for music. By the end she was standing in the middle of a pile of clothes. When she reached across to Jason, it seemed to him like the curtain coming down after an overwhelming performance.

"Come on, the water'll be overflowing if we don't hurry up."

Jason had only ever made love to Lizzie in the open air, in clearings, once even in a haystack. She had been his summer girl, while he would always associate Zoë with this extraordinary winter. She would always make him think of snow and ice, but also of a warm bed, a refuge under the pillows, where they entwined their shivering limbs until they sang with warmth.

And now a hot bath. Their bodies were islands in a sea of bursting pomegranate foam, Zoë's breasts were scented fruit. He stroked them with his softened hands, sucked on them until the nipples hardened like little buds, while she took him into herself, her face just out of the water, framed by a garland of dark plant-like fronds that at every movement separated into different shapes and then came together again. Foam flew as, amongst the swirl of the water, she cried out loud and had to grip the edge of the bath, panting, in order not to sink down, and then she couldn't help laughing when she saw his dripping face above her and later, as she was getting out of the bath, became aware of the water flooding across the floor.

When Jason woke up the next morning Zoë was already dressed, sitting on the edge of the bed, sending a text message.

"Good morning, Mr Dormouse," she said, without looking up from her mobile. "My father is wondering why I'm in England. He wants me to come to London to meet his new girl-friend. Someone called Fiona. I'm just writing to say that I can't at the moment."

She was in a particularly good mood, ready to find everything wonderful: the English breakfast, the flooded plain that they later crossed by train, even Taunton Station. The B&B they finally settled on was near it at the end of a cul de sac, a small villa whose ground floor had been turned by the owner into a little sculpture gallery.

"My pride and joy," said Mr Pyke, glowing with satisfaction, as he took Zoë and Jason up to their room. "My wooden carvings keep me company. I never get bored when I'm with them. I'm divorced, you know, and have been living here for a good eight years. And where do you come from? I can tell the lady isn't local – I've got a good ear for these things. Let me guess: Canadian? French?"

"French it is."

"Ah, vive la France!"

Mr Pyke hummed a couple of snatches from the *Marseillaise* before giving them the keys to the room and the main entrance and taking leave of Zoë with an exaggerated bow.

"He may be a bit bonkers, but at least he's friendly," giggled Zoë after he had left. "But now let's be serious. We've got work to do."

Jason opened Zoë's rucksack and began pouring its contents onto the bed.

"Watch out, don't scrumple my blouses. I folded them up carefully. And as soon as you've put your clothes in the cupboard you can put my blouses and the other stuff back in the rucksack. I'm moving on tomorrow and I'll need the rucksack."

Jason didn't like being reminded of the coming days. Zoë alone in Southcombe! What would she find? More important and more worrying was the question what would happen to her there. She tried to reassure him that in the first instance it was only a question of finding out who, if anyone, was this year's Apple Queen. Jason kept on thinking of dangers that Zoë would be exposed to.

"It's not a good idea to let you go to Southcombe on your own. I ought to be going with you, Zoë. You don't know these people. They'll do anything to preserve their wassailing."

"And we're ready to do anything to put a stop to it. Don't forget that, Jason. We've got a job to do, and we'll do it."

"And then there's Miles. He didn't find us in St Valéry, and that makes me worried. Something must have happened, otherwise he'd have come across us. He only needed to keep his ear to the ground and he'd have found out that you lied. You yourself told me that time in La Civette that I was known as the local hermit. If he's given up looking for me in St Valéry there must be a reason for it. Not knowing what that reason is makes me scared. Just imagine him having come back to South-combe. What'll you do if you meet him on the street? I don't dare think of it."

"In that case don't think of it. We can't change our minds now. I'm going to Southcombe tomorrow, whe-ther Miles is there or not. And you'll stay here, please, and make sure you don't get involved in any stupid ad-ventures. That could only make things more difficult."

"Yes, Mummy Zoë. Am I allowed to say anything?"

"No, I'm afraid not for the moment."

The next day Jason had a heavy heart as Zoë packed her red rucksack to leave. He feared for her in South-combe, dreading the thought of her encountering Miles there. The fact that he had not come after them in France seemed to indicate that the Wolf had returned to home territory. But Zoë dismissed his fears.

"I'm the last person he'll be looking out for there. Besides, I don't believe he'd even recognize me. He bare-ly looked at me, you see, all the time he was … I wasn't a person to him, just a thing he had to destroy. He prob-ably thinks he succeeded."

Zoë shivered and forced herself to sound brisk and unafraid.

"I'll send you texts to keep you up to date. I've got a map with me, and once I've got the apple tree behind me everything'll be all right. And then you'll be able to go back to your own village at last. Isn't that a reason to be happy?"

"Yes, of course," admitted Jason, "but …"

He just had time to kiss Zoë and press a note into her hand before the doors closed and the bus set off.

There were nine stops to Southcombe, about twenty minutes in the bus through dilapidated suburbs which only gradually gave way to Somerset's lush rural landscape. Outside the 40 Commando Royal Marines camp in Pen Elm two uniformed soldiers got on to the bus and talked about a colleague who had recently been killed in Afghanistan. Zoë shuddered and looked down at the hand-written note in her hand. "Zoë," she read, "you are the most wonderful woman in the world. I love you more than my own life. For God's sake, take care!!! Come back, I need you. Your Jason."

In Southcombe everything looked quite different from the way that it had been described to her. The pub was bigger and lighter than she had imagined it, and she would never have expected Mulberry Lane to be so narrow or so thickly bordered by trees and shrubs. Birch Cottage, on the other hand, more or less matched her expectations: Jason had described the house as Victorian, dark and creepy. Zoë knew what he meant from her experience of London. In Hampstead Heath, where her father's great-aunt had lived, there were whole streets of

Victorian villas like that with bay windows, dark, damp corners and little towers smothered by ivy. As a small child she had always had a queasy feeling when going through Auntie Mabel's road, especially under a cloud-laden sky.

Now, as she opened the door to Birch Cottage, she remembered that road in London and her slight feeling of anxiety about a calamity that she could not name. At least today she knew why her heart was beating so wildly. After all, she was on the point of getting to know Mrs Moore, the mother of the girl that Jason had loved and had seen die in such a cruel way.

At her first touch of the bell Zoë could hear the barking of excited dogs, and when the door opened a terrier squeezed through the gap and began sniffing around her legs. Another stayed two feet away, panting loudly.

"Maisie, stop that now. Heel! I do apologize, she's such a naughty little thing, I just don't know what to do with her. But do come in! You must be the lady who rang me from France the day before yesterday … Miss Cox?"

"Yes. I'd like a room for a couple of nights, but I don't know exactly how long I'll be staying."

"That's not a problem. At the moment I've only one guest, and I'm not expecting any others this month. Somerset isn't particularly attractive to tourists in February. What brings you here, if I may ask? Do you have friends or relatives in the village?"

"No, I'm going on to Exeter. I'm waiting for a friend who's going to fly direct from Nice. We're thinking of studying in England next year and want to visit various possible universities beforehand. Exeter's got a good reputation."

"There was never any choice like that in my day. You young people have so many options these days, it's enough to make one envious."

Zoë was given the blue room at the rear of the house, the one with, as Mrs Moore proudly declared, a view over unspoiled woodland.

"How lovely," cried Zoë. "It'd be great to stay a bit longer and have a holiday here."

Mrs Moore tightened the corners of her mouth into a polite smile. She was evidently used to receiving compliments on her house.

"I hope you enjoy your stay at Birch Cottage, Miss Cox. Just let me know if you need anything. I gave you the keys, didn't I? I'll be out for a couple of hours this afternoon. There's a funeral in the village."

The room was tasteful and well supplied: Mrs Moore hadn't stinted with the soaps, shampoos, tea-bags and biscuits. Zoë examined everything with curiosity, passed her hand over the silk bed-cover, felt the heavy material of the curtains and opened drawers in which she found besides the hair-dryer and the Bible the most recent numbers of *Country Life* and *Dog Fancy*.

If Jason hadn't told her the story of Lizzie she might have been inclined to like Mrs Moore. She thought of her own mother and tried to imagine what it would have been like to grow up as the daughter of a discreet and reasonable woman like this instead of a coquettish prima donna who could never deal with the ageing process, let alone reconcile herself to it. But, polished as Mrs Moore was in her manners, Zoë could not let herself forget that she had allowed her own daughter to take the path leading to her doom.

"That's all very well," Zoë said to herself aloud, "but thoughts like these aren't going to get me anywhere. What do I do now?"

Jason had given her a couple of names and addresses that she had written down in a notebook. And there was the apple tree in Greenhill Park. If he had told the truth ... She shuddered to think of it and turned back to her list of names. She decided to go through them in order and made her way first to the Kings Arms. There was just one guest sitting at the corner table by the fireplace drinking cider. The barmaid was filing her fingernails wearily while the barman wrote up the week's new menus on the blackboard.

Zoë sat down at the bar and ordered tea, at which the barmaid raised her eyebrows in surprise, put the file behind her ear and stood up.

"Tea?" she asked doubtfully. "You want tea?"

"Yes, please. And there's something I wanted to ask, too. It's about Mr Harper. I've heard that he works here. Is that right?"

"Yes, but not at the moment. Why?"

The barman stopped writing and pointed to the kitchen: "Rupert's the chef here. He doesn't arrive until five. And maybe a bit later today because of the funeral."

Zoë took her tea and put her hands round the cup to warm them.

"You're looking for Rupert Harper, are you?"

The question came from the corner by the fireplace. The man had put down his newspaper and was looking at Zoë with unconcealed curiosity. He was Asian, dressed in a fashionable suit and steel-framed glasses.

"That's right," replied Zoë cautiously.

"So am I. I'm waiting for him here."

Zoë burned her tongue on the tea because she drank it so fast, but she was suddenly in a hurry to get out of the pub and into the open air. The stranger seemed to want to engage her in conversation, He even introduced himself by name and asked her for hers. But this kind of chance encounter in the village was what she was keenest to avoid. What did this Ahmed Haider think he was doing, sticking his nose in like this? Anyway Jason hadn't mentioned him at all and the man's pushiness made her suspicious. She left with an abrupt "'Bye", and when she was outside the first thing she did was send Jason a text: *"Do you know an Ahmed Haider? Z. xxx"*

She wasn't alone for long. Haider caught up with her outside the primary school and to her irritation addressed her as "Mademoiselle".

"You must be French, aren't you?"

"So what?"

"Your English is almost faultless. I congratulate you! Don't you think it's strange that there should be two people wanting to speak to Rupert Harper today?"

Zoë thought for a while before replying. Of course the stranger was right, it really was strange, it could hardly be pure chance. At that moment her mobile rang. It was Jason texting her back: "*No. Be careful. J. xxx*"

"I'm sorry, what were you just saying?"

"I was wondering whether perhaps we've got the same reason for wanting to talk to Rupert Harper."

"I doubt it so let's each of us go our own way. I don't like people accosting me in the street, Mr Haider! That doesn't work with me."

He tried to justify himself but Zoë had already turned away and, because of the church bells which had just begun to ring out above them, didn't hear what he called after her.

Luckily she had jotted down Rupert and Sue Harper's address in her notebook and once she had shaken off Haider by doing a tour of the village she knocked on their door. Jason had told her that he had lived in very cramped conditions with his sister and Rupert, and he hadn't exaggerated. As one in a line of identical terraced villas, the Harpers' looked particularly small, not least because of the bush that took up the whole of the tiny front garden.

A small child opened the door, naked apart from his Pampers.

"Hello, I'm Zoë. Are your parents in?"

The boy stood silently in the doorway and stared at her with big brown eyes. Only when Zoë repeated her question did he breathe "Yes" and then run back down the corridor, shouting, "Daddy, Daddy", until Rupert Harper came down the stairs. Big on ego as well as muscles, thought Zoë as he stood in front of her, legs astride. The sweaty T-shirt and the towel round his neck showed that he had just come in from some kind of sporting activity.

"I'm not buying anything and I'm not signing any petitions. Apart from that I haven't got time, I'm dashing over to the church for a funeral. You're not getting anything from me."

"No, no, that's not why I'm here. I've got some news for Sue, your wife."

Rupert Harper's face darkened.

"In that case you're a bit too late. She's been dead for over two months. Who are you?"

"My name is Zoë Cox and I wanted to …, I was supposed to pass on greetings to your wife. But of course I didn't know … My sincerest condolences, Mr Harper. My visit must seem terribly tasteless."

"Whose greetings?"

"Her brother's."

"Hang on a moment … you don't mean Jason, do you?"

"Yes, I do."

Harper spat on to the tarmac, not noticing that the child had just squeezed through his legs and was scurrying away towards the nearest parked car.

"I just don't get it, that idiot getting in touch after five years … What an arsehole! Who'd have thought it? And even then he hasn't got the guts to come himself, no, he sends some girl in advance. Shit, I've never known such a fucking coward. What I'd like to know is …"

His first sentence had made Zoë redden with rage.

"Mr Harper," she interrupted him, spluttering, " Jason is not a coward, I am not 'some girl'… and you should look after your child better." She jumped into the road as she spoke, snatching the child out of the path of a car which was turning the corner

"And what about some clothes? Really, in this weather!"

Zoë went back to Birch Cottage, raging but also worried. She had scarcely closed the door to her room before she rang Jason's number. She had to inform him of his sister's death as gently as possible, but above all she wanted reassurance from him that everything else was in order and she had done the right thing. But had she?

"Jason, Jason, please answer," she begged, and shook her mobile as if she could magic his voice out of it. When he hadn't answered after she had rung for the fourth time she angrily threw the mobile into a corner of the room and sat down cross-legged on the bed.

Even though the church was at the end of the village, the bells sounded almost as loud here as they had at the Harpers', who lived opposite it. Zoë was surprised that they made such a noise and looked at her watch: ten to three. The house itself was silent. She couldn't hear anybody moving or the dogs barking and she could hear nothing from the room next to hers when she pressed her ear to the wall. She was alone in the house. Hadn't Mrs Moore announced that she would be at a funeral in the afternoon?

Zoë opened the door to her room a crack and listened. A clock was ticking on the wall and there were some sparrows twittering in the garden. She went down the stairs on tiptoe and looked round the rooms that she had simply walked past when she arrived. Not that she was interested in fine crockery, silver cutlery or Wedgwood vases. But amidst these old-fashioned pieces of bric-a-brac Mrs Moore had put framed photos of her family. Photos of her husband and her son at every stage in their lives and a small number, just four, of Lizzie.

So that was Jason's girlfriend. At last she had a face and was no longer the ghostlike being that Zoë had sometimes imagined as extraordinarily beautiful, and sometimes as just shapeless and ungainly. When she looked closer she could see that she was neither the one nor the other, in fact criteria like that were irrelevant given the quite extraordinary expression in her eyes. Zoë turned a frame around and read that the photo dated from 2005, the year in which Lizzie died. The girl was wearing a purple and black striped blouse that was so tight over her chest that the white bra was visible between the buttons. The piercing on her left eyebrow was the only piece of jewellery she wore. Lizzie was pouting, but you could see that it wasn't out of feminine coquetry but because she was having to pose for a photo against her will or else because she resented the photographer. Her eyes, green or light brown, were heavily made up, but no eyeliner, however thick, no eyelashes, however gooily black, could conceal the uneasy expression in her eyes.

Jason had told Zoë how in love he and Lizzie had been during this year. But the photo, so it seemed to Zoë, showed a girl who was raging with anger, and, as Zoë now knew, the girl had been raging not just against her mother but against the whole village. She was the first and only Apple Queen who had had the courage to rebel against her fate – and had lost. All this Zoë felt she could read in Lizzie's eyes and mouth.

But she hadn't come to Southcombe just to look at photos of Jason's former girlfriend. She must use the time for more urgent things. Funerals don't last for ever. Mrs Moore could be back at any moment.

Chapter 24

Simon Lee's funeral brought the whole of South-combe together in St Michael's. The afternoon was cold but sunny and the air smelled of freshly mown grass and pine resin, which encouraged the vicar at the beginning of his sermon to weave the theme of regeneration and decay into his eulogy of the dead man and to contrast the horror of 'poor Simon's' last hours with the miracle of rebirth in nature. He spoke in a deep, well-trained voice and after every sentence, during which his glasses would slide down his nose, he inserted a pause, looking over them at the faces of his audience to reassure himself of the effect he was having.

For Vera this was the first time since the wassailing ceremony that she had seen the whole village gathered together. Mrs Moore was there, sitting – of course – in the front row, elegant in her navy blue suit and white silk blouse. On her left was Tom's mother, stouter, almost portly, who had hidden her fiery hair under a dark scarf for the occasion. Geoff Skinner wasn't seated next to his wife, but Vera discovered him on the other side of the aisle between Mr Lee and another gentleman who evidently had difficulty sitting still during the sermon and kept on bending forward, whispering to them both. Even Greg was present. He stood right at the back by himself, leaning against a pillar, the only person in the congregation wearing uniform. When their eyes met he greeted Vera with a friendly nod of the head and she returned the greeting, disconcerted but also relieved to have got through the next awkward encounter with him.

By contrast with the wassailing ceremony, wine was distributed instead of cider and Christian songs were sung instead of pagan ones. Vera was only half-listening, alternately studying the sparkling Burne-Jones window and the coffin covered with wreaths. She sensed tension, and now and then caught looks in her direction that were not without a certain antipathy. If Nadja hadn't insisted that her mother accompany her to the funeral she would probably have stayed at home. The memories of Robert's burial service were still too painful, she had argued, and in any case she hadn't known this poor man, Simon Lee, personally, so why should she go to his funeral? But Nadja had persisted: "It's still a relative of Mr Lee's, and you know him personally. Here in Southcombe attending people's funerals is considered an act of kindness towards the bereaved. Even if you're going back at the end of the year, you belong to us until then. People wouldn't like it if you weren't there."

"People? Do you mean Mr Lee? Or Mrs Moore, perhaps."

"No, not only them. Everybody here thinks like that."

"You too?"

"This is where I live, Mum. When will you get that into your head? I live in Southcombe, Somerset, and not in Bern – I haven't lived there for years. You'll just have to get used to the fact. I've made up my mind to make my roots here and fit in. You have to if you're going to lead a normal life in the village."

How reasonable Nadja sounded, and how right she was in the end. In any case, what harm could an hour in church do?

"At his birth Simon was perhaps not one of ours," Vera heard the vicar announce, "he was, as some of you may recall, born in Devon of parents who, in reprehensible neglect of their sacred duties, left the child in front of the gates of St Mary's Redcliffe in Bristol after he had scarcely been weaned. And this, dear parishioners, in the depths of winter! Let us imagine in our own bodies the suffering of that child, let us suffer for him in our thoughts.

"But God had a plan for Simon. He sent a compassionate soul who took care of that child and brought him to the clinic at Greenhill Park, where he, as we all know, received not only nourishment and a roof over his head but also acceptance in a loving family, in the midst of which he was able to grow and thrive. Truly, the goodness of God knows no limits. Where there is need He finds good people ready to sacrifice themselves in order to relieve that need. Again and again we find these godly souls, and they existed then when little Simon needed them.

"Yes, let us use this sad event also to recall the wonderful parents with whom our dear Simon, after a fulfilled life, can now be reunited in God. Sadly Dr Reginald Lee and his wife Aldusa Emily left us many years ago, but their charitable acts continue to illuminate Southcombe and they themselves live on amongst us, so to speak, in their two sons William and Miles. Dr Lee's life's work as a doctor and as director of Greenhill Park needs no further explanation. It remains, as I am sure you will all agree, unforgettable. Not a day passes when someone here in Southcombe, but also in more distant places, does not think back with gratitude to childhood years spent under Mr Lee's competent and compassionate care in Greenhill Park. Indeed, everyone who has grown up in a place like Greenhill Park can speak of their good fortune, yes, of their privilege to have done so. For even if God called to Himself the good-hearted Aldusa Emily much too early – so early indeed that one might be tempted to rail against His will – much too early, I say, it was not too early for her to have instilled in her three boys the fear of God, Christian humility and the highest moral virtues, and thus to send them on their life's paths armed against all evil. Was she not, while she was still amongst us, an inspiring example to us all, and is she not, since she passed from our sight but not from our minds, beloved as a saint?

"But to return to Simon, to return to our good fortune, our privilege to have been able to count as one of our friends a simple soul with a big heart …"

At this point Vera's thoughts wandered. Like Craig Brett, she had heard enough to make a connection between Greenhill Park and the wassailing ritual. Aldusa! So it was here, with this woman, that all the threads came together. While the vicar turned out further rhetorical phrases, Vera let her eyes range over the congregation stiffly and silently listening to his words and waited impatiently for the end of the sermon. He went on, however, at quite excessive length. Then there were prayers, hymns, the Eucharist.

The service lasted an hour and a half. Finally Vera could follow the coffin towards the exit, walking between Nadja and Tom. The cemetery was bathed in dazzling sunlight, but the Lees' family grave, a dark, ivy-covered mausoleum, stood in the shadow of two yew trees next to the wall which ran along the side of the Co-op down to the main road. Vera waited until the coffin had been lowered into the grave and the mass of people had thinned out so that she could look more closely at the burial plot. An angel with broken wings was kneeling beside the tomb, its eye sockets black with lichen and pockets of water in the folds of its gown, which had collected mouldy leaves and pine-needles. Its broken index finger pointed to the door of the mausoleum in which a long list of names had been engraved, the oldest of which were weathered and almost unreadable.

Reginald Arthur Lee's name stood out from the others in size, and it was the only one followed by a list of professional honours. The list was long and covered not only medicine but also pharmacy and psychology. Beside this shining eminence no other member of the family, neither antecedent nor descendant, seemed to have been in any way remarkable, not even the wife on whom the vicar had showered such extreme praise in his sermon. Aldusa Emily Lee, née Amory, had been born in 1920 in Washford and died in Greenhill Park, Southcombe, in 1951.

Thirty-one years old ... that was young to die. Vera asked Tom, who was standing beside her, whether he had any idea how the poor woman had died. He shook his mop of hair and said, "How would I know? That's decades ago. But where's Nadja? Straightaway after the service we were going to go and stay with friends in St Ives for the weekend. If we don't get moving it won't be worth making the journey."

The clock on the church tower had just struck half-past four. Tom looked round impatiently and waved his arms in the hope that Nadja would catch sight of him from one corner of the cemetery or other. But she didn't react. Vera saw her standing in front of the church porch, looking down at her toes while talking to Tom's father. Both of them seemed to have forgotten the world around them and were looking very serious. From a distance it even seemed to Vera as if Geoff were looking for words to cheer up his daughter-in-law or perhaps console her. For a moment his hand rested on her arm. Before he withdrew it he gripped her wrist or patted her on the back of her hand, Vera couldn't see exactly.

"There she is, with your father, look."

"Nadja!"

She jumped as if awaking from a dark dream. Relief at being able to leave Geoff was written all over her face. Her smile was that false one with which she could so skilfully ward off unpleasant questions. However, Vera had no time to make any enquiries. Nadja hugged her before she could say anything.

"Dearest, dearest Mum! Thank you for coming. I know it wasn't exactly exciting, but it had to be done. Shall we go, Tom? I've finished packing. As far as I'm concerned we don't need to go home before we get on our way."

"Good. Let's be off then. See you soon, Vera."

The two of them made their way to the cemetery gate and went up Church Street to their car. Tom held Nadja's hand and pulled her forward with a quick, springing step. Vera heard her protest briefly while she tried her best to keep up with him.

"What a lovely couple. That's your daughter, isn't it?"

Vera turned round, startled. She knew the voice, and it was the last one she would have expected to hear in this place.

"Mr Haider, but …"

"Well, if the mountain won't come to Muhammad … You didn't reply to my telephone calls, so here I am. But not only because of you. I'm a keen reader of the *Somerset Gazette* and I saw the report of Simon Lee's death at Blue Anchor. I didn't want to miss the funeral."

"I was there, too, and now I'm going home."

"Yes, I saw you in the church. I was sitting to the side behind a pillar. Did you know Mr Lee?"

Should she give him an answer? For a long time she scrutinized this man who had appeared out of nowhere and was astonished by the way he managed to pester her with questions again after only a couple of moments.

"Mr Haider, to tell the truth I don't know what we have to say to each other. In Watchet you were unable to give me any useful information and I don't seem to have helped you in any way."

"But that was several weeks ago. Weeks in which we have both – I assume – made progress in our investigations. But neither perhaps with a complete understanding of what's going on here. We should trade information."

What Haider was saying was what Vera was thinking. She too had the feeling that she lacked important pieces of the puzzle that she needed in order for the whole thing to make sense. Nevertheless she could not bring herself to collaborate with this man. His skill at worming things out of her still made Vera mistrustful. She remembered all too clearly how inferior she had felt to him in Watchet. She didn't want to be caught in his net a second time.

"Our priorities aren't the same, Mr Haider."

"Please, Mrs Wyler. It's very important to me to have a conversation with you. I'll be entirely frank. I'm on the point of filling in the gaps in the story that Brett was working on before he died. Brett … let's put it like this … wanted to make his film about Southcombe without me, and I have to admit that for a long time I resented that. But now I've seen his notes I understand him better. Southcombe's wassailing could be the story of the decade, a real scoop that would make waves beyond these shores. Unfortunately the material he left behind is incomplete. That's why I'm here. I want to make this story public. Do you understand? The wassailing ritual here is a barbaric monstrosity that must be stopped at all costs. Worldwide coverage could make that happen. A press scoop is one thing. The other is that this year the role of Apple Queen has been given to your daughter. The whole village is crazy about her. But it won't last."

"Yes," Vera admitted ruefully. "That's what I suspect, and that's what worries me."

"And rightly. None of the women previously elected Apple Queen here has lived longer than a year. Brett researched the Apple Queens back to the nineties. With one exception they all died a natural death during the year of their reign. There is no reason to suppose that a different fate is awaiting this year's Queen. It must be stopped. Or to put it differently: we must stop it."

"But you say yourself that the cause of death has always been a natural one. That's where I get stuck."

"If you count suicide as a natural death. But that raises further questions. It's one of the gaps I've got to fill in before I can publish the whole story. What was it that Craig Brett wanted to fetch from your house? Do you remember? Did you find it?"

338

"All you're really interested in is the scoop, isn't it? What happens to my daughter is of no interest to you. Why should I help you?"

"I can't stop you from seeing things like that. You're right that we may have different reasons for wanting to expose the secret of Southcombe, but is that so bad if in the end it's in both our interests?"

Haider stared at her so intensely while he spoke that Vera automatically took a step back before answering: "No, of course not. I suppose you're right. It's time for us to share what we know. I don't trust the police. In fact, I don't trust anyone here."

"I don't come from this village. Like you. Can't that be our common ground?"

"Shall we go over to the café to have a talk? It'll be full of people who've been to the funeral service, but I'm sure we'll find somewhere to sit."

Helen Dean had anticipated the rush of customers and had squeezed in some extra tables and chairs. Little pink and green flags dangled over the tables, an obtrusive aroma of violet came from the scented candles next to the till, and there were vases full of tulips and little baskets of home-made brownies everywhere. Vera and Haider had to share a four-person table with two ladies who were discussing their impressions of the funeral over tea and cakes: "Perhaps the vicar could have said a bit more about poor Simon's life, don't you think? He wasn't much seen in the village recently. Nobody really knows what he got up to."

"I think he was working on the building site. But just between you and me, what the vicar said was way over the top. Simon was no angel. He spent more time in the pub than he did at home: that's the kind of person he was."

"I'm afraid this café isn't quite the right place for our discussion," whispered Vera. "I'm sorry, I think it's best if we go somewhere else."

"I won't offer you a Black Rat cider this time, but let's just have a coffee and then we'll see. First, though, there's this."

Ahmed Haider drew a roll of photocopies out of his coat pocket and put them on the table in front of Vera.

"There, you see. These are the last pages Craig Brett photocopied in the Taunton archive last summer. For weeks I've been puzzling my head over why he was so preoccupied with these."

Vera glanced at the copies, without however completely unrolling them, and asked in a low voice: "You were here in January at the ritual and tried to take photos yourself. Was that something to do with these?"

Haider nodded: "I didn't want to alarm people by taking a camcorder, especially since Brett had already filmed enough material. Stills would have been enough for my records. But as I'm sure you saw, my camera copped it. That would have been okay, but the worst thing is that I missed the rest of the ritual. They literally chased me away, maybe because I look foreign, but in the end I don't think that's the reason why. I'm lucky no one reported me to the police."

"I don't think that would have been a problem. The police didn't have any reason to take things any further. You weren't guilty of anything."

"I'm not so sure about that, but please, do me a favour and look at these pictures closely. They must be part of the solution to the puzzle or Brett wouldn't have spent so long over them."

Vera spread out the copies between the coffee cups and flower vases, doing her best to protect them from the inquisitive glances of the two local ladies. It was no good. Both of them leaned over, squinting to get a better look. Vera gave them a reproving glance and put the sheets on her lap. They were photos of the Southcombe wassailing ritual from various years as well as the same ritual in other villages of Somerset and even the neighbouring county, Gloucestershire.

"At first sight all the photos seem to show the same thing. The slices of toast dipped in cider, the cider being poured over the tree roots, the gun being fired into the sky, the Morris dancers, the Apple Queen. Yes, that's exactly what happened this year," Vera commented as quietly as possible.

Nevertheless the phrase 'Apple Queen' stirred the interest of the whole café. For a fraction of a second there was a pause, glances were exchanged, people held their breath, and finally the two ladies turned their heads to Vera at the same time and one of them said in a tone of absolute delight: "Oh, isn't your daughter this year's Apple Queen? Such a charming young woman, I do congratulate you. That's wonderful. We haven't been granted such a beautiful and deserving Queen for years. Thanks to her we're bound to have the best crop of the century next year."

As thanks for this compliment Vera could only manage a tightening of the corners of her mouth. Nadja was the last thing she wanted to discuss with these cake-eating old crows. Everyone was nice to her face, everyone loved and admired Nadja and lost no opportunity to show it. But that was only on the surface. Underneath there were forces at work that were intent on harming her child. Never before had Vera felt so uncomfortable and so threatened in the midst of this cosy British 'niceness'.

"I can't stay here, Mr Haider. I can't breathe. Please, let's get out. I can't stand it."

Without waiting for his response, she had got up and slipped into her coat under the astonished eyes of the two ladies. Haider did not hold her back. Vera forced her way through the chairs to the exit and the open air, where she took a deep breath before beginning to laugh in the middle of the pavement – she laughed out loud, hysterically, like someone who has just escaped death and cannot believe their good fortune.

When she looked round for Haider he was still standing in the café with the photocopies squashed under his arm, exchanging a few words with Helen Dean at the till. Through the window Vera could see him pulling out his wallet, taking coins out one by one and pushing them across the counter to Helen Dean with outstretched fingers. The hand gestures reminded her of Nadja's. It was the same carefulness with which she had smoothed the soil round her rose in the garden. And earlier still – yes, that was it, there was once before when Nadja as a child of the city had treated soil so lovingly that it had disconcerted her. But when had that been? And where?

"I thought you were going to run away from me," he joked as he came out. "That's not the first time today. There was a young girl in there who thought I was trying to chat her up. I ask you, do I look that kind of person? Well, obviously I do …"

"Mr Haider," Vera said, interrupting him as he reached her, "I think I know now what it was about these photos that so preoccupied Craig Brett. It's as if scales had fallen from my eyes. Yes, I'm sure I've found a clue. Come on. We must go to Greenhill Park."

"To the apple tree?"

"Exactly. If my theory is right we'll find something there. I've no idea what, but at least I know where we'll find it."

In the twilight the apple tree seemed even sparser than it had on the night of the wassailing ceremony. Bare and bent, it rose out of the earth, so withered that one would scarcely have believed it would come to life again if it weren't for the tiny buds that could be seen on the branches. The bits of string that Nadja had used to tie on the slices of toast were dangling in the wind. Vera counted three of them, but remembered that she had hung up one for each of the four points of the compass and at the end one remaining slice on the lowest branch.

Vera stood with her back towards the barracks and checked the view down the valley.

"This is more or less exactly where I stood during the wassailing ceremony. After the Morris dance Nadja went up to the tree from the right and hung up the slices of toast, going clockwise."

Ahmed Haider nodded: "Yes, I remember. Then I started to take flash photos. That was the mistake that cost me my Nikon."

"It's a great pity that nothing came of your pictures. Otherwise you would have caught on camera something that no one before you ever had. No wonder Brett never found what he was looking for in the photos. Like the two of us, he experienced it at the wassailing ritual but didn't find it documented anywhere."

Vera squatted in front of the tree and began to sweep away the damp foliage around the stem. The soil was still hard from the recent frosts, but where the two men, Paddy and his colleague, had dug a hole almost two months earlier, she came to looser earth. She had to move aside a little for Ahmed Haider, but he didn't think of getting his hands dirty in order to help her. He stood with his hands in his coat pockets and looked alternately down at her and across the park to the first houses of Southcombe.

Vera's fingers were soon numb with cold. The deeper she dug, the more compacted the soil became, but she went on scrabbling. There was no stopping her. She broke roots and pulled out stones until at last she reached something soft.

"There it is at last," she cried out. "That must be it!"

"Not so loud, Mrs Wyler. I'm afraid we've got a visitor."

"A visitor!!"

Vera was at once on her feet and following Ahmed Haider's gaze. A figure had turned on to the footpath by the Kings Arms and was coming up the hill directly towards them. Whoever it was was carrying a map and studying it as they walked.

"We must come back some other time. If we're caught here, it'll …"

"Don't panic, Mrs Wyler. You don't seriously think we're going to be gunned down like in a western, do you?"

"That's more or less what happened to Lizzie less than fifty yards from here. But perhaps you don't know who I'm talking about."

"Mrs Moore's daughter, yes, of course I know. I've done my homework. That wasn't really difficult since Brett had put together a whole file on her. Lizzie died because she refused to accept the role she was given. But we're just – hang on a moment, that's the girl from this afternoon."

Vera wanted to escape in the direction of the barracks and was astonished to see a smile cross Haider's lips.

"You here, Mademoiselle? So our paths cross again. My goodness, bumping into each other by chance twice in one day."

Vera wiped her hands clean on her jeans and came nearer in order to see the girl who planted herself so confidently in front of Haider and replied in unusually melodious English: "You can count yourself lucky that I've got a speedy and reliable source of information, otherwise I wouldn't flatter you by replying. But when I last spoke to him my boyfriend told me who you are and the fact that you work for Channel 4 News. You're OK. And the fact that we're meeting here in front of the apple tree is hardly by chance."

Vera had placed herself in front of the hole in order to hide it from the girl, but she nodded towards it. "I see you've got here before me. I'm not sorry about that, because this particular job is one I've been dreading for days. By the way, my name is Zoë Cox. And yours?"

When she heard Vera's name she had to hold back an exclamation of astonishment.

"The mother of Nadja Wyler?"

"Yes. Do you know Nadja? Are you one of her friends?"

"No, I've only read her name. But I suggest we put off telling each other what we know because it's going to get dark soon. I daren't imagine what would happen if we were caught here then. So I can assume we three have all come here for the same purpose, can I? If not, that really would be too much of a coincidence, wouldn't it, Mr Haider?"

Zoë's eyes twinkled as she walked past him to the apple tree and kneeled down beside Vera in front of the hole.

"I've brought a plastic bag to put the purse in. Here."

Vera wanted to ask Zoë hundreds of questions. She couldn't understand what this self-assured girl was doing in Greenhill Park and why she so obviously knew what was going on. She moved aside a bit of soil in order to gain time, but Zoë didn't stir from her side and followed her movements closely.

Ahmed Haider looked down, sniffing:

"Ugh, what's that?"

"The leather purse that Nadja had to bury here during the wassailing ceremony, don't you remember?" answered Vera.

There was little left of it. Mouldy and chewed, the leather fell apart in Vera's fingers and beneath it there was a slippery, glistening mass in which maggots and tangles of worms had made their home. Nausea made Vera hold her breath; she had to look away and take a couple of deep breaths before she could look at the purse again. Zoë had also gone quiet, and her hand trembled as she held out the plastic bag to Vera, saying: "Here, quick, I can't bear the sight of it any longer."

Vera gripped the purse with her fingertips and let it fall together with its contents into the plastic bag. For a while she contemplated it and then turned away in disgust.

"For God's sake, that stinks to high heaven. I've never smelled anything as revolting in my life. Is that … meat?"

"Yes, you could say so," replied Zoë, and added after a solemn pause: "What we have dug up here is the heart of last year's Apple Queen."

"What? Sue Harper's heart?" cried Vera, putting her hands in front of her mouth in horror. "That's impossible!" For a moment her head spun, she had to lean on Zoë and wait with closed eyes for the shock to pass. When she pulled herself together she saw that the girl was in just as bad a state. She was as white as chalk and stared at the bag in her hands as if she were hypnotized.

Haider was the only one who remained composed about the discovery. He just said, "*Mashallah*, human sacrifice," while Vera and Zoë carefully filled the hole in again. "So that's what Brett's scoop was about: human sacrifice in Somerset. In the twenty-first century!"

Vera turned to Zoë and asked, "Did you know Sue Harper?"

"No, not personally. She is … she was my boyfriend's sister. Until today Jason didn't know that his sister had died. And he certainly didn't know about the circumstances. But we should have this heart examined forensically as soon as possible. It's our strongest piece of evidence. That will alert the police to what's been going on and hopefully stop this murderous conspiracy once and for all."

Haider had reservations about this course of action: "The first thing is for us to get away from here. If anyone in the village gets wind of our having dug up the heart we'll all be in for it. And above all we could be putting this year's Apple Queen in danger."

"No, I don't think so," replied Zoë. "The village needs its Apple Queen. Nothing will happen to her before the autumn. But I can't go back to Mrs Moore's now. What if she finds out what we've done?"

"She doesn't know everything that happens here even if she thinks she does," said Vera. "We've filled in the hole and nobody is likely to find out that the heart is missing until the next ceremony."

"Jason is certain that everyone here in Southcombe is involved. Everyone, even the police. If that's right, then Rupert Harper will have told Mrs Moore long ago that I'm in the village and that Jason can't be far away."

"I don't understand everything you say," said Vera, "but I think we need to get away from here, don't you?"

"Of course, you're right. Come on, let's get moving," said Zoë, and speeded up. "This afternoon I was stupid enough to look up Rupert Harper and tell him who I was. If the whole village is involved then I need to get away fast. Jason and I had better change our base too …"

Vera and Ahmed Haider just looked at her questioningly, and so on the way back Zoë began to explain Jason's history with Lizzie Moore and how he had fled the village and gone into hiding after her murder.

"It was he who told me about you, by the way, Mr Haider. He did some research for me in Taunton library's internet café this afternoon and came across some interesting stuff by you and Craig Brett. But how can I get to Taunton now, are there are any more buses?"

"I'll drive you, Miss Cox," Vera offered. "That seems safest. What about your luggage? Do you dare fetch it from Mrs Moore's?"

"No, never. I'm not going to set foot in that house again. Too bad about my pyjamas and toothbrush. Luckily I've got the most important things with me here."

Triumphantly Zoë tugged a couple of scrumpled pieces of paper out of her trouser pocket and said: "This is our second piece of evidence. I nicked these this afternoon while Mrs Moore was out. She had a ring-binder full of stuff about the organization around the wassailing ritual. They call it 'The Aldusa Circle' and it all started here in Greenhill Park in the fifties. But it was only in the nineties that the circle became a village institution. All the details were there in the ring-binder but I couldn't take that or Mrs Moore would have noticed at once. But if there are just a few pages missing it may take her a while to realize. That gives us a bit of time."

Haider immediately jumped in: "I'd like to take a look. May I?"

"No, not now and not here. It's too dark for reading anyway. Let's make sure we're safe first, and then we can read. Where are you staying, Mr Haider?"

He smiled: "Three guesses."

"Not …"

"Yes, indeed. I'm staying at Birch Cottage, the same as you. It's the only B&B in Southcombe. So our rooms are next to each other."

"You can stay with me at Station House if you want to. There's enough room there," offered Vera.

"Station House? But that's not safe either," Zoë protested. "The house belongs to Mrs Moore, and we can't take the risk. Even if you do pay a pretty hefty rent."

"How do you know that?"

"Mrs Moore is a model book-keeper. Her files are completely up to date. So I've been able to read how much you pay into her account, on which day of the month, but also how much other things … oh it's so horrific I can hardly bear to say it … well, Mrs Moore kept accounts of these so-called 'heart operations', costing three hundred pounds each. I think we can guess what they involved. All paid in cash to a certain Simon Lee."

While she spoke Zoë held the plastic bag as far away from herself as she could and avoided looking at it. She tried to keep calm but Vera could tell from her trembling voice that the young woman was just as shaken as Vera herself was.

"Three hundred pounds," added Zoë reflectively. "It's not much, is it, for desecrating the bodies of innocent women? Is it far to your car, Vera? I think you should both come back to Taunton with me and we can find a new B&B."

"I must drop in at Station House first," Vera told them. "I can collect my clothes and pictures later, when this is all over, but I did find what Craig Brett was so keen to get his hands on: Lizzie's diary from the time she was the Apple Queen. Her entries contain overwhelming proof of what's been going on here. Together with …

what we found this afternoon we've got everything we need to put the ringleaders behind bars."

"And your daughter?" enquired Haider.

"Nadja would never come away of her own free will. I'm afraid she's fallen for the part she's been given here, hook, line and sinker, and just wouldn't believe there's anything sinister behind it. In any case, she's gone away for the weekend."

"That's not a good sign, Mrs Wyler," said Zoë doubtfully. "If I were you I'd ring her and make up a reason for her to come to Taunton."

"But she only left today. Tom's got friends in St Ives. The two of them are coming back tomorrow evening."

"Tom?"

"Tom Skinner, her husband. A charming young man. His family have lived here for generations."

As Vera spoke Haider and Zoë exchanged glances.

"But if he's from an old Southcombe family," said the girl tentatively, "don't you think there's a good chance they'll be involved in the ritual?"

Vera closed her eyes as images of the wassailing night flashed before her: the Green Man welcoming his daughter-in-law; Marion Skinner's all too evident enthusiasm for anything connected to it. The girl could well be right.

Chapter 25

Nadja had never been by car from Southcombe to the furthest point of Cornwall. Even if she was looking forward to seeing Tom's friends Mike and Jenny and getting to know the famous coastal town of St Ives, she had no great enthusiasm for the long journey. She had packed sandwiches and iced tea and once they had set off studied the map so as remind herself of the route.

"Launceston seems to be about half-way," she said. "We could stop and have a coffee there and then I can take over the driving. I'll have a bit of a snooze first. You can leave the radio on, music doesn't disturb me."

Tom didn't like talking when he drove and she couldn't usually get much more out of him than monosyllabic replies, but this time all she heard was an unintelligible mumble before stretching out her legs, yawning and closing her eyes. Although she was tired she found it difficult to relax. Images of the funeral swam through her mind, individual phrases that the vicar had used echoed in her, and then in particular there was Tom's abrupt way of driving, which shook her awake at every set of lights and threw her off balance at every corner. In general Tom had become more absent-minded than normal in recent days and, so it seemed to her, haunted by an un-happiness that she hadn't known in him before. The question of children had driven a wedge between them, the first since their marriage four years earlier. However, they hardly talked about it any longer. The discussions had soon ended in silent assent. Tom had won and it was up to her now to deal with the prospect of a marriage without children. Nadja tried not to think about it any more, but there were moments in which the desire for children took control of her like an enormous hunger and threw her into despair. Tom did not understand it, did not even try to, but at the first sign would withdraw and wait until Nadja had overcome the crisis and was herself again: jolly, uncomplicated, conforming.

"Tom, why are you so tense? It makes me feel ill when you drive like this."

"—"

"Tom?"

"What is it?"

Nadja opened one eye and saw through the wind-screen trees flying past, outlined against a darkening sky.

"We're not even on the motorway!"

Tom murmured hoarsely, "No," and briefly put his hand on Nadja's thigh to reassure her.

"Have a good snooze."

"But we're on the wrong road, Tom. We should have been on the motorway ages ago. This is an A road, look."

Nadja had sat up in her seat and was looking with wide open eyes out into the darkness while Tom still refused to say anything. The road was bordered on both sides by hedges and snaked gently through the countryside, but it soon seemed to Nadja that she recognised these curves and could tell when the next one was coming.

"Stop, Tom. This isn't the way to Cornwall. You're heading for Minehead. Can't you read the signs? We've just passed the turning to Vellow."

Tom cleared his throat without showing any indication of wanting to stop the car in one of the lay-bys.

"Say something, Tom. I can't bear talking to a brick wall."

"We're not going to Cornwall today, Nadja," Tom finally decided to reply.

"You mean we're not going to Mike and Jenny's? Where are we going, then?"

"I'm taking you to the old Amory Cider Farm for a couple of days."

"No, please don't do that. What do you think you're up to?"

"Those are the instructions. Bill and Eileen have shown me the plan. It's part of your training."

Nadja's fingers gripped the door handle and she was about to burst out in protest when Tom added: "But I'm going to stay with you. Apparently I'm supposed to be trained with you."

"Aha. And where is this Cider Farm, if you don't mind?"

"In Washford. Do you remember when we visited Cleeve Abbey together? More or less diagonally opposite there's a biggish building with the sign 'Amory Cider Farm'."

"Cleeve Abbey? That was the romantic ruined monastery beside a stream, wasn't it? Where we afterwards went and had a picnic on the edge of a wood and saw a dead deer?"

"Yes, that's the place. We should be arriving soon."

"I don't remember a Cider Farm, though."

"It hasn't been in use for a long time. It's almost a ruin like Cleeve Abbey."

Nadja sat still in her seat for a while thinking about what Tom had said.

"Mike and Jenny never invited us, did they?"

"No."

"I thought it was a bit strange anyway that they should come up with an invitation after such a long time. It's not as if we knew them that well. And I don't even think he likes me."

"That's just you. He can be a bit loutish, but he's OK. I always thought it was a pity they moved away from Southcombe. I know you and Jenny would have become best friends."

"I've got Helen. She's enough for me. She really is a best, best friend. And until the end of the year I've got my mother. In a way she's a friend, although she sometimes gets on my nerves with her worrying."

Tom had become calmer during the course of the conversation. He felt more at ease since telling Nadja the truth and was relieved that she had shown so little resistance to the change of plan.

They had scarcely driven half an hour when, just before they reached Washford, Tom turned into Station Road, which was already shrouded in darkness at this time of the evening. After a few yards the façade of the abbey came into view on the left hand side, lit up by lights set in various corners of the garden, which gave it an orange hue. The gates were shut and the sign showing the opening times and entry prices stood beside them, hanging crookedly in the wind.

"An owl," cried Nadja, and as she did so a night-bird, alarmed by the car, stretched its wings out quite close to them and slid silently across the abbey garden to the next tree.

Amory Cider Farm consisted of a tall rectangular building covered in ivy which could easily have been missed from the road. This evening there were lights to be seen in the upper storey, and when Tom drove over the stone bridge and parked between two cars at the end of the gravel drive a ground floor light also went on before the double door opened and William Lee stepped out. In front of the building, as he came out, walking with outstretched arms towards Tom and Nadja, the florist seemed even smaller and more compact than usual.

"Well, what do you think of my old shed? Great! But don't just stand out there, come in, everything's ready for you."

Nadja, clinging to Tom's arm, hesitated.

"So, come on, then," said Tom impatiently. Nadja thought she heard in his voice exactly the same uncertainty that she herself felt. She wanted to whisper something to him as they crossed the threshold into the house but Tom pretended not to hear and followed Mr Lee along the corridor into a room that because of its spartan furnishing looked more like a cell than a visitor's room: bed, table and chair had all seen better days, and the only decoration on the wall, the tattered sepia photo of a cider press from way back, gave the same impression of advancing dilapidation. Nadja shivered.

"This is your room," said Mr Lee proudly, as if offering Nadja a suite in a five star hotel. "It used to belong to my mother. She slept in this bed and worked at this table. I can't imagine a more fitting home for our Apple Queen. Tom's accommodation will be in a different wing of the house. I'll take him there now and then we'll meet again in the hall, where I'll explain what I've planned for you in the coming days."

"Wait a moment, why can't Tom and I be together? I don't want to be alone here."

"The regulations insist on separate quarters. And we don't want to go against them on the first evening, do we? It'll only be for two or three days. Just be patient, Nadja."

Before Nadja could think of an answer, the florist pushed Tom out of the room and closed the door after him. Nadja at once put her ear to the door to discover whether, for his part, Tom would resist, but she only heard steps resounding down the corridor, and when she tried to look out she found the door bolted. Mr Lee had used a moment of inattention to lock her in! And Tom was letting himself be led away without any idea of what was going on.

"Tom, Tom," she cried and beat against the door with her fists. "Mr Lee, please let me out of here."

She banged and screamed until she was exhausted, but in vain. No one came back.

Exasperated, she searched her pockets for her mobile, but could not find it. She had had it with her during the funeral, for she remembered having switched if off before the sermon. But what had happened next? In vain she struggled to remember the time between the burial and the moment when she had got into the car with Tom. She could see herself with her mother walking out of the church and exchanging a couple of words with Helen, and she remembered exactly how Tom's father had caught up with her in front of the porch, comforting her for Tom's strange behaviour. She had wept and Mr Skinner had stroked her hand in a fatherly way while asking her for patience. "It'll be alright in the end, Nadja," he had said. "Everything will be fine by the autumn. Be patient until then."

Had Tom's father taken her mobile? What a ridiculous idea! It was more likely that it had fallen out of her bag in the car. In any case she didn't have it with her and she cursed her carelessness.

And the window? Nadja pulled the curtain aside and looked through the iron bars to a field at the end of which a stream flowed behind poplar trees, the same stream that snaked its way through the gardens of Cleeve Abbey. She could even make out the orange glow of the illuminated abbey, but apart from that Amory Cider Farm stood alone in the far-flung, flat landscape.

Looking vainly round the room for any other means of escape, she struggled with the idea that Mr Lee had enticed her here in order to keep her prisoner in his decaying ancestral home. At least Tom was there, close by, and the milk drink and the cakes that Mr Lee had put ready for her on a silver tray showed that he only meant well. The sight of the biscuits decorated with brightly coloured icing placated her, and when, after a while, she had accepted that no one else would be visiting her during the evening she sat down at the table and began to eat. The milk had a strong taste of vanilla but she enjoyed the ginger and coconut biscuits and in the end ate them all.

Was she afraid? That was what she asked herself while she ate and later when she with some difficulty got up from the table and slipped between the coarse sheets, still in her clothes. Her head was buzzing, the ceiling was turning and the photograph on the wall suddenly became two photographs. If she stared at it for long enough it would even turn into four photographs, while the table and the chair began to rock even more wildly, as if she were on board boat in a storm.

It was no better if she closed her eyes. The grotesque faces that emerged out of the night refused to go away. They leant over her face, their grins revealing their rotten teeth and their lolling tongues. Nadja vainly tried to dispel them, she screamed and raged, buried her face in the pillow, but there they were again, grinning and lolling, while an unspeakable weight was holding down her body and pressing her through the bed deep into the earth, or no, perhaps it was liquid lead that was being pumped into her veins and now it was metal flowing through her instead of blood, travelling down to the tips of her fingers and toes and back to her heart – her heart, which beat and beat and beat, struggling to shift this great mass that was increasingly solidifying the whole of her body, even her brain, so that she could no longer think, no longer feel – until there was absolutely nothing of her left.

"Jason? Hi, it's me. I … Yes, yes, of course, everything's OK here. I've got so much to tell you. If only you knew! But it'll have to wait. We're just walking back from the apple tree into the village and now we all want to go into Taunton … Yes, Taunton. Things have got a bit out of hand here and we'd rather not stay any longer. Ask Mr Pyke whether he's got two more rooms free. From now. We're going to take the next bus, or if not then we'll definitely take the next but one … We, that is: Mr Ahmed Haider, the film man – you know – and the mother of this year's Apple Queen, a Swiss lady. No, they're not together. That's why they need two rooms. – Would you ever have thought that a foreigner could become Apple Queen in Southcombe? … Nor me, but … No, the mother says she's gone away with her husband for the weekend … What? … He's called Tom Skinner, and I don't suppose he's Swiss … Yes, I think I've got it right, Tom Skinner. Why? … A school friend of yours? That's wonderful … Right. But then … No, I told you they

361

wouldn't be back until tomorrow … Right, I'll pass it on. We'll be back soon … Yes, love you too … bye, bye …"

When Nadja woke up the following morning she did not recognise the room she found herself in, nor could she remember how she had arrived there. The half empty glass of milk drink and the biscuit crumbs on the table aroused a distant memory but, with no before and no after, she felt like an island in a vast sea of forgetting: alone and lost.

Her watch showed half past nine. Light-headed from the deep sleep, Nadja tottered into the bathroom, which seemed as alien as if she had never been in it before. Only when she had washed her face in cold water did the previous evening partially come back to her and with it her unease. She was still not afraid, but she could feel her anger growing at the thought of the way in which she and Tom had let themselves be tricked so easily.

Mr Lee seemed to have reckoned with her being in a bad mood. At ten he unbolted the door and entered the room with a vase of yellow tulips which he placed on the table, humbly begging Nadja for her forgiveness.

"I know, Nadja, I know. I shouldn't have locked you in. But it was for your own protection. You are so valuable to all of us that I didn't want there to be any risk."

"Where's Tom? I want to talk to Tom."

"That's not easy, I'm afraid. Tom has driven back to Southcombe. He's got to go to work tomorrow and …"

"That's not what Tom told me. He thought he would stay here and be trained with me."

"Yes, my dear. He will. But not yet. First and foremost it's all about you. Did you at least sleep well in my mother's bed?"

Nadja didn't reply. What could she say about the black hole she had fallen into and out of which she would only with difficulty be able to escape. Shrugging her shoulders she moved away from Mr Lee, keeping her eye on the door, which had remained open a crack. She was determined not to let herself be surprised into spending the whole day locked in.

"Come on, don't be angry, I've prepared breakfast for you in the hall, and after that we can make a start with your training."

Mr Lee hadn't exaggerated. The room was so big and so richly decorated that there could be no doubt that it deserved to be called a hall. With its high windows framed by satin curtains, the portraits of ancestors and the two crystal candelabra, the hall reminded Nadja of black and white comedies from the fifties starring eccentric aristocrats in their haunted castles.

"Please eat as much as you like. And don't forget your pills. Here's a glass of spinach-apple drink with my special herbal mixture, as well. You'll see how that puts you in top form."

Mr Lee had put together a lavish breakfast and watched with satisfaction as she eagerly attacked it.

"Afterwards I'd like to ring Tom, please. And my mother, too, she doesn't know that I'm here."

"We'll see about that later," replied Mr Lee evasively, and when Nadja had drunk the last drop of tea he moved his chair nearer and asked: "Is it alright with you, Nadja, if we start right away?"

"You mean now, at the breakfast table? No, I told you I wanted to make some phone calls first."

Nadja tried to stand up but her legs refused to obey her. The same great heaviness began to paralyse her limbs that had kept her nailed to the bed the evening before. It wasn't an unpleasant heaviness: on the contrary, she was aware that her speech and her movements were becoming sluggish and her thoughts were slipping into a vacuum. She put her head on the table, closed her eyes and let Mr Lee's words fall over her like water from a refreshing stream. His voice was soothing and what he was saying stood out clearly from the all-embracing haziness that she was increasingly dipping into.

"So why not here? We're not in school. You don't need to write things down or copy from the blackboard. All you have to do is sit still and listen. So far I have told you about your role at the next wassailing ceremony and explained what the village expects from you and what it is prepared to give you in return. You have been wonderfully understanding and we are very pleased with you. In these next few days, though, we shall be going over to a trickier phase that requires a certain psychological preparation."

"But we could have done that just as well in your shop in Southcombe. Now I'd like to ... change my clothes ... and ... brush my teeth ... and make ... the phone calls." It cost Nadja a great effort to get the words out.

"Of course. You can do all that, but only after my little introduction. The reason for having you brought to my family home is that it is so important for you to understand the historical background of your role and the way that you yourself are heir to a whole line of Apple Queens. The practice of wassailing goes back far into the middle ages, you've read something of that already, but now we're talking about the Apple Queen herself. We're talking about you, Nadja, and how you have to fit into our customs."

"The Apple … Queen is … something from … the middle ages, like the … wassailing. I thought, oh … what … did I think? … It goes back to … this St Al … Aldusa, that you are … always … talking about."

"Aldusa is my mother's name."

"Aha! I don't mean her … what I mean is … the Aldusa of your wassailing circle. The Aldusa from the … middle ages in the church."

"And if I now reveal to you that our first Apple Queen dates from 1951?"

"1951?! I don't … understand."

Nadja grabbed the chewed core of a pear, separated the stalk and began to play with it. She was still enjoying listening to Mr Lee, but he was beating around the bush. Even more than usually, she thought. As if he didn't know how to tackle the heart of the matter, perhaps because he found it embarrassing or perhaps because he was afraid of her reaction. Or was it she who was failing to grasp the heart of the matter?

"You're listening, aren't you, Nadja," Mr Lee checked before he went on. "What I wanted to say is this: Southcombe's wassailing, which the whole village meanwhile holds in high honour, in reality goes back to my mother."

"Your mother? Then it's … not something religious … I mean … not like baptism and marriage."

"Wait, let me finish. My mother …"

"But what's your mother got to do with the Aldusa in the church?"

"There's no direct connection. We, that is to say my father and I, established the connection."

"I don't like that at all. I don't want … to be involved … It all sounds … like hocus … hocus-pocus."

"No, calm down, Nadja. You'll soon understand the connection. Let me tell you a bit about my mother. She was a wonderful woman and all of us in the village have a great deal to thank her for."

"That's what … the vicar said in the church. What does the village have to thank her for … specifically?"

"Nothing less than its prosperity."

"But that's not possible. Your … mother has been dead … for a long time!"

"Yes, that's right in one way, but in another way it isn't. She married my father when she was young, and she had already had two children from him when she became pregnant for a third time at the age of thirty. This time she was to have a girl. Just imagine, we boys were to have a sister. Miles and I were over the moon. A sister!"

"Weren't you … three boys? Miles, you and this … Simon who was buried yesterday?"

"Yes, but Simon never really belonged. Mother adopted him because she had a big heart, but, as things are in life, love cannot be forced. Miles and Simon couldn't stand each other, and in any case Simon was a bit odd, he preferred to go his own way. When Mother told us she was expecting a girl he showed absolutely no emotion whereas Miles and I spontaneously joined in her joy."

Nadja smiled doubtfully. Mr Lee, who decades later could still get worked up over the birth of a sister and whose eyes were even starting to glisten.

"You're lucky … I would have … would have liked to … have a sister. But I'm an only child … I think my mother … was … too old to … to have any more children … It just wasn't to be."

Mr Lee looked down at his hands which lay folded on the table.

"It obviously wasn't to be for us, either. Our mother had a miscarriage in the fifth month. Little Aldusa was born dead."

"What? You gave the … well … you gave the child a … name?"

"Of course. What are you thinking of? She had my mother's name. My mother insisted. It was still her child. And so it was important to her as well that the child should make a contribution to the world in spite of its only having had a brief existence. For my mother held the view that we all, from the queen to the bin-man and to a piece of rock, we all have a task to fulfil on this earth. Yes, you may smile and shake your head, you refuse to believe that even a piece of rock has its task in the world."

"Alright, if you insist … And so what … was your little sister's task?"

"For you to understand that properly I'd first like to ask you if you know where you are at the moment."

"What a question. … In your … family home, of course. You told me … yourself."

"Right, the family home on my mother's side. My mother grew up here on Amory Cider Farm."

Mr Lee made a pause and checked in Nadja's eyes how she reacted to the three words.

"Doesn't that mean anything to you?"

"No. What should it mean to me? … I come from Switzerland … Cider … isn't so important for us. People there prefer beer … or wine."

"Until the seventies Amory Cider was the best and most celebrated cider of Somerset. You can ask anyone in the village and they'll confirm that."

"What … what has that got to do with your sister?"

"Everything, Nadja, absolutely everything. She is the one who made Amory Cider what it was for twenty years: the most successful brand of cider in Somerset."

Nadja dropped the pear stalk onto the plate and let out a long sigh.

"Mr Lee, please … can't I finally get … washed … and changed? I don't feel good … in my old … clothes. You can go on talking afterwards."

"No, wait, it won't last long. You'll have plenty of time to get changed during the lunch break. Where was I?"

"–"

"That's right, the most successful cider in Somerset. The surprising thing is that after the War Amory Cider was a brand that no one in Somerset knew or took seriously," Mr Lee went on, undeterred. "The business figures were even so bad that my grandfather thought about stopping production and emigrating to join relatives in Nebraska. That was the difficult time when my mother had her miscarriage. – By the way, have you got any idea what a five month old foetus looks like?"

"No … but that … that's something I'd prefer not … to imagine too precisely."

"Mother showed her to me and Miles. 'That's your little sister,' she said, 'isn't she beautiful?' I can still see her sitting in bed – no, Nadja, not in the bed you slept in last night, it was in Greenhill Park – I can still see how gently she held baby Aldusa in her arms and smiled so blissfully at her as if she didn't know that the baby wasn't alive. Miles and I had to sit beside her on the bed and admire her and stroke her. Mother couldn't have stood it if we had run away, so we sat there and took it in turns to hold baby Aldusa in our arms. She was a tiny bundle, covered in blood, with minute little hands and a head that was much too big. Her eyelids seemed huge, and her

369

mouth, a thin red line that looked like a knife wound. Can you understand what I mean when I tell you Miles and I will never forget our little sister? That image will always be with us, always!"

Nadja didn't dare make a sound. The growing fervour of her teacher was gradually beginning to unsettle her.

"And do you know what Mother then said to us?"

Nadja shook her head.

"She said that she would have the girl baptised in her name and then laid to rest amongst the roots of an apple tree."

"Really? Did she ... really say that?"

"Yes, and that's what happened on the next day."

"But you can't simply ... bury a ... child under a ... tree! There are cemeteries for that."

"No one needed to know, and no one paid any attention. My parents buried my sister the following evening under the oldest apple tree of Amory Farm. Then there was a service, and then ..."

"And then?"

"Then came the great catastrophe. Two days later Mother died of childbed fever."

Mr Lee poured himself a cup of tea to strengthen himself and said: "You're fortunate because you still have a mother. But when Miles and I were young lads we lost mother and sister at one stroke."

"That must be ... terrible, Mr Lee. I feel very ... sorry for you and your brother."

"That's alright. I don't want to talk about that any more at the moment. These painful memories are not central to the whole business. What's more important is what happened later."

Without wanting to, Nadja had become enthralled by Mr Lee's story. She hung on his lips and begged him to go on.

"A couple of months later our trees began to bear fruit the same as every year. But this time the fruit, Nadja, was like fruit you've never seen in your life, bursting with juicy sweetness and especially in such unimaginable quantities that my grandfather didn't know what was going on. Never in his whole life had his trees produced so many apples. It was the harvest of his life, a blessing that gave the company a real boost. Little Aldusa had fed the tree and with it all the trees on the farm so that they produced apples as if there were no tomorrow. Can you understand this miracle, Nadja? Can you get your head round it and feel it in your beautiful young body?"

"I don't know, Mr Lee. But what's the business with … Aldusa in the church?"

"Oh, her! The figure in the church has never been identified. No one knows whether it's a saint or a pagan fertility symbol. When Mother died and the miracle of the apple harvest happened, Father regularly repeated this miracle in the name of his dead wife and daughter, and so with time the belief in St Aldusa grew up and gradually merged with the unknown figure in the church."

"How do you mean 'repeated'?"

"If a dead child under an apple tree could have such an effect on the following year's crop, the obvious thing was to try it again."

"But that's not … possible."

"In a children's home it is."

"?"

"Don't you understand what I'm trying to say?"

"No. Or … You mean children from the home were … buried under the apple tree."

Mr Lee nodded solemnly.

"But children don't die … just when you need them to."

"No, of course not. But they can be helped along."

Nadja shook her head in disbelief: "No, Mr Lee, that's not possible. I must be misunderstanding you because that would be …"

"Murder?"

Nadja nodded silently.

"What a big word that is! No, Nadja, Father just helped them along. He did it for the good of the community. And always in Aldusa's name. For decades now we in Southcombe have had the most fertile soil and the best crops far and wide. Unfortunately Amory Cider Farm closed after the death of my grandfather because of bad management by his heirs, but Southcombe is flourishing, and this it owes very largely to my far-sighted father – and now to me!"

"… It all sounds … like … like a horror story, but I believe you're telling the truth."

"What is important, girl, is not your believing but a deeper knowing and feeling. You must feel these creative forces in the depths of your being. But that'll come, don't worry. That's what we're here for, you and I. In the end we'll make a worthy Apple Queen out of you, I'm confident of that. – Right, and now I'll help you back into your room. Tom has left your bag here. You can wash and get changed and while you're resting you can think about everything I've said."

"She's still not answering."

"Try again later," Haider advised. "Perhaps they're just driving through an area where there's no signal. There are lots of places like that in Cornwall, especially by the coast."

"Or try Tom," Zoë suggested.

Vera alternately rang his and Nadja's numbers, but neither of them answered. When she told the others she made an effort not to show any of the worry that was beginning to preoccupy her.

"Perhaps we should go to the police after all," she said. "Nadja isn't normally like this. She's always very good about answering her phone. And Tom too."

"I think it's too early to get the police involved. I'm quite certain no harm will come to her. She's bound to be back tomorrow as planned."

"I don't suppose you've got children, Mr Haider, otherwise you wouldn't talk like that."

Zoë added a conciliatory note to the discussion: "Maybe Mr Haider is right. Let's at least wait and hear what Jason thinks. He knows everyone who has anything to do with the wassailing, and he may have a suggestion. Didn't he say that Tom was a school friend of his? In small villages that's inevitable because everyone goes to school with everyone. Give me Tom's number and I'll pass it on to Jason. Perhaps he'll have more success than you. Tom will have stored your number on his mobile, but he won't know Jason's number so perhaps he'll reply to him."

"Do you mean that Tom doesn't want to speak to me?"

"No idea, but that's possible."

Chapter 26

"Hello?"

"Tom?"

"Who's that?"

"Don't you recognize my voice any longer?"

"N-No. Should I?"

"Well, five years is a long time."

"Jason!"

"Spot on. How are things with you?"

"How did you get my number?"

"That's my business. It wasn't hard."

"Look …"

"I asked you how things were. Or is this a bad time to talk?"

"No, of course not. I'm just a bit taken by surprise and don't quite know what to say or where to start."

"I hear you're married. Congratulations."

"Thanks. And you, have you got hooked up yet?"

"No, not yet. How's work? Are you still in computers?"

"Yes, till something better turns up. These days you cling on to what you've got."

"Where are you now, Tom?"

"At home. Why? Is the reception bad?"

"No, I can hear you fine. And where's your wife?"

"Here with me, of course. But what are all these questions about. Why are you acting so funny, man? Are you high? Or drunk?"

"No chance. I'm the same as I always was, never touch those things."

"Great to hear you after all this time. I've often wondered what happened to you."

"Yes, likewise."

"There was a time when people in the village said you'd decamped to Morocco with a woman. Someone said they saw you in a bazaar there."

"People here obviously want to believe that I'm living an exciting life. But Africa's not for me. Too hot, too dirty. And anyway …"

"Perhaps you're ringing because … well, because of that business in Greenhill Park. There's no more news, I'm afraid. Still nothing."

"I've known that for a long time. That business in Greenhill Park – you can call it by its proper name: Lizzie's murder. That's what it was and I think it's better to be straightforward."

"Yes, of course. I'm still so terribly sorry, Jason, believe me. I often think about it."

"No need, Tom. Because it's your turn soon, if I'm correctly informed. Your wife is this year's Apple Queen, isn't she?"

"Yes."

"So now it's my turn to congratulate you."

"Thank you, thank you. Nadja is a wonderful Apple Queen. You should have seen her at the wassailing ceremony. The whole of Southcombe was at her feet."

"How is she now?"

"She's doing her duty and I'm supporting her as best I can."

"Tom, do you love your wife?"

"Hey, Jason, stop talking crap. Of course I love her. She's a fantastic woman, I couldn't wish for anyone better."

"But by the end of the year you'll be a widower if everything follows the village's crazy plan. Do you really want that?"

"Jason, Jason, you're going a bit far now. Why should I discuss all this on the phone? And especially with you, since you've been away five years. You don't belong to the village any longer. You can't judge these things properly any more. It's best if you leave us in peace. We get on fine without outsiders."

"I'm not an outsider. I know about the wassailing just as well as you do, and because of Lizzie I know more than most people in the village."

"What was your reason for ringing, Jason?"

"Among other things, because I wanted to speak to your wife."

"But you can't, not now."

"I thought she was with you."

"She doesn't know you. What reason should I give her?"

"Tell her that I want to say hello to her as my old friend's wife."

"No chance."

"She isn't with you at all, is she? You lied to me earlier, didn't you?"

"Jason, stop this nonsense. In the end it's got nothing to do with you where she is. I don't know if you've got a girlfriend, but if you have I don't want to speak to her."

"I have got one, but in contrast to your wife she is not in mortal danger. There's no circle of fanatics fixed on her death."

"Listen to yourself. You used not to talk like that."

"Quite right, Tom. I used to think like you, and what was the result? Lizzie died and I've spent five years in absolute misery. But that's the end of it! I don't know your wife, don't even know if I'd like her or not. But that's not relevant. I don't want her to end up like Lizzie and the others. That's all. Fuck your apple crops."

"You've lost all … sense of respect."

"For God's sake, tell me, where is your wife?"

"Calm down. Nadja is being well looked after at the moment. No one is harming her. I guarantee it. Just now she is being trained."

"Trained? Where?"

"Stop it, Jason. I'm going to put the phone down if you get worked up like this. It doesn't do any good."

"Where is she being trained? Can't you at least tell me that?"

"That's enough, Jason."

"Tom!"

"Goodbye."

"Damn!"

After he too had pressed the 'End' button on his mobile, Jason stood at the window for a while, irritated but also strangely relieved, staring at the fountain in the garden which Mr Pyke had turned into a bird feeder. A blackbird was at that moment hopping up and down the edge of the basin and chasing away any other birds that dared to come near.

He and Tom had been best friends at school, but after that they had gone their separate ways. They had met in the pub now and then and chatted about the good old days, but the friendship had become more casual on each occasion. The last time they had passed each other in the village, scarcely a week before Jason made his get-away, they had done no more than nod to each other. And now? Hearing Tom's voice again after so many years had left Jason without emotion.

Jason scarcely dared to admit to himself how free he felt after this telephone conversation, how happy in the knowledge that Southcombe, its people and its practices had lost their power over him. He hardly thought of Sue, she hadn't meant anything to him for years now. Nothing more tied him to the village and now, with his sister's death, the last family bond was broken.

For the first time in five years he could think of Southcombe without his heart racing.

Tom hadn't wanted to reveal where his wife was at the moment, but he must have forgotten that Lizzie had gone through the same ordeals. She too had been 'trained': it hadn't worked, but all the same they had made the attempt. Luckily for Jason, Lizzie had never taken her oath of silence seriously but had always told him exactly what happened to her and what people tried to convince her of. She had also told him what had happened during her 'training' at the old Cider Farm in Washford.

Jason's eyes clouded over at the thought of that evening in the Kings Arms when Lizzie had exuberantly told all and sundry about her escapade. Poor Lizzie! She had experienced what the Swiss woman would now have to go through. He was willing to bet this year's Queen was being taught in the same place.

Zoë had rung Jason half an hour earlier about the extra rooms. He didn't want to wait until she arrived with the filmmaker and the Swiss mother because they would then only insist on going with him. He sent Zoë a text and scribbled a couple of lines on the back of his EasyJet boarding card, which he left clearly visible on the window ledge. Then he leapt down the stairs and knocked on the kitchen door. Through the frosted glass he could see Mr Pyke going back and fore as he hummed an aria from 'The Magic Flute'.

"Is there a problem with the room?" he asked, a cigarette in the corner of his mouth.

"No, everything's fine. It's something quite different. Excuse me for troubling you but I've got a big ask to put to you. I'll understand if you say No, but there's no harm in asking."

"Well I never. You really seem quite worked up. I hope it's nothing bad. Please come in, I'm just frying up some bubble and squeak. My neighbour gave me the cabbage – the best organic cabbage there is."

"Thank you, no, I'm afraid I haven't got time at the moment. – Mr Pyke, could you possibly lend me your car for a couple of hours? Please!"

"My car? That's a strange request. None of my visitors has ever asked me for that."

"I'll leave you my watch as security, all my cash – there, two hundred and sixty pounds – even my passport if you want it. I promise that you'll have your car back tonight. And I'll pay you a good rate for it."

Mr Pyke wasn't a man to make rush decisions, but by the end Jason was able to persuade him that he wouldn't make off with his car.

"That nice French girlfriend of yours, right, she's coming back soon and she's bringing me some new visitors, isn't she? Alright then, if you insist. It's only an old wreck of a car anyway. But do watch out, sometimes the accelerator gets stuck, and the gears aren't quite what they were."

Jason soon got used to driving on the left again. Even by the time he was leaving Taunton it was as if he had never been out of the country. He kept looking away from the road, searching for familiar landmarks in the darkness. There had been a lot of building since he made his escape. In some places estates had grown up where earlier there had been fields, blocks of brick and concrete unlovingly strewn across the landscape with garages and fenced gardens, all approximately identical: Taunton's tentacles reaching out into the peaceful landscape of Somerset.

Only after the road off to Combe Florey did he find the land on both sides of the A358 had changed little, and he was surprised how much of it had remained in his memory and how precisely he was still able to estimate the distance between the villages.

It took him a good half hour to reach Washford. Even from some distance away he could see the lights of the village pub and in front of it the signpost to Cleeve Abbey. As a precaution he parked the car away from the orange light of the abbey, but before he got out and despite the smell of stale tobacco smoke in the car, he sat for a moment with half closed eyes in order to collect himself. He had no idea what was awaiting him in the coming hours, knew only that he had done the right thing by not dragging Zoë and the others into it. It was his job to free the Apple Queen from the clutches of her would-be murderers, this was the unexpected second chance that he had been granted through Zoë. He must take it.

He took his mobile out of his coat pocket and read what Zoë had replied: "Why??? Just coming, will do it all together. Where are you going? Z." Without answering he switched it off.

How dark and lonely the lanes were by this time in the evening. It had been exactly the same in St Valéry. Since he didn't know precisely where Amory Cider Farm was he was afraid of missing it and so he walked slowly, looking into every corner that he passed.

In the end it wasn't the house that he recognised but the car, which he found after about two hundred yards, parked on the side of the road. A Landrover Freelander, and not any old one: no, it was the silver-grey one with the Chinese charm in the form of a knot hanging on the mirror, the tank that Miles used to block the High Street with whenever he fancied parking in front of Bill's flower shop. Miles! So he was here! No doubt about that, unless he'd passed the car on to his brother in the meantime. Or they had both come.

While he circled the car and turned into the drive leading to Cider Farm, Jason couldn't help thinking of Rich and Frances' chateau. Things had been the other way round there: he had been barricaded inside and Miles had lurked around outside. The tricks that fate played!

Anxious to avoid the gravel and instead to walk on the softer grass border, he approached the house on tiptoe. What he could see in the darkness impressed him more through its dilapidation than its monumental dimensions: crumbling plasterwork, 'Amory Farm' – in distorted, scarcely legible writing above a rotten cornice fascia – and on the ground fragments of tiles that the wind had blown off the roof. The lights were on in two rooms on the ground floor, but the drawn curtains prevented him from seeing inside. He checked that no doors or windows were open at the front of the house and cautiously felt his way towards the rear. There he came across a corrugated iron shed whose doors were falling off their hinges. Inside there were all sorts of machines for processing fruit – presses, pumps and shredders – rusting away in peace and still gently exuding the sour scent of fermented apples, as if cider production had stopped only months, not years, before. Behind the shed was an orchard, and beside it was a rubbish bin full of paper for recycling, rows of spraying machines and tractors as well as a lines of big plastic containers in which all kinds of tubes and hoses, rolls of adhesive, bottles of methylated spirits, scissors and knives lay in a heap. The knives were rusty, too, Jason discovered when he took several of them and tested their blades. But a rusty blade was better than none at all, and two blades were better than one. With two knives in his pocket Jason returned to the house to explore further.

He didn't have any luck. The cellar door gave way, but at the end of the tunnel, which was full of cider barrels, he came to a door that was bolted. What had he imagined? Open doors in the winter? A red carpet laid out for him and the Apple Queen handed over without resistance? No, he had to take a different approach, preferably involving cunning.

He went back to the car and sat in the passenger seat. He had acquired two knives which he could use for self-defence in an emergency, but what he now needed was something small that, if he judged Mr Pyke correctly, he should be able to find in the car. Praying that he would, he opened the glove compartment and began to root around in it. He turned up a glasses case, an open packet of Marlboro, papers and at the bottom – yes, a box of matches.

"Yes," said Nadja hesitantly after drinking another sip of tea, "I can see it. It is standing in front of me. Now it's beginning to grow. Not high into the sky, no, this is where it's growing, here, towards me, and the heavens are rocking it, the twigs are reaching for the sun, the apples are also suns, no, they are moons, your face is also a moon."

She could hear herself speaking as if she were standing outside, as if through a loudspeaker in the corner of the room. But the room didn't have corners any more, and those eyes that stared at her did not belong to any face, did not even belong together, for one flew in one direction, the other in the opposite direction. But that couldn't be right either, for there were no directions any longer, just this tree that grew and shrank and grew again and was right on top of her, so close that she could breathe the scent of its fruit and with her hand touch its knobbly skin, which burned. While the leaves stroked her cheeks and neck, the burning went deeper, through her pores and lungs into her heart, which stood still until she no longer knew where the tree was growing, whether it was in front of her eyes or in her and through her. But then suddenly she felt that it was she who was growing and had leaves which shook in the autumn wind and it was she that bore all the apples which fell from her arms onto the world, her gift –

"Can you feel it now, Nadja, your tree?"

Nadja nodded weakly. Every movement caused a tremor that she could feel reaching into the core of her being. Clods of earth swelled to the size of mountains, and how distant her toes suddenly were, distant on the horizon, but when she stayed calm she was rooted to the earth as if no wind, no axe could bend or break her.

But where was this earth? And who did the mouth belong to that twisted and showed its teeth while saying, "Sit down now and drink a sip of water"?

Was she sitting? Was she drinking?

And why suddenly this excitement when she just wanted to close her eyes and go to sleep on the fluffy carpet of flowers, why such loud voices that weren't hers. She was silent and almost asleep, but there was Mr Lee's voice and another voice which now shouted just beside her ear, "Where are the fire extinguishers in this bloody place? Are there any?" – and then disappeared upstairs and downstairs with curses which coloured her sleep a glowing yellow like the suns on the tree, her apples.

A chill spread over her body, a draft of wind swept in through the crack of an open door. She drew her knees up and clenched her hands under her chin and in the warmth of her own breath she became smaller, younger, almost unborn, her mouth a red line, her eyelids large and arched, while the other voice said: "Leave her there. We can worry about her later. The shed's on fire, get it?"

On fire? How they would crackle, her great limbs, if she burned. Blazing fiercely, the twigs quickly black, the trunk turned to charcoal, then ashes trickling down onto the earth. That's where it always goes back to, whether tree or apple or child – always back into the earth.

Those steps! They sent dull tremors through the earth, with one ear she could clearly hear the waves beneath her, and with the other she could equally clearly hear a wheezing and puffing, and there was this sudden heaviness, this giddiness and the feeling of floating, no, of dangling with her feet in the void and one arm hanging down, in her head a funeral dance of colours and sounds. Because the tree now began to shrink and its roots grabbed at the air. Because she suddenly felt so cold, as cold as death.

She wanted to open her eyes but the lids bore down too heavily on them, and with her other senses she could not understand why she hung so shrivelled in the air and felt material on her cheeks, not the soft material of the flowered meadow on which she had begun to dream that she was lying after the tea but a cold, damp weave that smelled alien, with buttons that pressed into her flesh.

And then these shouts in the distance and how she was being shaken, and over her head more wheezing, louder than before. She had to open her eyes, otherwise she would fall – but from what height? And onto what?

A jolt and after that an eternity of floating before she slid ever further down, hit her head and lay flat, her arms and legs outstretched, really lay, happy except for the chill and the voices above her, snarling animals and she herself perhaps their prey.

Once again she tried to open her eyes and this time at least she could see where she was lying: under the open sky at the edge of a road, her head in the grass, her feet on the road. But she wasn't alone. Beside her there were two people grabbing at each other and grappling with each other, not silently like the leaves of her tree in the wind but panting and cursing. They fell over and got up again, grabbed each other and pulled and tore, and neither would give way.

Into what strange dream had she now tumbled, seeing Mr Lee in it? Normally he sent her off alone on her journeys and stood waiting on the edge, her pole-star, so that she could find her way back. But perhaps Mr Lee didn't want her to find her way back any more and was fighting – for that was exactly what he seemed to be doing – fighting with evil forces that were trying to lead her away, back to a life that was no longer hers. What wouldn't she have given to help Mr Lee! But her limbs felt like lead and every slightest movement made things go black in front of her eyes. When one of the men shouted the sounds would cut wounds in her flesh so that she awoke with a start, dulled by pain but for a moment fully awake, with all her senses present. Then she saw the other man who was trying to tear her away from Mr Lee, saw him and indistinctly yet another man, who came running from the other side of the road, his hair flying, something flashing in his hand. She could smell the grass, the sweat and the fear of the men wrestling and tasted disaster in her dry mouth while things were still undecided – that was all so clear before the night flowed once again through her head and the spiral turned her back into herself.

And then in the midst of this dizziness a bang. Sharp, short, it left behind a silence so deep that between one second and the next it touched eternity. Nadja lay paralysed. She saw the two men next to her fall to their knees and then collapse onto the grass. Each of them had pulled the other down, each gripped the other, but only one of them lifted his head above the chest of the other, reached his hand out, slid away from the body of the other and crawled over to her. From the other side of the road came bloodcurdling cries of "Bill! Bill!", followed by neither shots nor curses but only by loud sobs of despair.

Once again she felt herself being grasped under the knees and an arm being pushed under her back to lift her up. When he held her securely he didn't begin to run as earlier but turned towards the road and shouted: "Stop it now, Miles. It's over."

But why couldn't she stand on her own two legs? As soon as she opened her eyes the world turned again and she saw what was not possible: an orange coloured sky and, stretched out on the side of the road, Mr Lee with dark splashes on his shirt and face.

"Miles?" repeated the stranger.

"–"

"You look after your brother. I'll call an ambulance and a fire-engine."

The stranger waited a moment for a reply, but Miles – what Miles? – came silently across the road and kneeled down beside Mr Lee, bending over him until his forehead touched the shirt with the splashes on it, and howled like a wolf.

The stranger finally moved. He had not yet spoken a word to her. Now he did, whispered something to her, his mouth close to her ear, but the safety he was talking about – what was that? Here it was fruit trees that were always safe, trees like her were revered. Even if she wasn't perhaps a tree, who could tell her exactly who she was and where she was being carried, into what dream, what car? And where were they were going?

Chapter 27

Vera followed the nurse down the twisting corridors into Room 302. For two days Nadja had been in one of the six beds separated by curtains, suffering the after-effects of a powerful cocktail of hallucinogens and sedatives.

It was Vera's fourth visit. Since Jason had rescued her daughter from the Cider Farm and taken her directly to Musgrove Hospital in Taunton, Nadja had occasionally emerged from her coma, but after briefly opening her eyes had returned immediately to a deep sleep. Whether or not she was conscious during these brief moments the doctors were uncertain: however, they told Vera they were confident the patient would recover from her drugged state.

"Your daughter has been very lucky. We found high levels of altropine and scopolomine in her blood. Any increase in the dose could have had serious consequences. Now she just needs time to clear the drugs from her system. You'll have your daughter back with you soon, Mrs Wyler."

Every time she sat by Nadja's bed Vera had mixed feelings. She prayed that Nadja would wake up soon and that everything would be just the same as before. At the same time she was afraid of the moment when her daughter realized that the Southcombe idyll no longer existed. And, worse, that it had never been more than an illusion.

The first thing that Nadja asked when she woke up in the middle of the second night was not what had happened to her but why Tom wasn't there. "Where is he? We were at a funeral together and then we drove to friends in St Ives and …"

The memory of the car journey suddenly made her shake with fear. She tried to throw off the blankets and jump out of the bed, but the room started spinning around her and she fell back on to her pillows.

"Tell me, Mum, where's Tom?" she pleaded. The look in her eyes told Vera that though Nadja was still confused she knew that something bad had happened. Have we had a crash? Is he …?"

"No, no, don't get worked up, Nadja. Tom is fine. He just can't come at the moment, that's all. And that's why I'm here."

Nadja accepted the explanation without visible emotion. She turned onto her side, sighing, closed her eyes and was silent. Vera thought she had fallen asleep again when, after a while, Nadja threw another question at her: "I've got a vague memory that Tom told me lies. We didn't actually drive to St Ives. But where did we go? Do you know?"

"Tom took you to Mr Lee in Washford."

"Washford? Why Washford?"

Vera tried as circumspectly as she could to explain what had happened in the last two days. She didn't want to deceive Nadja, simply spare her. Nadja would discover soon enough the darker facts surrounding the wassailing ritual. But she wasn't so easy to satisfy."

"You're just beating about the bush, Mum. You may be right that I was somewhere with Mr Lee, even if I can't remember anything about it, but what I want to know is what's up with Tom. Why he told me lies."

"He thought you wouldn't go and see Mr Lee of your own free will – perhaps that's the reason."

"No, that can't be it. I'm always happy to go to Mr Lee. Aha, now it's slowly coming back. I was a tree. No, I am a tree. I'm growing and I'm sprouting roots and … Or …, oh, I don't know any longer what I am. But come on, please tell me where Tom is!"

"You're going to have to be brave. He's at the police station in Bristol at the moment."

It was out in the open, the word Vera had wanted to avoid. Tom and the rest of his family were helping the police with their enquiries. Nadja stared at her mother, eyes wide open. She wanted to speak but at first only a slight gurgling sound came from her mouth, while her breathing became faster and more laboured.

"What is it, Nadja? Are you not feeling well? I'll go and get a nurse."

"No, no, it'll soon be over." She sat up in bed to breathe more easily, head bowed, a picture of misery in her loosely tied hospital gown sagging off one shoulder.

"What crime has he committed?" she asked quietly.

"Well, it's actually more complicated than a single crime," said Vera carefully. "But lie down again, otherwise you'll catch cold."

Nadja ignored this advice and drummed her fists against her thighs in an outburst of anger. "In all these months you've been reproaching me for not facing up to things … Yes, let me finish, that is exactly what you think, isn't it? You think I like to avoid anything unpleasant if I can. But you're no better, are you? What have you been doing here ever since you sat down? You've been fobbing me off with half-truths. But I want to know, and I want to know now. What has happened to my husband, and why isn't he here with me?"

"Nadja, you haven't recovered yet."

"No! You're only making things easy for yourself. Tell me everything."

"Right, if you insist I'll tell you. Ever since you were chosen to be Apple Queen you have been undergoing systematic training in suicide."

"Who's been doing that?"

"Mr Lee. He gave you drugs that messed with your mind. The vitamin pills, for example, contained traces of various plants from the nightshade family."

"I've no idea what you're talking about," said Nadja defiantly.

"Plants like belladonna and thorn apple. They contain dangerous substances, and the day before yesterday Mr Lee increased the dose and must have given you a special kind of sage too so that you would be helpless against him. He planned to push you so far that you would take your life in the autumn."

"I'd never do that."

"It's pretty certain that you would have done. Sue Harper did, and other Apple Queens before her."

"You're just using scare tactics to turn me against my new home!"

"No, Nadja. I'm not."

"But I don't understand. Why would Mr Lee want me to take my own life?"

"It wasn't just him. He and the whole village believed in the power of human sacrifice. After an Apple Queen has died her heart is cut out and buried under the apple tree during the wassailing ceremony by the new Queen, in order to feed the tree and assure the village of a good harvest to come."

"No! That can't be …"

"It is, Nadja. You don't want to be spared the truth so I'll tell you quite openly: you yourself buried Sue Harper's heart under the apple tree in January and …"

"Stop, Mum, please, I can't bear it!"

Nadja blocked her ears, trembling, and stared with a look of blank horror past Vera at the wall. For a moment she was silent and motionless and then she breathed: "The leather purse?"

Vera nodded and put her hand on her daughter's arm to soothe her.

"That's enough for now. We can talk about this later."

"No. I want to hear it all."

"If you're sure? Well, while we speak the police are in Greenhill Park searching for further evidence."

Nadja listened without interrupting.

"Eileen Moore was Mr Lee's associate. She helped him to groom the Apple Queen and prepare her for death. The thing that will be most difficult for you to accept, Nadja, is that Tom too knew what your fate was to be at the end of the year."

At the mention of her husband's name Nadja's face creased in sorrow but she controlled herself.

"It's not Tom's fault in the end. Even as a child he was made familiar with the wassailing rituals, like all the young people in the village. Together with Mrs Moore and Tom's mother, Mr Lee has had psychological control over Southcombe for years. Mrs Moore and Mrs Skinner used to be nurse and cook at Greenhill Park. They worked under Mr Lee's father and fell under his spell. He seems to have had an extraordinary charisma. He could order anybody to do anything and they'd obey him. In any case the tradition of the Apple Queen in this barbaric form goes back to him, and when he died and his son took up this tradition in the nineties he found willing accomplices in both women."

"But what's happened to Tom?"

"I don't know. There's probably no crime he can be charged with. He was just somebody who went along with things."

"He lied to me and stood by while they planned to murder me."

"Well, Nadja, you'll have some thinking to do and you'll have to decide how you want things to continue between you two. Whether you can clear the air between you and ..."

"Yes, Mum, I've understood. But that's my business. When I want your advice I'll ask for it. – And how are things with you? Are you going to be staying in Station House?"

"No, certainly not. I think I'll break off my stay in England and go back to Bern. Mrs Moore was arrested this morning, by the way."

"Poor Eileen."

"She was expecting it. When the police called she had destroyed all the evidence and was sitting with a case packed in the lounge."

"What's happening to the dogs?"

"They've been put in a dogs' home for the moment. Would you like to adopt them perhaps?"

"Maybe, who knows? And Tom's parents?"

"I'm afraid Marion and Geoffrey won't get off as lightly as Tom. Marion is denying everything but we've got enough evidence to incriminate her."

"Who are 'we'?"

"Don't you think I've told you enough for one day?"

"When can I go home? Has the doctor said anything?"

"No, but in your position I wouldn't be so impatient to go there. As you can imagine, the village is in terrible turmoil and the police are nosing around everywhere.

You can still think about whether you'd like to come back to Bern with me and stay a few weeks in Switzerland until things have calmed down."

"Bern?"

"Why not? After all, it's your home town. How long is it since you were last there?"

"An eternity."

Chapter 28

As he did every morning, Mr Pyke filled up his fountain with bird food and collected the leaves that had fallen onto the lawn over night. After breakfast he had made his studio at the end of the garden available to Jason and Ahmed Haider so that they could discuss the 'extraordinary events in Southcombe' without being disturbed.

"My sculptures are as silent as the grave," he had assured them, "whereas in the house you can always get interrupted by a phone call or by someone arriving at the door wanting a room. As you'll see, the two glass walls mean that you can use this room for morning light and for afternoon light. Ideal for filming. Especially ideal for my sculptures."

And indeed, even on this grey March morning, the light really brought Mr Pyke's three-dimensional figures to life.

They were slender wooden sculptures, most of them small-scale female torsos standing on pedestals, lined up along the wall. In their unfinished state they gave the impression of having to be freed from the material as if from bandages that were constricting them. Jason examined each one with a mixture of distaste and fascination while Haider cleared the work-table of spatulas, messy overalls and pieces of chalk so that he could put his recorder on it. Perhaps because he was used to spotless surroundings at home, he seemed unwilling to sit on the stool and avoided touching the table with his arms and hands.

"Right, everything's ready now. We can get started. If you don't mind I'll begin by asking you a few questions and then I'd be grateful for a free description of the most recent events."

"Okay, fire away."

Jason sat down opposite Haider. He was tense but the window, which offered a view from the garden gate as far as the fence at the back, gave him enough composure to at least sit still. Although he had liked Haider from the first he now had the feeling that with this interview he was agreeing to expose himself to the whole world. But he was there of his own free will, Haider hadn't forced him. The film-maker, as if reading his thoughts, held his finger hovering over the start button and said: "We'll just pass over any questions you don't want to answer. And please relax. Our conversation will never be broadcast in this form, I'm just recording it because my memory isn't the best and I prefer not to take notes. What we discuss here is just to help my memory."

Jason nodded, then Haider pressed the button and began: "Jason Collings, you lived your first twenty-three years in Southcombe, Somerset, the village that for the past two days has stood in the centre of a horrific scandal. You have admitted to being familiar with the satanic practices of the local wassailing ritual even as a child. Can you describe to me what it's like to live with a knowledge of this kind? For outsiders it's very difficult to imagine."

Jason thought for a moment, bent forwards and spoke cautiously into the microphone: "I'm not trying to excuse myself, but if you grow up in a community where every member – and I mean literally every single member – fervently believes something, at first it doesn't even occur to you to question it. I remember that even in kindergarten the teacher told us about wassailing and its background. Not in all its brutal details, of course, but with songs and games and so on. For example, within the limits of our understanding we learned how to make compost and what compost is good for. In the autumn we had to bring apples from our orchards and compare them with each other, judge which apples were juicier and sweeter, and work out the reasons. Looking back, of course, I can see the conditioning that lies at the core of teaching like that, but at the time I felt myself as a child somehow tied into the processes of nature, and this gave me a sense of security."

"How was it with the girls? At some stage they must have had a suspicion that wassailing was potentially life-threatening for them."

"No, not really. Even a word like 'life-threatening' was wrongly chosen from our point of view. There was only ever the word 'life-giving': everything that died, whether human, animal or plant, gave life."

"Isn't that a rather one-sided view of death?"

"Yes, of course, I can see that too since I got away. But in those days in Southcombe there was only one way of looking at things. To die as Apple Queen meant giving, participating in the growth of nature. So our teachers always only told the girls how important and fulfilling their contribution to nature was, without going into any disturbing detail. The result was that for the young girls these Apple Queens were heroines like princesses or pop-stars. We sang songs which celebrated the Apple Queen, and when children's performances were put on all the girls would fight to be the Queen. I think that if you start early enough with drumming stories like that into children's heads they internalise them and consider them the most natural thing in the world."

"When did you first become aware that during the wassailing ritual the fertility of the tree was guaranteed not only by cider and slices of toast but also by the sacrifice of a human heart?"

"That isn't a straightforward question because I now know the list of the women who died and could reply that even at the wassailing of 1997 I knew what happened to poor Mrs Rees Mogg. I was sixteen at the time. But I think I knew what happened in this case without quite realising the significance of what I knew. It was only three years later and especially in 2002, when young Judith Selwyn was sacrificed, that I was fully in the picture."

"Did you know Judith personally?"

"Of course, that's unavoidable in a village: you just know people. She was our postman's daughter. I often saw her at the post office counter, and sometimes we exchanged a few words. She had just accepted a job in Scandinavia as an au pair when she was elected Apple Queen. After that there was no question of her leaving the village, and in the autumn she threw herself under a bus, as planned."

"How did you feel about attending that wassailing ceremony?"

"What do you mean?"

"I mean, did you find it particularly difficult or stressful? After all, Judith was only nineteen and her whole life lay in front of her."

"I don't remember particular feelings. You mustn't forget that the role of Apple Queen was seen as a distinction. Judith was very proud of it, despite her increasing depression. And her parents too felt themselves honoured. They're simple people and perhaps they felt it gave them higher status in the village."

"But as we know, not all the Apple Queens accepted their fate with so little resistance. There is one striking exception. Tell us."

Jason folded his arms and swallowed a couple of times. His mouth had become dry from talking, and although he was expecting this question, it struck him like a slap in the face. What could he say? Didn't Haider know enough already to imagine Lizzie?

As he tried to put his sentences together he could see Zoë tripping towards the garden gate and couldn't help smiling. Lovely Zoë. She was wearing a long lemon-coloured pullover and black leggings. Haider turned around too when he noticed the expression on Jason's face. Before going to bed the evening before she had announced that she would have a lie-in the following morning and have breakfast later than Jason: "You haven't got time for me anyway. While you tell Haider the story of your life I'm going to take things easy. I may stay in our room, but I may nip out. Perhaps I'll stir up Taunton a bit, or else make a pilgrimage back to Musgrove Hospital. I suppose the Apple Queen will have to wake up sometime."

Zoë waved at them both, smiling, and with an elegant twist slipped out through the garden gate.

"I … I'd rather leave that out, if you don't mind."

Haider frowned and went on to the next question: "Right. How would you judge the position of the Lee brothers in the village, and how do you see their relationship to each other?"

"There were three of them but Simon never counted somehow. He was considered the village idiot and no one really knew how he earned his living or what he did during the day. He lived alone in a room above the hairdresser's, and if you wanted to see him you would have to go to the Kings Arms. In reality he was marginalized and I suppose led a sad life. Bill and Miles never really accepted him as their brother. They had each other and that was enough for the two of them even though they couldn't have been more different. Miles was always a bully. As children we were all scared of him. Sometimes he would hit us for no reason at all, just for the fun of seeing us cry. Bill was the one who seemed the most normal. That must sound strange now it turns out he was the craziest of the three."

"Bill Lee cured all kinds of illnesses in the village. His knowledge of herbal medicine must have been impressive. But above all he managed to manipulate the whole village. What was so special about him that everyone joined in with his fantasy?"

Jason shrugged his shoulders and admitted that he didn't have an answer to that question.

"It must be connected to his father. Reginald Lee was considered the protector of the village. He cared for the wellbeing of the people there, distributed medicines, practised the laying on of hands and occasionally did things behind closed doors that could be called exorcisms. But that was all before I was born, I'm a bit vague about it, it's only what I've been told."

"One last question. What exactly happened in Washford on the night of the fourteenth to the fifteenth of March this year?"

"Oh, I don't like to think about it. I did everything wrong that you possibly could do wrong, and by doing that I risked the life of the Apple Queen, a certain Nadja Wyler from Switzerland, and maybe my own as well. But I …"

At this moment Mr Pyke appeared at the window and lifted up in front of them a tray with steaming coffee mugs on it. Haider at once pressed the button on his recorder and stood up to open the door.

"How kind of you, thank you very much. Just pass the tray through to me."

"I thought that you'd need a bit of strengthening. What you're doing here must be very tiring. – And since I'm here, Mr Haider, there's something that's occurred to me. I'd be very grateful if before you leave you could write a sentence in Arabic in my visitors' book. Arabic is one thing I'm lacking. I had a Chinese family here once, and a few weeks ago a student from Colombia, but never anyone from Arabia, no, never."

"I come from Pakistan, Mr Pyke. Of course I'd be pleased to write something in Urdu and Dari, but I'm afraid I can't help with Arabic."

"Can't you?!"

"No, but the script is more or less the same."

"Oh right, then that's fine. I just like exotic things, you understand? Signs of something exotic look good in a visitors' book, they make other visitors gawp in surprise. It's better than Tripadvisor – but there I am standing around and getting in the way of your work! Here's the coffee. If you need anything else there's a bell there. After all journalists from Channel 4 News deserve special treatment."

After Haider had shut the door behind Mr Pyke he encouraged Jason to continue his account.

"My train for London leaves at a quarter to two. We haven't got a lot of time. And your contribution is valuable, Mr Collings. Without it Brett's film would have no ending."

"What happened that evening is quickly told. The Lees still owned their old family estate, the Amory Cider Farm in Washford, which had stopped functioning long ago – everyone in the village knew that. In addition I found out from an earlier Apple Queen that Bill Lee used to carry out a kind of intensive training there that was designed to produce in the chosen women the fantasy that they were one with the apple tree. When I learned that this year's Apple Queen, a Swiss lady, had possibly been abducted, the memory of the Cider Farm came back to me. I drove over there and since I assumed that both brothers were in the house I could think of nothing better than setting the shed on fire in order to get them out of the house. When Bill and Miles saw the fire out-side and started trying to put it out they left Miss Wyler lying in the house, unconscious. It's obvious, I'd have done the same. In any case I thought I'd got it all sorted out when I found Miss Wyler in the drawing-room and carried her out into the open air. Unfortunately my car was too far away for me to be able to drive off with her straightaway. Bill heard my steps on the asphalt and ran after me. Half way to the car he caught me from behind and knocked me over, which may have been a bit of luck because when I left Miss Wyler lying in the grass in order to stand up again, at least she wasn't in Miles' line of fire. The shot was of course aimed at me, but it hit his brother."

"You talk modestly about luck and belittle your own achievements."

"No, not at all. My greatest stroke of luck was Miles' reaction, which I couldn't have foreseen. That's what Nadja Skinner and I owe our lives to. I still don't understand it. It would have been the easiest thing in the world for Miles to shoot us. No witnesses far and wide, we were the ideal distance away, two shots and it would all have been over. I'd never have had time to escape or hide, and Miss Wyler certainly wouldn't. But no, it was as if all the life suddenly drained out of Miles when he saw his brother lying on the side of the road. He was suddenly not thinking of us any longer at all. And that was after he had sworn he would kill me and I had lived for five years in mortal terror of him. But life has its strange turns. Just as Miles' lust for murder was suddenly extinguished the night before last, so was I also freed from my fear. It was almost as if I was drunk as I went to the car with Miss Wyler in my arms, expecting at any moment to be shot in the back but experiencing no fear. At that moment I felt that I was invulnerable. It sounds strange but I can't explain it any better. It was a moment … how shall I put it? … a moment of grace, yes grace, that's the word."

Neither of them had touched their coffee. Silently they now drank it, and finally Jason asked: "What exactly are you planning to do with this material?"

"Channel 4 News has given me an earlier slot for Craig Brett's film. Southcombe is in the headlines right round the country, and they want to build on that momentum. The film is practically ready, but of course the latest developments are missing, the solution to the mystery, so to speak. I've agreed to do a second in-depth film on Southcombe's wassailing ritual at some later stage and for that I'd very much like to have you and Miss Wyler there as guests."

"I've still got a job in France that I can't just run away from, and that's why I'm planning to leave England in the next few days. That is to say, if the police let me. After all, I've set a shed on fire and will have to answer for that."

"That shouldn't be a problem. We'll pay for your air fare."

"And how is it with Brett's documentation of the wassailing ceremony? Could I have a look sometime?"

"You'll have to ask the police about that. I gave them the most important stuff … but of course not to Greg Jones."

"No, of course not. What an idiot! Corruption, forgery, abuse of office – he'll pay a lot for all that."

"He certainly will. But as long as he hides behind silence, like Miles, we'll never know exactly how Brett and Simon Lee died. Perhaps they were natural deaths, who knows."

"I don't think you even believe that yourself."

"I'm afraid I must be going, Mr Collings. It's getting late. However, I'd like to welcome you and Mademoiselle Cox to London sometime soon. At the latest for the broadcast. How about that?"

Chapter 29

When the bus from Taunton stopped in front of the Kings Arms in Southcombe, Jason and Zoë found that the pub and the drive up to Greenhill Park were closed off by barriers. Sight-seers had been arriving since the early morning in order to watch the police digging round the apple tree, and the streets of the village were thronged by journalists and television teams questioning people.

"I guess we can forget your little pilgrimage," said Zoë. "I'd prefer to take the next bus straight back to Taunton."

"I hadn't reckoned with crowds like this. There's not much point in staying. I'll have to come another time, alone perhaps. But instead of going back to Taunton we could take the next bus and go on to the sea. It's not far, and then you could at least have seen the Bristol Channel. It's the English answer to the bay of the Somme at St Valéry, so to speak. What do you think?"

Zoë gave him a mischievous look and snuggled into his arms.

"You're relieved, admit it."

Zoë had this gift of being able to find words for what he half knew but could not quite admit to himself.

This time the correctness of her insight went straight to his conscience. While holding her in his arms and breathing in the warm scent of her hair he could feel the blood rise to his cheeks and knew from that how right she was. Yes, he was relieved, and it embarrassed him. He had lain awake in the night and imagined how he would go up the drive to Greenhill Park alone, and in a moment of solemn reflection would cast off his five-year nightmare. He saw himself standing still for a couple of minutes in the barracks, summoning Lizzie back to his mind in every beautiful and every brutal detail, in peace. Then he saw himself going back to Zoë, who had been waiting for him at the Kings Arms, and saying to her that he had now taken final leave of Lizzie and was free for a new future. How easy this had all seemed in the night, and how honestly he had meant it when in the morning he suggested that they should go to Southcombe together.

The bus-stop where they were standing was the same old steel construction with panes of glass disfigured by dirt and graffiti. There were obscene messages for waiting passengers to read, telephone numbers, tattered stickers and initials in paint-sprayed hearts saying that A and S loved each other, as did K and E, as well as P and D. Jason recognised individual markings from earlier and was grateful that he and Lizzie had never been tempted to immortalise their names in this way. Looking over the top of Zoë's head, he scanned the bus timetable and said: "The next bus goes in eight minutes."

They drove to Watchet. From her window seat Zoë could quietly watch the hilly landscape of Somerset passing by, and in Watchet too she was silent as she walked beside Jason, who led her through the little town and then showed her the marina with the bronze statue of Coleridge's 'Ancient Mariner' and, from the pier, the distant coast of Wales.

As always, there was a strong wind in the harbour, but today it brought with it a long forgotten mildness that was almost intoxicating.

"Wales isn't all that far from here," said Zoë, after gazing silently across the sea for a while. "You get the feeling it wouldn't be so difficult to swim across."

"Sixteen miles? Can you swim that far in one go?"

"I don't suppose so. I'm hopeless at swimming. What about you?"

"I wouldn't exactly call myself hopeless, but I couldn't get as far as Wales."

"In any case I don't think this is very like the bay of the Somme. The sand is much darker here, and there are none of these extraordinary cliffs in St Valéry. Our bay is more inviting. In the summer there are even sheep grazing on the islands of grass in the middle of the sand, which gives their meat a slight flavour of sea-salt. I can't imagine that here. Here it is lonely and, yes, somehow creepy."

"Perhaps you think the estuary is creepy because it reminds you of what happened nearby."

"You may be right. I'm thinking especially about poor old Simon who met his end in the mud. Do you really think that was an accident?"

"No, anyone who grows up in this area knows the danger of these beaches. And what do you think the poor devil was doing there on his own at night, anyway? No, it certainly wasn't an accident. But Miles won't talk and the sea has washed away all the traces. What can you do?"

"Not a lot, I agree. Nevertheless …, but let's forget about that for the moment."

Zoë squeezed her hand into Jason's trouser pocket, snuggled up closer to him and buried her face in his jacket. She liked the smell of Jason's clothes and enjoyed the warmth that came through the material from his body. When she looked up again, blinking, and he reached down for her mouth she abandoned herself to his kiss. After the past difficult days Jason was finally thawing.

"You know, Jason," she said, "when we arrived I thought we'd manage to put your past to rest – I mean Lizzie and everything that was connected with her. I used to think that a genuine and lasting relationship is only possible if you're a hundred per cent open and tell each other everything. But that's an illusion. You told me your secret because I put pressure on you, and I …"

"No, Zoë, that's not true. I don't regret for a moment having told you everything. Otherwise we'd never have come here and the wassailing ritual would carry on claiming victims."

"Of course, that's not what I mean. I just want to reassure you that it's OK if we give Lizzie a place in our relationship. It was stupid to think that a visit to Greenhill Park would be enough to free you from your past. Things aren't that simple. She belongs to your history, and what happened to her will live on in your memories for a long time, for ever. That's why I say, don't let's deny Lizzie, let's take her on board. And above all please don't think that you are obliged to tell me every little detail of your thoughts and feelings for her. We need space and we need secrets in order to be able to breathe, so let's allow each other to have them."

Holding each other close, they looked out across the sea that restlessly slapped against the pier. Zoë's words needed no further explanation. Silently she and Jason stood by the harbour and allowed themselves to be overwhelmed by a heady feeling of happiness, knowing that they had become a couple.

Alexandra Lavizzari was born in Basel, where she went on to study Anthropology and Islamic Studies. She has spent periods of her life in Nepal, Pakistan, Thailand and Italy, and now lives in Somerset. In addition to shorter, more occasional pieces, she has published more than twenty books. These include novels, literary biographies, short stories, children's stories, poetry and books about oriental art. She is also a keen painter and photographer.

12350356R00232

Printed in Great Britain
by Amazon.co.uk, Ltd.,
Marston Gate.